D0929950

The Bucket Flower

The Bucket Flower

Donald Robert Wilson

Pineapple Press, Inc.
Sarasota, Florida

Inquiries should be addressed to:

Pineapple Press, Inc.
P.O. Box 3889
Sarasota, Florida 34230

www.pineapplepress.com

Library of Congress Cataloging-in-Publication Data

Wilson, Donald Robert,
  The bucket flower / Donald Robert Wilson.-- 1st ed.
      p. cm.
  ISBN-13: 978-1-56164-369-1 (alk. paper)
  ISBN-10: 1-56164-369-6 (alk. paper)
  1. Women botanists--Fiction. 2. Florida--Fiction. I. Title.
  PS3623.I5786B83 2006
  813'.6--dc22

                                                              2006004356

First Edition
10 9 8 7 6 5 4 3 2 1

Printed in the United States of America

To Regina

Chapter 1

Boston, Massachusetts, March 18, 1893

*H*er knuckles were white as she gripped the tablecloth. "Papa," Beth said, "I've decided to go to Florida."

Walter Sprague put down his soup spoon and touched his napkin to the corners of his moustache before speaking. "What has brought forth this sudden declaration, Elizabeth?" he asked. He looked at Mama accusingly.

Mama's eyes widened with her soup spoon suspended halfway to her lips. Had it been a mistake not to include Mama in her plans? No. Between Mama's fear of upsetting Papa and her adherence to custom, she would have invented reasons to support him.

"It's . . . it's about my graduate study," she replied, having practiced her words over and over. At that moment the gaslights flickered, reflecting her own fear of awakening the fire-breathing dragon. Her graduate study alone was a sore spot, let alone mentioning a long trip. "My mentor, Alice Katherine Adams, has suggested the Everglades as an excellent resource for my thesis. I'm required to complete a field study before I receive my master's degree."

She looked across at Aunt Sarah for support, having waited for Sunday evening when her aunt customarily came to dinner. With his sister present, Papa might react less vehemently. Aunt Sarah was concentrating on adjusting the forks beside her soup plate.

"I allowed your mother to talk me into sending you to Wellesley to become a better conversationalist at dinner parties, not to become a scientific bluestocking. I must say, Elizabeth, I cannot see much change. You're not very clever with witty repartee. Now you're involved in this ridiculous master's degree when there's no place for female scientists. A college degree, much less a master's degree, for a woman is nonsense."

"Papa's right, dear," said Mama. "You know that men are reluctant to marry a woman with a college degree. Why must you continue with this additional time wasting? People will consider you a spinster before you're twenty-four."

"I'm not interested in marrying yet, Mama. We've talked about that," she said, trying to keep the sharpness of her tone in check. She had expected this response.

"Don't tell me you're thinking about looking for a position when you're all finished with your education," said Papa. "You have no business taking a job away from a man with a family to support. A woman's place is in the home." That was his familiar stand when it came to women acquiring a profession. Then came a mystifying statement: "It's more important that you remain in Boston right now."

"Why is it necessary for me to stay here, Papa?" Staying at home had never been an issue before, although she had seldom been farther away from home than Duxbury or Newburyport.

"If you insist upon continuing with your pointless studies, there's always the plant life in the Public Garden." He had yet to return to eating his soup.

"School children study the flora in the Public Garden, Papa. Botanists search for and examine new species."

"Then look in the Berkshires or the White Mountains. There's no need to flounce off to Florida."

She decided not to be sidetracked by the sting of the word *flounce*. "The White Mountains have already been scoured by botanists and trampled by hikers and campers." She was still looking at her father, but sensed Mama and Aunt Sarah watching this exchange with concern. One did not stand up to Papa without experiencing his gruff retorts and eventual subjugation by the force of his anger and determination. "Doctor Adams has suggested Florida's western Everglades as an excellent area where very little botanical study has taken place. Florida's swamps are the homes for hundreds of plant species still unnamed, some rare, others yet to be discovered. Mama, remember the lecture you and I attended with Mr. Cushing last fall? Pliny Reasoner's trek along the Fakahatchee River in 1887 was what inspired me."

Papa glared the length of the dining room table at Mama as if this whole thing were her fault.

Her mother adjusted her chiffon shawl nervously. "People will gossip, dear. They'll surmise that you are in confinement. By seeming to go away to avoid a scandal, you will surround the family with embarrassment."

"I can't help what your wicked-minded friends will imagine, Mama. The only other places to get a similar experience are Africa or South America."

"Good heavens!" exclaimed Aunt Sarah. Perhaps it had been a mistake to start this argument in the presence of Papa's older sister after all.

"What does this woman—your mentor—know about Florida?" asked Papa. "It's a distant, uncivilized place where yellow fever and malaria are rampant."

"Oh," said Mama softly, raising a hand to her throat. "Surely you don't want to travel to a place where those diseases exist, dear."

There had been outbreaks of yellow fever, but none in the past two years. Before she could reply, Papa spoke again.

"This woman sounds like a feather-head to suggest traveling to the wilds of Florida. I assume she plans to accompany you."

Beth resented his referring to Dr. Adams as "this woman." She was tempted to defend her mentor, but decided to stay on course and gripped the table again. "I plan to go alone."

"Unheard of. Young ladies do not travel alone. I forbid it." His voice reverberated from the dining room's black walnut paneling, overriding Mama's gasp. Even Aunt Sarah had looked up in alarm.

She had prepared herself for this. "Papa, this is 1893. Women travel alone all the time. I've seen them on the train to Wellesley."

"Working women, perhaps," he said disdainfully. "Common people. But not ladies, for long distances, overnight, to strange hotels. Certainly not to Florida's swamps. This discussion is closed." He pointed at her. "Dismiss these insane notions from your mind, Elizabeth." He returned his attention to his soup.

She paused for a moment, knowing what turmoil to expect from what she was about to say. Seldom had she stood up to Papa, and even then it had been about minor issues that Mama had supported and helped her win. Now her mother remained silent. "Papa, I'm twenty-three. An adult. I intend to go whether you approve or not." The words came out tremulously, but nevertheless they had been said.

Papa lowered his soup spoon slowly. His hand was shaking and his face was as red as she had ever seen it. Aunt Sarah's presence made him attempt to contain himself. "I am amazed to hear your defiance, Elizabeth, especially in front of your mother and Aunt Sarah. You will not go. I forbid it, and will not advance you one penny for such an outlandish venture."

She had anticipated this threat. "I have my trust fund from Grandfather Jackson, Papa. I am now of age and intend to draw from it." Grandfather Jackson's portrait, hanging above the marble fireplace behind Aunt Sarah, looked down with approval.

Papa's forehead furrowed. "I've always been against women handling money, and tonight you've given me a good example why they shouldn't. You are naïve and see life through rose-colored glasses, Elizabeth. Some no-account will steal your money before you are able to turn around. This is the thanks your mother and I get for sending you to college. You've become headstrong and are jeopardizing your main purpose in life—to marry and have children."

"I see Elizabeth as an independent thinker, Walter, but not headstrong," said Aunt Sarah, speaking for the first time. "I didn't realize you considered me a failure because I never married and had children."

"Elizabeth is smart and can take care of herself, Papa," added Mama. "She has never embarrassed the family." Papa had overreached himself and the women were closing ranks. She saw a slight glimmer of hope for their support.

Papa sputtered a few times and pulled at his high wing-tip collar, but held his ground. "I still refuse to allow our daughter to travel alone to the depths of Florida or any other far away place, Harriet," he said, looking at Mama. Then, turning toward his daughter, "If you are suggesting that I escort you, I cannot. Business is not good right now, and the company requires my attention here in Boston."

"Well then," interjected Aunt Sarah, "Elizabeth can accompany me when I go to St. Augustine for the cure." The suggestion came as a surprise, giving even more support than she had dreamed of. But at what cost? Was Aunt Sarah to be Papa's surrogate in Florida?

"The cure?" asked Mama. "I hope you're not ill." Mama seldom mentioned illness, even to her sister-in-law.

"I've had a lingering cough for months and this winter has got me down. I need a change, and Florida's warm sun will help." Beth failed to recall ever having heard Aunt Sarah cough.

"No one goes to Florida except those with consumption or those who go there to die," growled Papa. "It's a silly idea. Besides, the season is almost over."

"Nonsense," replied Aunt Sarah, now sitting ramrod straight like her brother. "We'll leave this week and have the whole month of April there. We'll stay at Flagler's new hotel, the Ponce de Leon, and have a grand time. During the day Elizabeth can search for all the plants her heart desires."

The tension had subsided, but to tell Aunt Sarah that St. Augustine wasn't the part of Florida she intended to explore might change all that. "Thank you, Aunt Sarah," she said before Papa could object, realizing that losing so easily was not acceptable to him. "I'd like to go to St. Augustine with you."

The conversation had confirmed to her that there were more reasons to get away than just field studies in botany. Here was her chance to break away from Papa's dominance and Mama's obsession with the family's position in Boston society, which was so confining. Her parents' concern about offending Boston's "Ancients and Honorables" by breaking the rules of social etiquette was suffocating her.

For a moment, silence echoed around the high-ceilinged dining room while everyone waited for Papa to react. Papa's face was still red and his mustache bristled, but his voice was much softer as he spoke. "If you two insist upon this foolish venture, then I will make arrangements for the two of you to have a first-class stateroom aboard the *City of Providence*, which sails on the thirtieth for Jacksonville and Key West. A sea voyage will be healthful and invigorating." This was Papa's way of maintaining control in defeat. The *Providence* was one of his ships, and the crew answered to him; she was doomed to be under his influence.

"Oh, no," said Aunt Sarah, raising her hands. "I will never go anywhere by ship again. When I went to Europe I was deathly sick during both crossings. I would have walked home if I had that choice. We'll take the train, Walter. It goes all the way to St. Augustine now."

Papa glared at Aunt Sarah. "A stateroom is a much more civilized way to travel. You never know what common people you will encounter on a train, mostly drummers. They don't just sell their wares, they're a wanton lot. The cars are dirty, noisy, too hot or too cold, and the food, when available, is inedible."

"We'll get reservations for a stateroom in a hotel car," said Aunt Sarah bravely. "They have all the modern conveniences at hand, including meals, all in one car, and we won't have to move about the train once we leave Jersey City." Aunt Sarah had traveled before, but it mattered little to Elizabeth whether they went by Papa's steamer or by train as long as they were able to go.

Sunday was the maid's night off, and Mrs. Faraday, the cook, had cleared the soup dishes. The dinner had continued without further upset. Papa was unusually quiet while Mama and Aunt Sarah engaged in small talk. Their conversation gave her the opportunity to absorb what had taken place. That she was accompanying Aunt Sarah to Florida in a few days was hard to believe. She hadn't won, exactly, but she hadn't lost, either. Aunt Sarah, in her mid-sixties, had certain limitations as a traveling companion. Once they were in Florida she planned to find out how close to the Everglades they were. How to arrange a few days away from Aunt

Sarah for exploration was a problem, but this evening was not the time to worry about that.

"You know, Sarah," said Papa, ending the quiet moment while Mrs. Faraday had served the Indian pudding, "I expect you to be the perfect chaperone and never let Elizabeth out of your sight. Louts will be attracted to her like bears to honey." He pointed that threatening finger again. "If anything happens to her, anything at all, I will hold you responsible."

"Papa, I know how to deal with untoward gentlemen. You forget all the Harvard men I've had to fend off at cotillions."

"These men will not be from Harvard, Elizabeth, and they will not be gentlemen requesting a place on your dance card. If you insist upon going, you will encounter all kinds of riffraff, and you will not be treated like a lady. If you ever need help, don't expect to receive any. Distrust any man who attempts to be friendly. They'll be after your money—or worse." This was the closest her father ever came to admitting that sexual drives existed. "At best, you'll be ignored. You will find the train schedules to be unreliable. You'll have to change trains frequently, stay over in questionable hotels, and often take a ferry or cross a city to reach the next railway line. And these are unsettled times. Grover Cleveland will be inaugurated within a few days, and who knows what vermin that will bring into office. I predict that you will return to Boston within a week—if you get back at all."

"It's a man's world out there, dear," said Mama vaguely.

"We'll be able to take care of ourselves," said Aunt Sarah. "You'd think I have never traveled before."

As they rose from the table, Papa asked, "Elizabeth, have you told Edward Cushing about your travel plans?" The thought of Mr. Cushing caused her to shudder. He competed with Papa in the shipping business. Mama had included the obnoxious man in their social plans more frequently as of late.

She paused, puzzled. "Why need I discuss anything with Mr. Cushing, Papa?"

"He might be slighted by your leaving Boston just now."

"Why is that?"

"I believe he will be making a proposal of marriage to you very soon."

Chapter 2

*E*dward Cushing was the least desirable man in the world. The past three days had not helped to lessen the repugnance associated with the idea of an engagement to that man. The thought of marriage to him called up nightmarish images, which she quickly cast aside. Much to her relief, his name had not been brought up again, but she was certain that her parents had invited him to tonight's dinner party. Somehow she had to get through the evening without appearing to be self-conscious and embarrassed by his presence.

Beth knew no man that she cared to be engaged to at this moment except Michael Otis, but Michael was already married to her best friend, Mary. Both Mary and her husband were expected to arrive for dinner at any moment.

How fortunate it was that she had planned to go away now. Living at home was becoming more and more like prison. Leaving tomorrow morning meant escaping further dominance by Papa and Mama and at least postponing a proposal from Mr. Cushing. For her parents to consider her marriage to Mr. Cushing without even consulting her was beyond belief.

The Bucket Flower

From her rocker she looked around her third-floor bedroom. She would miss this room and its stairway to her hideaway in the turret. The latest issue of *McClure's* lay in her lap, unable to hold her interest. The impending dinner party was intended to be a bon voyage celebration for her and Aunt Sarah, but the fact that Edward Cushing might be lurking downstairs destroyed any pleasant anticipation.

The past three days had slipped by in the wink of an eye despite her eagerness to get away. Never in her wildest dreams had she expected to leave so soon. Aunt Sarah had obtained the train tickets, but there had been so much preparation for their trip. Which gowns and dresses should she take, and which ones should be left behind? Dresses for traveling, walking, morning, balls, and parties. For sporting events she decided upon long skirts and shirtwaists with leg-of-mutton sleeves. Then there were the hats, the scarves, the shoes, the unmentionables, and her jewelry. She hoped she had made the right decisions. Fortunately Mama had been busy with plans for this evening's farewell dinner. It had been difficult to limit herself to three Saratogas and the one valise to carry with her on the train. Then, too, there had been arrangements to be made about her trust fund and the train ride out to Wellesley to borrow a microscope from Dr. Adams. Thanks to her mentor, the microscope and other equipment were being shipped separately to St. Augustine.

Voices rose from the second floor. The guests were already arriving. Once the ladies had completed their primping after depositing their cloaks and hats in the master bedroom, Mama planned to have them congregate in the second-floor drawing room, and her presence was required. After all, the hastily arranged dinner was a going-away affair in her honor.

She stood and made one final appraisal before the full-length mirror. Her carefully coiffed, long, blonde tresses were in place. The pearl necklace and matching pearl earrings were appropriate for an unattached lady. She had chosen a simple satin dinner dress, which added modest curves to her slim figure. But no matter how much she tightened her corset or let out the bodice, she still looked like a string bean. She had long known that an hourglass figure like those Gibson Girls she admired in *Harper's Bazaar* was beyond her natural capabilities. Unless hoop skirts and bustles came back into vogue, she would need additional padding in the right places.

Mama had insisted on making tonight's dinner party formal. After reluctantly donning her gloves and picking up her fan, she descended to the second floor and turned toward the drawing room, which was surprisingly quiet. The voices had retreated to the first-floor parlor adjoining the dining room. To her great dismay, instead of the guests she had expected, there stood Mr. Cushing alone before the fire. Mama had set a trap!

If Mr. Cushing hadn't seen her, she would have slipped past the archway and continued on down the stairs. Instead, she pushed the button beside the door that switched on the electric lights. Mama preferred the gaslight's gentle glow, but now was no time for a romantic setting. The electric lights gave Mr. Cushing the yellow-gray face of a walking cadaver. Her worst fears were realized: for the first time they were without a chaperone.

The fact that Edward Lawrence Cushing II was the heir to the Oceanic Steamship Lines was of little interest to her. She knew that a year ago his father had died, leaving him in control of the company. Oceanic competed with Papa's Atlantic and Southern Steamship Company, a smaller firm. That Mr. Cushing desired to absorb Papa's line into his own was no secret. The merger would make the company the largest trans-Atlantic line on the western side of the Atlantic. It had become evident that Papa also had designs upon combining the two steamship lines into one. He had said in private that it was a matter of becoming a partner or running the risk of being driven out of business.

Marrying Mr. Cushing had never entered her mind until Papa had broached the subject. But now here he was, towering over her, his purpose clear. Was she expected to be Papa's gift to Cushing to sweeten the transaction, or had her father added her to the merger to land her a husband? She wasn't sure which reason was more distasteful.

The reason for certain events of the past few months involving Mr. Cushing now became evident. Mr. Cushing had invited Mama and Papa to a concert, and she was included as an afterthought, or so she had surmised at the time. The bleak, shabby Music Hall, combined with Mr.

Cushing's dreary personality, scuttled an evening that even an excellent program by the Boston Symphony couldn't salvage. Despite that disaster, Mama had invited Mr. Cushing to join the family at two dinner parties, a lecture, the theater, and an evening of parlor games. The latter turned out to be worse than the Music Hall fiasco. Even "Bulls and Bears" failed to hold his attention. Mr. Cushing had no more interest or aptitude for silly pastimes than Papa had. At first it had been difficult to understand why Mama and Papa were befriending this strange man. But it became clear that Papa shared his business interests, and Mama admired his social standing with Boston's Old Guard. He was related in some hard-to-follow way to both Oliver Wendell Holmes and Ralph Waldo Emerson. He was also a Harvard graduate and a Presbyterian.

"Good evening, Mr. Cushing," she said, careful to avoid smiling. This was no occasion for him to get encouragement from her.

"Good evening to you, Miss Sprague." He bowed slightly. The spasmodic twitch under his left eye was active this evening. His long, thin face and scraggly, drooping moustache depressed her. "Please sit down over here." He was at least ten years her senior, and in her imagination the washed-out color of his hair and his sallow complexion made him look much older.

Being in the same room with him was always awkward, and now, knowing his plans for her, being forced to be alone and face-to-face like this was even more intolerable. "We're expected in the parlor downstairs, Mr. Cushing. Dinner will be served shortly."

"There's something I wish to say to you," he said, taking her arm in a viselike grip. "It will only take a moment." She had little choice but to sit as he guided her to a chair. He sat facing her, squinting through his gold-rimmed pince-nez. "I have a ring," he said as he reached into his coat pocket and produced a small velvet box.

"Aren't you forgetting something?" she asked, frantic to find a way to prevent this scene from proceeding any further. Since swooning might be misunderstood, she arose from the chair.

"Oh, yes. I have a letter of proposal right here." He replaced the box and reached inside his coat for an envelope which he held out to her as he stood.

"I don't wish to accept that, Mr. Cushing." Accepting the envelope required a reply. A reply involved further embarrassment and hurt feelings. She wished she and Aunt Sarah were already on their way to St. Augustine.

"But why not, Miss Sprague?" His left eye was twitching more than ever. "I have asked your father for your hand in marriage, and he has consented. Aren't you afraid of becoming a spinster? College graduates aren't considered to be good homemakers, you know. I'm giving you the chance of a lifetime. Naturally, you will be expected to give up further studies."

"The few times we have met do not amount to a courtship, Mr. Cushing. You hardly know me." Good manners prevented her from adding, "and I don't want to know you." She added, "I will not give up my graduate studies." She was also tempted to suggest that his being unmarried at thirty-three raised questions, but only said, "There are worse things than being a spinster, Mr. Cushing." She whirled toward the archway.

"Miss Sprague." The sharp edge to his voice made her stop and turn. "There is much riding upon this engagement, you know, much more than merely a young lady's whims."

"Come, Mr. Cushing, the other guests are waiting downstairs," she said, giving him no choice but to follow her down the stairway leading to the main hall.

"Ah, here come Elizabeth and Mr. Cushing!" gushed Mama from the foot of the stairs. The look of joy on her mother's face grated against her own feelings. The other guests were in the parlor.

"Did he ask you?" Mama whispered in her ear.

"No, Mama." That was the truth. No question had been asked, and he had returned the envelope to his pocket.

Cousin Daniel stepped forward from the group as they entered the parlor. "Cousin Elizabeth! How good it is to see you." He was wearing a clawhammer coat and cummerbund along with patent leather oxfords, as were all the gentlemen except one. He kissed her longer and harder than was proper for kissing cousins, but it told her that he and the others had not been made aware of the impending proposal. Mama had invited her stocky nephew to round out the table, always balancing the number of gentlemen and ladies.

Looking past her cousin, she observed the ladies' long, sweeping dinner gowns of Chantilly, lilac satin, fawn silk, emerald, and black velvet polonaise. Most of the ladies wore their hair pulled into a roll or knot at the back. Mary McKay Otis' was swept up from the forehead in a pompadour, and Grace Sumner's hair was piled on top and pinned carelessly in a knot. The ladies, except Grace, decorated their hair with aigrettes, wreaths of silver blossoms, gold net, lace, ribbons, or pearls. Diamonds, broaches, pendants, earrings and bracelets abounded.

Grace's fiancé, Patrick Muldoon, was the only gentleman not wearing a formal dinner suit. A shabby coat several sizes too large hung from his bony frame. And Grace and Patrick were not wearing gloves. Grace knew the custom for formal dinners and wore none, she guessed, because Patrick didn't own any. Grace had been known in college for her daring social gaffes. Mr. Muldoon was a fisherman and very likely the first Irishman to enter the Sprague mansion by the front door. It would be intriguing to know what Grace's family thought of this redheaded young man.

Eleven guests were there for dinner. Other invited couples had made their apologies. The short notice, Mama said, was the problem, but she knew that most Bunker Hill and Back Bay families never intended to be seen in the Sprague home.

Stepping past her cousin to greet the other guests, she spoke to the Tremonts and the Burroughses, friends of her parents, then to Aunt Sarah. Her college friends, Mary and Grace, were next. With them were Patrick, and at last, Mary's husband, dear Michael.

"That's a lovely gown, Elizabeth," he said.

She hoped that the redness she felt creeping up her neck went unnoticed as she talked with Michael.

Mrs. Faraday opened the sliding doors to the dining room and announced dinner, and the procession began. As was the custom, Papa escorted the senior lady, Aunt Sarah, followed by the Tremonts, then the Burroughses. Next came Mary and Michael and then Grace and Patrick.

"My arm, Elizabeth," said Mr. Cushing, more in the tone of a command than an invitation. But she ignored his proffered arm and walked beside him without touching. Mama, the hostess, accompanied by Cousin Daniel, brought up the rear. She endured the formality of each gentleman seating his lady to his left. Cushing took off his gloves and sat beside her. Like the other ladies, she then removed her gloves and placed them in her lap, resisting the wild inclination to stuff them into Mr. Cushing's water glass. Across the table Grace and Mr. Muldoon seemed oblivious to the formalities.

She dreaded having to sit through dinner beside Mr. Cushing, but Michael sat on her left, and Grace and Mr. Muldoon were across from her. She intended to converse with her friends as much as possible.

The ten-course dinner proceeded smoothly. Mrs. Faraday was assisted by their two maids, Eileen, the Irish one, and the new Norwegian girl whose name she hadn't learned. Mrs. Faraday had outdone herself with the lobster sauté and the veal cutlets. Mama had seen to it that the appropriate wine was served with each course. Michael and Mary had their heads together. Fortunately Mama was conversing with Mr. Cushing, leaving her the opportunity to explain her trip to Grace across the table. On Grace's right, Mr. Muldoon was relating a long story to Mrs. Burroughs. At one point he reached across her for a dinner roll, startling the elderly woman. She was amused to see Cousin Daniel, who was being ignored, attempting to stifle a yawn.

After coffee and liqueurs were served, Papa got to his feet. She expected her father was going to suggest to the ladies that they repair to the parlor while the gentlemen join him in the library for a cigar. Instead, standing stiffly erect as always, he said, "Ladies and Gentlemen, I am proposing a toast. As you may have heard, our darling daughter, Elizabeth, has been planning a trip to Florida. I had intended to wish her bon voyage, but instead, I take this opportunity to congratulate Elizabeth Julia Sprague and Mr. Edward Lawrence Cushing II on the announcement of their engagement to be married!"

Amidst the ohs and ahs around the table, she sat stunned, at first not certain she had heard correctly. Looking at Mama she saw a flash of startled ignorance which transformed into a weak smile. Across the table, Grace, who was seldom shocked by anything, sat with her mouth open.

Near Papa's end of the table Aunt Sarah had her napkin to her mouth, but the upper half of her face was whiter than usual. Mr. Cushing nodded at the others, accepting their congratulations.

"Mr. Cushing, say something!" Elizabeth said in his ear, sure he would have to correct his misunderstanding.

Cushing arose, holding his glass in his hand. "I offer a toast to my future mother-in-law, the gracious Mrs. Sprague, and my future father-in-law and partner in—"

"No! No! There's been a mistake!" She jumped to her feet. "I'm not marrying Mr. Cushing!"

Papa's face turned beet red. "Sit down, Elizabeth, you are upsetting our guests."

She looked at Mama for help, but Mama's expression was pleading for her daughter to comply, mixed with the consternation of knowing she had already made up her mind to rebel.

Papa was still standing at the head of the table, trembling. "There will be no trip to Florida, Elizabeth."

"I am going if I have to crawl there on my hands and my knees, Papa!" She heard Mama's gasp, but across the table Grace was grinning at her.

Aunt Sarah interrupted the stunned silence that followed with a calm voice. "A two-month trip to Florida might be just the thing to calm Elizabeth and give her proper time to reconsider such an, ah, um, interesting proposal."

"Elizabeth," Papa said through clenched teeth, "you have embarrassed our guests and your mother and have subjected our family to scandal. You owe everyone, and especially Mr. Cushing, an apology." The humiliation was too great to remain in the room. She ran into the hall and up two flights of stairs and flopped on her bed, sobbing as she had as a child.

The dining room walls had closed in on her as if she were in a torture chamber. Her parents had sold her to Mr. Cushing with the world watching. The scandal of her rebellion would spread all over Boston by tomorrow; Mrs. Burroughs and Mrs. Tremont would see to that. To allow it to appear as if she had accepted Mr. Cushing's proposal, and then later refute it would have been just as bad. Not only had she defied Papa, but she did it in front of guests. She had violated the social conventions regarding poise, family solidarity, display of temper, and creating a scene. She had brought shame onto her parents, and she did it before non-family—the Burroughses, the Tremonts, and worst of all, her friends.

If a man had to ask for her hand in marriage, why wasn't it, she asked herself between sobs, someone like Michael Otis and not Edward Cushing? Mama had taught her from an early age that two standards existed, one for men, and the other for women, and that men in general were beasts. Edward Cushing was one of them. She had always promised herself to search for one who was not.

Michael was a real gentleman, handsome, and from a good family. She had known him ever since their third year in college, his at Harvard, hers at Wellesley. At a college-sponsored dance she had met him and introduced him to Mary. From that moment it was obvious that Mary and Michael were meant for each other. She envied Mary but loved her as much as Michael and shared in the happiness of their courtship. She admired Michael's handsome features, his gentleness, courteousness, and gallantry. He was a churchgoer and an excellent dancer. Where Papa was haughty and arrogant, Michael was dignified and gracious.

Edward Cushing was like Papa and had no sensitivity for her feelings or preferences. Only Mr. Cushing was worse—he lacked the dignity and the handsome features of Michael or Papa. Above all, he had grabbed her hurtfully by the arm and had forced her into a chair in the drawing room, causing her to suspect that cruelty lurked just below the veneer of his gentlemanly behavior.

It seemed as if she had been lying on the bed for hours, but perhaps it had been only minutes before she heard a light tapping on the door frame. She hadn't closed her door, and someone was hesitating in the doorway. Expecting to see her mother, she buried her head in her pillow.

"Beth?" Mary was the one who had started calling her "Beth" when they met at Dana Hall. Only Mary and Grace called her that. She sat up slowly, dabbing at her eyes with her handkerchief.

"Oh, Mary," she sobbed, indicating that her best friend should come sit beside her on the bed.

Mary had difficulty climbing up on the high bed in her dinner dress but finally succeeded. She sat close by without saying anything. She had placed a bag at the foot of the bed.

"Oh, Mary, what have I done?"

"Did you accept Mr. Cushing's proposal of marriage?"

"He never proposed. He started to hand me a ring, and then he offered a letter of proposal, but I refused it."

"Then you've done nothing wrong, Beth. Your father must have misunderstood."

"I'm not certain of that, Mary. Papa and Mr. Cushing have been planning a marriage without informing me. And you saw how Mr. Cushing went right ahead as if the engagement was a foregone conclusion. Then I embarrassed everyone present with my outburst."

Mary put her arm around her. "Everyone will understand once they know the truth. Are you still planning to go to Florida tomorrow?"

"I will go tonight if I can—and never come back."

"I brought you a going-away present." Mary withdrew a box with a large bow from the bag and handed it to her.

"Oh, Mary! What a thoughtful gift!"she said as she unwrapped the Kodak Brownie and several rolls of film. "I should have thought about using a camera. This will come in handy with strange plants."

Mary laughed. "Don't forget to take pictures of the young gentlemen you meet."

"Where is Aunt Sarah? She'll never want to go to Florida with me now."

"I'm right here, dear." Aunt Sarah was in the doorway. "Tomorrow morning can't come soon enough for either of us."

"Aunt Sarah, if Mama and Papa insist on this nightmare of an engagement, then I will never return from Florida. Thank you for helping me escape."

Chapter 3

St. Augustine, Florida, March 25, 1893

"What could possibly go wrong with my traveling in the Everglades, Aunt Sarah? This isn't the wild west." She still had only a vague idea of where the Big Cypress Swamp was and sensed that it was not near St. Augustine. She had looked at a map of the Florida Peninsula in Papa's atlas. It showed the lower half of the state as disappointingly blank; there were no roads or cities, only the word *Everglades* stretching from one coast to the other under a large lake

The thirty-hour train ride had dragged like the lectures in economics and history at Wellesley. There hadn't been that much to see from their stateroom window. Near the cities, dreary factories and warehouses slid by. The rural areas were a monotonous blur of barren trees with infrequent glimpses of rivers. Farther south there had been an occasional shanty with little Negro children and chickens running about. The meals had been considerably less than haute cuisine, and her sleep had been fitful in the uncomfortable upper berth. To pass the time she read *The Adventures of Sherlock Holmes* while Aunt Sarah relied upon issues of *Leslie's Weekly* and the *Ladies Home Journal*.

When she reached into her valise, she discovered that Mama had slipped in a bottle of styptic balsam. She had never had to use it, but knew the tincture was to quell excessive bleeding during her debilitating periods. She returned the bottle to her valise without showing it to Aunt Sarah. Dear Mama and her going-away present.

When it was dark outside, she could see her reflection in the window. It reminded her of her mother's still-beautiful face, the blonde hair with wisps of gray swept up in a pompadour. The blue, oval eyes looking back at her from the image pleaded for her not to leave home. The beginnings of crow's feet and creases around Mama's mouth were accentuated with worry. People said that the daughter resembled a young Harriet Jackson Sprague, but she hoped she possessed a more determined and less cowed manner than her mother.

Mama was mild-mannered and friendly—too friendly with the servants, according to Papa. Friends were the more-recently arrived matrons of Back Bay, but casual acquaintances were all that had developed with the older families that her mother sorely wished would recognize the Spragues.

With Papa, Mama was wishy-washy and subservient. Mama had confided to her before she had gone away to Dana Hall about women who fought for abolition, for prohibition, and the right to vote. Her mother had admired these women, but never dared to speak out in behalf of their causes. Papa, of course, had forbidden discussion of these subjects or the allegiance to any movement more liberal than the church ladies' guild.

Inside her book an envelope had been inserted. Her name on the outside was in handwriting unfamiliar to her. The message inside read:

> March 20, 1893
> Dear Miss Sprague,
> It gives me great pleasure to ask for the honor of your hand in marriage. The favor of your reply will be appreciated.
>> Sincerely,
>> Edward Lawrence Cushing

Mama must have placed Mr. Cushing's envelope in the book. The act said more than words could have expressed. Mama had been a party to the continuing nightmare. She handed the note to her aunt.

"I found this letter in my valise, Aunt Sarah."

Her aunt read the note and then looked up. "He doesn't waste any words, does he?"

"I've received invitations to tea that were more flowery than that."

"'The favor of your reply will be appreciated' sounds like a business letter. Is this the first time you've seen this proposal?"

"Yes."

Aunt Sarah shook her gray head. "Your father has been domineering ever since he was a little boy, but knowing how much he loves you, his lack of understanding in this matter is unbelievable. There's something I want to say, Elizabeth, before I lose the will to say it, and then I promise you won't hear of it again."

She put down *Sherlock Holmes*, expecting her aunt was about to lecture her about last night's embarrassing scene in the dining room.

Aunt Sarah set her jaw as if about to address a distasteful subject. "I don't like Edward Cushing, but I think you should mull over his proposal of marriage for a while before rejecting it out of hand. The Cushings are old Boston money, one of the richest and most well-established families."

"I don't care to marry a man for his money, Aunt Sarah."

"I hope not, but there are other factors to keep in mind," said her aunt, closing her magazine. It appeared that a long lecture was coming.

"I don't love Mr. Cushing."

"Love has many faces, Elizabeth, and it's much more than that first infatuation with a gentleman's good looks and gallant style. Love grows from a sense of duty, loyalty, trust, and shared experiences."

"How does a sense of duty have anything to do with love, Aunt Sarah?" How did Aunt Sarah, who had never married, have knowledge on this subject? Was it possible that her aunt had experienced a secret love affair at one time?

"Lasting love comes from the caring attention a woman gives a man and a man returns. The woman is the heart and soul of the family. She provides the warmth. The husband provides a home and the necessities of life. He is the protector and has the strength a family requires. Each relies upon the other, and in time love grows, even if it isn't there at first. I wish I had understood that when I was young."

Aunt Sarah must have turned down a suitor that she didn't love. Knowing that there was more to come, she remained silent.

"There are other considerations." Her aunt paused, looking out the window as if organizing her thoughts. Turning back to her, she said, "Cunard and White Star Lines are taking away business from Atlantic and Southern at the moment. A merging of our company with Mr. Cushing's Oceanic ought to help them both."

The mention of "our company" reminded her of her Aunt's share in Papa's firm.

"A marriage to Mr. Cushing seals that merger. Then there's your mother, who has always aspired to be absorbed into the respected Old Guard in Boston. The only way she will ever come close to achieving that goal is if you marry into one of the First Families like the Cushings. Face the fact that the older families consider the Spragues members of the codfish aristocracy. You might want to take into account what obligations you have to your parents and what that will mean to you years from now." The older woman took her hand.

She was taken aback by the coldness of her aunt's grasp.

"Against that you must weigh your personal goals, what you are striving for in your education, what you will accomplish by your present actions, and what it will mean to you over the years. As I said, Elizabeth, I don't like the gentleman, but perhaps Mr. Cushing has some hidden qualities. All I ask is that you promise me you'll consider his proposal carefully before giving him an answer."

That had been on the train. Now they were sitting in high-backed wicker chairs in the formal courtyard garden at the Ponce de Leon Hotel. Even in the shade of the palms the warmth was like an early summer day in Boston. It had been snowing the morning they left Back Bay. Strains of music drifted from the vaulted dining room where an ensemble still entertained patrons enjoying a late lunch. Gently falling water from a nearby fountain was the only other sound they heard. The bougainvillea and hibiscus were in bloom, and the heavy fragrance of gardenias was in the air.

"Well, we'll wait and see what Mr. Flagler has to say about your traveling all about the state," replied Aunt Sarah. "You know that I am obliged to keep an eye on you, but I'm too old to travel into the wilderness."

"Then I will hire a guide," she said boldly, possessed with a restlessness that came from waiting all week. Papa still maintained a certain amount of control over their lives, even at a distance. He had telegraphed Henry Flagler, a business acquaintance of his who owned the hotel, and insisted that they meet him. She was tempted to balk at Papa's demand except for the fact that Mr. Flagler knew Florida and might be able to guide her to places where she could do her research. The problem was that Mr. Flagler had been at Lake Worth this past week and had been unable to meet with them until this afternoon.

At a quarter to three they mounted a victoria drawn by two bays to go to the Flagler home, Kirkside. She was thankful she had brought summer dresses with her, and even these were too warm with their long sleeves. She had already shed one petticoat and hoped Aunt Sarah hadn't noticed. For this afternoon visit she had chosen a yellow dress with silver brocade and a coordinated flower-trimmed bonnet. Her skirt was short enough to reveal her matching shoes. Hopefully Aunt Sarah wouldn't be too warm in her light blue dress with darker satin stripes and puffed shoulders and ruffles. At least she had given up wearing a shawl. Sarah's wide-brimmed hat was wreathed with crimson roses and draped with a blue veil. They both wore gloves and carried parasols the same color as their dresses for protection against the warm afternoon sun.

As they rode, Beth reflected upon the past week. She had been eager to delve into her studies, but the time hadn't been wasted. Aunt Sarah turned out to be an excellent companion, setting a fast pace and enjoying everything. They had explored old Fort Marion with its cannons, parapets, and dungeon, and visited the alligator farm on Anastasia Island.

"What are you smiling at?" asked her aunt.

"I was remembering how you had to force yourself to look at the ugly alligators, but fell in love with the sea lions, which are just as ugly in their own way."

They had walked the sea wall and looked in the little curio shops along sandy St. George Street. Narrow streets with overhanging balconies and moss-covered walls had charmed them both. They enjoyed watching artists sketching and painting on many street corners. She had been surprised to learn that St. Augustine was older than Boston.

Aunt Sarah had remarked on how there were no tearooms for ladies to stop for refreshment while saloons for the men abounded. It reminded her of the double standards which existed for men and women. The man was dominant and the woman subservient. Men drank and swore, made unreasonable demands, and committed ugly deeds, and yet they looked for respect, trust, and love from their womenfolk. Papa, while demanding, at least behaved like a gentleman.

She marveled at the hotel, an experience in itself, with its great rotunda and the grand parlor. Aunt Sarah studied the Old World murals and paintings adorning the walls and ceilings. Continuing a custom from home, they took afternoon tea on the loggia overlooking the formal gardens. Both enjoyed the excellent cuisine accompanied by an orchestra in the vaulted dining hall. And every evening she had been pleasantly overwhelmed by invitations to dance in the casino ballroom.

Kirkside was two blocks from the hotel. Around the grounds stood a newly constructed four-foot wall which was being painted by two Negro workmen. Once through the gate, they saw a two-story frame structure built in the colonial style. The lawn was neatly trimmed and several workmen were planting shrubs and trees. Other workmen were painting the exterior of the newly completed house. The easygoing architectural style and grounds echoed the relaxed way of life she had found here in Florida.

As a footman helped Aunt Sarah down from the carriage she chuckled. "We could have walked here."

They were met at the door by a black butler who escorted them into a parlor after they handed him their cards. Mrs. Flagler held court regally from a large, red velvet chair.

"Miss Sarah Sprague and Miss Elizabeth Sprague," intoned the butler. She wondered if the woman expected them to curtsy.

"How do you do?" said the middle-aged lady without rising. "I am Ida Flagler. Please be seated."

"I'm Sarah Sprague, and this is my niece, Elizabeth." They sat opposite on a small sofa.

"Mr. Flagler will be here shortly. He has just returned from Lake Worth where he is building a new hotel. He wants to change the name of the village to Palm Beach. His railroad will go there any day now, you know. He works so hard I hardly ever see him," Mrs. Flagler said sadly.

The queenly face was a beautiful oval with fair skin. Her hair puffed out in a brown bouffant cloud. It seemed too early in the day for her elaborate emerald gown and diamond-studded tiara. The regal lady's brown eyes bored through Beth in an unsettling way. "At least we have many colorful guests. Last month the Vanderbilts were here, and in January, the Rockefellers. We expect President Cleveland may come next season."

"We have been looking forward to meeting you both," said Aunt Sarah.

"Papa has said so many nice things about you," Beth added to be polite.

"Yes. I remember meeting Mr. Sprague at the Ponce de Leon in the fall. He was here with your mother. She could pass for your sister, I must say."

Mrs. Flagler must be confused. Mama hated to travel and had never accompanied Papa on his southern business trips. She was stunned and didn't dare look at Aunt Sarah.

"Ah, here we are!" In strode a tall, distinguished man in a three-piece suit. "I'm Henry Flagler, and I'm sorry to be late." His wife let them introduce themselves. He wore his gray hair short, and had blue eyes behind a pince-nez. He stood erect and had a commanding air about him that made one understand how he had become rich in oil and owned railroads and huge hotels. His face and build reminded her of Papa. "Ah, Miss Sprague," he said to Aunt Sarah, "it's an honor to meet you." Then turning to her he asked, "How is your father, Elizabeth?"

"He's in good health, sir," she answered.

He sat in a parlor chair and crossed his long limbs. "Are you comfortable at the Ponce de Leon?"

"Oh, yes!" they both answered at once.

"It's a grand hotel," added Aunt Sarah.

"Thank you. As you may have heard, I'm now building a new one at Palm Beach. Next year you will be able to ride there on my East Coast Lines. In a few years you will be able to travel all the way to the Miami River and a village there called Fort Dallas." He changed the subject without warning. "In his telegram your father said you wish to do a little exploring, Miss Sprague."

"Yes, sir. Actually, I'm a botanist, and I wish to study the flora of south Florida."

"Very commendable. An excellent hobby. I trust you've been admiring the greenery around St. Augustine?"

Irritated by his assumption that botany had to be a hobby, Beth felt the redness creeping up her neck. "Yes. Aunt Sarah and I have been enjoying the sights of the city this first week, but we'd like to see more of the state."

"Well, someday soon you must take the train inland to Palatka and go for a cruise on the St. Johns River down to the Oklawaha. There you will see what the real Florida is like. Not only will you satisfy your curiosity about the plant life, but the wildlife as well. It will make a grand overnight trip if you take the early train."

"That sounds like an excellent idea, sir, but actually, I was hoping you might suggest a guide to show me the Everglades."

"The Everglades! Oh, my. Well, they present a challenge, especially for a young lady. Very few men have traversed the Everglades. My engineers have scouted the area and tell me it's too dangerous to lay tracks across the southern section of the peninsula."

"I was expecting to record the plant life in the cypress swamp," she said, her hopes diminishing rapidly.

"What you are suggesting men must do thoroughly and soon. Otherwise there will be no record of what Florida was once like. No portion of the western sections of our country is so unknown to us as southwest Florida. It's a worthless jungle with nothing in it but flies, mosquitoes, and Indians. Someday soon the Everglades will be drained. Henry Disston started the project more than ten years ago." His voice rose in both pitch and volume, and he used his arms to demonstrate

Florida's expanse. "When it's done, millions of acres of new farmland will stretch from the Atlantic to the Gulf of Mexico, all the way from Lake Okeechobee to Cape Sable. Along both coasts there will be railroads and magnificent hotels, and the cypress and pine forests will be cut to provide the lumber. Florida will become the nation's breadbasket, and a mecca not only for consumptives, but also for tourists."

What he was saying was difficult to imagine. "That sounds wonderful, Mr. Flagler." She wanted to ask how all this was to be done if his engineers felt it was impossible to build a railroad across the Everglades. But instead, she asked, "How does one get to the Everglades from here?"

"Well, one can take a steamer to Key West or a train to Tampa. Another way is to take a train inland to Kissimmee and then a riverboat south to Lake Okeechobee. From the lake southward the Everglades spreads all the way to Cape Sable. A man must walk with water up to his armpits and sawgrass higher than his reach for a distance of fifty miles. Once you've seen one part of it, you've seen it all."

"How can I get to the cypress swamps?"

"The riverboats continue on through the lake and westward down the Caloosahatchee River, which has been dredged by Henry Disston. From there one has to hike twenty miles or so through pine forests before getting to the swamps. But those swamps are dangerous. They tell of bears, wild boars, alligators, panthers, millions of mosquitoes, and poisonous snakes. My engineers brought back a rumor that a swamp ape bigger than a man roams in those bogs. But even if no predatory animals existed, the swamp miasmas—the poisonous gases that rise from the stagnant waters—will kill a man."

She happened to glance at Mrs. Flagler, who was staring at her—or more accurately, staring through her. The lady's eyes were wide and wild.

"What about yellow fever and malaria?" asked Aunt Sarah.

Mr. Flagler nodded. "There have been outbreaks of yellow fever in past years, and malaria can be contracted in any tropical area."

Each bit of discouraging information had made her spirits sink lower, but to turn around and go back meant defeat. Papa would be proven right if she returned to the oppressive life that awaited her in Back Bay. And there lurked the horrible Edward Cushing, waiting for her to accept his proposal of marriage backed by the insistence of both of her parents.

"I want to go," she said.

Mr. Flagler shook his head and smiled condescendingly. "I'm sorry, but such a trip for two ladies would be unthinkable. I have failed to mention that the trains and riverboats are frequented by gamblers and ruffians, and the swamps are known to be hideouts for murderers and thieves."

Aunt Sarah shook as if casting off a chill. "Oh, I refuse to go to a place like that! St. Augustine is rustic enough for me."

She was relieved to hear her aunt's reaction and said, "I'll hire a guide or a Pinkerton detective, then."

Aunt Sarah patted her on the knee. "We'll talk about that when we return to the hotel."

"If you are determined to go, I happen to know a botanist who lives in Fort Myers." He turned to his wife. "What is his name, Ida?"

"The Duke of Marlborough," Mrs. Flagler said, still staring at her. "My side of the family is related, you know."

"Worthington. That's it. Doctor Worthington. He's an excellent man to give you information about the interior of south Florida. I will telegraph him."

Her hopes began to rise slightly. "Thank you, Mr. Flagler. I'd appreciate that."

"I can't let Elizabeth go," said Aunt Sarah. "I promised Walter to keep her under my wing."

"Are you a descendant of Queen Elizabeth?" asked Mrs. Flagler.

"Perhaps I can get my son, Harry, to escort you to Fort Myers," said Mr. Flagler, ignoring his wife. "It's at least a three-day trip depending which route you take." He described the three different routes in more detail, and the riverboat seemed to travel closest to where she wanted to be.

"Harry has gone back to New York, dear," said Mrs. Flagler, returning to reality. "You know how he hates Florida."

He scowled for the first time and said nothing.

Aunt Sarah rose to her feet. "Thank you, Mr. Flagler. We must be going. I know you're a busy man. You've been most helpful in showing us how impossible travel through the Everglades would be."

"Invest in Florida, Miss Sprague," he said to Aunt Sarah as he stood. "The state is growing rapidly and is already becoming the nation's vacation paradise."

As they were escorted to the front door by Mr. Flagler, she expressed her appreciation and promised to take the trip to the Oklawaha River.

As the carriage carried them back to the hotel, Aunt Sarah prattled on about Mrs. Flagler's gown and regal fantasies and Mr. Flagler's commanding but cordial manner. It was evident that all possibilities of traveling through the Everglades had been dismissed.

Mrs. Flagler's comment about meeting Papa with Mama last fall weighed as heavily on her head as one of the flat irons in Mrs. Faraday's kitchen might have. She struggled to dismiss the remark as the chatter of an unstable woman. Mrs. Flagler's stare had been frightening, and some of her comments wild. Surely the lady was mad. Aunt Sarah had overlooked the statement about Mama like a true lady should, and was determined to see no evil, speak no evil, and hear no evil. That Papa could have taken up with a loose woman seemed unthinkable. Proud, churchgoing Papa, who stood as stiff as a ramrod, was always proper at home, insisting upon the strictest decorum from his wife and daughter.

But then she recalled the summer day she had wandered from home in search of her father. She had been eleven or twelve and had walked all the way from Dartmouth Street, past the Commons, down State Street to Atlantic Avenue, expecting Papa to be pleasantly surprised by her appearance at his office. Although frightened to be alone on the city streets and eyed by strangers seeing a little girl without an escort, she pressed on. The saloons, drunken sailors, loud waterfront noises, and the smells from the fishing boats and the harbor itself kept her and Mama closer to home most of the time. The company's outer office was empty. When she opened the door to Papa's office that she and Mama had visited on rare occasions, she saw no one at first. Then a slight noise made her look behind Papa's huge, mahogany desk where she saw him lying on top of a young woman.

On the way home in his carriage, Papa explained how he had tripped and fallen and how he and Miss Murchison, his secretary, had landed on the floor. He seemed much more concerned that Mama would be furious about their daughter having wandered so far from home, and insisted for her protection that her jaunt would be their little secret. Nothing more was ever said about her excursion to the waterfront, and she had put aside the incident until now.

She felt her face grow hot as the image of Papa on top of Miss Murchison eleven years ago came roaring back. Had her naïveté clouded her vision of Papa's true nature? Her social life had been as innocent as Sunday school. The ladies and gentlemen she had associated with at college dances and parties had always followed strict rules of propriety. Well, Grace was different of course, but her friend had behaved acceptably in their group. Those who didn't had been ostracized. One time Grace was nearly expelled for some undisclosed reason until the intervention by powerful connections her parents had at Wellesley. She was aware that not all men and women were as pure in thought and deed as her close group of friends. For Papa to be one of those other people had been impossible to accept—until now.

The Flaglers' behavior was not too different from her own parents. Mr. Flagler boasted about his plans for the development of Florida, oblivious to Mrs. Flagler's sitting there imagining that she was of royal lineage. Papa was absorbed by expanding his steamship line while Mama dreamed of the Sprague family being included in the higher circles of Bostonian society. Mama blamed the legends surrounding Grandfather Sprague, a rowdy sea captain, for holding them back. These stories, she claimed, were still whispered around the upper class.

Mr. Flagler's description of the Everglades was depressing, and his none-too-subtle inferences about the inabilities of women hadn't been lost on her. There had to be a way for her to get to the Big Cypress Swamp and the Fakahatchee River. Among the young gentlemen guests at the hotel there must be one willing to escort her to Fort Myers and beyond. A plan was starting to form.

Chapter 4

"Watch out for these dandies, dear," Aunt Sarah had said at the beginning of the first week in St. Augustine. "They are a caution, as smooth as glass, and their motives are just as transparent." But most gentlemen at the hotel showed more refinement than some students from Harvard she had encountered. She had waltzed in the casino ballroom for the fourth night in a row and even danced the daring two-step. Because there were more gentlemen than ladies, she had been asked to dance almost every dance by a variety of gentlemen, most of whom had gray hair. To her dismay, Aunt Sarah was present every minute at first, but managed to remain in the background. As time went on and she was always in mixed company, her aunt mingled more with the mothers of the other young ladies.

The hotel's activities were entertaining but pointless, and the desire to start her botanical exploration made her restless until she met Mr. Davis. One evening she decided to wear a whale-boned light-blue brocade with raised silver designs, and matching gloves and dancing slippers. The second gentlemen who asked her to dance, a Mr. Davis from Philadelphia, introduced her to his group of friends about her age. Before the evening was over, she was invited to join them at the indoor swimming pool the next morning.

She soon discovered that the other two ladies and three gentlemen had become acquainted within the last few days. Millie Dalton was in St. Augustine with her mother from Pittsburgh, and Henrietta Thompson and her parents were from New York. Henrietta, she soon discovered, was a complainer, but otherwise pleasant enough. Mr. Davis was the most gentlemanly, and also charming and funny. Mr. Everett was also from Boston and the person with whom she had the most in common. Mr. Bolton, from Baltimore, was the most reserved. Now there were six in their early twenties who enjoyed each other's company and began to attend social activities together day after day. Before long she was addressing the other ladies by their Christian names, but used surnames when addressing the gentlemen.

On that first morning together, the six new friends had bathed in the indoor pool, but every day thereafter they agreed they preferred the ocean. She was self-conscious in her bathing attire at first, but Millie and Henrietta had similar black bathing wear that extended from their necks to their ankles and included a cap and bathing slippers. The gentlemen were appropriately covered as well, but looked foolish in their close-fitting bathing suits that made them all limbs in a spidery sort of way. The ladies' clothing prevented all movement in the water except for walking slowly. Nevertheless, they managed to play keep away and dodgeball, games which often degenerated into happy splashing battles.

Along with the others she fell into a routine of tennis and bathing most mornings and a different activity every afternoon. At first the tennis was played by the gentlemen while the ladies cheered them on. But as each morning wore on, the ladies were encouraged to take part. Never having played the game before, she felt awkward and foolish at first. Then she discovered she was no more inept at returning the ball than the other ladies; they all had the disadvantage of playing in their long dresses. Beth lost track of time. One week blended into the next, and she found herself regretting that the season was coming to a close.

April's clear days were like Massachusetts in September. She was delighted on one such day when Mr. Everett, the most aggressive of the "St. Augustine Six," as they called themselves, chartered a schooner complete with food, drink, and a crew. They sailed down the coast into a stiff breeze that made it difficult for the ladies to keep on their broad-brimmed hats. Millie Dalton became queasy as soon as they hit open water, and Henrietta Thompson shrieked every time the schooner heeled.

The schooner was tame after the small sloops she had sailed in from the time she was a little girl. Beyond his business, Papa's only known interests were the Tavern Club and his sloop. Her earliest memory of sailing was with Mama and Papa on Narragansett Bay. Then after moving from Providence, there were many Sunday afternoons on Boston Harbor. Most of these experiences were both exhilarating and demeaning. Papa at the tiller was a daring sailor, and he ordered Mama about as if she were a galley slave. But today's sail was exhausting from the salt spray, the wind, and the sun, and by late afternoon she was happy to return to the hotel in time for dinner with Aunt Sarah.

The next afternoon she cheered on the quiet Mr. Bolton as he rode in a horsemanship competition, a weekly event at the hotel. "Oh, there's Mr. Flagler," she said to the others. "That lovely lady with him must be his daughter."

"That's Mary Lily Keenan," said Millie Dalton in an awed voice. "Mother said that she's Mr. Flagler's mistress." She looked at the young woman on Flagler's arm with greater interest and noticed that the others were staring, too.

On another afternoon they watched the hotel staff play baseball. Friday evenings they attended the amusing cake walk. The Negro bellhops and waiters strutted down an aisle formed by the other dancers, bowing and bending in mock imitation of the white Southern aristocracy of the past. Mr. Everett was selected among other distinguished hotel patrons to judge the dancers and award prizes. Later Mr. Davis, trying to imitate the buck dance with his head back, briskly strutting, made the others laugh. But they laughed even harder when he failed miserably at the double shuffle.

The young gentlemen smoked cigarettes during the day, reserving cigars for after dinner. Mr. Bolton, she noted, often borrowed Turkish Orientals from Mr. Davis, or Three Kings from Mr. Everett, claiming to be "just out" of his domestic brand of Cameos.

She thought less often of the rift with her parents and Mr. Cushing's engagement offer. Aunt Sarah asked if she had responded to Mr. Cushing, reminding her that the letter required an answer. If his letter deserved a response, there was no rush. A well-thought-out reply, even though negative, might be considered more final than offhanded remarks. But she admitted to herself that she was merely putting off an unpleasant task.

In spare moments she had made notes and sketched the unusual palms, flowers, and beautiful shrubbery around the hotel, aware that these plants were already well known. What was needed was a trip to the hinterlands as Mr. Flagler had suggested.

After making inquiries, a hotel clerk told her of a friend who had fished on the Oklawaha River and gave her directions. She had been awaiting the proper moment to mention the jaunt to her friends. Now she suggested a train ride to Palatka where they could charter a boat and explore the river. She related how Mr. Flagler had suggested the excursion and mentioned the wildlife, strange flowers, and trees they would see. Explaining that the trip might take at least two days with an overnight at a hotel along the river added to their enthusiasm. Everyone was excited by her idea except for Mr. Bolton. He agreed to participate, but seemed to be only marginally interested.

When she revealed their plans to Aunt Sarah at dinner, her aunt insisted on going along, and no amount of cajoling, explaining, or pleading changed her mind. "You're looking for trouble," responded her aunt. After dressing in a sweeping pale green satin-striped gown and matching ensemble, she joined her group in the ballroom and explained her dilemma with embarrassment.

The exuberant Mr. Everett said, "That's an excellent idea. Perhaps other family members might like to go on the outing." The others had little concern, and in the end Millie Dalton's mother agreed to accompany Aunt Sarah, and her predicament was settled.

"I think it should be a camping trip," she told her aunt at bedtime. "That's a better way to get a look at the plant life."

"Land sakes! I'm not looking forward to this excursion. I dislike alligators, I have little interest in the greenery, and I abhor mosquitoes.

We will stay in a hotel or not go at all." The statement was the strongest she had ever heard Aunt Sarah make. She knew that the success of their excursion depended upon her giving in to her aunt on this matter.

On the morning of their trip the "St. Augustine Six," accompanied by Aunt Sarah and Mrs. Dalton, boarded an open-ended wooden railway car. She was embarrassed by the rustic train which was plain and uncomfortable compared with the plush hotel car she had taken from Jersey City with Aunt Sarah. The four-wheel car had slat seats with cast iron arms. There was no separate smoking car, and spittoons were everywhere. The others didn't seem to mind until black smoke from the locomotive blew through the open windows. This distressed the ladies because of their elaborate hats and dresses.

By ten o'clock they were in Palatka. The men negotiated the rental of a small steam-driven riverboat, which Mr. Bolton claimed to know how to run. The owner, however, insisted on sending along a colored "engineer" to operate the steam boiler. Again she was embarrassed, this time by the boat, which was a dowdy affair with a low, flat roof extending from one end to the other with a small, rusty smokestack protruding from its middle.

After stowing their overnight valises and basket lunches prepared by the hotel, they set off down the river. She sat on a bench with Millie and Henrietta. Mrs. Dalton and Aunt Sarah were behind them. Beyond the little steam engine were the men. Mr. Everett steered the boat while Mr. Bolton helped the Negro feed the fire with wood supplied at Palatka.

Almost immediately they spotted alligators along the banks. She felt nervous about these reptiles which, unlike the ones at the alligator farm, were free to swim out to the boat if they chose. Millie and Mrs. Dalton had not seen alligators before and were excited.

"I wish those birds would go away," whined Henrietta. A myriad of flapping wings fluttered all around the boat like huge snowflakes. The mangroves on the right-hand shore were almost white with birds.

Having studied Elliot Coues' *Key to North American Birds* in preparation for her trip, she was able to identify the long-legged egrets and the ibises with their curved beaks. They remarked about the hundreds of fish just below the surface. Mr. Davis thought they were catfish.

"I wish I'd brought my fishing pole," he said.

With only a slight breeze to provide relief from the hot sun, she was grateful for the shade of the boat's roof. The river was like an elongated lake with dense vegetation encroaching on both sides of the water's edge. She had brought her notebook with her and was disappointed in not being able to examine any flora closely even though they were near the vegetation on the right. No signs of human habitation cluttered the riverbanks, and they saw just one fishing boat. The alligators were too numerous to count.

When they decided to stop for lunch, Mr. Everett pulled in close enough to the shore for Mr. Davis to tie up to an overhanging branch. Before the ladies were able to spread out the lunch, the passengers were attacked by swarms of mosquitoes. They had not been a bother while out in the stream with a breeze caused by their forward motion. Henrietta screamed as the others swatted until Mr. Davis was able to untie the boat and Mr. Everett could steer away from the shore. Everyone agreed eating was more pleasant once they were under way and the mosquitoes had disappeared.

"How far is it to the first town?" asked Mr. Everett over the chug-chugging of the engine.

Everyone looked at Beth since she had planned the trip.

"We must come to a fork in the river before we come to Pomona," she said, hoping the hotel clerk had given her accurate information.

"How much farther after that?" Mr. Everett persisted.

"It can't be far. Didn't you ask the man who rented us the boat?"

"I thought you had gotten directions at the hotel."

"Maybe we should turn back," said Mrs. Dalton.

"There's a fork up ahead," said Mr. Davis, pointing over Mr. Everett's shoulder. "The town can't be much beyond that."

After the fork were more forks as the river meandered like a maze among a cluster of grassy islands. All the waterways between the islands looked the same to her. She wasn't certain whether the St. Johns River had divided into two or more streams, but she directed Mr. Everett to keep to the right as she had been told at the hotel. "We must be on the Oklawaha River now." The birds were more plentiful than ever.

The river narrowed, and no other boats were to be seen. After a time they passed a shanty on the left shore.

"Perhaps we should stop and inquire," said Mr. Davis.

"We'll stop at the next shack we see," said Mr. Everett.

Her anxiety increased as the little steamer chugged on until mid afternoon without their seeing other evidence of humans. "Maybe that shanty was Pomona," suggested Aunt Sarah. Someone snickered. The others remained quiet.

All at once a loud thump at the bow sent a shudder through the little boat. Henrietta shrieked and several others responded with an assortment of gasps. Mr. Davis stood up and looked over the side. "We hit an alligator," he exclaimed, watching the stunned reptile float past, "and bloodied the old bugger!" The boat seemed no worse for the encounter and chugged on.

After another hour Mrs. Dalton said, "We should turn around and go back. We don't want to get caught out here after dark."

"It will be dark before we can get back," said Mr. Davis. "Our only choice is to go on until we come to a town. We don't have enough fuel to get back." A glance at the woodpile confirmed for her that their fuel was more than half gone. The boatman should have sold them more wood. The Negro seemed unconcerned even though the stream was now hardly twice the width of the boat.

"We could go ashore and scavenge for wood," suggested Mr. Davis.

"How could we get through that thicket?" Beth asked. The branches over the water created an impenetrable tangle as if it had been woven.

"There's no town out here," said Mr. Everett. "I'm turning the boat around and heading back to that shanty we passed—if no one has a better suggestion."

"What if there's a town around the next bend?" asked Mr. Davis.

She went to the Negro. "Is there a town around the bend?" she asked.

"Ah dunno," he replied with a shrug.

"Sakes alive! Turn around now, please," said Mrs. Dalton with murmurs of agreement from the others. No one objected as Mr. Everett maneuvered the boat around in the narrow space. "If we're lucky, we'll have enough wood to get back to that shack."

"We passed that shanty almost three hours ago," said Millie. "We'll be lucky to get there before dark."

"What if the shanty's empty?" asked Henrietta Thompson in a whining voice.

"Then we can stay there for the night," said Mr. Everett in a cheerful voice. "We have the river current to help us in this direction. We'll be fine." Beth appreciated his attempt at cheering them up, but she had not noticed any current to speak of.

"It's a good thing we brought more than enough food for lunch," said Aunt Sarah. "There's a little left over for supper."

"Maybe we ought to save it for breakfast," said Mr. Bolton dourly, his first remark in hours. Beth knew that two sandwiches, several oranges, and a little lemonade remained.

They traveled downstream for several hours with Mr. Everett still at the wheel. Mr. Bolton threw the last stick of wood into the firebox. The sun was low in the western sky, and their conversation, which had been lively until mid-afternoon, dwindled down to almost nothing. She watched the right-hand shore, but nothing was there except buttonwood with occasional tall palms standing behind them.

"We must have passed it by now," said Henrietta in a whiny voice that was getting on Beth's nerves.

The sun was behind the trees on the western shore. They had less than an hour of daylight. "There it is!" shouted Mr. Davis from the bow. Just then the little steam engine sputtered into silence. Two poles were found aboard which Mr. Davis and Mr. Bolton used to move them toward the shanty.

A barking dog greeted them at a small, rickety pier.

As they drew near, a man carrying a rifle came down to the river's edge. Behind him stood a woman and three children. "This hyar's private prop'ty." He was wearing a battered straw hat and ragged overalls. His feet were bare, and his bearded face appeared to be none too friendly.

"Sir, can you tell us where Pomona is?" she called. The boat had stopped about ten feet from the pier.

"Hit's over thar on t'other river," the man said, pointing behind them. "You cain't get thar from hyar."

"Sir," said Mrs. Dalton. "Can your wife put us up for the night?"

"We haint got nary room for ussens." The shanty was smaller than the boat, and she wondered how all five of them could lie horizontally at one time.

"Sir," called Mr. Davis, "can you sell us some firewood?" Two woodpiles were stacked beside the shanty.

"I was a-fixin' to trade that buttonwood to the charcoal folks."

"I mean your stove wood over there. The other logs are too long. I'll give you five dollars for the whole pile."

The man's eyes bulged, but he said, "You'll hafta tote it yerselves." For the first time he pointed his rifle away from the boat.

"Done," said Mr. Everett as he poled the boat to the dock.

"Sir, might we talk to your wife while they load the wood?" asked Aunt Sarah.

The man hesitated for a moment and then said, "I reckon." Once Mr. Davis and Mr. Bolton had secured the boat to the narrow dock, the gentlemen helped the ladies ashore. Beth felt stiff after sitting for hours, and walking around would have felt better if she hadn't had to relieve herself so urgently.

Aunt Sarah went directly to the woman, who was wearing a ragged homespun dress faded to a dull gray. Her aunt said a few words to the woman and then dashed around the back of the shanty. She understood. They had been without the use of a toilet since Palatka, and her aunt had spotted the outhouse behind the shack.

While they waited, there was little to do but stand around and slap at the mosquitoes. The three children, dressed in rags, hung shyly behind their mother. Even among the poorest immigrants in Boston she had not seen such poverty. Both the man and his wife stared at their dresses. All at once she felt out of place here in this small clearing beside the river. Without a word the woman went to the river's edge and came back with a bucket of water and a dipper. The water was the color of weak tea. Only Mr. Bolton drank.

Once everyone had a turn at the outhouse, Mrs. Dalton asked the woman, "Do you have any food you're willing to sell us?"

The woman looked at her husband. "The missus can fix you some collards 'n' cooter, or atter the sun comes up I can fotch you a sloosh of catfish."

"What are 'collards and cooter'?" asked Mrs. Dalton cautiously.

"Greens 'n' turtle meat." The man still held his rifle in one hand.

The group looked at one another. No one seemed to be that hungry.

"We thank you kindly for the wood," said Mr. Everett handing the man a five-dollar bill. "As soon as the boiler heats up we'll be on our way." Mr. Bolton was already on his hands and knees working at the firebox while the Negro was turning valves.

By the time they got under way, darkness had enveloped them. The stars did little to reveal the difference between the blackness of the water and the growth on either side. They crept along with Mr. Everett in the bow as lookout. The mosquitoes had followed them onto the boat and didn't give up until the moon rose and they made better headway. She noticed that Mr. Everett was careful to stay in the middle of the river.

After dividing the remaining sandwiches into small pieces, everyone was quiet. A few people appeared to be attempting sleep in an upright position. The sole noise was the mesmerizing chug of the steam engine.

Beth was unable to sleep. She had talked everyone into this pointless trip. With embarrassment she reflected upon how badly the day had gone. Her attempt at learning more about the flora was a disaster as well. The few plants she had been able to sketch were buttonwood, alligator flag, and grasses and lilies in the river. Her vision of Florida's interior had changed. She had expected to see towns along the river and hotels and restaurants. The interior was wild and unpeopled. To be alone and defenseless frightened her. Forging ahead to the Everglades alone was less attractive now.

The other choice was to return to Boston with Aunt Sarah, and that option provided terrors of its own. Admitting defeat to Papa was unthinkable. Papa always won, and he was always right. She remembered Papa forever berating Mama for initiating her own plans or ideas; every action, every idea, had to be his. He was the supreme master of the house and never let anyone forget it. That was why he hadn't allowed them to have a butler. Mama's role was relegated to planning the afternoon tea and negotiating with the seamstress. Papa even gave orders to the servants, and in a way, Mama had even less discretion than Mrs. Faraday. Beth could never understand the double standard Mama allowed for Papa—he committed countless selfish acts and yet she respected and loved him. Was it fear? Mama tried to make Papa the center of her life and be his helper and servant. Yet he always blamed her for whatever went wrong.

Going back to Boston meant having to contend with Mr. Cushing. Living with him would be worse than Mama's problems with Papa. Mama and Papa expected her to marry him, live in the city, and be Mr. Cushing's slave—a slave, at least, to the endless customs to be observed. At best, life would be a long string of boring teas, dinner parties, and calling cards. That last night at the dinner party she had broken almost every rule in the book, and hopefully now Mr. Cushing had given up on her anyway. The other option was to live as Aunt Sarah did, as a spinster and alone. With all its unknown dangers yet to be encountered, Florida still presented a better choice.

They had returned to Palatka close to midnight and remained at the Putnam House until the morning train carried them back to St. Augustine. Almost everyone had been kind to her for suggesting the trip up the Oklawaha. The gentlemen were enthusiastic about the adventure, except for Mr. Bolton, who said nothing as usual. The ladies were less pleased, but considered the experience "interesting," save for Henrietta's saying that the trip had been dreadful. That comment was less disappointing than the fact that the day had given her little opportunity to study the plant life in detail. Aunt Sarah was unusually quiet and pale.

When they arrived back at the Ponce de Leon, a telegram awaited her from Edward Cushing. He would arrive in St. Augustine in seven days.

Chapter 5

*T*he next few days slipped by too quickly. She was reminded of the weekends during her senior year at Wellesley. Life had been a merry-go-round of parties and dances, and the moods of both the young ladies and the gentlemen had been light and carefree. But now her outlook was different from the others. While everyone should have time out to play, more serious matters needed to be addressed. Mama had said this was a man's world. Women who allowed themselves to be confined to the strict, customary roles were contributing to that ancient tradition. She admired women like Elizabeth Cady Stanton and Julia Ward Howe. Other women like Susan B. Anthony and Carrie Nation worked toward prohibition, women's suffrage, and other rights for women. But even more than these ladies, she revered professional women like her mentor, Alice Katherine Adams, who was among the first women to attain a doctoral degree. Even fewer women were like Dr. Adams, a professional who was also married and had children. Custom was against a woman becoming educated, achieving professional status, and raising a family if she chose. Was she expecting too much of herself by aiming for that goal? She decided she was not. Now was the time for her to get on with her reason for being here.

Another worry was Aunt Sarah. After her return from the Oklawaha trip, she remained confined to her room for the next two days. Her aunt pooh-poohed all concerns for her health and reassured her that she was just overtired. True to her promise, she was up and around again on the third day, but still looking pale.

Planning the immediate future was imperative. Without telling anyone, she assessed the three gentlemen, looking for that male companion who might escort her into Florida's interior. The excursion up the Oklawaha had helped her determine which gentleman was to be her partner on the trip into the Big Cypress Swamp. No one was capable of holding a candle to Mary's Michael Otis, of course, but at least one of them might qualify as an acceptable escort to accompany her down the Fakahatchee River. Her decision had to be made soon, since they had to leave before Mr. Cushing arrived.

Of the three, Mr. Everett ranked as her favorite, perhaps because he was also from Boston and they had much in common. But Mr. Everett, in addition to being from a good family, was a gentleman and very kind. His assertiveness on their river trip, and his agreeableness toward inviting their family members to join the "St. Augustine Six" impressed her.

It took several days to confront Mr. Everett alone, but at last she managed to corner him in the garden before dinner. "Would you like to take a trip across Florida with me, Mr. Everett?" she asked. She was horrified; the phrasing wasn't at all like she had practiced.

He stared open-mouthed at her proposal and then finally spoke. "What a courageous idea! It's an honor to be asked to escort you across Florida, but unfortunately I'm going to Europe with my parents in a little over two weeks. Then I must be in Newport for the season." He appeared to be disappointed.

She was stunned. She hadn't considered that he might have other plans. She felt the redness rising up her neck as she mumbled an embarrassed apology and hurried into the dining room to have dinner with Aunt Sarah. Her aunt told her she had received a telegram from Papa confirming Edward Cushing's arrival in Jacksonville on one of Oceanic's ships in three days. Until this moment, her ideas about a trip across the state were hypothetical. Now she was determined to break away, even if it meant going alone.

The number of guests at the hotel, which had never been overflowing thanks to the panic on Wall Street, was even fewer now as the season came to a close. Still looking for an escort, she made her plans without informing Aunt Sarah. Mr. Davis was also a good candidate—intelligent, full of fun and adventure. But she asked him what his immediate plans were before revealing her own. Mr. Davis, she was disappointed to learn, was leaving for a family gathering in Saratoga in the morning followed by an excursion to the Chicago World's Fair.

That left the enigmatic Mr. Bolton, of whom she expected little— not that he wasn't a gentleman, but he was quiet, and she had difficulty knowing what he was thinking. On the trip up the Oklawaha, he had worked with the Negro at the boiler, a positive quality. He had been almost as frenetic as Henrietta Thompson when there had been mosquitoes around. Nevertheless, he was her last hope. She waited for a favorable moment to speak to Mr. Bolton alone. She came up to him in the grand foyer while Aunt Sarah was on the far side of the room making arrangements for the handling of their trunks. Her aunt had agreed to leave St. Augustine before Mr. Cushing arrived.

"Mr. Bolton, when Aunt Sarah heads north tomorrow, I plan to travel across the peninsula to Fort Myers, and I will require an escort. I was wondering if you might be willing to favor me with your company. We would observe all the social proprieties, of course." Approaching a gentleman in such a fashion was embarrassing, especially a second time, and her words sounded stilted.

He looked at her without expression, making it difficult to predict his response. Then, to her satisfaction, he said, "Yes, Miss Sprague, I'd be delighted to accompany you, and naturally we will observe all the social proprieties." Surely he realized that for two unattached persons of opposite sexes to be traveling across the state together was highly improper. "There is just one thing," he added.

"Yes, Mr. Bolton, what is it?"

"I'm a little short of cash until I get back to Baltimore."

"No need to concern yourself, Mr. Bolton," she said. "I can extend you a loan until we return." She was disappointed that it had come to this, but in effect, she was paying for him to accompany her. He hesitated, and it looked as if he had something else to say. She waited.

"I wonder if you could make me an advance to settle up my hotel bill." His eyes darted about as if he were embarrassed to have to reveal to a lady his lack of funds.

After Aunt Sarah had gone back to her room, she told the clerk that there had been a change in plans and to have two of her trunks put on the train through Palatka to Tampa instead of New York. The day before she had shipped her botanical equipment to the Hotel Hendry in Fort Myers, hoping that by now Dr. Worthington had received a telegram from Mr. Flagler. Fortunately the train to Palatka was scheduled to leave before Aunt Sarah's train headed north. She had asked Mr. Bolton to meet her on the train.

Deceiving Aunt Sarah was hateful. The dear lady had been so kind and patient, but there was no way for her aunt to allow her niece to go off on her own with a male escort. In the note she planned to leave at the hotel desk at the last minute, she thanked Aunt Sarah for accompanying her to Florida, apologized for running away, and explained her reasons.

The next morning she told her aunt that she wanted to say good-bye to a few friends and thereby needed to take a separate carriage to the railway depot.

"Oh, I almost forgot," said Aunt Sarah. "This is the strangest thing. I received a letter from your father, and in it he included a check for you for twenty-five dollars. Without any further explanation he said the check was for your allowance. Also, this telegram came for you last night."

"Maybe Papa has come around to accept my decision about Mr. Cushing," she said as she opened the telegram.

ELIZABETH.
SINCE YOU ARE INCAPABLE OF HANDLING YOUR
INHERITANCE FROM HUBERT JACKSON, I HAVE
ARRANGED TO BECOME TRUSTEE OF YOUR ACCOUNT
UNTIL YOU CAN PROVE YOU HAVE RETURNED

TO YOUR SENSES. I WILL SEND YOU A MONTHLY
ALLOWANCE OF TWENTY-FIVE DOLLARS THROUGH
YOUR AUNT SARAH.

WALTER HARRISON SPRAGUE

She numbly handed the telegram to her aunt. "Oh! Aunt Sarah! How
could he do this? It's my money, and I'm of age."

"Probably it was very easy, dear. All he had to do, I suppose, was
convince a friendly judge at his club that you are incompetent and have
himself named as your guardian."

"By 'returning to my senses,' he means when I agree to marry Edward
Cushing."

Aunt Sarah sighed. "Yes. In all my born days I've never heard of such
a despicable act. I'm ashamed to say he's my brother."

"What am I to do now?" She collapsed into a chair, unable to stop
the tears. "I can't afford to complete my master's thesis. I can't travel
on twenty-five dollars a month." She realized that Edward Cushing's
expected arrival the following day was no coincidence and felt the walls
closing in around her. The one hundred dollars she had loaned to Mr.
Bolton had left her almost penniless and stranded without being able to
tap her inheritance.

Her aunt sat down beside her. "I have money, dear. Not a lot of it, but
I can make you a loan until all this is straightened out."

"I will not agree to marry Mr. Cushing."

"I know. I can write you a check for four hundred dollars. If you need
more, I will be able to send it to you wherever you may be. Send me a
letter at Arlington Street telling me where you are, and I'll keep your
secret."

She looked up. Aunt Sarah was smiling. Her aunt *knew.* "Aunt Sarah,
I didn't want to deceive you."

"I know, dear. During unusual times a body has to do unusual things.
It's better that I know nothing more. But I will see to it that your third
trunk is shipped back to Boston."

She stood and hugged her aunt.

After departing from breakfast early, she picked up her valise and took a carriage to the train. She boarded a sooty car like the one they had ridden to Palatka one week earlier. Mr. Bolton must be in the other car and would come searching for her once the train was moving.

Nervously waiting for the train to start, she looked out the window, half expecting that Aunt Sarah had changed her mind and was coming after her. She breathed a sigh of relief as the train jerked forward. Mr. Bolton was not among the other passengers in this car. One row behind her on the opposite side sat an older man, mostly bald, whose remaining hair and mustache were a reddish-gray. He was staring at her and did not look away when she noticed. Wishing Mr. Bolton was already beside her she placed her valise on the seat to prevent a stranger from sitting there.

She reached into the valise for *The Biography of Charles Darwin* to hold as if reading. She hoped to look nonchalant. She had started the book at the hotel. Her hand closed around an unfamiliar object, which made her look into the bag. To her astonishment, she held in her hand a small, chrome-plated gun. It had to be Aunt Sarah's double-barreled derringer. How it came to be among her possessions she had no idea. Then she saw the envelope. Inside was a note. It read:

May 7, 1893
Dear Elizabeth,

I understand why you are running away, but I cannot fathom how you have found so much courage to do it. I wish you safe journey. I have done everything in my power to keep you safe. Mr. Moses Gallagher is a reliable man.

Your father will be more favorably disposed toward his sister if it appears as if I had known nothing about any of this.

Love,
Aunt Sarah

P.S. Have you sent your reply to Mr. Cushing yet?

She looked at the derringer again. The chrome-plated weapon was so small she could cover it with her hands. The twin barrels were over one another instead of side-by-side as one would expect. Hunting through the valise for any other unexpected gifts, she found none. She read the note again. Aunt Sarah hadn't explained who Mr. Gallagher was. The dear lady had known about her niece's plans and had not attempted to stop her. She felt as if she had underestimated her aunt from the start and was embarrassed that it had taken so long to discover what a good friend she had.

Inside her valise she had pinned the name of the botanist in Fort Myers that Mr. Flagler had promised to contact, Dr. Worthington. Mr. Flagler, being the busy business tycoon that he was, had probably forgotten to send the telegram as he had promised.

Mr. Gallagher remained a mystery.

Where was Mr. Bolton? Had he missed the train? Continuing on alone was not a pleasant prospect, but she was determined to meet Dr. Worthington and get a clear picture of the situation in the Big Cypress Swamp. The conditions that Mr. Flagler had described, with bears, alligators, and other beasts, couldn't be that bad.

She imagined that the man with the reddish-gray mustache was staring at the back of her head again. Being unable to help herself, she turned around. He was still there, his large, round, blue eyes staring rudely at her as if he had never looked away.

She hadn't noticed the other man approaching from the opposite direction until he was standing over her. In his hand he held a silver flask, which he brandished in her face. With his other hand he lifted her valise into the aisle and stuffed his fat body into the seat beside her before she could protest.

"Want a drink, lady?" he asked. "Ralph Henry Prichett is my name." He was clad in a threadbare black suit, black boots, and a bowler hat that he had forgotten to remove in the presence of a lady. His face was fleshy and unshaven, his eyes were watery, and an unkempt mustache and bushy sideburns made him out to be a totally unsatisfactory traveling companion. He punctuated his offer with a one-hundred-proof belch.

"Please replace my valise on the seat and sit somewhere else, sir" she snapped. "My husband is coming right back." Her bravado was short-lived. She had no idea how to deal with this cave dweller. She might threaten him with the derringer except for his having put the valise beyond her reach.

"You called me 'sir.' Now that's nice. It's the sign of a true lady, and a beautiful one, too." Both Papa and Mr. Flagler had warned her about ruffians like this one.

A hand on the drunk's shoulder made him turn toward the aisle. There stood the little man with the reddish-gray mustache.

"Excuse me, sir, you're sitting in my seat."

"The lady prefers my comp'ny. They's plenny other—" Suddenly the big man jumped from the seat with an agility that bewildered her. Then she understood the reason: The little man was standing in the aisle and had opened his suit coat just enough for both of them to see a holstered revolver.

"Please excuse that unpleasantness, Miss Sprague," said the little man with the gun. He returned her valise to the seat beside her. Prichett took a few steps away, then turned and gave them both a vengeful glare before heading toward the front of the train. "I should have come forward sooner. Please let me introduce myself. I am Moses Gallagher." Everything had happened so quietly and quickly that the other passengers were not aware.

"I met your aunt, Miss Sarah Sprague, in St. Augustine, and since you and I were both going in the same direction, I promised to look out for you." Just then a cloud of sooty train smoke blew through the car making it hard to breathe for a moment.

"Thank you, Mr. Gallagher," she said with a cough, waving away the smoke. "I appreciate your timely arrival." She put the valise on the floor near her feet. "Won't you please sit down?" Relief flooded over her.

"Thank you, Miss Sprague. I was wondering how I might broach an introduction without startling you. That bummer solved the problem for me." He was mostly bald and wore his remaining reddish-gray hair close-cut. His most outstanding feature was his large, blue eyes. He was wearing a garish plaid three-piece suit with gaiters. His moustache and clothes were meticulously cared for. She guessed he must be in his early fifties.

"Aunt Sarah is full of surprises," she said with a laugh. "How did you meet her?"

"I was one of the two Pinkerton detectives at the Ponce de Leon. Your aunt asked me, in my official capacity as a hotel detective, to keep an eye on you. That was my pleasure, but in so doing I discovered your plan to go to Fort Myers. You shipped two crates to the Hotel Hendry and later confirmed your intentions when you had two Saratogas put on the train to Tampa. Since the hotel is closing for the season, and I was headed in this direction, I was pleased to take on other work."

"I don't recall seeing you at the hotel," she said.

"I'll accept that as a compliment, Miss Sprague. My job was to stay in the background and keep an eye on everyone. Have you seen this man?" He withdrew a photograph from his pocket. It showed the head and shoulders of a young man with dark hair.

"No. Who is he?"

"Someone I've been hired to track down. It's one of three jobs I presently hold."

"What's the third one?" she asked, amused.

"I also sell Dr. Corey's Cosmic Compound. It provides me with a little extra income and a way to meet people. My case is on the other seat. I can provide you with a bottle of Dr. Corey's elixir for just one dollar."

"No, thank you. Aunt Sarah must have been shocked to know that I had arranged to have a young gentleman escort me to Fort Myers."

"Ah, you must mean Mr. Bolton. I'm sorry to say he had to make a sudden trip back to Baltimore."

"Oh, dear, I hope nothing serious happened," she said.

"Not at all. Mr. Bolton, who wasn't as affluent as he might have led people to believe, came into some money and was induced to go home."

"Are you saying that Aunt Sarah bribed Mr. Bolton?"

"Oh, I didn't say that. You might say it. In fact, you just did." He smiled at his not-too-subtle way of conveying his meaning. "I don't suppose I could get you to change your mind and go back to Boston?"

"No, Mr. Gallagher. I am determined to accomplish what I've started."

"South Florida is no place for a lady to be traveling alone. You'll see many more men like that drunkard. And to expect to go into the swamp is foolhardy. Beside that, this heat and humidity gets worse in the summer. You should go north now and come back in November if you must."

She knew that going north now meant never coming back.

Mr. Gallagher excused himself and went through the cars asking if anyone had seen the man in the photograph and did the same with the ticket agent at Palatka. The Pinkerton man was clean-cut and had a pleasant smile, but then Papa's words came back to her: "Some no-account can steal your money before you are able to turn around." But then, who was he to talk? He had separated her from her inheritance.

What Papa had said about many changes and unreliable schedules returned when they boarded the train for Sanford. "You're going to Tampa, then?" she asked, wondering how long Aunt Sarah had arranged to have him escort her.

"Not if I can convince you to go to Fort Myers by a more direct route, Miss Sprague, or I can get you to go back to Boston."

"I don't think I should change my plans, Mr. Gallagher. What are the advantages of taking a different train?"

"It's not a train. From Kissimmee there's a river steamer that goes across Lake Okeechobee and down the Caloosahatchee River all the way to Fort Myers. Miss Sprague told me you're interested in botany. You will see much more from the boat than you can from a train going forty miles an hour. Furthermore, the steamer leaves tomorrow morning, while if you go to Tampa, you have to change trains again, and then take a boat from Punta Gorda. You might have to wait a few days for a schooner that will take you to Fort Myers."

"I could take a carriage from Punta Gorda to Fort Myers," she said.

Mr. Gallagher shook his head. "Carriages get stuck in the sand. There are no roads to speak of, and two broad rivers to cross. The steamer has staterooms, serves meals, and is a more relaxed way to travel. Also, you'd have the pleasure of my company," he said with a wry smile.

"I have shipped my trunks to Tampa," she said, only half sold on Mr. Gallagher's suggestion. Despite Aunt Sarah's affirmation, she didn't know this man.

"With your permission, I will talk to the baggage smashers and see to it that they are taken off the train when we get to Kissimmee and transferred to the steamer."

She hesitated. Mr. Gallagher appeared to be a trustworthy gentleman, and Aunt Sarah had vouched for him. His pleasant disposition and protective manner were positive attributes. She had liked the river route when Mr. Flagler mentioned it. Traveling on the rivers appealed to her, knowing that route would bring her closer to the Everglades. And by changing to the steamer she might avoid further confrontation with that bully, Mr. Prichett. But on the other hand, Mr. Gallagher was still a stranger, and they were headed into an unknown region.

"I can understand your hesitation, Miss Sprague. You should be careful. But let me show you something." He removed a billfolder from his pocket and withdrew an identification card indicating that Moses Abraham Gallagher was a Pinkerton detective. "I am a happily married man, Miss Sprague. My wife, Fanny and I have seven children, I go to church most Sundays, and I imbibe only on holidays. I can assure you I'm harmless."

She smiled at this last statement. But he wasn't exactly harmless—he carried a gun. Then she had to laugh at herself: So did she. "All right, Mr. Gallagher. I will take the steamer to Fort Myers provided that I can get a private stateroom."

When they changed to the Tampa train at Sanford, she was relieved to see that this car was slightly better with painted interior, worn velvet seats, with a little more foot room, oil lamps, and a stove. A stove in this heat! The air was so hot and muggy even with the stove out, her clothes stuck to her. What would the heat and humidity be like in the summer?

Then they noticed that the abominable Mr. Prichett had boarded the train as well.

Chapter 6

Kissimmee, Florida, May 7, 1893

*B*oarding the riverboat tomorrow morning didn't seem like such a good idea now that she knew what Kissimmee was like. From her hotel bed, the shouting through the open window from the dirt street one story below sounded as if the men were in her room. The cowmen were drunk and wild, their language vulgar. Evidently the saloons stayed open all night. Kissimmee was like the Western cow towns described in the dime novels about Indians, gunfighters, and pioneers that she had occasionally borrowed from Grace. Just then three shots rang out from the street below. She stuffed her fist in her mouth to avoid crying out in fear. Mr. Gallagher's room was next to hers. All she had to do was pound on the wall, but there was little he could do about the noise in the street.

As it was, she had clung to him all evening. They had arrived in Kissimmee in a downpour. Few women were about, and those she saw appeared to be rough and common. The men were loud and coarse, and she was relieved to be escorted by the gentlemanly Mr. Gallagher. The staff at the hotel were rude, the restaurant smelled of stale cigar smoke, spittoons were everywhere, and the food had been barely edible. Her room was a bare box with a lumpy bed. The worst part was the stained chamber pot and the bathroom at the end of the hall. If Kissimmee was like this, what must Fort Myers be like? Everyone had tried to warn her. South Florida was no place for her to be traipsing about.

The one bright spot had been Mr. Gallagher. He guided her around the tough men on the street, and thoughtfully suggested she rest in her hotel room while he promoted his case of Dr. Corey's Cosmic Compound. During that horrible dinner he had told her about his wife and seven children. At the hotel desk he had shown the photograph to the clerk and had asked if the man had been in the hotel. He asked the same question of the waiter as well. "That's my other job," he reminded her. "This man" he said, waving the photograph, "is from Philadelphia, and I've been hired to find him and bring him back. The Everglades are notorious for being a hiding place for men running from the law." After dinner he started making the rounds of the other patrons in the dining room as she left for her room.

She tossed about on the uncomfortable mattress. The heat, even in the middle of the night, was oppressive. Her nightgown stuck to her body like wet bathing attire. The fear of someone bursting into her room kept her from lying there naked. Never in the hottest months of the summer had she ever experienced weather this uncomfortable, and this was only May. As if Mother Nature wished to prove herself, lightning flashed through the window, and distant thunder rolled around the sky.

Their home in Back Bay didn't seem so formidable now. Mama's subservient life was far better than this uncivilized extreme in Kissimmee. Perhaps her mother's preoccupation with social standing was a diversion from what she knew about Papa's escapades. Mr. Flagler had Mary Lily Keenan. Did Mama guess that Papa had a mistress who was young enough to be his daughter? Papa was always at his office, at the Tavern Club, or away on business. Mama must have known the truth and immersed herself in her silly calling cards. Men were beasts, Mama had always said, but she had never dreamed her mother had been talking about Papa.

She indistinctly remembered Papa moving the family from Providence to Boston when she was four. His purpose was to expand his father's shipping company. Her memories of their lives in Providence were like looking at a stereopticon in flickering candlelight. But recollections of Mama from the time they had moved to Dartmouth Street were of unending social events: teas, visits, visitors, dinner parties, and the ever-present calling cards for every occasion and non-occasion. She deplored Mama's preoccupation with the cards. Mama insisted they were obligatory for every situation, including luncheons, weddings, dinners, card parties, evening entertainments, afternoon teas, and sick friends. Then another card was required in return; the cycle was never ending. And then there were the bent corners, each conveying a special meaning she had refused to memorize.

Papa had arranged for a tutor to teach his daughter to read, write, and cipher, and Mama placed herself in the role of social instructor. She taught her daughter the etiquette a lady should follow at dinner parties, teas, on meeting a gentleman on the street, and of course, the rules of those infernal calling cards and the language of the fan. Those subtle messages directed at gentlemen seemed ridiculous to her, and she had never used or remembered them. Then there were the customs of courtship, which Beth had never taken seriously, and which were horribly disregarded by Mr. Cushing with Papa's help and Mama's silent acquiescence.

Every step she took with Mr. Gallagher removed her farther from civilization. For the first time she had to admit to herself that she yearned to be back in her own bed in Boston. The Boston waterfront, not far from Papa's office, was like Sunday school compared with this wild town. Seeing these men act in the manner they did explained a lot about Mama's "beasts." Papa's puritanical ways might be just a thin veneer over his true self, but surely he didn't act like these cowmen when he was away from Mama.

Going back home meant defeat. Suffering Papa's harangue was not a pleasant prospect. But this uncivilized world was not for her. There must be a better life, if not in Boston, then perhaps in another Northern city. In the morning she would board the first train for Jacksonville and home.

Chapter 7

*T*he sunlight brought the world back from hell. It had rained in the early morning and the downpour had cleared the air. The street was quiet as the drunks were sleeping off their night of revelry. Knowing that they were leaving Kissimmee helped her to forget the declaration made in the darkness. Beth did not disclose her nighttime fears to Mr. Gallagher and now had the courage to continue on one more lap of her journey. The daylight had lifted her spirits.

Then she saw the *City of Athens*. When Mr. Gallagher had used the word "steamer," she had pictured Papa's ships. This boat was about the same length as a railroad car and resembled a two-story wooden box on a raft propelled by a paddle wheel at the stern. A single smoke stack rose in the middle and belched black smoke into the sky. It was a barge, or at best a work boat; the *Slum of Athens* would be a more fitting name.

The dock buzzed with activity as the last barrels, bolts of cloth, and cord wood were being loaded onto the main deck from horse-drawn wagons. As she crossed a short gangplank with Mr. Gallagher, they were met by a member of the crew who led them to their cabins on the upper deck. She had trouble keeping her eyes from this homely creature, unable to decide whether the person was a man or a woman.

"I'm Pepper Douglas," the person said, leaving the question unsettled. This wiry creature, even shorter than her, must be a woman, she decided, and was the first one she had ever seen wearing trousers and a work shirt. Her graying hair was cut short and was thin on top.

The tiny "stateroom" on the upper deck was an oversize oven. Through a narrow door she saw a double bunk. The floor barely provided enough space to stand in. At the end of the narrow box was a straight chair and a wash stand. No drawers or closets existed for unpacking. "How long is this trip?" she asked.

"Three days and two nights," said Mr. Gallagher as he entered the cabin next to hers.

Wishing she hadn't listened to Mr. Gallagher, she dropped her valise on the lower bunk and left the stifling heat of the cabin to stand by the rail. The still air was rancid with the odors of wood smoke, dead fish, and horse dung. Pepper Douglas and a Negro man had already hefted the gangplank and were pulling in the lines. For the first time she was watching a woman involved in strenuous labor, and the sight was worth writing to Mary and Grace about. Mr. Gallagher was nowhere to be seen.

As soon as they were under way, Pepper appeared on the upper deck and came straight along the narrow passageway to her. "Hit's nice to have other womenfolk on board. Someone to talk to. Thar's blamed few now that the weather is gittin' warm. I'm Pepper Douglas. My husband's the pilot." Her voice had a high-pitched nasal twang that seemed typical of most Floridians she had encountered.

"I'm Elizabeth Sprague from Boston." The way Pepper was clothed and her taking part in manual labor made the woman unique. Her face was thin, tanned, and wrinkled. She was missing a front tooth, and her protruding ears might have been better off hidden by longer hair. Her left eye stared off to the side, but her trousers were the woman's most remarkable feature.

"That's a mighty purdy dress you're wearin, Miz Sprague. I heered of Boston, but hain't been futher than Jacksonville. I'm hopin' to go to Key West someday. I was borned on a boat on St. Johns River and lived my whole life on Floridy's rivers." Pepper had an unassuming, matter-of-fact way that she found unusual but engaging. The woman's face clouded and a scowl formed. "Hyar comes no good."

She turned away from Pepper and was startled to see Ralph Prichett heading toward her. Now she wished she had stayed on the train to Tampa.

"Ah, look who's here, the lovely lady from the train." A yellow-toothed grin lay in the shade of his huge mustache. She was surprised that she had missed seeing the ugly mole on his right cheek when he had accosted her on the train. He appeared to be closer to sober than he had been the previous day, but his face was still flushed. Once again she was separated from her valise and Aunt Sarah's derringer.

She remained silent, hoping he would be discouraged and move on.

"Will you be so kind as to have lunch with me today?" he asked her.

Even though Prichett towered over Pepper, she stepped up to him, hands on hips, and said, "Don't you get rambunctious with this lady. You all eat together in the salon, Prichett. You know thet. Ussens air talkin' hyar. Why don't you go and see if you cain't rustle up a game of draw poker?" He stepped back. The man must have tangled with Pepper before, and Pepper had won.

"I'll see you later, then, beautiful lady," he said to Beth, ignoring Pepper, but carefully stepping around her as he walked away.

"Don't trust him, Miz Sprague," Pepper said as she watched him head toward the salon. "He's the most ornery, no-account scalawag in Floridy." Pepper departed but returned immediately carrying a wooden box for her to sit on. The passageway was too narrow for chairs. "Now, I have to be fixin' the vittles for you hongry passengers."

"Do I need to dress for lunch?"

Pepper looked at her from head to toe. "Whut's thet thar yer wearin'?" The little woman turned, strode aft along the passageway, and disappeared into the galley.

Beth was left to watch the canal disappear behind them as the *City of Athens* pushed its way into a lake. The air was cleaner but still hot even in the shade of the overhanging roof. The chump-chump-chump of the paddle wheel was hypnotizing, and she was content to sit at the rail and watch the water flow by. Last night's fears had dissolved, and she was resigned to living out the next three days aboard even though Mr. Prichett was there, too.

Mr. Gallagher appeared from the deck below. "Well, Miss Sprague, this is better than sitting on a dirty train, isn't it? I presume you're aware that our friend, Mr. Prichett, is on board."

"Yes, I saw him, Mr. Gallagher."

"I wanted to see if you're all right before we start a poker game."

"I'm fine, thank you, Mr. Gallagher." After he entered the salon, she opened the door to her room and took out the derringer to carry with her as long as men like Mr. Prichett were around. She opened the drawstrings to her reticule. The little weapon fit easily inside. She never intended to shoot it, but the weapon might come in handy to keep a coward like Prichett in his place.

At the sound of a cow bell Beth entered the "salon" for lunch. The narrow room had bare gray walls and a long table that seated twelve. Light came from one window and a door at each end that gave access to the passageways on either side. Mr. Gallagher and Mr. Prichett, who was puffing on a cigar, were playing poker with three rough-looking men she had never seen before. It was unsettling to see that Mr. Prichett had a silver flask set beside his plate. Papa would never have allowed the cigar or whiskey at the dinner table. Beth sat at the opposite end with a young couple, the Fishers, who were moving from Connecticut to a town named Ritta on Lake Okeechobee. She was pleased to see Mr. Gallagher leave the card game and move to a chair beside her. He introduced himself to the others as being from Weehawken, New Jersey. Empty chairs served as a buffer between the diners and the poker players. Pepper Douglas appeared from a door in the back wall and served large platters of boiled sweet potatoes, greasy venison steak, corn bread, and a pitcher of hot coffee. Pepper's cooking was better than that at the hotel. Until now she hadn't realized how hungry she was.

Beth observed that the four remaining players continued to smoke, drink, and concentrate on their cards in spite of being in the presence of ladies. Their foul language and cigar smoke assaulted her senses as she tried to eat. She remembered the rule that a lady sees and hears nothing she ought not to, and acted accordingly. Mrs. Fisher, on the other hand, stared open-mouthed at the offenders. Mr. Gallagher talked the most, attempting to drown out the poker players, she thought.

"Although no one asked, I'm a purveyor of patent medicines," offered Mr. Gallagher. "I have a cure for every illness known to man, and for a few that haven't been discovered yet. This magic elixir is all in one bottle. Doctor Corey's Cosmic Compound will cure bad breath, baldness, cancer, colds, colic, constipation, coughs, cramps, croup, chicken pox, depression of the spirits, diarrhea, diphtheria, debility in males, dyspepsia, falling of the womb, fevers, headaches, inflammation of the lungs and kidneys, influenza, liver complaint, loss of voice, measles, mumps, nervousness, pains, pregnancy, seasickness, sore throats, spasms, and whooping cough."

Everyone laughed, including Mr. Gallagher. The drummer had a ringing baritone voice that made his chant almost a song.

"Can you do that again?" asked Mr. Fisher.

"Certainly, sir," said Mr. Gallagher, and he sang out the cures in rapid order. She watched the others, but no one seemed to mind the mention of diseases while they were eating any more than they minded the rudeness of the men playing poker and smoking cigars while they ate.

"Can you prove that your elixir can cure all those diseases?" asked Mrs. Fisher.

Mr. Gallagher pretended to be offended. "Why do I have the feeling you don't believe me? Can you prove that they don't?" he countered. "Actually, I can truthfully speak for colds and coughs personally," he confided. "But I have an affidavit signed by Dr. Corey himself in which he swears that he had scientifically proven the magical qualities of his Cosmic Compound."

Looking at her protector she said, "Mr. Gallagher, don't you believe in the power of prayer, hope, and self-will as more effective cures?"

"A positive attitude always helps, Miss Sprague, but you can't imagine the miraculous restorative powers of Doctor Corey's Cosmic Compound until you've tried it."

"How much does a bottle cost?" asked Mrs. Fisher.

"One thin silver dollar a bottle, ma'am, to keep you and your husband healthy out here in the Florida hinterlands."

"I suppose," mused Mrs. Fisher, "considering that there aren't that many doctors down here, that we might buy a bottle to be safe." Mr. Fisher rolled his eyes but remained silent.

Since Mr. Gallagher had saved her from Mr. Prichett on the train, she wasn't about to scoff at his patent medicine humbug. Mrs. Fisher's purchase was the first sale she had seen him make.

"You couldn't make a wiser decision, Mrs. Fisher. I just happen to have my case with me. How about you, Miss Sprague? Are you ready to make a wise purchase of the magic potion?"

"No thank you, Mr. Gallagher." She looked over her shoulder and asked, "Why are we stopping, Pepper?"

"This hyar is Turkey Hammock. The pilot stops hyar to wood up and drop off supplies."

Once the meal was over, she went back to the narrow outside passageway alongside her room to get relief from the smoke-filled salon. Following Mrs. Fisher's move, she removed her hat and left it on her bed. She was down to one petticoat and was still hot. She envied Pepper Douglas in her trousers which must be cooler than a long skirt. Enduring the poker players in the salon or lying in her hot cabin were not particularly good options. She decided it was better to sit on the box by the rail and observe the bank of the river they had entered after Turkey Hammock.

She happened to glance toward the back of the steamer and saw Mr. Prichett. He was standing at the doorway of the salon, unmoving, staring at her. This time she was prepared and slipped her hand inside her handbag and onto the derringer. Turning toward Prichett, she stared back, but her heart was beating wildly. He slipped back into the salon, and she removed her hand from the gun. He had disappeared for now, but sometime there had to be a face-to-face confrontation with the man.

The steamer had plowed its way through a series of lakes and canals. The monotonous scenery and the rhythmic beat of the paddle wheel made her drowsy. Resisting the temptation to lie down in her ovenlike room, she moved her seat box to the opposite passageway to remain in the shade as the sun moved past its zenith. The scrape of a boot on the deck behind her made her whirl and reach for the derringer at the same time.

"I'm sorry if I startled you, Miss Sprague," said Mr. Gallagher. His plaid suit and drummer's traveling case concealed well his job as a Pinkerton detective. "Are you enjoying your trip?" He had a free and easy way about him that was inoffensive.

"Florida is very different from Boston, Mr. Gallagher."

"Yes it is. I've traveled all over this great country and never cease to be amazed at all the wonderful and different people and places." He looked over Beth's shoulder at her sketch book. "I see you've been sketching the plant life along the banks. Are flowers a hobby of yours?"

"No, sir. I'm a botanist, and I'm going down to the Fakahatchee River to research the flora."

"A botanist! That's a man's trade, isn't it?" he asked, leaning against the railing.

Beth bridled at his remark. "Not necessarily. There's no reason a woman can't do everything a man can do, Mr. Gallagher. Pepper Douglas cooks, lifts gangplanks, and wears trousers."

"No offense, Miss Sprague. It's just that you don't see many ladies such as yourself doing men's work."

"What makes 'work' belong to men?" she asked, surprised at herself for saying that. Except for her studies, she had never worked a minute of her life.

"Well, it's always been that way," he said apologetically. "Men have certain things they do, and women have . . . others. I guess I've stuck my foot in my mouth, haven't I?"

She smiled. "I have something to prove, Mr. Gallagher. My father and most men think women are incapable of being more than housewives and mothers. Women like my mother know better but are afraid to speak out and act. Others like Elizabeth Cady Stanton and Susan B. Anthony talk and write about women's rights. But it's those like my professor, Alice Katherine Adams, who demonstrate to the world that women are as capable as men. They get an education, do good work, and have a family as well."

"What I'm trying to say is that you'd never catch my wife out here doing what you are. She's been happy staying home taking care of our children."

"How old are your children, Mr. Gallagher?" she asked, hoping to change the subject.

"Well, let's see. The oldest of the seven is Robert, who's fifteen. The youngest is Diana. She's two, a redhead, and I think she'll be a fire-eater like you."

"What is a fire-eater, Mr. Gallagher?"

"An aggressive lady who goes to prohibition meetings and marches as a suffragette, makes speeches, and writes for a newspaper."

"Although I'm favorably disposed to those causes, I've never thought of myself as being aggressive, and I've never been involved. My mother has gone to meetings to listen to Julia Ward Howe and Elizabeth Cady Stanton when that great lady was in Boston. In fact, Mama named me Elizabeth Julia without Papa's realizing the significance of those two names. Papa was always angry when he found out Mama had attended a meeting; women's rights were never discussed in our house."

Mr. Gallagher laughed. "If Mrs. Gallagher ever wanted to go to meetings like that, I'd let her go, but you women will never get the vote as long as the WCTU exists."

"What do you mean, Mr. Gallagher?"

"Men will never support the women's vote as long as you insist on depriving us of our liquor."

"There are more important reasons than that. Don't you think your wife should have the right to vote?"

"I don't know. I've never thought about it. What's the point? The wife makes up her husband's mind, and then he votes."

From his wry smile she wasn't sure he was joshing her or was serious.

"Where is this Fakahootchee River you're headed for?"

She laughed. "Fakahatchee. It's in the Everglades, in the Big Cypress Swamp, actually. You must travel a lot, Mr. Gallagher."

"I go all over creation. I love detective work and selling, but I don't want to be on the road forever. Someday I hope to save up enough money to buy a farm."

Once, as a little girl, she had visited a farm in Massachusetts. The cold farmhouse and the smells made it difficult to understand why someone wanted to live on one, but she remained silent. She had never known a detective or a drummer before and decided this one was nice in spite of what Papa had said.

"Does the trouble on Wall Street hurt your business, Mr. Gallagher?" she asked for something to say.

"On the contrary, Miss Sprague. The bad times make men nervous, and I have an elixir that will calm their nerves."

Thankfully Pepper Douglas came up to them before he got started on his puffery again.

"Hello, Mrs. Douglas," she said.

"You kin call me Pepper, Miz Sprague."

"And you can call me Beth, Pepper." In Boston she never would have permitted herself such informality.

"And you can call me anything you like except late to dinner." Mr. Gallagher laughed at his own joke. "If you ladies will excuse me, I will try to convince those men in the salon that Doctor Corey's Cosmic Compound will improve their poker playing."

"Where are we, Pepper?" she asked after Mr. Gallagher had left them. "Was that Lake Okeechobee back there?"

"Thet thar were Lake Tow-hope and then Cypress and Kissimmee. This hyar's the Kissimmee River. We have a goodly ways to go to get to Tantie, the big lake."

The waterway was narrow and as twisty as a snake, unworthy of being called a river. Great blue herons stood poised for flight among the lily pads and sawgrass, watching for fish. Here and there orange groves or fields of grazing cattle lined the river, but more often its banks were crowded with willows, cattails, ferns, and custard palms. Here and there the dog fennel stood ten feet tall with white flowering heads. Beth's sketch book lay in her lap, ready to capture images of as many live plants as time allowed. She was thrilled to spot deer, rabbits, and raccoons among the trees. Occasionally the pilot reversed the steamer to navigate a sharp turn around a backward loop. Offshoots of the river appeared with no markers, reminding her of the Oklawaha. How the captain knew which branch to take was mystifying. Along the banks were alligators by the dozen. They passed little settlements with curious names like Grape

Hammock, Bay Hammock, Kicco, Shell Hammock, and Alligator Bluff. At many villages the steamer stopped to "wood up" or drop off supplies. In the distance was black smoke that after an hour became a steamer off to the right, apparently marooned in sawgrass.

"Thet's the *Cincinnati*, another wet-ass boat. We'll pass her atter awhile," said Pepper.

How that was possible was hard for her to understand, but she decided to wait and see. She wasn't about to ask about a wet-ass boat either. With all the twists and turns their headway seemed negligible.

Abruptly gun shots rang out on the opposite side of the steamer. She followed Pepper around to the other passageway as fast as she was able in her long dress. The firing continued while they looked cautiously around the corner. The men who had been playing poker were lined up along the upper deck shooting at alligators. The creatures were no more than thirty feet away and were writhing and slipping into the water.

"Why are the men doing that, Pepper?" she asked. She was relieved to see that Mr. Gallagher did not have a gun in his hands.

"'Cause they hain't got no senst. I reckon hit don't do no harm."

"But they're defenseless creatures, Pepper."

"You wouldn't think so iffen you was swimmin' in the river."

It was pointless to say anything else as the *City of Athens* moved on and many alligators lay dead, and others that were unable to slip into the water were still thrashing about in pain.

The birds were more numerous than ever, and Pepper pointed out wood ducks, teal, pin tail, and mallards. Some species must have numbered in the thousands. The shooters turned their attention to the birds and shot down several dozen before they lost interest. Fortunately for the wildlife, after that the men went back to their poker.

After making many twists and turns, the *Cincinnati* gradually grew larger, and after two hours the riverboat was upon them. She saw that the boat was a smaller steamer carrying lumber. The two vessels passed close enough for a man to hop across from one to the other. Rowdy men occupied the upper deck and brandished rifles. Evidently they, too, had been shooting alligators. Much yelling and cursing crossed back and forth between both passengers and crew. A ruffian called across to her with a coarse invitation that made the other men laugh, but she pretended not to hear. As the *Cincinnati*'s paddle wheel at its stern splashed by, she began to understand why they were called "wet-ass" boats.

For supper that night Pepper served up beef stew and biscuits that Beth found to be tasty. Not long after supper she retreated to her cabin and went to sleep. In the darkness of the night she was awakened by a low, persistent sound. After a moment, she realized someone was working at the lock on her door.

"Who's there?" she asked tremulously. The door flew open, and a tall, stout figure was silhouetted in the doorway. She pounded the wall for Mr. Gallagher and screamed at the same time. The man was undoubtedly Mr. Prichett, now full of whiskey and ready for something more exciting than poker.

The dark form loomed over her as she lay in the bottom bunk. She pounded on the wall with one hand, and groped for the derringer with the other. Her screams failed to scare the intruder away. His hands were almost on her when it seemed as if he were backing away. Prichett's silhouette grew smaller, and suddenly he was lying in the outside passageway with another, smaller figure standing over him in the darkness. At first it appeared as if Mr. Gallagher had dropped Prichett, but it turned out to be Pepper who had grabbed the big man by the arm and had somehow forced him to the deck. Mr. Prichett had been drunk, as she suspected, and swore that he thought he was entering his own cabin, a lie that no one believed. Mr. Gallagher had slept throughout the whole disturbance.

Beth was unable to get back to sleep. Mr. Prichett was still on board, and she knew that sooner or later he would have to be stopped.

Chapter

8

*I*n the morning the river was still a watery snake winding its way though the sawgrass. The steamer was already under way, progressing downstream at the same slow, tentative pace as the day before. The birds were more abundant than ever. She had brought Coues' *Key to North American Birds* along, and was able to identify the birds for herself this time. Along with the now-familiar egrets, ibis, and herons, she spotted curlew and snipe.

Tiring of watching the birds, Beth leaned against the rail, and for some reason Papa came to mind. In his office and not thinking about her, he was most likely sitting behind his desk, glowering at the latest employee to displease him. He had been that way at home, often aiming a brooding look of annoyance at Mama, a servant, or her.

When Papa was annoyed his mustache bristled. If he had been a bird, his feathers would have been ruffled, a sign that he had been angered by someone who had broken one of his many strict rules. How does a man cause his mustache to bristle? She twisted her mouth and ran her tongue under her upper lip, but she needed a mirror and a mustache to observe the effect. Whatever he did, he was unaware of the results; it just happened.

Papa always made the rules for Mama and her, and infractions were not taken lightly. His rules extended from table manners to what women should do and say. He had never laid a hand on Mama, and had stopped using a paddle on his daughter when she went away to boarding school at Dana Hall. But his demeaning words were more stinging and lasting than a slap in the face.

The scene she had made in the dining room would have launched a scathing diatribe if no guests had been in the house. What made it so bad were the many different social blunders she had committed all at once: her emotional outburst in front of their guests, her defiance, her refusal to accept Edward Cushing's proposal, and most damaging of all, Papa's embarrassment. Fortunately for her, Mary and Michael Otis, as well as Aunt Sarah, had stayed the night. In the morning she had departed for the depot before the other guests had left and thus had escaped his verbal beating.

Having lost the opportunity to upbraid and belittle her, Papa took the opposite tack and had left the mansion before daybreak. Their gardener and coachman, Mr. Steeves, had made two trips to the depot, one before daylight with their trunks, and the second with Aunt Sarah, Mama, Mary, and Beth in the brougham pulled by two high-stepping mares. It had been snowing lightly, but not enough to warrant the cutter, which she loved for gliding through the snow. The serenity of the falling snow had been in contrast to the turmoil she felt at departure.

Papa had always been stern, with a sense of humor that revealed itself only when the joke was at someone else's expense, usually Mama's. From the time Beth was a little girl, she was unable to recall a lighthearted moment. She admitted to herself that she had always loved her father, but he had never given Mama or her the kindness and gentleness a woman needed. She reflected upon the small bit of irony in still loving him after learning about his dalliance, and even after his attempt to arrange a marriage for her. But the bittersweet fact was that she could never speak to him or live in the same house with him again. Her resolve to continue her quest was strong.

Her thoughts were interrupted by the passing of another steamer, the *Octavia*, which seemed to be as ugly as the *City of Athens*, but carried freight exclusively and had no upper deck for passengers.

She was shocked to see Pepper coming toward her smoking a pipe. The eccentric woman took her to the wheelhouse to meet her husband, the pilot. Mr. Douglas was as tall as Pepper was short and kept his eyes on the river. He let his wife explain how there were no beacons or buoys, and how he had to be on the lookout for silver streaks and ripples. The silver streaks were caused by snags that might puncture the hull, and ripples signified the presence of sandbars. The skipper also had to get around bends without allowing the current to push them sideways.

"Why don't we ever see the Fishers on deck?" she asked Pepper later.

"Them's newlyweds," said her friend with a wink and a sly smile as if that explained everything.

At the noonday meal Pepper served them meat reminiscent of a veal cutlet, dipped in flour and fried in fat, but the meat was too pink and tough.

"Thet thar's gator steak," answered Pepper when Mrs. Fisher asked what was on her plate. "Seven cents a pound." Beth pushed away her plate, and Mrs. Fisher did the same. The men at both ends of the table laughed and continued to fork down their food.

By late afternoon she learned they were coming to the river's mouth. Any change was welcome after the monotonous backing and filling the steamer had performed under the skillful hands of Mr. Douglas. After one last stop to wood up, the river widened, and soon they were in the lake she had heard referred to as both "Tantie" and "Okeechobee."

They stopped for the night at an outpost called Buckhead on the north shore. The oncoming darkness filled her with trepidation. She was unable to rely upon Mr. Gallagher, who had slept through Pepper's decking of Mr. Prichett, and the lock to her door was still broken. Placing the derringer under her pillow helped little in falling asleep. Prichett was still on board, and who was to say that he wouldn't try to attack her again? Then there were the other three rowdies who looked none too trustworthy themselves.

The Bucket Flower

The night turned out to be uneventful, and early daylight was filtering through her cabin window when she awoke. The steamer had left Buckhead behind in the fog, moving faster than the skipper had been able to go during the first two days. The water was glassy calm under the gray blanket. How Mr. Douglas knew where he was heading was a mystery. After an hour the sun burned through, and she was amazed that the lake was so large. The shoreline, which was low and flat anyway, had disappeared, and with the exception of occasional grass patches, she could see no land on either side for more than an hour. A breeze came up, changing the mirrored surface of the water into textured patterns.

At last Beth saw a single tree ahead and to the right, which Pepper had told her to look for. The flat-topped cypress with a nail keg and small flag on top marked the entrance to the three-mile canal. To the right, a group of tar paper shacks appeared; Pepper said they were occupied by fishermen. Earlier her guide had pointed out huge schools of catfish to her.

On the south side of the lake lay unbroken sawgrass waving and glistening in the sun all the way to the horizon like a gigantic playing field. A shiver ran through her as she realized she was looking at the Everglades that Mr. Flagler had described to her. The huge expanse of open space was stunning—Beth was both amazed and defeated. The sawgrass stretched before her endlessly. The tops of the grass were yellow, and the overall view presented an immense golden plain as flat as any she had ever seen. Without trees the sky was enormous. The pale blue overhead was interrupted in the southeast by huge, billowing clouds, thunderheads with a pale orange tint that cauliflowered larger and larger as she watched. On the distant horizon beneath the clouds, heavy rain showers were in progress. Within one dark area she spotted a lightning bolt, too far away for the sound of thunder to travel to her ears.

After a short stop where the Fishers disembarked, the steamer plowed through a series of shallow lakes. One, called Lettuce Lake, gave the appearance of a vegetable garden covered with a lettucelike growth. Once across, the steamer stopped, and Pepper and the Negro clambered over the paddlewheel to scrape off the tangled weeds. The next lake was so shallow Beth could see the bottom close by. The absence of towns made her feel lonesome and a long way from Boston. After more than an hour of passing through the lakes, the current flowed through a rocky channel, and Pepper, passing by, announced to her that they were on the Caloosahatchee River.

At first the land was flat and open with pines or an occasional raised clump of trees that Pepper called hammocks. Then they passed fields of sugar cane, grazing cattle, and orange groves. But even these suggestions of civilization failed to lift Beth's spirits; every turn of the paddlewheel plunged her farther into the wilderness.

At lunch they were distracted by one of the poker players, whose loud vociferations revealed that he had been drinking too much. Apparently he was losing steadily and getting angrier with each hand. The situation was becoming more tense by the minute. Mr. Gallagher suggested to the ladies that they leave the salon. Gathering up several slices of Pepper's bread, Beth retreated to sit on her box in the open passageway.

The growth on the riverbanks had changed to bald cypress, sabal palms, and swamp oaks. A great variety of birds, including flocks of white egrets, dotted the trees and sky. Impressive mossy cypresses towered above everything else. The river became crooked with high banks of ten to fifteen feet, but was more passable than the Kissimmee had been. Near a place called Fort Thompson, she was shaken by Pepper's account of this steamer, the *City of Athens*, sinking at this spot several years earlier. At one sharp turn in the river the Negro jumped ashore and looped a rope around a palm tree to keep the current from running the steamer aground.

The men were still yelling in the salon, and between the heat and the tension Beth had the almost uncontrollable desire to jump overboard. The boat was too small to hold so much anger. She felt like something bad was going to happen.

The woods were thick. Oak and cypress branches formed a canopy above the river. She did her best to sketch the colorful air plants and vines growing on the trees as the steamer drifted by. For the first time she had a close look at roseate spoonbills, which Pepper called pink chickens. She refrained from asking Pepper if that was a dish served aboard.

At a village facetiously named Belle City was a store. "This hyar's jus' a one-horse town, Miz Sprague," said Pepper. But curiosity made her follow

Mr. Gallagher ashore when they stopped to wood up and take on cargo. She was disappointed to see that the general store sold nothing but the basic foodstuffs, dry goods, and notions. The Quaker Oats brought back memories of home and Mrs. Faraday making breakfast. Why was she obsessed with thoughts of home? The most exotic objects for sale were sewing machines, Allen's root beer extract, Towle's Log Cabin syrup, and Hall's Sicilian hair renewer. The storekeeper and his son, both in a dirty aprons, helped Pepper and the Negro load aboard smelly skins of alligator, otter, deer, and raccoons. Mr. Gallagher explained that the storekeeper engaged in barter with the Indians. He showed his photograph of the man he was tracking to the men ashore as he had at every stop.

At Fort Denaud Pepper helped the men load lumber from a saw mill. Later on they passed two Indians in a canoe. One was wearing a derby hat and the other had on a top hat. Both wore black vests over calico shirts. As they were the first Indians she had ever seen, she had expected a few head feathers, at least.

Evidently Mr. Gallagher preferred standing on deck to sitting in the smoky salon where the tension was still high, as evidenced by the shouting. "What good will it do for you to draw pictures of every plant in the Everglades?" he asked.

"Botanists do more than draw pictures, Mr. Gallagher. Among other things, we seek economic uses for newly discovered species. Many of these plants are edible, some have fibers that might be used in rope or cloth, and others might have medicinal uses."

"Just like Doctor Corey's Cosmic Compound."

"Perhaps," she said dryly. "Studying the means of pollination and other characteristics may result in developing hybrid species of fruits and vegetables that will grow faster or larger. We also study the soil to see what kinds of agriculture the Everglades might support."

She was tired of sitting on the box, and Mr. Gallagher's presence was wearing thin. Fort Myers could not appear soon enough. From the salon came more angry shouts. The men were yelling at each other in a high-pitched argument. One was accusing another of cheating. A shot rang out. The single blast was more ominous than when the men shot fusillades at the wildlife. Mr. Gallagher ran to investigate while she sat frozen at the rail.

Mr. Prichett dashed out the door of the salon and down the open passageway away from where she was sitting. Mr. Gallagher ducked into the companionway to avoid being shoved aside as one of the gamblers fled up the passageway toward her, gun in hand. A second man leaped from the doorway and fired at the man running in her direction. She jumped up, realizing that she was in the line of fire, but the door to her cabin was on the other side. Before she could turn the corner at the front, the first man grabbed her and used her to shield himself from the second man farther back. Her reticule with the derringer in it had slipped to the deck. The second man ducked into the companionway at midships. Mr. Gallagher had disappeared. With great force the man pulled her backward and around the corner at the front.

For what seemed like several minutes, all was quiet except for the distant chugging of the steam engine and the sloshing of the paddle wheel and a louder pounding which was her heart. The smell of rotten whiskey and stale sweat engulfed Beth as the man's huge arm crushed her against him. She was afraid to struggle or scream, not certain how the drunk would react. Her captor and his pursuer peered at each other, each waiting to get off a shot if the other stepped into the passageway.

Suddenly there was a voice close behind them. "Put down your gun, Toby, or I'll blow your head off," said Mr. Gallagher calmly. He must have crossed through the salon and dashed forward the full length of the steamer on the other side and across the front. She couldn't see him, but from the sound of his voice, the little man was close enough to be pointing his gun upward at the drunk's head.

"Frank's gonna kill me iffen I doan have a gun," her captor whined.

"Let Miss Sprague go and put down your gun or I'll kill you." His voice was still calm, but the tone left little doubt about his resolve. For whatever reason, whether it was the liquor, fear, or insanity, the drunk tried pulling her around toward Mr. Gallagher, and was met with the loud roar of a pistol.

It was springtime, and as she lay in the open coffin, she could see the blossoms of the Public Garden above her head. From somewhere out of sight she could hear the voices of both Mama and Papa. Mama was weeping, and Papa, in his gruff, matter-of-fact way, was telling her that he knew this would happen.

When she awoke, she was lying on her bunk, and Pepper was bending over her, wiping her face with a cool, wet cloth. "Was I shot?" she asked.

"No, Miz Beth. You was a little too close fer comfort, though. You got blooded when Mister Gallagher shot him. Thet fool had jus' kilt his friend in the salon an' t'other one woulda kilt him iffen Mister Gallagher dint." She was hearing Pepper's voice over the ringing in her ears. In a few minutes she was able to sit up, and when Pepper left, she changed her dress, deciding to throw away the bloody one. As she came out on deck she was still shaking. She gripped the rail to steady herself. If friends shot one another, what did enemies do in this part of the world?

After attending to the two bodies, Pepper joined her on deck.

"Where's Mr. Gallagher?" she asked Pepper.

"He's in the salon havin' a drink or two. He don't cotton to killin' a man."

The sun was disappearing into violet clouds on the horizon turning their faces and the wall behind them blood red. After a place Pepper called Alva, the river widened to several hundred feet, and the current slowed. Nothing but the monotonous throb of the steam piston and slosh, slosh, slosh of the stern wheel broke the superficial serenity of twilight, and it was hard to accept that hardly an hour ago two men had been killed.

Then the river widened to more than a mile as they approached Fort Myers at dusk. How much wilder than Kissimmee could this village be? The farther into the wilderness they went, the more barbaric it had become. Mr. Gallagher had told her he was planning on sailing down the coast the next day. His commitment to Aunt Sarah had been fulfilled. She was now on her own and at the mercy of Mr. Prichett or other ruffians already lurking in Fort Myers. Nothing but drunkenness, lust, and violence were to be found here in untamed Florida. When the *City of Athens* headed back tomorrow, she decided she would be on it, and heading home.

Chapter

9

Fort Myers, Florida, May 11, 1893

*B*eth sensed someone behind her even before she heard the floor squeak. She turned and her heart pounded. The lecherous Mr. Prichett loomed above her and was grinning evilly.

"Well, well, dearie, here we are, alone at last."

After a quiet night and breakfast at the Hotel Hendry, she had climbed the stairs back to her room. Her steamer trunks and the two crates she had sent ahead were waiting downstairs. All she had to do was retrieve her valise and go down to the river where the *City of Athens* was leaving for Kissimmee within the hour. Within three days she would be in Jacksonville, and thirty hours later in New York. A few more minutes and she could have been rid of Mr. Prichett forever.

After a brief questioning last night about the killings on the steamer, she, Mr. Gallagher, and Mr. Prichett had been allowed to go to the hotel. The third poker player had disappeared. The local sheriff had seemed indifferent, as if killings happened every day, and the lives of two strangers mattered little.

No one else was in sight. Prichett's huge form filled the hotel corridor as he approached. He came so close that his paunch was pressing her into the wall, and his foul odors enveloped her. Instead of groping for her door key, her hand went for the derringer. Just as she gripped the handle, he grabbed her by the shoulders. "Now don't hurry off. Let's have a little chat together in my room." It was difficult to twist the gun in his direction as he pressed against her. He forced her toward the door diagonally opposite hers as the gun went off. A look of incredulity spread across his face which quickly turned to horrible realization and pain. His hands dropped from her shoulders as his knees buckled and he slumped to the floor. She couldn't remember having pulled the trigger.

The hour which followed was a blur. At first she heard no other noise than Mr. Prichett's yelling. For a moment she hesitated between hiding in her room or running from the hotel. In a daze, she was led into a small, crowded room downstairs behind the hotel desk overflowing with the sheriff, the hotel manager, a doctor, the reporter-editor-publisher of the *Fort Myers Press*, and several other men who may have been hotel guests.

Overwhelming her at this moment was having missed the *City of Athens* for its return trip to Kissimmee. Living under the influence of Papa and Mama seemed tolerable now compared to facing the possibility of going to jail for shooting a man. A marriage to Edward Cushing was a better alternative than trembling in fear of being attacked day or night. Remaining in Boston the rest of one's days as a spinster appeared to be a better solution than living in this uncivilized, remote place for one minute more. Papa had been right to warn her about south Florida. What had Dr. Adams been thinking to send her here?

The roomful of men stared at her with morbid curiosity. The sheriff was a man of about forty who looked more like an unshaven store clerk than an officer of the law. He seemed more interested in this shooting that had happened in his town, particularly when the shooter had been party to a killing hardly fourteen hours earlier. But even so, he treated her with respect and there was a certain air of restraint about both him and the other men in the room. After having her describe what had happened, he asked, "If he was facing you, Miss Sprague, how were you able to shoot him in the back?" His question didn't make sense.

"I don't know, sir," she sobbed. It was then that she remembered having heard a door in the hall closing immediately after the gunshot.

"Did you know he was unarmed?"

"He was pushing me into his room! I was frightened." She no longer cared how she looked or sounded. "He tried to attack me on the riverboat."

"Why are you in Fort Myers?" he asked.

"I'm from Boston. I am a botanist. I'm here to study the plants of the region."

He seemed unimpressed. "Let me see your pistol, Miss Sprague," he said. She removed the tiny derringer from her handbag and handed it to him. After inspecting it carefully, he said, "This little toy hasn't been fired. Is this the only weapon you carry?"

"Yes, sir."

"Did you see the man who shot him?"

His question was as strange as his earlier one. "I thought I had pulled the trigger. I didn't see anyone else. Is he dead?"

"Haw!" The guffaw came from someone in the back.

"We wish," said the sheriff. "It was just a shoulder wound, but your little pea shooter would hardly have tickled him."

"Who shot him, then?" Mr. Gallagher was short enough to have shot Prichett from behind and then ducked into his room without her seeing him. It was prudent not to mention the Pinkerton man's name at this time. Most likely her protector had no interest in being connected with two shootings within twenty-four hours.

The sheriff's demeanor had transformed into an attitude of indifference. "We'll probably never know. Prichett is always causing trouble. He has more enemies than a cat has meows. He calls himself a private detective, but no one around here would hire him. Let him figure it out for himself. Whoever it was deserves a medal. You can go now, Miss Sprague." It didn't seem as if there would be any further investigation.

Still dazed as she walked from the room, she hardly noticed the woman who approached her.

"Miss Sprague? I am Marian Worthington. Welcome to Paradise."

The lady's smile was genuine, and she held out her hand. "I have come to invite you to stay with us. My husband received a telegram from Mr. Flagler more than two weeks ago, and we've been expecting you."

She took the lady's hand but could barely speak. "May I sit down, Mrs. Worthington? I feel faint." She gathered her composure as Marian Worthington talked. The woman, about fifty, was round-faced, with a body to match. She wore a pince-nez, her dress was plain by Bostonian standards, and on her head was a coal scuttle bonnet. This lady seemed to be unaware of the shooting that had taken place earlier.

"I sent you a message last night saying I was taking the steamer back to Kissimmee this morning."

"Oh," said Mrs. Worthington, putting her hand to her mouth. "Since the messenger brought your note this morning, we thought you were leaving *tomorrow* morning. I came to invite you to stay overnight with us. We had been hoping you could stay longer. We don't get many visitors."

The story of what had happened in the hotel's upstairs hallway and how she had missed the boat shocked Mrs. Worthington.

"Well, then, since you're already packed, please come stay overnight with us, or longer if you can, and perhaps we can make up for this terrible experience."

Mrs. Worthington led her outside the hotel to a buggy pulled by a sleepy mare. Seeing the woman drive the carriage was remarkable, something ladies never did in Boston.

"I came as soon as I knew you were here. My husband, Ben, was engrossed in a very important task—fishing." She rolled her eyes but smiled at the same time. "I'll send Homer after your trunks later." Mrs. Worthington clucked at the horse and held the reins confidently.

The idea of Mama driving a carriage or meeting someone at the depot alone made her smile. "I had hoped to meet your husband, but I hadn't expected to stay with you, Mrs. Worthington. I had planned on staying at the hotel. I don't wish to be an imposition."

"Nonsense. Ben and I enjoy company. Please call me Marian."

Marian pointed out several landmarks as the carriage crunched along the gravelly road. The one wide, unpaved street with several narrow side streets reminded her too much of Kissimmee. A few brick and cement buildings and several false-front stores stared back at her: the Packer and Blount General Store, two or three saloons, a blacksmith shop, a post office that labeled the town as "Myers," and on a side street, the schoolhouse. The whole town cried out for paint and repairs, but palms had been planted along the river front, which almost made up for the rest.

At the docks were two schooners in the process of loading or unloading goods. The *City of Athens* had already disappeared up the river. She was going to miss Pepper Douglas. That outlandish woman had become her friend in their three short days together. As soon as she met Mrs. Worthington she had a good feeling about the lady and decided that an overnight at the Worthington home was better than staying at the hotel. Mr. Prichett had more reasons than ever to track her down.

They rode along the river, passing corrals of scrawny cattle. The cattlemen wore sombreros and stood or sat around listlessly in the heat watching the two women drive by. Fort Myers had been described by Pepper as another cow town, but except for the incident at the hotel, the town, at least in daylight, was much quieter than Kissimmee had been at night. As they rode slowly down the road, they passed a few comfortable-looking frame houses along the river.

"That home, Seminole Lodge, is owned by Thomas Edison," Marian pointed out. "We're neighbors, but he hasn't been here in several years. Ben keeps an eye on the place for him." The house was a pleasant one with broad verandas. She found it fascinating that such a prominent person, whose famous laboratory was in New Jersey, owned property this far away.

Marian drove the horses into a driveway several houses farther along the river. The house was similar to the Edison home in that it, too, had wide verandas and several shade trees on a lawn that swept down to the Caloosahatchee River. The horses stopped beside the veranda steps without being told. A Negro came from the back of the house and took the reins.

"Homer, please take the runabout to the hotel and pick up Miss Sprague's trunks, valise, and two crates."

As soon as they were in the house, she felt more relaxed. All the windows were open, and a light breeze drifted in from the river. Marian was forthright, friendly, without affectations, and made her feel immediately at home. She sensed that life was slower here, and that she could enjoy this section of Fort Myers.

"Why don't you walk out to the dock and meet Ben while I get Phoebe started with lunch."

The river seemed more like a large lake. The opposite shore must have been two miles away, and the surface was mirrorlike near the shore. The Worthington dock stretched out into the river, and near the end sat a man with a floppy straw hat and a fishing pole. His bare feet dangled just above the water. Before she got close he waved and then held his hand up as if he wanted her to stop. In a loud voice he recited:

"There was a fish that caught a man.

And then a great fight began.

He struggled and twisted,

Pulled and resisted,

And swam all the way to—what rhymes with 'man'?"

"Japan?" she offered.

"And swam all the way to Japan." He jumped up and laughed. "Thanks for coming, Miss Sprague. Now I don't have to sit here and pretend that the fish are going to start biting any minute. I don't think they like my rhymes. I'm Ben Worthington." He stuck out his hand.

She laughed as she shook his hand. "I'm Elizabeth Sprague, Dr. Worthington. Thank you for seeing me." He was as short as Mr. Gallagher, but with a Humpty-Dumpty frame. She guessed he might be in his fifties.

When they entered the house, Dr. Worthington went straight to his wife and gave her a kiss. Having witnessed few expressions of love at Dartmouth Street, Beth was unsettled. Whatever affection existed between Mama and Papa was reserved for times when they were alone. She could not remember when Papa had kissed her last, if ever. Mama's attention had come in the form of reading to her, followed by a bedtime kiss. But even that had ceased after they had moved from Providence.

As Beth looked back, she realized that Mama's metamorphosis came when they moved from Providence to Back Bay. From that point on it seemed as if Mama's goal in life was to make a favorable impression upon Boston's First Families. Her mother's persistent pursuit of the Boston elite had shaped every comment and action. During dinner parties Mama had sent her to eat in the kitchen with Mrs. Faraday. She felt as if she had been relegated to a station lower than the servants. When she became a resident student at Dana Hall, it seemed at the time to be a rejection by both parents. Even their relationships with their Providence relatives withered to infrequent letters. But Mama's efforts to ascend to Boston's high society were futile against a mountain too steep to climb.

For lunch Marian made her husband put his shoes on, and it was amusing that such a discussion was necessary. Papa never sat at the table without coat and tie, let alone shoes, even for breakfast. Dr. Worthington had on an open shirt, trousers, and shoes by demand.

"Did Ben inflict his poetry on you?" asked Marian as they sat down.

"Dr. Worthington treated me to a poem about a fish." She was interested to see that the Worthingtons did not sit at opposite ends of the table, but close to each other at one end.

"Please call me Ben, Elizabeth, or I might be persuaded to torment you with another poem."

"Oh, no," said Marian with a laugh. "One poem a day is enough, Ben. He's been vexing me with his impromptu poems for twenty-three years, and he seldom recites the same one twice."

Lunch was served by a Negro woman.

"This is Phoebe, our cook," said Marian. "Phoebe, this is Miss Sprague."

"How-de-dew, Miz Sprague. Ah hopes you like our pickens." She set before them plates of cucumber salad.

"I'm sure I will." She had never been introduced to a servant before, and Mrs. Faraday had never been introduced to her parents' guests.

"Henry Flagler sent me a telegram saying you have an interest in the flora and fauna of southwest Florida, Elizabeth," said Dr. Worthington.

"I was going to write my master's degree thesis on the plant life of the area."

"Was? Have you changed your mind?"

"Well, finally I've been convinced that Florida is too wild for a woman to be traipsing around alone." They were shocked to hear about the two killings aboard the steamer.

"Elizabeth had a another dreadful encounter this morning at the hotel," said Marian. She proceeded to relate the incident to her husband.

"That's a terrible way to be introduced to Fort Myers, Elizabeth." said Dr. Worthington. "But that shouldn't deter you from your studies."

She asked them to call her "Beth" and then told them about her other encounters with Mr. Prichett. The Worthingtons shook their heads but didn't seem too surprised.

Phoebe brought in hush puppies next, and Marian explained they were fish balls rolled in fine cornmeal and fried in fat.

"You can conduct your work from right here, Beth. Have the flora brought to you as I do with the animals," said Dr. Worthington.

"Animals?" she asked. "I was told you were a botanist."

Dr. Worthington abruptly threw a fish ball across the room which was snatched out of the air by an old dog that had just entered from the kitchen. "That's Towser. He owns the place. I'm a zoologist, but don't let that bother you. I'm not sure Henry knows the difference. I have contacts with people who can bring you specimens from the swamp, Seminoles who know their way around and aren't afraid of the snakes and alligators. They bring me gators, panthers, anything I want, alive or dead."

She was disappointed. She had expected his experience in her field to be helpful. But that mattered little since she was returning home. "Doesn't that limit your learning about animals' habitats," she asked, "their lairs, their enemies, their food?"

"I suppose it does a little, but I'm not about to wade around in waist-deep water playing tag with poisonous snakes and gators. I can tell what an animal eats and doesn't eat and where it's been from inspecting the contents of its stomach and what gets entangled in or lives in its fur. I've even trained the Indians to bring me footprints and scat."

"That might be harder to do with plants," she said.

"Yes, especially with trees," said Dr. Worthington with a laugh. "But we occasionally take short camping trips. Let's do that while you're here. It's better than not studying our natural surroundings at all."

A camping trip! That's what she had wanted to do on the Oklawaha.

"After lunch I'll show you my laboratory, and we can share the space."

"The sharing will happen while Ben's fishing, which is most of the time," interjected Marian with a smile.

"Now, that's not fair, Marian. These studies progress slowly."

"Mmmm," replied her hostess.

"I don't wish to impose. I can stay at the hotel." She sounded to herself as if she had changed her mind.

"You can stay with us," said Marian. "We have plenty of room and it will be a pleasure having another woman around."

"I can pay room and board," she said. The Worthingtons were so friendly and informal. Here was an oasis in south Florida she might enjoy.

"Nonsense," said Dr. Worthington. "What's it cost to add another cup of water to the soup?"

Phoebe next served cold turkey slices and green beans.

"Then it's decided. You'll stay with us for a while," said Marian.

Their generous offer made heading north seem less desirable. It was pleasant beside the Caloosahatchee with these friendly people. For dessert they had lemon ice, a treat she hadn't expected to find in this warm climate.

"Thank you," she said. "I'll stay a few days."

Chapter 10

"*T*hat's a rattlesnake," said Dr. Worthington.

He was showing Beth his laboratory. She was standing as far back from the cages as possible. The snake was coiled and apparently asleep. Its diameter was larger than her upper arm. The cages were stacked in a back room, and all except four were empty.

"These four critters, the snake, the opossum, racoon, and fox, were all the Seminoles had for me this trip."

Even though the cages were clean, she felt sorry for the racoon and the fox, but she had little sympathy for the ugly opossum or the snake. "What do you keep in the large cages?" she asked.

"At different times I've had black bears, panthers, and a wild boar once. There's a market for these animals in the northern cities, and when I get an order from a zoo, the Indians get me what I need. Poisonous snakes are in great demand, but the Indians don't like to bring them in alive, and Marian can't sleep when they're on the property—when she knows about them," he said pointedly. He looked at the snake and recited:

"The rattler is my friend,
And will be till the end.
When he shakes his tail
I hit the trail,
On that you can depend."

Outside he showed her a cement enclosure that contained a small pool and a three-foot alligator. "Once in a while someone will bring me an injured deer or a pelican, which I try to mend and then let go as soon as they're well." Leaning over the wall, he rubbed the alligator on its snout with a stick. The beast slowly opened its jaws revealing rows of vicious-looking teeth. He then placed the end of the stick in the alligator's mouth. Its jaws snapped shut so violently that she jumped. "You don't want to mess with these babies." He closed his eyes for a moment and then said:

"An old gator slept in the sun
Waiting for me to run.
When he took hold of my leg
I could do nothing but beg,
Which pleased the old son of a gun."

Beth had been bored by the poetry her professors had inflicted upon her at Wellesley, but she enjoyed Dr. Worthington's little rhymes—although she hoped he was a better zoologist than he was a poet. That a scientist was in the business of selling wild animals to northern zoos was surprising, but it was in the interest of educating the public, she supposed.

They ate dinner under the light of a kerosene lamp. Marian said, "A few days after we come back from our camping trip, we're going to Ohio for the summer. You are welcome to stay here. Phoebe and Homer will keep the house open for you."

"Oh, no. I couldn't impose upon you like that. Whatever information I can gather between now and the end of the camping trip will have to suffice, and then I will return to Boston."

"You're welcome to stay as long as you wish," said Dr. Worthington, "but when you do head for Boston, may I suggest you consider taking the schooner to Key West and then a steamer to New York. You'll find it much less harrowing than crossing the peninsula again."

"We'll be sailing in the opposite direction, to New Orleans," said Marian, "and then up the Mississippi. In the meantime I can take you in the buggy to the unsettled areas near here to inspect the native growth."

"I don't want to keep you from all you have to do before heading north."

"Nonsense. If you weren't here, I'd be passing the time by reading while Ben is napping on the pier pretending to fish."

"I resent that, Marian," he said gruffly, but with a grin. "Just for that I will challenge Miss Sprague to a game of chess or checkers, and you can read."

"Good," said Marian. "I'd prefer to read for a change."

The following week was a great relief after the unpleasant trip from St. Augustine. In the space Dr. Worthington had given her to set up her microscope and books, Beth inspected the contents of her crates. Most of her equipment had been delivered intact; only a few vials for the collection of soil samples had been broken. Marian turned out to be a delightful partner who showed her woods and fields where there was natural growth she could dig up and bring back to the laboratory to inspect and record in more detail. It was unfortunate that they were not closer to the Big Cypress Swamp.

In between long periods of fishing from the dock, Dr. Worthington went about gathering equipment and supplies for their forthcoming camping expedition. She was impressed by the quantity of equipment he had, but his preparation went all too slowly.

While Dr. Worthington fished, Beth penned letters to Aunt Sarah, Mary, and Grace. Aunt Sarah would need to know where to send another check, and she wrote to her aunt that the next stop after Fort Myers was to be Key West. To Mary and Grace she related all the happenings since St. Augustine, including thorough descriptions of Pepper Douglas, Mr. Gallagher, and Mr. Prichett. She decided to wait until she was about to leave for Key West before writing to Mama. There was no point in revealing her whereabouts, although Marian told her it might take weeks for her letters to get to Boston. A letter to Papa was out of the question; his actions had built an impenetrable wall between them.

"You can also send a telegram from Punta Rassa," said Marian. "It's three miles from here." She decided she wanted to leave Fort Myers before Papa found out where she was. He might hire someone to look for her and drag her home like a stray dog.

When the day for their camping trip arrived, Dr. Worthington left early and returned with a motorized boat named the *Mina*, which he tied up at the dock. "This is Tom Edison's boat," he told her. "He lets me use it whenever I want in exchange for looking out for his place. It's a great arrangement since he's never here." The craft was smaller and better kept than the boat they had rented on the Oklawaha River. She peered at the naphtha engine, which ran without a firebox. Dr. Worthington lashed a canoe, which she noticed held his fishing equipment, alongside the *Mina*.

Once the tents and other paraphernalia had been loaded on board, they headed down the river with Dr. Worthington at the helm. She hadn't expected Phoebe and her husband to come along. Homer, Beth noticed uneasily, brought a rifle aboard and stowed it with the other equipment. Marian sat in the bow holding her hat. "I sit up here, even though it's breezy, because I'm afraid of that engine. One never knows when it might blow up."

The river was broad, but Dr. Worthington pointed out sandbars just beneath the surface on one side and then the other. A few were marked by branches thrust into the bottom. Dr. Worthington negotiated the unseen channels carefully. She was pleased to see the water was becoming clearer and bluer as they approached the mouth of the river.

After a while he said, "That's Punta Rassa up ahead." After pulling up to the dock none too gently, he led her into the large building that served as both a hotel and telegraph office. After sending Aunt Sarah a telegram saying that Key West was her next destination, they were under way again. The telegraph operator charged her two dollars and fifty cents, but the telegram would reach Aunt Sarah before her letter.

"Cattle and farm produce are shipped from here to Key West and Havana for the Spanish Army." Dr. Worthington pointed out the Sanibel lighthouse and Matanzas Pass as they motored into Estero Bay.

He called their attention to the birds, pointing to frigate birds soaring in great arcs and brown pelicans skimming along, then rising up and plummeting like an arrow into the water after a fish.

"Oh, oh, I know what's coming next," said Marian in mock distaste.

"Marian knows me too well," said Dr. Worthington.

> "The pelican is a funny bird;
> Its bill is really absurd.
> It can hold several fish;
> They're his favorite dish,
> But from turtles he has demurred."

Without warning the *Mina* suddenly ground to a stop.

"You'd better forget the poetry, Ben," said Marian, "and concentrate on where we're going."

"It's an oyster bar," said Dr. Worthington excitedly. He and Homer jumped off into shallow water with their boots on and shoveled up a bucket of oysters for their dinner before pushing the boat back into deeper water.

"Look at those fish!" she said excitedly. "What are they?" Scores of large silvery black bodies frolicked alongside the *Mina*.

"Those aren't fish," said Dr. Worthington. "They're porpoises, sometimes called dolphins—small-toothed whales."

"I can feel another poem coming," said Marian.

"No, this is a true story," said Dr. Worthington. "This schooner that used to sail between Cedar Key and Key West was a bad-luck boat. It had sprung a leak and sunk. It had capsized another time, and it had gone aground so many times that the skipper changed its name to *Accident*. One time this drummer showed up in Punta Rassa, and the telegraph operator asked him, 'Did you come by *Accident*?' 'No,' said the drummer, 'I came on porpoise.'"

"Don't laugh, Beth," Marian told her. "You encourage him." But neither of them were able to control themselves.

"Those are mangrove islands," explained Dr. Worthington as they passed several clumps of trees surrounded by water.

"What is all that white on the trees?" she asked.

"That's Florida snow," he answered.

"Bird droppings," Marian whispered. Then aloud she said, "The egrets nest on those islands by the tens of thousands at night. Look at the great blue herons standing over there."

The sun was overhead, and Dr. Worthington turned off the engine.

"Why are we stopping, Ben?" asked Marian.

He pointed toward the shore. "We're going up Survey Creek over there. Let's eat lunch before the swamp angels find us."

"Mosquitoes," Marian translated for her. "Leave it to Ben to be thinking of food, but it's a good idea this time." Phoebe had prepared crabmeat sandwiches and lemonade.

After lunch Dr. Worthington steered into the mouth of a small river. "This is Survey Creek," he said. "We'll find a campsite two or three miles up. That's Braxton Comer's plantation over there. He grows pineapples, coconuts, and bananas." They saw Negroes working in the fields.

A little farther along Dr. Worthington stopped the engine again and they glided silently upstream. A large live oak overhung the water above the mangroves, looking as if it were ready to fall onto the boat at any moment. Sabal palms were clumped together on one side, their long-dead lower fronds hanging down like coarse lions' manes. On the other side was a flock of white-plumed wood storks wading in the shallow water. Their black, wrinkled, bald heads were ugly, and Beth shuddered. The still water mirrored everything above it in darker, inverted patterns. The peace and beauty was hypnotizing until they were attacked by a swarm of mosquitoes.

"Time for the mosquito netting," said Marian, handing her a bottle of citronella to rub on her hands and face. "We also have Bee Brand insect powder." Her hostess had prepared nets to fit over their broad-brimmed hats and tie around their necks. Now she understood why Marian had suggested she wear a scarf. For the first time in Florida Beth was happy to have worn long sleeves. "Tuck your skirt around your ankles."

Dr. Worthington started up the engine again, and they wended their way up the narrowing creek. Farther on, a little break in the undergrowth revealed a muddy bank on which three lethargic alligators reclined, eyeing the humans suspiciously. The mangroves hanging over the creek formed a tunnel and scraped the roof of the *Mina*. The undergrowth was so thick Beth thought they had come to the end of the creek until at the last moment she saw a narrow break to the right and another narrow strip of dark water ahead.

The farther they penetrated the wilderness, the more nervous Beth became. After a time they approached a pine tree grove with palmettos on the south bank. The water was deep enough for Dr. Worthington to steer the *Mina* up to the pine-needle-covered shore. Phoebe and Homer, who had been quietly shucking the oysters, became talkative as they unloaded the equipment and set up the tents. Dr. Worthington paddled away from the *Mina* in the canoe and started to fish. Beth sat with Marian on wooden tubs that doubled as storage and seating. As soon as the three tents were set up, Homer began collecting firewood and dead palm fronds, which Marian explained made smoke when they burned and helped keep the mosquitoes away. "You can't have enough protection against those nasty insects." Phoebe set up a folding table and unpacked the cooking and tableware needed for dinner.

Except for the saw palmettos, the area was open under the slash pines, devoid of wild animals, and safe enough to explore. "Marian, do you mind if I take my sketch book and start inspecting the plant life?"

"That's why we came, dear. But be careful where you step. There can always be snakes underfoot."

Beth hesitated at the thought of snakes, but then pushed herself. This might be her last chance to get out into the wild. Watching the ground where she was headed, she lifted her skirt and stepped cautiously over dead logs and around the saw palmettos. Pepper Douglas' trousers or the bicycle bloomers she had seen a few daring women wearing in New York were more suitable for trekking through the underbrush. She had never owned a bicycle, let alone worn bloomers, because Mama accepted the general belief that bicycling was harmful to a lady's health. Strolling under the slash pines, the going was easy at first, but soon brush and thorny vines were grabbing at her mosquito netting and skirt, and she changed direction. The mosquitoes were even thicker here, and she had to keep brushing them off her hands in spite of the citronella.

She sketched a typical slash pine and drew a detailed picture of its rust brown and grayish bark and wished she could record its color. The yellowish candle-like new growth of a feathery-topped young pine was another sketch. She was careful to detail the new shoots of the saw palmetto and the vicious-looking spikes on the stems of the mature plants. So many plants—gallberry, goldenrod, milkwort, and many whose names she didn't know. Her excitement grew. Here was where she wanted to be; this was what she had imagined it to be like along the Fakahatchee River.

Beth lost track of time and distance. Suddenly there was a presence among the trees. They saw each other at the same moment, and neither moved. The deer was staring at her, unafraid and motionless. The thrill of seeing the animal made her shiver, and it may have been that little movement that made the sleek animal bolt noiselessly into the thicket.

The desire to continue on was mixed with the need to find her way back to the camp. All the while Beth had kept in mind the direction of the creek, but now when she turned around, nothing looked familiar. Heading in the direction her instinct told her she had come, all the pines and saw palmettos looked alike. The sun was hidden by the taller trees, and was no help. She felt the cold fingers of panic creeping up into her head and forced herself to push them away, walk slowly, and look at the ground for snakes and footprints. Just then there was the banging of metal on metal off to her right. Relieved, she headed in the direction of the sound, and soon the tents were in sight. Phoebe was striking a large metal spoon against a pot until catching sight of her.

"Thank you, Phoebe. I might have had trouble finding my way back if you hadn't made some noise."

"Supper time, Miz Elizabeth." The afternoon had flown by. The table had been set. Homer had two fires going: one which had supper cooking over it, and a smaller one in which dried fan palms popped and crackled and gave off pungent smoke which stung her eyes but helped keep the mosquitoes at bay.

"Did you find anything new?" asked Marian as she handed her a fan palm to help keep away the mosquitoes.

"Oh, yes! I could spend a week here studying these flowers and plants. Thank you both for bringing me."

After a dinner of fried oysters, catfish, canned vegetables, lemonade, and lemon cake, they discussed her walk and the sketches she had made.

She told them about the deer she had seen.

"Those are beautiful pictures," exclaimed Marian. "You can become an artist if you ever decide against being a botanist."

"We have to be careful out here," warned Dr. Worthington. "From now on we should walk with someone else when leaving the campsite. Most of the animals are harmless if they hear you in time and have a chance to get away, but if startled or feel their young are threatened, they may attack."

"Which one is the most dangerous?" she asked.

"You're looking at him," he said with a smile. "Man is the most dangerous predator of all to the flora and fauna. But I know you're asking about the animals. The wild boar will attack without being provoked, but it's unlikely you'll see one around here. There has been talk of one or more apelike creatures larger than a man having been seen in the swamps miles to the southeast from here, but its existence is highly improbable."

"Mr. Flagler had mentioned the swamp apes," she said. "What makes you think they don't exist?"

"The presence of apes in the wild on this continent is unknown. Unless one escaped from a zoo or a circus or floated over here on a log from Africa, it's unlikely any species of that kind exists in North America. Besides, an ape brought up in captivity has little chance of survival among wolves, panthers, bears, poisonous snakes, and alligators."

Darkening shadows danced around outside the firelight. Beth was glad she wasn't out here alone. Phoebe and Homer were invited to join their circle around the fire and they talked for a while longer and then sang "Faith of Our Fathers," "Rock of Ages," and "Battle Hymn of the Republic" before retiring to their tents. She had a tent to herself, the Worthingtons had another beside it, and Phoebe and Homer had a smaller one on the other side. She watched Phoebe look fearfully out into the darkness as she circled the campfire.

"Pull up that sleeping bag tight around your neck if you don't want some critter crawling in to keep you company during the night," called Dr. Worthington. Beth shivered even though the evening was still warm. The shrill whine of the mosquitoes outside the netting was ominous enough.

The Worthingtons had even brought a commode which Homer had set up in the bushes and she had reluctantly used earlier, but she promised herself to suffer through the night without using it again. She had never slept on a cot before, and wasn't sure she would be able to tonight. She dismissed the possibility of a swamp ape entering her tent, but the idea of a snake slithering into her sleeping bag stayed with her.

Beth awakened to the sound of murmuring voices and the clatter of pots. Daylight seeped through the tent fabric. She had fallen asleep after hours of tossing and turning in the hot sleeping bag, but was afraid of removing it. Her face and hands itched from mosquito bites she had gotten in spite of all the precautions. When she opened the tent flap, Dr. Worthington was already sitting on a tub drinking coffee and Phoebe was preparing breakfast.

"Good morning," he said softly. "Did you sleep well?"

"Yes, thank you," she lied.

"Marian is still sleeping," he said, pointing toward their tent.

"No, I'm not," said his wife's voice from within the tent, "and neither are the mosquitoes." After a few moments Marian pulled back the tent flap and squinted at the sunlight. Beth hoped she didn't look as disheveled as Marian did.

After breakfast and a cursory attempt at washing their faces and hands in pans of tea-colored water from the creek, they were ready for the day's activities.

A shot rang out in the distance. She looked at Dr. Worthington, startled.

"That's Homer. He's hunting down our dinner. I hope he bagged a deer."

She hoped that it wasn't the deer she had seen yesterday afternoon.

Marian went with her to find plants along the creek and was almost as excited as she was in finding a dainty little blue flower and other new plants. In the afternoon Dr. Worthington took her farther up the creek in the canoe while Marian napped in the Worthington tent. He wasn't as much fun as Marian had been. She felt that he was with her solely for the purpose of protecting her from whatever dangers might arise, and became restless with her search after the first half hour. But she made full use of the time and kept up her investigation until they heard Phoebe banging on the pots again. As they approached camp, they were met by mouth-watering smells of roasting venison. Before they could eat, the daily thunderstorm passed through, but this time the downpour seemed harder than usual. For a time it appeared as if their tents might be washed away.

Somehow Homer had kept the fire going, and after the rain shower they had venison for dinner. Since she was hungry, Beth avoided thinking about the deer she had spotted the day before.

"Thank you both for a very worthwhile day," she said. "This experience inspires me to reconsider going into the Big Cypress Swamp."

"You have no idea how different that would be," said Dr. Worthington. "Here we have all the comforts of living in a hotel. In the swamp are more of everything—more swamp angels, more snakes and animals, and more water everywhere. This spring has been unusually wet."

After dark around the campfire Phoebe told them the story of the night folks and how they spirited people into the woods, never to be seen again. They again sang hymns before retiring, but Phoebe's tale followed Beth into her sleep.

On the second morning everyone assisted in loading the boat after breakfast. Beth placed on board a box containing her collected samples of flowers and small plants to be dried and pressed once they were back in Fort Myers. She felt as if she had just begun to learn about the local flora, but looked forward to returning to the Worthington home and a refreshing bath.

The time had come to be moving on. After all, it was impossible to stay with the Worthingtons forever. Being alone again was not a pleasant thought. Prichett was in Fort Myers recovering from his wound and might seek revenge even though she wasn't the one who shot him. In spite of that, she made her decision. The camping trip had inspired her to find a guide to escort her through the Big Cypress Swamp.

Chapter
11

"*I*'ve decided to continue on to the Big Cypress Swamp," she said.

On the return trip up through Estero Bay Beth sat near Dr. Worthington. She had two questions she wished to ask him.

"Dr. Worthington, these three days have been wonderful. I've learned so much. I've decided to go farther into the Everglades. You certainly know how to conquer the wilderness. Would you and Marian be willing to delay your trip north long enough to be my escort?"

"I'm flattered that you should ask, Beth. A foray like that could be beneficial to both of us in our respective fields. But even if I were going to be here, a trek like that is beyond the staminas of an old geezer like me and a young lady like you. It might be worth considering if we could do it by boat. Please don't think that what we experienced the last three days is anything like what is to be faced in the cypress swamp. This spring has been unusually wet, and you'd be walking in water up to your—well, you'd be wet all the time. My going with you is a moot point, however, because Marian and I cannot delay our trip north. I have a convention to attend and several speeches to make."

Beth hadn't expected him to change their plans and so was not disappointed. She had noted his disinterest in her work the preceding afternoon and suspected he preferred working in his laboratory to being in the field. This brought her to her second question:

"Might it be possible for you to find a guide for me before you head north?"

Dr. Worthington seemed to concentrate on steering the boat and didn't answer for a while. Then at last he said, "Guides are a dime a dozen, Beth. The problem is in finding one with both knowledge of the cypress swamp and the integrity to lead you through it safely. My suggestion is that you take a boat to Marco, Allen River, or Chokoloskee, and hire a fisherman with a skiff to accompany you through the Ten Thousand Islands and up a river or two."

She remembered her experience on the Oklawaha and how little she had learned about the flora from a boat.

"Are there mangroves there?"

"Everywhere."

"Then to investigate the area I need to see, I must come in from the land side and avoid the mangroves."

Dr. Worthington shrugged but remained silent, his eyes on his course across Estero Bay.

If she had to return to Boston now, at least she had tasted the wild, had gathered a few specimens, and had almost filled one sketch book. But she had barely scratched the surface; there must be hundreds of species waiting to be discovered. *Time* was needed to study the form and structure of new plants, how they grow and reproduce and are affected by their surrounding conditions. It might take months of observation to learn how a plant manufactures, digests, and uses food. It was impossible to learn in one short trip what method is used to get rid of waste materials, why some plants are resistant to insects, and by what means others produce natural fertilizers. To expect to study the different kinds of cells under a microscope was unworkable, too; a laboratory in the swamp was needed for that. Even mere classification of the genus and species she encountered was guesswork without a taxonomic guide.

Dr. Adams must not have had any idea of the problems to be faced. Before the end of her senior year, her mentor had encouraged her to pursue cytology, the up-and-coming cellular study of plants. But she was afraid people would see her as just another female in an office, a secretary or at best a librarian. The lure of being a field botanist was much stronger than being cooped up in a laboratory or a museum. But now that she was here, time was needed to study the effects of climate and water supply and the availability of nutrients in the soil. Discovering the possible economic uses of new-found plants also took time. The best to be expected of herself was to record, collect, and press specimens for the Wellesley herbarium, and ship a crate of live plants for their greenhouse. Classification had to wait until she had access to the reference books.

The thought of going to the general store brought back the dread of seeing Mr. Prichett again, but it was a necessary step in preparation for her trip—a trip she knew she had to make. Her decision made, Homer drove her in the runabout to see what supplies were available at Packer and Blount's for her forthcoming foray into the cypress swamp. At the bank she found a draft for more money than she expected or needed from dear Aunt Sarah. The general store was well supplied; they had the food and dry goods and most of the equipment she needed. On the shelves she was reassured to find products that she had known from home—Borden's condensed milk, Van Camps beans, Chase and Sanborn coffee, and bottles of Heinz ketchup. She added two of each to her box of supplies, glad Homer was there to help her carry them. When she realized the runabout was going to be overflowing, she stopped. There would have to be a second trip on another day.

As they passed the Hotel Hendry on the return trip to the Worthingtons, all the bad memories of that place came flooding back. The odds of seeing Mr. Prichett again were slim, but there he was with his left arm in a sling, sitting on the hotel porch. Why wasn't he in jail? He glared at her as they passed, and she imagined she could feel his eyes still upon her back as they rode down the street. Now that he knew she was still in Fort Myers, the fear that he might try to find her was discomforting.

After dinner she said, "Dr. Worthington, I've made a list of provisions and equipment, and I'd appreciate your looking it over and seeing if there's anything I've missed. I've based my list on our camping trip and then added several other items I saw at Packer and Blount's." She expected his experience to be helpful, but she also wanted to remind him to help her look for a guide.

Dr. Worthington took her list, sat down, and studied the full page in her careful, handwritten script. "You're planning an African safari," he said after a cursory glance at the list. "How many bearers were you planning to hire?"

"I can hire a horse and wagon, two if necessary," she said defensively.

Dr. Worthington shook his head. "Horses and wagons can't travel where you want to go. You must travel much lighter than this, Beth. I'm willing to lend you the tents, but why do you need two tents?"

"One for the guide, one for me."

"You can't carry tents and cots along with everything else you have on your list."

"Where would we sleep?" Snakes and mosquitoes!

"In the open. Seminoles prefer that anyway. How long were you planning to be gone?"

"I was planning on two weeks the first time. Why does the guide have to be an Indian?"

He shook his head. "Knowing the swamps is an Indian's way of life. Any white man who claims to know his way around the Big Cypress Swamp must either be a poacher, a bandit hiding from the law, or a liar." He looked again at the list. "Two weeks is too long, Beth. Why do you need fifty pounds of salt pork?"

"The salted and smoked meat will keep, and we can eat it three meals a day." She had expected him to add items to her list, not to be criticizing what was already there.

"Your guide should be shooting your food. Who is going to use the sixty pounds of flour?"

"The guide will be doing the cooking. We'll need biscuits and bread."

"You'll be lucky if I can find a guide who will take a woman into the swamp at all, let alone one who is willing to do the cooking." This was a new Dr. Worthington, and he was upset with her for some reason.

"Well, I'll do the cooking," she said. She wasn't about to admit that she had never boiled water. She could learn.

"A guide might carry his own bedroll and his rifle, but you'll have to tote everything else," he said.

She didn't want to admit that one large wagon was needed to carry her two trunks, the two crates of botanical equipment, and the provisions and equipment she and Homer had hidden in the laboratory. "Is it possible to hire Indians to carry my supplies?"

"That's not in their nature. They hunt, fish, and carve dugout canoes."

Marian had entered the room in the middle of the conversation and sat beside her husband. Now she said softly, "Don't you see, Beth, that what you've set out to do is impossible, especially for a woman?" Having another woman talk like that was devastating.

"You might charter a boat and return to Survey Creek or go up Trout Creek or other little rivers on excursions like the one we just made," Dr. Worthington said more kindly.

She was unable to answer him. The tears in her eyes made it impossible for her to look at the Worthingtons. She hadn't dared to tell them that her plan was to trek all the way through the swamp to Allen River or Chokoloskee. Nor had she mentioned that she had already bought half of the supplies that day.

The next morning Beth overheard the Worthingtons talking in the dining room as she came down the stairs. "I'm worried about Beth, Ben," Marian was saying. "She shouldn't be traveling into the Big Cypress Swamp alone."

"Then try to talk some sense into her," said Dr. Worthington. "She's determined to give it a try, and she hasn't the foggiest idea what it will be like. She won't last even one day."

Beth retreated up the stairs with a hollow feeling in her stomach. The urge to cry was strong, but that wouldn't help. When she returned for breakfast, Phoebe told her that Dr. Worthington had "done gone" for the day and that "Miz Worthenting" had a meeting of the Ladies' Guild and had left with him. The house was quiet and she had the time to write letters. She read a little of William Dean Howells' *The Rise of Silas Lapham*, which she had found in Dr. Worthington's library, but when she tired of that, she went into the kitchen. Phoebe was cutting up vegetables for dinner.

"Phoebe, can you teach me how to cook?"

"Ah allow ah doan know how ter cook, Miz Sprague. This chile jus' throws things inter thuh pot, an' when they's done, Ah throws 'em onter thuh plates, and mos' of thuh time folks make 'miration."

It didn't appear as if she was going to learn much here. She had no idea what questions to ask. She wished she had watched Mrs. Faraday more often before she had gone away to school.

Phoebe went on with her chopping as if she weren't there. Pulling up a stool, she sat and watched the thin, black hand manipulate the knife while the fingers of the other hand held the carrots without getting cut.

"Have you been doing that all your life, Phoebe?"

"No. I wuz a-fixin' breakfus this mawnin."

"No," she said, trying not to laugh, "I meant have you been a cook all your life?"

"No. Ah wuz a kitchen helper till mah mammy died. Then Ah wuz de cook for de big house till de war ended. Atter dat Ah cooked for black folks mostly ontil Miz Worthenting hired me an' Homer."

Having lived through the war, Phoebe must have been a slave. She wanted to know more, but hesitated to use the word. "Were you on a plantation, Phoebe?"

"Yessem. An' Homer wuz, too. In Georgy. Homer excaped to Floridy an' came back atter de war to marry me."

"That sounds like true love," she said, impressed.

"He liked thuh way Ah throws the food onter his plate, Ah reckon."

She saw the twinkle in Phoebe's eye. This cook of thirty years had been joshing her from the outset of their conversation.

"Miz Worthenting tol' me you is goin' inter de cypress swamp?"

"Yes. I study plants."

Phoebe shook her head without replying.

"Why do you ask, Phoebe?"

"Thet's an all-fired bad place, Miz Sprague. They's a heap o' evil spirits out there. You orter stay put." The cook's eyes grew large and she raised her arms as she said, "Den dere's de miasmas dat rise outta de swamp at night an' poison a soul." Even though Beth tried to put aside this woman's gibberish, a chill swept through her which made her shiver.

"Dem evil spirits'll gobble up a bucket flower like you."

"What's a bucket flower, Phoebe?" she asked, not sure she wanted to know.

"You's a lady, Ma'am, wif fine dresses and high fallutin' ways, an' no way cud you wrastle dem evil spirits in de swamp. Homer hid dere in de war an' he say dat's no place for human be'ens."

Wanting to hear no more of evil spirits, Beth went out the kitchen door and along the path to the dock. She felt that Phoebe had given her an oblique answer to what she meant by a bucket flower. The river was calm, and the day, like most days here, was hot and humid with huge thunderheads building in the east that would descend upon them later in the day. Seeking to soothe her emotions, which had been roiled by Phoebe's dire predictions and the description of her, Beth walked out on the dock.

Engrossed in watching a schooner heading out toward the Gulf and parts unknown, she felt more than heard a footstep on the dock behind her. She turned and smiled, expecting that Dr. Worthington had returned and was about to recite a poem. She changed her smile to a scowl. It was Mr. Prichett. His arm was no longer in a sling, and his face contorted into its usual lustful leer. For the moment the two stood, perhaps twenty feet apart, staring at each other. Assessing her situation, she felt more helpless than she had ever been. She was surrounded by water, and if she had to jump, she would drown. Her derringer was in the house, and the only other person in sight was Phoebe standing in the kitchen door watching them. As Prichett advanced toward her, she retreated backwards, step-by-step, closer and closer to the end, careful not to lose her footing.

"Well, Missy, naow we're going to get down to bizness." He edged closer.

"I didn't shoot you, Mr. Prichett."

"The sheriff will think you did when he finds out I been hired to drag you back to Boston like a thief, and you tried to stop me."

His words stunned her. The sheriff had said that no one in Fort Myers would hire him. Could Papa have somehow wormed the information about her from Aunt Sarah and hired this man sight unseen? Out of the corner of her eye she saw Phoebe in motion now, running down the path, something bright in her hand flashed in the sunlight.

His sneer increased. "We kin have a good time all the way to Boston."

It might be a good time for him, but she knew it would be perdition for her. Her feet were now on the last broad plank of the dock. "I'll jump in and drown before I'll let you touch me," she bluffed.

Phoebe was now on the dock, but hidden behind Prichett's massive body. Bare feet made little noise until the cook was close. He stopped, not wanting to lose his reward as the result of a drowning, then was distracted by the sound behind him and turned halfway. Seeing her only chance, she threw herself at him. Her small body had little effect upon his massive bulk. He turned back toward her. In the next moment Phoebe jumped on his back, jabbing at his shoulder with her small vegetable knife. She again threw herself against him, but the two small women were not enough to overcome the large man. Like a raging bull with a couple of angry dogs biting on his flanks, he shook himself free with a roar. As she fell backwards onto the deck, she saw Phoebe falling in the opposite direction. Instead of pursuing his attack, he leapt over Phoebe and ran toward the shore with the blade from Phoebe's paring knife sticking from his shoulder. Then she saw the reason for his flight. Homer was running across the lawn with a rake in his hands. She helped Phoebe to her feet, and they clung to each other as they watched. Both men reached the end of the dock at the same time. Homer swung his rake wildly and missed. Prichett plowed through the smaller man without stopping, knocking him down. He ran across the lawn and disappeared around the front of the house. Phoebe still held the handle of her broken paring knife in her hand.

For the rest of the day she stayed close by Phoebe and carried the derringer with her in case Prichett returned. It was hard to believe that this man had been hired to escort her back to Boston. Leave it to Papa to have hired a private detective to find her and drag her home. He had to have the final say. If Prichett was telling the truth, how and why had Papa hired this particular ruffian to haul her back? This man had already attacked her twice. She wasn't about to allow herself to be placed in the control of this disreputable person.

When she heard carriage wheels in the driveway, at first she thought the sheriff might have believed Prichett and had come for her. But Dr. Worthington had picked up Marian at the church, and they arrived home just in time for dinner. At the table she told them how Phoebe and Homer had saved her from being kidnapped by Mr. Prichett. The Worthingtons were shocked by the violence occurring on their property, but were relieved that no one was hurt. Ben promised to report the attack to the sheriff in the morning.

After they had recovered from the news, Dr. Worthington said, "Well, Beth, your problems may be resolved sooner than you would have guessed. I was talking to a rancher I know named Beckett from Gopher Ridge. That's twenty-five or so miles southeast of here. He's willing to have you stay with his family at their ranch until a guide can be found. He says he knows a Seminole who is the best guide in southwest Florida. The Becketts aren't too well off—and they'll expect you to pay for your room and board, and you'll have to pay for the Indian guide as well."

"I can afford to pay expenses," she said, her hopes soaring. "But how far is the Fakahatchee River from Gopher Ridge?"

Dr. Worthington glanced at Marian before he answered. "Oh, about a twenty-mile walk due south from there, I guess. There are no roads, no trails, Beth."

"Will this man be able to carry my equipment as far as Gopher Ridge?"

"Mr. Beckett said he has a wagon pulled by a team of oxen that will have space for one trunk."

"But you know I have much more than just one trunk."

"Well, now is decision-making time," said Dr. Worthington. "Beckett said he has to carry supplies for other families back to Gopher Ridge and doesn't have that much space. He and his son are herding his cattle down to Punta Rassa for shipment to Havana and will be back here tomorrow morning. By that time you had better narrow down what you plan to take with you to one trunk. That includes your clothing, and also your supplies and equipment. Remember, Beth, you won't be attending any balls out in Gopher Ridge."

That remark hurt. "I'll walk beside the wagon and carry my valise in one hand and a sack of provisions in the other."

"That's a twenty-five-mile walk through sand, Beth."

"I can help you pack," offered Marian. "Whatever you decide to leave here we will store until you return, or we will ship it to you."

"I don't think you'll be getting any better offers than this," said Dr. Worthington. "I know this man a little. He's a Cracker but appears to be a good citizen and a Christian who will treat you fairly. By the way, he has his sixteen-year-old son with him."

She knew that Dr. Worthington was right about the offer being the best one she would get, and the quicker she could escape from Prichett, the better. The problem in accepting Mr. Beckett's offer was knowing what equipment, supplies, and clothing she needed to make the two-week trip into the interior successful. But she had to get away before Mr. Prichett convinced the sheriff that she had him shot to prevent his taking her back to Boston.

While Phoebe was in the kitchen, she asked, "Dr. Worthington, what is a bucket flower?"

He laughed. "You've been talking to Phoebe. A bucket flower is a potted plant, but Negroes also use it to describe a person who has been mollycoddled."

She looked at Marian for a translation, but her hostess said, "Well, we'd better get started if Mr. Beckett is coming in the morning." Nevertheless, she had an inkling what had been meant, and she felt herself blushing with embarrassment.

She forced herself to forget Phoebe's words and looked at her host. "Thank you, Dr. Worthington for making these arrangements for me, and thank you both for being my friends and being so kind and generous."

"You'd better save your thanks," said Dr. Worthington, "until you see how this whole venture works out."

Chapter
12

W hen Beth awoke, Marian was bending over her in the dark.

"Mr. Beckett is here, Beth. He wants to get an early start." She sat up, wide awake. Today was the beginning of her trek toward the Big Cypress Swamp—if Mr. Prichett didn't interfere.

With Marian's help she had been able to cram all vital clothing, equipment, and supplies into one trunk and her valise. She had eliminated the two crates and one of the trunks. Her only food was in her valise, a sandwich and drinking water for today. Gone were all her dresses, scarves, gloves, corsets, nightgowns, her lacy peignoir, and most of her hats, shoes, stockings, and petticoats. All cooking utensils she had bought were stored away except for one deep skillet, and one fork, spoon, and knife. The tents, cots, the microscope, the flats for drying and pressing plants, reference books, and the test tubes were to be left behind. She was taking three skirts and blouses and undergarments for three days with the intention of washing every night. The word *mollycoddled* still burned in her memory, but helped her to make some hard choices.

One last-minute decision involved her Kodak Brownie given to her by Mary. Except for one picture of the "St. Augustine Six" taken by Aunt

Sarah, she had been saving the film for now. On the Survey Creek trip it had been too dark under the trees for good pictures. Many plants were too small to get a good picture anyway, and the black and white snapshots were incapable of showing the true beauty of colorful blossoms. The camera had to be left behind.

Marian agreed to practical items such as citronella, candles, matches, soap, and of course, sanitary rags. Mama's bottle of styptic balsam was being left behind. But four items she insisted upon taking with her over Marian's strong arguments were mosquito netting, a sleeping bag, a poncho, and an extra blanket. No space remained for a pillow. Even then the trunk lid wouldn't close, and the extra blanket had to stay behind.

After a hurried breakfast everyone assembled on the front veranda. Mr. Beckett was waiting in the driveway with his oxen-drawn wagon.

"Here's a gift for you, Beth," said Dr. Worthington. "It's a compass. Trust it." There were tears in his eyes that were in contrast to his strong criticism of her list last evening.

"Good-bye, my dear," said Marian, giving her a firm hug with one arm. She withdrew her other hand from behind her back. "Here, Beth, I want you to take these. I think they will be a close fit." She was holding out the ankle-height brogans she had worn camping.

"I can't take these, Marian. You'll need them." She imagined people staring at her if she wore the heavy-soled half-boots, but they had been helpful to Marian on the camping trip.

"You can't wear slippers where you're going, and I won't be needing them in Ohio. I can buy a new pair while I'm there."

To refuse a gift was impolite even though the half-boots were ugly. "Thank you, Marian. You are very thoughtful and generous."

Phoebe, who had been standing in the back, came forward holding a tiny red flannel packet on a loop of string. "Take this, Miz Sprague."

"What is it?" she asked.

"A charm bag." Phoebe moved close, removed Beth's broad-brimmed hat and slipped the string over her head. "Dat'll keep the evil spirits away."

"What's in it?"

"Bones of a frog, piece of snakeskin, horse hairs, 'n' ashes."

She was sorry she had asked. "Thank you, Phoebe." She hugged the frail cook who was almost as short as she was. "Thank you for saving my life yesterday."

"Watch out for the night folks, Miz Sprague," said Phoebe. Homer had already put the trunk on the nearly empty wagon. She was flabbergasted to see that the only other items on the wagon were two blanket rolls, a milk can, and a jug.

"Marian, Dr. Worthington, thank you for everything. I'll come back and get my trunk and crates as soon as I can." She hugged Marian and shook hands with Ben.

Dr. Worthington helped her up onto the wagon, and she sat on her trunk. Mr. Beckett and his son walked beside the oxen as they slowly moved away from the Worthington home. She didn't dare look back.

Mr. Beckett stopped the oxen at the docks and again at Packer and Blount's to load supplies ordered by his neighbors in Gopher Ridge. The list had been dropped off the day before on the way to Punta Rassa. Now the wagon was full, but she figured that by stacking the crates and barrels differently she could have found room for her second trunk.

Mr. Beckett must have known what she was thinking. "Hit's not just the space things take up, but the weight the oxen can pull when we git inter the sand."

Every step of the way she feared Mr. Prichett would discover her slow escape and drag her to the sheriff. She sat atop her trunk as they started out from the store. A man standing in front of a saloon was staring at her. Her heart pounded, but it wasn't Ralph Prichett. The oxen were pulling the wagon away at a creeping pace. With her desire to be gone from Fort Myers, she was already impatient with their excruciatingly slow progress, her uncomfortable seat, and the muggy air.

Mr. Beckett was a plain man of average height in his mid-forties, she guessed. His face was long and lantern-jawed. When he spoke in that high, nasal twang of the Crackers, she noticed his teeth were stained brown by his chewing tobacco. He wore boots, an old work shirt, trousers held up by suspenders, and a floppy, broad-brimmed, sweat-stained hat. He slouched over as he walked with the weight of scratching out a living on his shoulders.

The ride continued to be maddeningly slow. The road, which had been a combination of crushed shells and sandstone, became sandier. Her broad-brimmed hat was too hot, but when she held it in her hand, the sun's rays were worse. The trace had gradually veered away from the river. They were plodding through scrubby, nondescript woodland. The ridged top of her trunk was painfully uncomfortable. Dr. Beckett had said the distance to Gopher Ridge was around twenty-five miles.

"Mr. Beckett, may I get off and walk for a while?"

"Hop off." Mr. Beckett stopped the team.

Underestimating the difficulty of getting down from the wagon in a skirt, she managed to tear the hem in the process. Carriages had steps, and she was accustomed to being helped down. Mollycoddled. In the past Mama's seamstress had taken care of these problems, or else the skirt was thrown away. This skirt was one of three she had with her, and she might have to wear it the way it was.

Walking on the rough road was more difficult than she had expected. To divert her mind from the heat, she decided to try to get Mr. Beckett to talk.

"Do you have other children, Mr. Beckett?"

"We have three others, Hannah, Billy, and Little Maggie."

"How old is Little Maggie?"

"Near about four. She's jus' knee-high to a kitten."

They trudged on in silence for a while. The lone object to break the monotony was an abandoned shack a considerable distance from the trail.

"Is Gopher Ridge as big as Fort Myers?"

"Nope. They's jus' six families. We built a school two years ago."

More silence.

"You goin' inter the swamp for plumes?" he asked.

"Excuse me?"

"Bird plumes. Ladies wear 'em onter their clothes. Seventy-five cents a plume."

"No, I'm going to learn more about the trees and flowers."

"Whyn't you read a book?"

"Because the flora, the plants you have here, are different from anywhere else."

He mulled over that for a while and then asked, "You fixin' ter write a book?"

"I hadn't thought about that. Perhaps I will when I learn about the cypress swamp. Will you be able to find me a guide?"

"The best dang guide in south Floridy. Big Jim Pantertail."

At mid-morning they rested at a small pond and let the oxen drink. Beth drank from the canteen Marian had given her while they were stopped. As thirsty as she was, the sulfurous taste of the warm water was less than enjoyable.

Once the wagon started moving again she walked in front with Hawley, who kept his position twenty feet ahead of the oxen with his eyes fixed on the ground. From the back, the lad was a younger image of his father—he wore work clothes, suspenders, and a floppy hat. He smiled shyly at her as she caught up with him. His teeth were white, and there was a coating of blond fuzz above his upper lip. At about sixteen, he was a little taller than she was.

"What are you looking for?" Beth asked.

"Snakes. Don't want 'em to spook the oxen."

That accounted for the long stick he was carrying. She dropped back one step.

"Is the family ranch large?" she asked him in order to avoid an awkward silence.

"It's about the same as t'others," he replied. "It's open range mostly."

"What is 'open range'?"

"No fences. Our cattle are branded and graze with those from the other ranches."

"Do you go to school or work on the ranch?" she asked.

"Ah work on the ranch mostly. When we git caught up, Ah go to school."

"Do you like school?"

"No, but Ah like reading. My mother tries to teach me some."

"What is your favorite book?"

"Last year Ah read *A Connecticut Yankee in King Arthur's Court*. Mrs. Brecht lent it to me. She's the school-marm. Ah like Mark Twain."

"I do, too," she said. They talked about books for a short time, but she discovered that his range of knowledge in literature was severely limited. Around noon they stopped and watered the oxen again. Mr. Beckett unwrapped a cold roasted chicken. He tore it in two and gave half to Hawley and offered a drumstick to her, which she declined.

She had started to eat the sandwich Phoebe had prepared when she saw movement far down the trace they had traveled. Her heart started pounding immediately. The heat and haze made it difficult to see clearly, but the apparition was moving closer. Now she was certain that a man on horseback was approaching. He was dressed in black and wore a black hat the same as she had seen Ralph Prichett wearing the day before. He came on slowly, allowing the horse to walk at a comfortable pace.

"Mr. Beckett!" she called, still staring down the trail behind them.

"What is it, Miz Sprague?"

She pointed at the slowly advancing horseman. "That's Ralph Prichett. He's the man who attacked me in Fort Myers and was shot. Please do something."

Mr. Beckett went over to the wagon and removed a rifle from his bedroll. "Hawley, you 'n' Miz Sprague stand beyond the oxen." He walked slowly toward the horseman who kept advancing at his slow, deadly pace. As she watched, Mr. Beckett raised his rifle and yelled at the horseman to stop. The rider stopped, and Mr. Beckett walked up to him, still pointing the gun at the intruder.

The two men talked for several minutes, and then to her bewilderment, Mr. Beckett pointed his rifle at the ground and allowed the man to pass. As he came closer, she gasped. This was not Ralph Prichett. The unarmed stranger lifted his hat as he passed and said, "The Lord be with you, Ma'am."

"Thet was a preacher goin' out to save the souls of the Seminoles at Brown's Landing," said Mr. Beckett as he brushed off the flies from his half-eaten chicken.

"I'm sorry, Mr. Beckett," she said, feeling her face turn scarlet.

"Hit's better to be careful than dead," he said matter-of-factly.

After eating they set off again. She walked a step behind Hawley. The going was slower than ever. The trail was nothing but two ruts in the sand. The wagon's wheels ground against limestone outcroppings that sometimes poked through the surface. They passed a second vacant shanty, the only other sign of humans. The sun bore down mercilessly, and this was still May.

Her limbs were stiff, her feet sore, and her clothes wet with perspiration. Hopefully they were nearing Gopher Ridge, but she was determined not to ask. They pushed on until the sun was low in the west, then stopped at a place Hawley called Halfway Pond. To her dismay that information gave her the answer to the unasked question. Tonight was to be her first time sleeping on the ground. She wished she had talked Marian into letting her bring a cot.

The canteen of water Marian had given her was empty. She reached into the wagon and pulled out the Becketts' water jug from beside the milk can, twisted off the cork and took a deep swallow. Whatever she tasted was the foulest liquid that had ever entered her mouth, and it burned all the way down. Her loud gasp drew the attention of Mr. Beckett and Hawley who were tending to the oxen. As she watched them through watery eyes, still holding the jug and wheezing, both broke out in laughter.

"The water is in the milk can, Miz Sprague," said Hawley, who was doubled over trying to contain himself.

She was too exhausted to be embarrassed. How was she to know which one held water? She had seen Mr. Beckett take a drink from the jug after lunch. How could a man drink that awful stuff? No wonder they called it firewater. If all liquor tasted like that, Carry Nation's war was soon to be won.

While Mr. Becket and his son prepared a fire, she considered her options for the night. Sleeping on the sand seemed easier than climbing into the wagon and getting her sleeping bag. But after a few minutes she worked up the energy to get what she needed from her trunk. Hawley gathered more firewood while Mr. Beckett heated salt pork and beans. After eating she was glad the Worthingtons had talked her out of bringing fifty pounds of salt pork. From her sleeping bag, she watched Mr. Beckett remove his jug from the wagon and settle himself against a tree. Hawley was already asleep nearby. Closing her eyes, she knew she could never go back to Fort Myers where Mr. Prichett was waiting for her. Or perhaps he was out there in the darkness waiting for them to go to sleep so that he could creep in and drag her away. She clasped Phoebe's charm bag in one hand, the derringer in the other, and tried to think of something more pleasant.

Chapter *13*

Gopher Ridge, May 25, 1893

*B*eth woke to rustling sounds, which turned out to be Mr. Beckett preparing breakfast. From the day before, she had learned that the bushes on the right were hers in which to complete her toilet. The men disappeared off to the left. While washing her face in a bucket of pond water Hawley had provided, she thought ahead. Today she was going to meet the rest of the Beckett family, and perhaps tomorrow the guide who was going to lead her through the swamp to Allen River. After a four- or five-day trek through the swamp, she would be on a boat to Key West and then heading back to Boston. She was eager to get started, but Mr. Beckett's breakfast of bacon, eggs, and coffee tasted as delicious as any breakfast she had ever eaten.

After walking a short distance, she asked if she could ride on the wagon. Her feet hurt, and pains shot up her limbs with every step. She sat on her trunk again, and Mr. Beckett sat on a barrel beside her while Hawley led the oxen.

"Miz Beckett's name is Carrie," he said. "She doesn't know you're comin'.'' After a while he added, "What's a fair price for room and board?"

She considered for a moment what they had charged in Kissimmee and at the Hotel Hendry in Fort Myers for two meals and a bed. "I guess around a dollar a day."

They rode on in silence for a while before Mr. Beckett replied, "This ain't no hotel, you understand, but Carrie sets a pretty good table."

"Well, how about a dollar and a half?" she suggested.

"I was thinking of fifty cents," he said. "You'd be sleeping upstairs in the toolshed. On the floor."

"Will Mrs. Beckett be satisfied with fifty cents?" she asked, suspecting that this conversation was not about the price, but about appeasing his wife. "Why don't you tell her I'll pay a dollar a day?"

"Well, let's see what she sez," he said as he climbed down from the wagon.

A lunch of cold beans from a can was tastier than she expected. The land was still as flat as ever, but the trees were taller and leafier, and the coarse grass was thicker and greener here. They had yet to pass an inhabited house.

Near mid-afternoon Beth spotted a farmhouse at last, and when they came to it, Mr. Beckett stopped and unloaded three of the boxes from the wagon. He talked with the woman for a moment. She suspected they were talking about her. Suddenly the woman put her hands to her face and ran into the house.

"Thet was Miz Jenkins. When I tol' her you was goin' inter the Glades she came a little onhitched. Her daughter, Emily, disappeared inter the swamp a little over three years ago. Gator gotched her prob'ly."

In close succession they dropped off supplies at four more farms before arriving at the Beckett ranch. The Becketts' neighbors were friendly and curious about her and why she was in Gopher Ridge. The children at each house stood around the wagon and stared at her, giving her an uneasy feeling.

The supplies for the Becketts were all that remained on the wagon with her trunk. The first five houses had been substantial two-story frame dwellings, but the Beckett home, just out of sight from their last stop, was a single-story log cabin. Close to the house stood a thatched-roofed open shelter, and some distance across the road was a small unpainted building that she guessed was the toolshed where she was to sleep. The building was on the edge of the clearing and backed up to the saw palmettos and slash pines. Where the road ended were animal pens. She had not known what to expect, and the ranch made her feel more lonely and farther away from home than ever.

As they drew closer, a barking dog came running out to greet them. Following the dog was a barefooted girl that had to be Little Maggie. She was clothed in a knee-length, worn, gray dress. Her hair was long and straggly. Hawley lifted her off the ground and swung her around.

As the oxen drew near the house, an unsmiling woman came out the door. She was wearing a plain, faded homespun dress that was short enough to reveal her bare feet and ankles. Her gray-brown hair hung down below her shoulders like so much untended Spanish moss.

"Stay here," said Mr. Beckett softly from beside the wagon. He walked over to his wife. They talked in undertones with glances at her. Possibly another family in Gopher Ridge might take in a boarder. If not, she had a long walk back to Fort Myers. After what seemed like a long time, he came back to the wagon.

"I'll show you the toolshed," he said.

He headed for the shed as she climbed down from the wagon and hurried after him. Mrs. Beckett stood motionless without saying anything and watched them. The double doors of the small building were open. A collection of rusting farm tools stood against the walls and lay on the dirt floor. Carrying her valise and Marian's brogans, she followed the rancher up a narrow, unpainted staircase outside the building. Stepping into the room was like becoming immersed in a hot bath. The one window was shut. What she saw was a small, unfinished room with a low, sloping roof and no furniture. In one corner an empty crate was lying on its side.

"When I have an extra hand he sleeps up here," Mr. Beckett said. "I'll get you a straw mattress. Miz Beckett agreed to a dollar a day. Hawley and I will fetch your trunk." She waited outside in the relative coolness compared to her attic room and noticed that Mr. Beckett carried his jug around to the back of the house while his son unloaded their supplies.

When the rancher returned, Hawley helped him carry her trunk up the narrow stairs.

"How much do I owe you for the trip from Fort Myers?" she asked Mr. Beckett when he descended.

"One dollar. We eat dinner jus' before sundown." He then led the oxen toward the animal pens.

She climbed the stairs to the room in the shed, but it was still uncomfortable even though the window had been opened. She discovered an object in the crate in the corner, a homemade rag doll, made of a stocking with button eyes and a mouth sewn on crudely. She tossed it back into the wooden box and descended to the outside.

In the east, orange-pink clouds towered above the trees. The underside of the clouds darkened to an ominous black that stretched down to the horizon. The house and the animal pens cast long shadows across the clearing in the late afternoon sun. Strolling toward the pens, she discovered that one held a large hog and several piglets. Nearby was a chicken coop. Another pen held two scrawny horses that looked at her hopefully. The oxen had been placed in a third pen, and the fourth and largest one held three small cows and two calves. Beyond the pens was a vegetable garden. Behind the log house stood a privy, and halfway between them were a well house and a wash table. From this vantage point she could see a small stone smokehouse nestled behind some bushes beyond the outhouse. The sun almost touched the trees in the west, and she headed toward the well to wash her face and hands before supper.

As she drew nearer to the house she saw that the thatched shelter served as their kitchen and eating area. In the front half was a cast-iron cookstove with a stovepipe sticking out away from the thatched roof. At the closer end was a sawbuck table and benches. As she approached the kitchen area, Mrs. Beckett was removing cornbread from the oven. She suspected Mrs. Beckett had not been pleased by the arrival of a stranger and another mouth to feed.

"Hello, Mrs. Beckett," she said. "My name is Elizabeth Sprague. My friends call me Beth."

Mrs. Beckett looked up and nodded. Her hair, which had been loose before, was now tied back in a knot.

Marian Worthington helped Phoebe by setting the table for some meals, and she said, "May I help you set the table or something?" The sawbuck table was bare except for a ring of wetness where a pot had rested.

"Hannah kin do it," the woman said without taking her eyes from the pot she was stirring.

Mr. Beckett approached carrying a bulky gray muslin bag that was the length of a body. "I have yer straw." This, she assumed, was to be her mattress. He set it against one of the posts that held up the thatched roof.

"Thank you," she said, trying to sound as if she meant it. She imagined herself shaping the bag into a flat surface by lying on it.

"Here is five dollars, Mr. Beckett." She had waited until his wife was present to hand him the money. "That will pay for the trip and four nights. I intend to move on as soon as the guide can be hired." Mrs. Beckett eyed the cash as it changed hands.

"That'll depend upon when Big Jim Pantertail shows up," he said.

"Sometimes he don't come around for weeks," said Mrs. Beckett sourly. Her husband gave her a dark look.

Hawley, Little Maggie, and an older girl approached the table, followed by the dog.

"This here is Hannah," Mr. Beckett said, indicating the older girl who appeared to be between twelve and fourteen years old. Hannah went about placing utensils and wooden plates at the table. Little Maggie hung back, peering out from behind Hawley.

"Hello, Hannah. My name is Beth."

"Hello," said Hannah, softly without looking up. She was frail and had an unhappy, down-turned mouth. Her hair was straggly like Little Maggie's and her mother's. Her dress was a shapeless homespun that hung halfway between her knees and bare feet. As she laid out the utensils it appeared as if she lacked full use of her left arm and hand.

Mrs. Beckett moved the pot from the stove to the table and this was a signal for everyone to sit down. Hawley and Little Maggie sat on one bench and Hannah on the other. Their parents sat on the boxes at either end. Mr. Beckett waved her to the space on the bench beside Hannah.

"Where's Billy?" Mrs. Beckett asked.

"Billy!" yelled her husband. A boy about ten came racing from the chicken coop with an egg in each hand and was about to sit close to his father when he spotted her, a stranger. He stopped and stared, and then ran around the table and sat between Hawley and Little Maggie all the while staring at her. He placed the eggs on the table and retrieved one more from his pocket.

Mr. Beckett looked up at the thatched roof and said, "God, thank you for this food, and bless everyone at this table."

"Amen," said Mrs. Beckett. While the Worthingtons had said grace before meals, Beth didn't expect to hear it in these rustic surroundings.

"This here is Miz Sprague," Mr. Beckett announced. "She's goin to be livin' in the toolshed for a few days." Both Little Maggie and Billy were staring at her. Hannah was looking down at her lap, and Hawley was already biting into a piece of cornbread.

Mrs. Beckett dished out what appeared to be a beef stew onto each plate passed to her. In the middle of the table was a platter of cornbread. The beverage was lukewarm tea poured from a metal pitcher into tin cups. The three-pronged fork was tin, too, and had an unwelcome metallic taste of its own. The beef possessed a smoky tang and was stringy, but she was hungry enough to get it down.

The bare-topped board table contrasted with dinner at home—no white tablecloth, no silverware placed just so, no gold-rimmed heirloom plates and dishes, no napkins or engraved napkin rings. No maids and no Mrs. Faraday. The dog was allowed to lie under the table.

Every once in a while Hannah rubbed her left shoulder as if trying to relieve the pain. The children were well behaved except for eating ravenously. Beth saw Little Maggie watching her and winked at the little girl. Maggie smiled back shyly and then hid her face behind Billy's arm.

"Watch out, Maggie, I'm trying to eat."

"How much did you get for the cattle?" Mrs. Beckett asked her husband. Beth assumed she was referring to the herd that he had driven to Punta Rassa.

"Nine dollars a head."

His wife shook her head. "Not much to show for a year's work. Did you bank the money?"

"I brung it home. They's talk of thet bank goin' under. Mebbe I can round up a few more before all the grass dries up or cattle thieves get 'em."

"They'll be skinnier'n hell," said his wife.

Thunder rumbled in the east.

"It sounds as if we'll get a storm," Beth said for something to hide her shock. The only other woman she had ever heard use profanity before, except for Pepper Douglas, was Grace, and that was done to annoy ladies at teas.

"Not tonight," said Mr. Beckett. "The wind is from the west and will keep them clouds where they is."

"We need the rain," said Mrs. Beckett.

"Hit rained more'n usual this spring," he explained to Beth, "and the swamp is full, but for the past month hit didn't never rain when hit's s'posed ter. The grass the cattle eat and the brush is plumb dried out."

"You goin' inter the swamp?" Mrs. Beckett asked her.

"Yes. I want to learn about the plants that grow there."

Mrs. Beckett shook her head without saying anything more.

"They's gators and snakes there!" exclaimed Maggie.

"And swamp apes!" added Billy.

"Thet's jus' a story," said Mr. Beckett.

"Hit was prob'ly one thet carried away Emily Jenkins," said Hawley.

"More'n likely a gator," said his father. "Stop try'n to scare Miz Sprague. You'd prob'ly be eaten up by the danged *gallnippers* afore enythin' else."

He slapped his arm, indicating that gallnippers was his word for Dr. Worthington's swamp angels. It was unsettling to see that the children were not reprimanded for entering into the adult conversation; they were treated as equals. "What's your dog's name?" she asked Billy.

He looked back at her with a blank expression then shrugged. "'Dawg,' Ah guess."

By the time the meal was over, the stew pot was empty, but everyone seemed to have had enough to eat. Mr. Beckett headed toward the animal pens with the dog ambling after him. Hannah and Billy gathered up the plates and utensils, and Hawley brought two buckets of water from the well. Mrs. Beckett watched to see that Billy helped Hannah with washing the dishes and then headed for the house. The lack of servants seemed to have no effect upon getting work accomplished.

Left at the table with nothing to do, she went for a short walk along the road they had arrived on. She needed to work out what she had seen and heard at supper. The talk of alligators, snakes, and the swamp ape was unnerving. The comment Mrs. Beckett had made haunted her even more. The Indian guide might not come around for weeks. The Becketts were hard-working people who didn't have much. She could understand why Mrs. Beckett didn't wish to have another mouth to feed. Staying here for more than a few days wasn't what she had planned. The tension between Beth and Mrs. Beckett was bound to grow unless the guide showed up soon.

The Beckett family differed from any she had ever known. They wore the plainest clothes, worn to the last threads, but patched and clean. They seemed to have none of the finer things and worked hard just to stay alive. The children helped with the work and were well behaved and reasonably happy, except for Hannah. An easiness in the relationship among the family members prevailed without words being spoken, an attribute that had been lacking in her home on Dartmouth Street.

She walked back to the outdoor kitchen and looked at her bag of straw and decided it wasn't going to get into the attic unless she carried it there. "This ain't no hotel," Mr. Beckett had said. The bag was lighter than she had expected and was easy to manage. Although the attic had cooled off slightly, it was still too uncomfortable to allow sleep. She flattened out her straw mattress and put her head down. It crunched noisily, but was better than lying on the bare floor. She unrolled her sleeping bag over the straw mattress and used a pile of her underclothes for a pillow. She had always slept with a down pillow until now. No one would be able to say that she was mollycoddled once this trip was over. From the open window she saw Mr. Beckett heading for the woods with his jug.

She went down the stairs and made a trip to the outhouse and the wash stand near the well. After washing her face and hands, she decided to walk a bit, but at dusk the mosquitoes were getting too numerous to tolerate, and she retreated to her attic. She had removed her blouse, skirt, and petticoat and lay in her chemise on top of the sleeping bag. Draping her mosquito netting over her as loosely as she could, she listened to the night sounds of Gopher Ridge. "Dawg" let out an occasional bark at something real or imagined in the dark. A shrill bird expressed its unhappiness among the pines, and above her head was the whining sound of the mosquitoes. Tomorrow she would have to fashion a tent with the mosquito netting.

Beth was drifting off to sleep when she heard footsteps on the stairs.

Chapter 14

*M*r. Prichett! She heard another footstep, and then a louder, stumbling sound, and then, "Damn!"

She reached for her valise and the derringer. Her heart was pounding as she waited for further movement. There was none. Then, after what seemed like hours, a heavy breathing sound developed into a snore. Whatever was there, *whoever* it was, had fallen asleep on the stairs.

"Clarence!" Mrs. Beckett's voice was angry. "Come down from thar!"

A groan from the stairs, and then slow footsteps descending. She heard Mrs. Beckett's scolding voice fading into the night. Her heart was still pounding as she lay with the derringer in her hand.

The next sound Beth heard was a child's tiny voice. Daylight had arrived. The voice was nearby in the attic. Little Maggie was sitting on the floor, facing the wooden crate that served as a doll house, and was talking to the rag doll.

"Good morning, Maggie."

Beth watched the child turn halfway toward her and with a shy smile say, "Mornin'," before returning her attention to the doll.

She slipped on her skirt, blouse, and Marian's half-boots, which she decided to wear around the ranch. "What's the dolly's name?"

"Bebe."

She held out her hand to the little girl. "Want to come with me?" She was anxious to start the day. Perhaps if she were lucky the Indian might show up and they could be on their way to the Fakahatchee River.

Mrs. Beckett was at the stove stirring a pot as she had the evening before.

"Good morning, Mrs. Beckett." She stood with Little Maggie, holding hands. Mr. Beckett and the other children were nowhere in sight.

"He prob'ly don't remember las' night. Hit won't happen agin. The 'shine is all gone. He wanted to grow cane and make his own squeezin's, but I put my foot down. He's a good man when he's not on a spree."

One by one the other children appeared and sat down at the table. Little Maggie sat close to her this time. The cornmeal mush was hard to get down, but she didn't want to offend Mrs. Beckett now that the woman was at least speaking to her. When she had almost finished her bowl of mush, Mr. Beckett appeared. She watched him uneasily as he sat down, bleary-eyed and apparently unaware of what had happened the night before.

After breakfast Mr. Beckett, Hawley, and Billy went about their chores while Hannah helped her mother clean up the kitchen. After washing up, she returned to the attic and found Little Maggie there again, playing with Bebe. The child had brought up a few small stones which most likely served as the doll's furniture. Then, to her horror, she saw that Maggie held the derringer in her hand. The little girl must have found the shiny chrome object on the floor where it had been from the time she had fallen asleep the night before. Gently removing it from Maggie's hand, she put it in her pocket. She then removed from her valise the jackknife and the tube of matches, determined to ask Mrs. Beckett to hide them as well as the gun in a place beyond Little Maggie's reach.

After gathering up her notebook and pencil, and then finding a long stick, she walked out into the clearing to inspect whatever wildflowers might be growing there. In the distance she saw Mr. Beckett and Hawley ride off in search of their range cattle. The clearing extended some distance to the east, but there were no cattle in sight.

In the afternoon she wandered farther into the pines without finding a single plant that she hadn't already recorded. She carried the stick with her and did see a black racer, which she hoped she remembered from her zoology classes as being nonvenomous. Nevertheless, the snake had scared her; snakes were fearsome and hateful.

The following day dragged by with nothing to do but wait for Big Jim Pantertail to appear. At supper she asked Mr. Beckett if he had talked to the Indian yet.

"You have to wait for the Indians to show up. They could be anywheres in the swamp. They don't git seen onless they wants to be seen."

Day after day she waited. She paid another four dollars in advance, to Mrs. Beckett this time. The compass Dr. Worthington had given her made little sense; it always pointed toward the north. Then she realized that if she went opposite to where the compass pointed, then she had to return due north to get back to where she started. The same was true if she went east, then she had to walk where the compass indicated was west to get back to the toolshed. Even so, she dared to explore just so far from the house for fear of getting lost. After she had searched a large area around the ranch, there was little else to do except wash her clothes, watch the animals in the pens, and help Mrs. Beckett in the chickee, which she learned was what the dining shelter was called. They had no books to lend her, and she had run out of new plants to sketch. Every afternoon the clouds piled up in the east, and the thunder threatened. Some days bolts of lightning streaked against the black eastern sky, but it never rained. Coming to Gopher Ridge seemed more and more to be a bad decision.

Then ten days after her arrival, Big Jim Pantertail appeared in the early morning. Mrs. Beckett fed him, and Mr. Beckett sat and talked with him at the table. She stayed well away from the Indian as she had been instructed. The Seminole wore a derby hat over his long, graying hair. A black vest partly covered a flowery calico shirt, and his lower half was covered with a skirt and leggings. His feet were bare. When they were through talking, Mr. Beckett saddled his horse and rode off to the east with the Indian on foot ahead of him, and she was left in a quandary.

A haze seemed to hang over the clearing, and she detected the pungent tang of wood smoke which became stronger as the day wore on. The rancher returned at supper time.

"There's a fire off to the east," he announced after unsaddling his horse. "Lightning. Hit's coming this way. Iffen it don't rain, we got troubles."

"We're safe here in the clearing," said Mrs. Beckett.

"Not iffen they's flames twenty feet tall 'n' flying embers. This here fire is half a mile wide. In the mornin' we'll load up the wagon, and you and Hannah'll take Little Maggie 'n' Billy 'n' enything you want to save and head outta here."

Mrs. Beckett appeared to be worried then and looked at her children. "Hannah can handle the oxen. I'm stayin' here."

"I'm stayin with Hawley," said Billy. "I kin fight the fire."

Hannah remained silent.

In the morning the smoke made it hard to see as far as the pens. Mr. Beckett, Hawley, and three men from the nearest ranches had already headed east to combat the blaze after opening the pens to allow the animals to escape. What the five of them could do with shovels against a wall of fire twenty feet high and a half-mile wide wasn't clear to Beth. Mrs. Beckett made no move to load the wagon or hitch up the oxen.

"Shouldn't we go, Mrs. Beckett?" she asked. "The children aren't safe here." Her trunk was packed and ready to drag down the stairs if the woman said the word.

"We're not leavin'," said Mrs. Beckett. "This here ranch is all we got, and we're gonna stay an' save it. You kin walk away iffen you want." The desire to leave was strong, but it didn't seem to be the appropriate thing to do, just walk away and leave the other woman and her children here alone. Besides, her trunk was in the toolshed, and it meant leaving all her possessions behind.

Just then action to the east caught their attention. Through the smoke, flames roared up a tall pine not more than a mile beyond the toolshed. An icy finger of fear ran up her back. Black smoke poured into the sky. The trees in between there and the clearing were not yet on fire. Time for escaping was getting short.

"The clearing'll save us. It'll go around." Mrs. Beckett disappeared behind the house and came back lugging a ladder which she propped up against the eaves. "Iffen eny sparks git onter the thatch, I'll go up the ladder. You pass me the bucket, Miz Sprague. Billy and Hannah, fotch a broom, a blanket, enything, and beat out any flames in the grass."

The smoke was now burning her eyes and making it hard to breathe. The breeze from the east was strengthening and hot. A deer came bounding past the house. Soon after, six or seven range cattle stampeded through the clearing. She wanted to run like the animals, but the children stood fast like their mother. Mrs. Beckett called everyone to the well, and they filled every bucket and pot they had, then carried them to the foot of the ladder.

Mr. Beckett, Hawley, and the other men were in sight now across the clearing. Whatever attempts they had made to divert the blaze had failed. Mrs. Beckett had been wrong; the fire was burning through the clearing, but the grass was lower, and no trees or saw palmetto were here. The flames were smaller and working their way harmlessly across the clearing.

Sparks and embers were flying by. One stung her face as it flew past. The men had now stopped and turned toward the fire in the clearing. The smoke burned her eyes as she watched the men making a stand just beyond the animal pens. Billy was ready to beat the fire away from the front of the tool shed where the flames had less to feed upon. Mrs. Beckett climbed part way up the ladder, ready to save the roof. "Dawg" stood at the corner of the house and barked incessantly at the flames.

The roaring inferno in the pines on the edges of the clearing was moving faster than the flames in the field. Tree after tree exploded into a huge torch. Underneath, the dry saw palmetto crackled and popped, fueling the frightening holocaust. The vanguard of the blaze was now beside them to the north and south of the open area. It had jumped the road to the north and was still heading west. There was no longer any place to run. Beth watched the advancing flames and knew that if they reached her, her life would end here. When the lesser blaze in the clearing reached the road, it sputtered out. But flying sparks and embers from the raging conflagration along the northern edge still landed all around them and on the thatched roof. The smoke was thicker than ever.

The men were trying to dig a firebreak to save the pens and chicken coop on the south edge of the clearing where there was no road to halt the blaze. Then, through the smoke, she noticed flames the others had not seen—the fire had worked its way closer in along the north side, where the underbrush had been allowed to grow too close to the toolshed. Flames were licking up the wooden wall where Billy was unable to see it. Her shouts to him were lost in the roar. She ran toward the shed; she might be able to pull her trunk to the door and slide it down the stairs. Sparks and flaming fragments as large as hats flew past her. She dashed up the stairs to the attic. The heat and smoke were intense. Grabbing the trunk, she started to slide it toward the door. To her amazement, there between the trunk and the wall, playing intently with her doll, was Little Maggie.

Flames were licking in the open window. She shoved the trunk aside, snatched up the little girl and with one hand pulled at the trunk. The roof was now on fire. The heat burned her face, and Maggie began to scream and gasp for air in the suddenly dense smoke. The trunk was stuck on a raised board in the rough floor. Reluctantly letting go of the trunk, she ran for the door and flew down the stairs, still surrounded by fire. She ran back toward the house holding Little Maggie in her arms, both of them coughing and wheezing.

Mrs. Beckett was on the roof fighting several small fires. Hannah was midway up the ladder holding a pan of water. The roof of the chickee was ablaze, but no one paid attention to that; the wind was blowing the sparks beyond the house. Turning back where she had just been, she saw the toolshed in full flame. Billy, now aware of what was happening behind him, stood helplessly and watched it burn.

The clearing was black with small fires burning themselves out here and there. The firestorm had roared by on either side. Fallen logs and stumps were still ablaze, but the major part of the conflagration had passed. The men had been unable to halt the blaze as it tore through the animal pens and the chicken coop. Mrs. Beckett was still astride the peak of the roof looking for any flare ups, and Billy was putting out isolated flames north of the house.

She was still holding Maggie when Mrs. Beckett came down the ladder. The woman put her arms around them both and sobbed, "Thank you, thank you!" Maggie had understood little of what had happened and was crying, too. Then the mother took the daughter gently from her and told the little girl not to cry. Maggie's hair was singed.

"I'm sorry," she said to Mrs. Beckett. "I didn't mean to let her get burned."

"You saved her life," said Little Maggie's mother. "I saw from the roof."

She felt a hand take hers. It was Hannah. "Thank you," said the girl, looking into her eyes for the first time.

Mr. Beckett came up with Billy and Hawley beside them. All three were black-faced and breathing hard. He looked at her and said, "What happened to you?"

Unclear as to what he meant, she ran her hand through her hair and was startled to discover that the long tresses on the back of her head were gone. Most of her hair had been singed away. She listened as Mrs. Beckett told him how their visitor had saved Little Maggie.

"God must have sent you here," he said to her and patted his little daughter on the head. To his wife he said, "Hawley 'n' me are goin' to round up the animals, iffen any of 'em lived. The oxen, our two milk cows, the heifers, one of the horses, and the pigs, are all missin'—and the range cattle." She had seen that the other horse had somehow survived and returned almost immediately.

The Becketts' log house and the outhouse were all that remained. The pens, the chicken coop, the chickee, the smoke house and most of their animals were lost. The toolshed was destroyed, including the harnesses and the wooden handles of their tools. In it had been her trunk and all of her possessions except those she had given to Mrs. Beckett for safe-keeping. She said nothing to the Becketts; her losses were insignificant next to theirs, but her hopes of exploring the swamp were dashed. She felt both sad and embarrassed over losing her golden locks, but knew they would grow back.

Where the chickee had stood were six posts and the cast-iron stove. The stove was still intact except for its pipe which had to be propped up. The table and benches were charred but useable. She helped Mrs. Beckett scavenge together a supper meal of beans and sow belly. Mr. Beckett and

Hawley were still looking for their animals. Then the raindrops started, large drops at first, and then a downpour. They scurried into the house with their suppers and ate in the main room.

"Iffen the rain had come three hours sooner, everythin' on the ranch might have been saved," said Mrs. Beckett sadly. "I don't know why I worked so hard to save the house. Hit ain't worth shucks. Iffen hit had burned we coulda built a regular frame house. We were goin' to do thet enyways, but now we'll have to build the other buildings first." The huge losses the Becketts suffered hung over her as they ate. Compared to her family, the Becketts had little to begin with, and now with the destruction of the outbuildings and loss of livestock, they would have to start all over again. She wished there was some way she could help them, but her money had been in her trunk, and now she had no way to help herself.

This was her first time inside the log house. The furniture was a mismatched collection of wooden chairs and one large table. There seemed to be no gas or electricity, or even a fireplace. The puncheon floor was bare. Beyond the main room were two smaller rooms, the bedrooms, and over them was a loft where Hawley and Billy slept. That night she was invited to sleep in Hannah's room in Little Maggie's bed, and Maggie slept with her parents.

Hawley came home at dusk. He had found several chickens, all dead. Mr. Beckett arrived an hour after dark, driving the two oxen before him. "Hit coulda been worse," he said. One oxen was burned on its foreleg, but not seriously. "T'other animals may still be runnin' before the fire iffen the rain didn't put hit out."

That night in the bedroom she asked Hannah what had happened to her shoulder.

"It happened when Daddy was chopping down a tree. I was standing too close. He was building this house."

The house looked as if it had been standing for years, and she had thought Hannah's accident had happened recently. "How old were you?"

"About Little Maggie's age."

Unable to fall asleep, she lay on Maggie's straw mattress, thinking of Hannah's injury. The parents seemed to ignore their older daughter while favoring Little Maggie and the boys.

Mr. Beckett set out early the next morning in search of the animals again while Hawley put together a rough enclosure to hold the oxen. The rancher's wife now treated her like a member of the family. Mrs. Beckett's first act of kindness was to cut her hair. Little remained on the back, and when the trimming was done, she felt her head and was dismayed at first. No Boston lady wore her hair this short; Mama would be shocked. She must look more like a man than a woman. As the day wore on, she began to recognize the freedom of having short hair. Now it required much less attention. It would have been an advantage had she been going into the swamp. She realized that her appearance mattered little to the Becketts. The important thing to them was that she had saved Little Maggie. Their gratitude was an embarrassment to her; she had gone into the burning building to save her trunk and found Maggie by accident.

Her blouse had been scorched in the back, and Mrs. Beckett loaned her one of Hawley's shirts to wear. Her remaining possessions were the derringer, the match case, and the jackknife that Mrs. Beckett had hidden in the house. The loss of her possessions was disheartening, but her main worry now was how to get to Key West, where a draft from Aunt Sarah would be waiting for her in a bank.

The one thing she was able to retrieve from the pile that had been the toolshed was her skillet. The notes and sketches she had made since leaving Fort Myers were now ashes. Another notebook filled previously had been left behind at the Worthington house. The loss was not serious; the plant life around Gopher Ridge outside the path of the fire was accessible. Now that almost everything she had with her was lost, she had resigned herself to reconstructing the notes that had burned.

By mid-morning other residents of Gopher Ridge had ridden up by horseback or wagon and offered their help. The Beckett Ranch was the farthest south; the fire had missed the others. They brought food, live chickens, and offers to help rebuild. Two men stayed to help Hawley put together the pens from charred lumber. Two others rode off to help look for the Beckett livestock as well as their own.

She watched Mr. Beckett return home at sunset driving before him three scrawny range cattle and a heifer. "This time we'll make the clearing bigger," he said. Then turning to her, he added, "I almost forgot. Big Jim Pantertail said he'd take you inter the swamp. His rheumatism is bad, but thataway you can keep up with him."

"I can't go," she said. "I have no clothes, and everything else has been burned." She explained how she would have no money until reaching Key West.

"We'll help you," said Mrs. Beckett. "An' what we don't have, other families in Gopher Ridge will lend us." It seemed as if the Becketts wanted to do everything possible to assist her, and the more they helped her, the less she felt like leaving them.

The Becketts were a remarkable family. They had lost more than half of all they owned, but they took it in stride as if it mattered little. She had heard not one word of complaint from either the parents or the children. How Mama would have carried on if a serious calamity had happened to her.

Two days later one more discouraging thing happened. Her debilitating period started. Mrs. Beckett was able to find for her old clothing that they tore into sanitary rags. She was determined that this setback was not going to prevent her from her journey. Mama had always insisted that she rest during her periods. Some of her classmates at Wellesley never did. She was determined to visit the swamp while the opportunity presented itself.

Mrs. Beckett's most radical but sensible idea was for her to wear trousers instead of a skirt. Ladies didn't wear trousers, but Pepper Douglas and a few brazen women she had seen up north wearing bicycle bloomers achieved a freedom of movement she envied. It seemed to make little difference out here on the ranch and in the swamp where no one would see her. Since she and Hawley were almost the same size, Mrs. Beckett shared a set of her son's clothes with her, promising Hawley to make new ones for him as soon as possible. Among items given by the other families were a small notebook and a knapsack from Mrs. Brecht, the children's teacher. The last article of clothing was an old slouch hat which needed adjustment to fit her head. With the hat, trousers, and

Marian's thick-soled brogans she was dressed like a miniature cowboy in one of Grace's dime novels.

Little Jimmy Pantertail showed up the next day to be Beth's guide. He was shorter and even more frail than his father. But what made her nervous were his eyes. They darted from one place to another, never making eye contact with her. Furthermore, his general bearing was insolent. She guessed he didn't cotton to the idea of escorting a woman, especially a white woman, anywhere.

"Where's Big Jim?" she asked.

"He sick."

"Do you know the swamp?"

"Yes. Much know," he said confidently, but his eyes darted about.

To go into the Big Cypress Swamp alone with this strange man was unsettling. How well did Mr. Beckett know this Indian? She wished he was here to ask.

"How long?" the Seminole asked.

"Four or five days," she said. "I may want to go to Allen River. I'll decide whether or not I wish to go tomorrow morning." That gave her the time to talk to the Becketts about Big Jim Pantertail's son. Her hopes for getting all the way to Allen River were sinking again. It would be better to wait for another guide or not go at all except that right now the Becketts had scarcely enough food for themselves and she was an extra burden.

"I wait to sun up. No longer." She hadn't expected the Indian to stay. What were they to do with him now? She explained to Mrs. Beckett what had been said, and the older woman shrugged.

"I don't know the son. He'll jus' set someplace and smoke. He can wait ontil you've talked to Clarence. Jus' keep Little Maggie away from him." That last comment made her all the more uneasy.

Mr. Beckett came back mid-morning. He had been looking for his animals again without success. When he rode up to the house, he came directly to her.

"There's a man here in Gopher Ridge lookin for you. Sez his name is Morrisey. Is this the man that gave you trouble in Fort Myers? I told him you went on to Brown's Landing, but he'll be back."

Beth felt her throat constrict. "That man's name was Prichett. I don't know anyone named Morrisey. Can you describe this man, please, Mr. Beckett?"

"A big man. Black suit, derby hat, mean face with a big mole beside his nose."

He was describing Mr. Prichett!

It seemed impossible that more than three months had passed since Papa's plot for her to marry Edward Cushing had been disclosed. Resentment toward Papa and revulsion for Mr. Cushing flooded over her in nauseous waves. To believe that he would use his own daughter as a pawn to expand his shipping company was still as hard to accept as it had been the morning they had left Boston. After Papa had learned that she was unwilling to marry Mr. Cushing, he had been as persistent as ever in forcing the engagement upon her.

She turned back toward Mr. Beckett. "Little Jimmy Pantertail is here. I have no choice but to leave with him."

"Where's his daddy?"

"Sick."

Mr. Beckett shook his head. "Most Seminoles are good, honest people. But I don't trust this 'un. They kinder suspicioned thet he might have done away with Jenkins' daughter, Emily. Don't go. Iffen you must skedaddle from this Prichett man, we'll hide you in the woods until he's gone."

She had no desire to go anywhere with the Indian, but now that Prichett was coming after her again, she had no choice. If she had to hide in the woods, it might as well be along the Fakahatchee Strand. If she were shanghaied back to Boston, she knew that somehow Papa would coerce her into marrying Mr. Cushing.

"My father is trying to force me back to Boston to marry a man I don't wish to marry. And this may be my one chance to explore the swamp, but I can't pay the Indian until I get to Key West."

"This un's knowed for his shecoonery. He's plumb bad."

"I have my derringer."

"Thet's near about as powerful as a sharpshooter's bite." She knew from hearing him talk with Harley that "sharpshooters" were horseflies.

"Iffen you must go, I'll take care of payin' him. I kin prob'ly git him down ter ten cents a day."

"Does he know the swamp?"

"He was born there, but don't trust 'im."

"I'll be careful. I must go before Mr. Prichett arrives."

Chapter 15

The Big Cypress Swamp, June 11, 1893

*T*he Beckett's ranch was soon out of sight, and after the first hour they had walked beyond the burn that had occurred four days earlier. With both excitement and trepidation, Beth was at last nearing the region she had come to study. They entered the pine forest at a pace too fast for her. She wanted to stop and examine species of flowers and other plants that were new to her.

"Slow down, please," she said.

Little Jimmy Pantertail pointed ahead and said, "Long way to go. Hurry."

There was no point in hurrying if she was unable to do what she had come for. She had to gain the upper hand with the Indian right now, or continuing with him was pointless. Her first battle with him back at the Beckett ranch had been lost. She had held out her knapsack for him to carry, but he had disdainfully refused. So now she said, "No. We stop," and made a point of crouching down to sketch a goldenrod, a common weed which was found everywhere. Jimmy stopped and came back and watched her. "All right, we can go, slowly now," Beth said, standing up.

Soon he was well ahead of her again, but when he noticed, he stopped, although in a petulant pose, and waited for her to complete a sketch and catch up.

Except for the mosquitoes and the heat, walking among the pines was pleasant. When there was a choice, she walked in the shaded areas. Underneath the trees were saw palmettos which she skirted carefully, aware of the spiny stalks. The branches of the pines were sparse enough to allow more hot sunlight than was welcome. Beth noted that on the branch ends of the slash pines were growing long, pale candles of new growth. In addition to the goldenrod were bachelor's buttons and saffron-headed milkwort.

Wearing trousers was easier but not much cooler than a skirt had been, and Marian's half-boots with Hawley's thick socks were heavy and not as comfortable as Beth had hoped. The knapsack chafed on her shoulders. It held her few possessions: one thin blanket, her skillet, a canteen of tea, a packet of dried beef, a notebook, pencil, matches, the jackknife, the derringer, one change of shirt, drawers, and socks, and, naturally, the sanitary rags.

Beth observed that the Seminole carried only his rifle and a thin bedroll, and unlike his father, wore trousers and a black, floppy hat over his long, black hair. The manner in which he carried himself was somehow insolent and seemed to be getting more so the deeper into the wilderness they walked. Her malaise over having chosen to come with him grew by the hour.

After gathering her belongings into the knapsack, she had said good-bye to all the Becketts and given Mrs. Beckett and all the children hugs. Mrs. Beckett had made her promise to return and said she was welcome anytime. The rancher's wife thanked her again for saving Little Maggie.

While looking for new species as they walked, she wondered if Mr. Prichett would follow her into the swamp. It wasn't likely. If he was afraid of little Pepper Douglas and Mr. Gallagher, he wouldn't be coming into the wilderness. When she had last seen him on the Worthingtons' dock, he had a small knife sticking into his shoulder. That was two weeks ago. Perhaps he had recovered from his wounds enough to come into the swamp with Papa's money as an incentive.

Papa was busy with his fleet of ships and hired hundreds of men to do his bidding. He always had to have the last word. How he had found and hired Prichett, of all the men in the world, was deeply ironic and mysterious. Papa wanted to have her dragged home in humiliation and lay upon her the fact that this was his world and she, his daughter, must obey. But she was determined to return to Boston on her terms after having successfully trekked through the Big Cypress Swamp. If she reached Allen River and then Key West as planned, her trip home might start as early as next week.

Jimmy had stopped, motionless, staring at something on the ground. She approached slowly and at first saw nothing. In a spot of sunlight, lying upon pine needles was a coiled snake. The reptile's dark diamonds upon a light brown background made it hard to distinguish among the dead leaves and pine needles. It was then that she heard the whirr of its vibrating tail that she might have assumed was the sound of an insect, if she had noticed at all.

The Indian pointed and said, "Bad fellow." Although Jimmy led the way, she decided to carry a stick from now on.

They entered another area of pines where fire had blackened the ground, this one more than a week ago. She noticed tender new growth already poking its way up through the ashes. In several places where the pine needles had burned, patches of bare limestone lay exposed. The bases of the trees around the border of the burn were scorched while the tops of the pines had been untouched by the fire. Closer into the center of the burn, the tops were brown or bare. In another burn that had happened perhaps a year ago, she noticed that the new growth had come back thicker than ever.

Beth had little idea about the time of day, but the sun was well past the zenith at those times when she did see it, and her stomach told her to stop and eat. On her tin plate she laid out the sandwich Mrs. Beckett had made for her and placed the bottle of lukewarm tea beside it. Jimmy crouched nearby watching her. She held out half her sandwich to him. "Dried, smoked beef and homemade bread." He shook his head and walked off a short distance and crouched again. He seemed anxious to get moving.

136

The Bucket Flower

Although the slash pines became fewer, the undergrowth grew thicker, and the ground underfoot was softer and wetter. To one side and then the other they passed dome-shaped clusters of taller trees with shorter, lighter-green needles—dwarf cypress, Beth guessed. Later they came to a pond covered with vegetation—a lettuce lake, smaller than the one the *City of Athens* had plowed through on the way to Fort Myers. It reminded her of a vegetable garden which she had once seen. A cloud of yellow butterflies danced in a ray of sunlight above the dense lettuce. Beth discovered Jimmy's real reason for skirting the water when she spied the eyes of a large, black alligator looking at her from among the floating weeds. That was one plant to be examined at another time.

Jimmy stopped and pointed into a thicket. She came up beside him and looked in the direction he was pointing. Seeing nothing unusual, Beth asked, "What do you see?"

"Panter."

As hard as she looked, she could not see the panther and wondered if he was just trying to scare her. He was being successful, and she was at his mercy. The farther they walked, the more helpless she became. Mr. Beckett's warning about the Indian kept circling through her head.

Ahead, the swamp spread before her in all directions. No true streams were revealed by a current, just shallow pools surrounded by thick growth. She saw that drainage was hindered by muck. Farther along they encountered an open grassland for a short distance and then the swamp again. The rat-a-tat-tat of a nearby woodpecker startled her.

Her limbs ached, her feet burned, and the knapsack became heavier, but Jimmy kept up his relentless pace in the sticky heat whenever she let him. The trees here were much taller, with featherlike needles, and their trunks were fluted at the base. These were bald cypress, so named, she knew, because they lost their needles in the winter. Long shadows from the cypress buttresses stretched across a flat strand covered with yellow top. Among the yellow top peeked marsh pinks and small, unnamed, purple flowers. Beth sketched one, and pulled it up to include the roots in her drawing. But only half of the root came free without a trowel. She decided to name the dainty little flowers "Maggies" after her little friend in Gopher Ridge. Its accurate classification and Latin name had to wait until she was back at Wellesley. For the time being she invented names of her own: Beth's wort, and even some pseudo Latin genera and species such as *Lavendera elizabethicus, Scarleta spragum, Vermilia bostonis, Magentus maria* after Mary, and *Verdantis harrieta* for Mama. Not having the resources with her for accurately classifying plants was frustrating.

Beyond a line of pines 100 yards off, Beth saw more light-green flats. Through the branches she glimpsed clouds stacking to the east like piles of pink cotton. If it rained she had no way to stay dry. The ground became wetter until the water was seeping into her brogans. Here the cypress were taller and their fluted bases stood in brownish water.

She followed Jimmy through brush along the edge of the water for a short distance. They were attempting to avoid the slough, but the higher land—higher by no more than a foot—was dense with thicket. The boughs Jimmy had pushed aside slapped back into Beth's face as she tried to keep up with him. Half of the time they were walking doubled over to avoid the vines and low branches. She shuddered at the possibility of snakes being above her, waiting to fall on her neck. Often the vines were above and below, leaving only small openings to crawl through. She laughed to herself. What would Mama say if she were here in her gown and petticoats? It was strange to think of Mama at this moment. The occasional clatter of dry palmetto fronds brought back the fire at the Becketts' and the popping sound they made while burning. She had scratched the backs of her hands several times in the thickets, and these scratches attracted mosquitoes and other little black insects.

Then suddenly they came upon a dugout canoe lying beside the water.

"Is this yours?" Beth asked. Of course it was. One doesn't walk all day through the wilderness and then find a canoe by accident when you need one. The Seminole knew where he was going and had planned ahead better than she had imagined. Getting to this point was why he had been pushing her to move faster all day. She felt more confident now about Little Jimmy Pantertail.

"Is this the Fakahatchee River?" she asked.

What he answered sounded like, "Okaloacoochee. We stay here," he said. "Get firewood." Jimmy picked up his rifle and walked away, but he had left his bedroll behind.

She sat on the overturned canoe and looked around her. The branches of the tall cypress far overhead combined with the lower trees brought on an early twilight underneath. Snowy egrets were perched on the trees all around her. The dark tunnel formed by the lowest branches was forbidding, and the water was black and still. The mosquitoes attacked in clouds and were voracious. Dr. Worthington had called them swamp angels. Swamp devils would have been more appropriate.

At last she was in the swamp—and alone. The last time she had seen the sun, it had already been low in the western sky. From where the sun had been in the morning, and where she had seen it last, it appeared as if they had been traveling more or less south all day, the direction she knew she had to go. But how far they had traveled she had no idea.

"Get firewood," the Seminole repeated when he returned. Squaws gathered firewood, bucks did the hunting. She knew this from Grace's dime novels, which she had read when she should have been memorizing the Latin names of plants.

"I'm not a squaw," she said.

"No fire, no food." He sat cross-legged on the ground. He wasn't about to move.

There were fallen branches everywhere. She tentatively stepped into the mushy undergrowth, dragged a few rotting pieces to the center of the clearing, and sat down. The Indian had disappeared once again, and she waited for him to return. A shot rang out, making her flinch. The shots fired at the poker player and Prichett were still with her. She went to her knapsack, withdrew her derringer, and put it in a trouser pocket. She still felt uneasy.

Before long Jimmy was back carrying a dead rabbit. Eating a furry animal was unappealing. She turned her back on the skinning and cleaning process to save whatever appetite she had left.

"Start fire," ordered the Indian. She had matches in her knapsack. But then what? She had never lit a match before, but knew it had to be struck against a hard object. The nearest tree, the bottom of the canoe, then finally exposed sandstone. She held the lighted match under a branch she had collected and looked up proudly at the Indian. He had stopped the cleaning process and was watching her with his mouth open. She dropped the match as it started to burn her fingers.

"You hold," he said, thrusting the bloody rabbit into her hands. She almost threw it into the water in disgust, but held the skinny carcass at arm's length, knowing that it was all that she was going to get to eat. He removed his large hunting knife from its sheath menacingly, but then turned his attention to the wood and cut a pile of tiny shavings from the driest log. He broke a handful of the smaller twigs and placed them one by one over the shavings as she watched. A lit match of his own inserted between the twigs and into the shavings produced a small spiral of smoke rising from the pile followed by a tiny tongue of fire. He placed a few of the thinner branches on top of the twigs which were beginning to burn.

"More wood," he ordered. "Dry."

"I thought Indians didn't have to use matches," she said, relieved to be passing the rabbit back to him, but then hurried off when he scowled.

Jimmy cut two pointed sticks and handed her one. He sliced the rabbit into small, thin strips. She watched him roast one over the flames on the stick and did the same. The meat was dry and smoky, but she was hungry enough to eat the stick and accepted another piece of meat. When nothing was left but the bones, he went to his bedroll and removed a tin can. He punctured the can with his knife, and after several stabs was able to bend the top back. The can looked like one she had seen in the Beckett's chickee before the fire. In fact, it had burn marks on it, but she remained silent. Perhaps Mrs. Beckett had given it to him.

Thunder pounded in the east, and she willed the beans to be heated before it rained. The already dim light was diminishing. She removed her tin plate and fork from her knapsack in preparation for her share of the canned beans. The Indian ate from the can and then handed it to her, a little remaining in the bottom. Squaw rations.

Her canteen was empty. "Boil the water before drinking it," Mrs. Beckett had said, but she couldn't have meant this awful stuff in the swamp. There was nothing she could do but fill her skillet with swamp water and place it on the coals.

"More wood," intoned Jimmy.

Flashes of lightning and claps of thunder were getting closer. The first, large raindrops were beginning to fall as the water began to boil. She grabbed the handle of the skillet and yelled as the pain shot up her arm. Jimmy laughed as she wrapped her spare shirt around the handle and poured the water into her canteen.

Jimmy propped up his dugout canoe and crawled under it. Beth rolled under a bush and wrapped her single blanket around her just as the skies opened up. She was too tired to worry about the water soaking through her blanket or notice the pain in her burnt hand.

She had scarcely closed her eyes when she woke to someone kicking her! In the first dim light of dawn, Jimmy said, "Get wood."

Beth jumped up. "Don't you kick me!" She raised her arm as if to hit him, and he laughed. His laughter foretold an experience she didn't wish to live through had she touched him. She had never raised her hand against anyone in her life, and here she was, alone with this strange man who Mr. Beckett had told her not to trust, miles from any other humans. Her derringer was still in her pocket, and she decided to keep it there from now on.

The light was brighter than when she had gone to sleep, but that wasn't saying much. A pall of mist hung over the swamp, and Mr. Flagler's and Phoebe's warnings about the poisonous swamp miasmas came back. She was cold and wet in spite of the hot, humid air. How much of this could one breathe before falling ill? The foliage overhead was so thick it kept out most of the light. In spite of the pains in her bones and muscles, she went about collecting sticks for a fire while wondering what they were going to eat for breakfast. A bird hidden in the branches above her was making a squeaky "Ki-dee-dee."

Jimmy had disappeared into the thicket and was gone longer than when he shot the rabbit. She had watched him make a fire the night before, and now attempted to do the same. With her little jackknife she scraped a small mound of shavings onto the ground. On the second try she had the chips smoldering, but no flame was produced. She needed drier wood. The third try with a fourth match was successful, and she had a smoky little blaze going. It helped keep the mosquitoes at bay, anyway.

Towering above her stood the trunk of a bald cypress she had been too tired to appreciate last night. Its height was overpowering. Beth felt like an ant standing underneath its green, lacy boughs. Looking up through the first, lower limbs, she could see that more trunk towered skyward to another cluster of branches, and then yet more trunk, disappearing among the feathery needles, taller than the Custom House in Boston. The fluted base stood in water, and the buttresses flowed out several feet in all directions. Here and there on the trunk were air plants and red-flowering bromeliads clinging to the bark. Around the base of the tree several vertical outgrowths protruded from the water, appearing to be separate, leafless gnarls of wood that looked to her like knees. Some of these knees were half as tall as she. Nearby was another, shorter, bald cypress, in a silent struggle for its life. Its attacker was a strangler fig. The smaller, vinelike tree wound itself like a giant snake around the cypress trunk, spiraling upwards and branching out new tentacles to aid it in a century-long assault that would eventually kill its stately victim.

In the distance she heard Jimmy's rifle. Her fire was still producing more smoke than flame.

Beneath the bald cypress, cabbage palms, gumbo limbo, ironwood, and other species new to Beth formed a lower canopy. On drier patches grew royal palms, much taller than the ones she had seen in St. Augustine and Fort Myers. In the dim light under these trees she saw myriad plant life too dark to have been observed the evening before. Ferns sprang forth in pale green fountains, some reaching over her head, and below them mushrooms dotted the dark humus. She had yet to become accustomed to the brown and green anoles that scampered everywhere.

When the Indian returned, he looked at her pathetic little fire, his eyes full of scorn, and said nothing. He was holding a wild turkey by its feet. He tossed the bird to Beth without a word, indicating that she should pull off its feathers. This unappetizing task took away any interest she had for breakfast even though her stomach was painfully hollow. But the Indian's scowl kept her at the unpleasant task while he coaxed the fire into a decent blaze. He grabbed the bird from her impatiently and with his knife tore off the skin and again cut the raw meat into thin strips as he had the rabbit.

The dried, smoky meat had little similarity to turkey she had eaten before, but knowing this was the only food she might eat all day, she cooked and ate several strips. Mrs. Beckett had wrapped four thick slices of dried beef in brown paper, which Beth was saving in her knapsack until she was absolutely desperate.

Having no other choice for drinking water, she filled her skillet again from the swamp. She held the skillet over the fire waiting for the water to boil while Jimmy stood around fretfully. When the handle became unbearably hot, she set the pan aside. Jimmy angrily kicked the fire apart and dumped over her skillet, wanting to start the day's journey.

Jimmy had shoved the dugout canoe into the water and was crouched beside it. After retrieving her skillet and canteen, she crawled into the canoe, finding it to be unsteady. Jimmy pushed off without a word and stood in the rear, poling them along. Her knapsack and his blanket roll and rifle lay between them. The mosquitoes followed the canoe. As soon as she had brushed off the backs of her hands and face, the nasty insects were back again by the dozens. Of all the equipment she had lost in the fire, she missed her mosquito netting the most. She used her spare shirt to protect as much of her face and neck as possible.

Through the water, Beth could often see the leaves on the bottom and realized how shallow it was in most places. From her crouched position she filled her canteen, knowing she had to have something to drink. The tealike color was caused by tannin from the tree roots, and she wasn't afraid to drink it, but didn't look forward to the taste. The stream, if it was a stream, stretched into pools twice the length of the canoe in places. She could touch the branches on both sides. Never once did she see an open reach; it appeared as if the swale had come to an end, and then a sudden turn to the right or left opened up. At times the route doubled back on itself, and soon she had lost all sense of direction.

At one point Jimmy grunted, and Beth turned carefully to see what he was looking at. He pointed his pole at a ripple in the water. The triangular head of a large snake made an arrow-shaped ripple, causing her to shudder. After that she kept her hands inside the canoe.

"Cottonmouth," he said.

Birds were almost everywhere she looked—the white ibis with its down-curved bill, titmice, several varieties of woodpeckers, and her favorite, the snowy egrets. Ugly-headed wood storks waded in the shallows and poked at the fish. The snake-necked anhingas dried their outstretched wings. Pairs of red-shouldered hawks sat on branches here and there. And a flock of disgusting turkey vultures fought over some unidentifiable flesh in the mud. She felt as if it were easier to recognize the birds than the plants. They were more distinctive, and since they traveled outside the swamp, were better known. A large brown bird with a long, curved beak was one she did not recognize. At another time they came upon a flock of wild turkeys, which thundered overhead as they approached.

Branches brushed past her, and several times she almost lost her hat before she decided to take it off. Above the canoe she spotted a snake and jammed the hat back on. Occasionally an opening permitted her to see the limbs of the bald cypress high above. The roof of the swamp was porous enough to allow a few rays of daylight through, and Beth realized from their greenish-gold hue that the sun was out even though none of the rays penetrated as far as the canoe. Even without the sunlight her shirt was damp from the heat and humidity.

They came upon six sorrel-sided white-tailed deer. The animals had already seen the approaching canoe and were watching warily. As one, they darted into the thicket and were not seen again. Farther on she saw a black shape loping through the underbrush.

"Bear," the Seminole said, and she shivered.

The canoe became stuck upon a mucky mass that had caught on a fallen log. Jimmy motioned for her to sit still, and he stepped out into the mud and slogged to the front end of the canoe. He was able to pull it over the mass and into the next irregular pool. At another time he made her climb out into the water when there was a muddy area ahead several lengths longer than the canoe. The muck oozed over the tops of her half-boots, but Beth had no choice but to lift and shove on the back end of the canoe while Jimmy pulled.

Most of the tall cypress grew in the water, their branches decorated with beards of Spanish moss. Around them were smaller trees and plants, most of which were new to Beth, some with small, unripe fruit and berries. She pulled out her notebook and sketched what she could, but Jimmy was impatient and pushed the canoe onward. Two great blue herons, who had been standing on their spindly legs watching them from one side, decided they were too close and flapped their great wings and flew away.

By late morning stomach cramps were making her bend over as she huddled in the canoe. Whether they were caused by hunger, the strange breakfast she had eaten, or her period, she could only guess. After the long hike yesterday, it had been a relief to crouch in the canoe at first. But now her limbs ached, and even sloughing through the mud might be an improvement to being motionless. The canoe's slow movement did little to discourage the mosquitoes, and the fan palm she had cut to ward them off was not helpful. Her skin felt lumpy from the mosquito bites, and she wondered if her face looked as bad as the backs of her hands.

At last the undergrowth crowded in, and there was no space for the canoe to move. With all the backtracking they had done, she was unable to guess how far they had come. Jimmy picked up his bedroll. "We walk," he said.

"Wait." Midday was as good a time as any to eat the dried smoked beef Mrs. Beckett had wrapped for her. The cramps must have been from hunger. Standing in the mud, she set down her knapsack on a fallen tree and unwrapped the brown paper but then dropped it with a shriek. During the night tiny ants had crawled into her knapsack and found her beef. She stared at the mud where hundreds of the little critters covered the meat, then slapped at her hands where others were crawling and biting. Looking at Jimmy, he seemed indifferent to her plight. She shook out her knapsack and brushed off the ants from her few belongings. Determined not to let the Indian see her cry, she drank a few sips of the warm water in her canteen and packed everything away again, leaving the meat behind.

With her hat pulled firmly down, her collar up, a fan palm in one hand to ward off mosquitoes and her walking stick in the other, Beth set off behind the Indian. As they trudged on, she knew conditions had to be better ahead. In her favorite daydream she had imagined the cypress swamp to be lined with wide paths like the Public Garden. She had pictured herself in the cool shade of tall trees sitting on a park bench beside a crystal stream sketching beautiful flowers. She wore a pink summer gown and a matching broad-brimmed hat, and her handsome guide held a parasol above her. The alligators and other animals kept a respectful distance on the opposite bank, and there were no mosquitoes.

Jimmy was moving at a pace too fast for her to keep up, as if he had someplace to be at a certain time. His insolence was insufferable, but she had no choice but to stay with him. The mud sucked at her half-boots; the Indian seemed to be picking the muddiest route. To her left she saw dry ground.

"Let's walk over there," she said.

When he ignored her, she moved to the left on her own, but kept him in sight. It wasn't long before she discovered the error of her decision. The ground was drier, but the thicket tore at her clothes and lashed out at her face and arms, knocking off her hat. With an extra effort she struggled to get back behind her guide and slog through the mud. The going was too rough to care about stopping and making records of the flora. At places they trod through water up to her knees, but it felt cool on her burning feet.

They entered a little clearing a few inches higher and a little drier than the rest of the swamp. Nearby was the tallest bald cypress she had yet seen. At its base she watched a purple gallinule high-stepping through a shallow pool, careful not to trip on its own overlarge feet.

"Stop here," Jimmy said. With relief Beth collapsed on the soft, thick layer of duff, a century's collection of dead leaves and decayed branches. She ached all over, was hungry, and her feet hurt. The Indian squatted down and watched her, making her nervous. If she were to lie back, she knew getting up again was going to be impossible. This was the time she had been looking for to study the species of plant life close by the clearing. And it might stop Jimmy from staring at her.

But before she could move he was on her, shoving her to the ground.

"No!" she screamed. On his face was a lustful grin. She tried to reach for the derringer, but her right arm was pinned under her. She kicked and twisted and managed to free her arm, actually with his help as he rolled her onto her back. The gun was jammed in her pocket, and it took several tugs to free it. At last she was able to shove the weapon into his face. He leapt back, and his expression transformed into surprise and fear.

The derringer had changed his attitude from lust to sullenness, and Jimmy slunk off to the opposite edge of the clearing and glowered at her. For the moment, at least, she was safe. But any time she turned her back, or after dark when she was too tired to stay awake, he might try to attack her again. If he knew she slept with the gun in her hand, he might restrain himself. But he had his rifle and a knife to bolster his courage. As they glared at each other across the small clearing, she dwelt upon her helplessness. They must be halfway between Gopher Ridge and Allen River, and she had no place to run. If she shot him, it would be impossible for her to find her way out of the swamp alone. Once he had figured that out, the derringer would be useless to her.

Beth's heart still pounded, but she was breathing normally again. The Indian crouched down and glared at her. She replaced the gun in her pocket. The best thing for now was to disappear until his anger subsided. Watching him carefully, she edged away from the clearing, keeping an eye on the tall cypress as well.

Her muscles cried out as she crouched down out of sight of the Indian, forcing herself to block out her dilemma by examining an unfamiliar succulent. Her hand shook uncontrollably from time to time as she tried to trace its parts, still unnerved by the Seminole's attack. She hated to think what might have happened if Aunt Sarah hadn't given her the derringer. It was hard to concentrate when she had to figure out what to do next. They must head back tomorrow morning. The problem was to keep Jimmy Pantertail at bay for two more nights. But even if she did, he could lead her anywhere during the day until she dropped from hunger or exhaustion. He wasn't about to take her back to civilization where she could report how he had attacked her.

Sketching in her notebook and brushing away mosquitoes at the same time was asinine when Little Jimmy Pantertail might be creeping up silently behind her. Her determination allowed just so much standing, crouching, sketching through tears, and swatting at swamp angels. The premature twilight was setting in, and she made herself head back, using the tall cypress as her guide. Arriving at the clearing still without a plan, she discovered that Jimmy had left and taken his rifle with him. He had gone out to hunt for their supper, no doubt. Why, then, was she crying?

Chapter 16

The Fakahatchee Strand, June 12, 1893

An icicle of fear stabbed her heart; the Indian had taken his blanket roll with him as well. Looking around for her knapsack for reassurance, she discovered that it, too, had disappeared. She noticed that Jimmy had left no footprints to or from the spot where he had been squatting. But a few paces away where the Indian had attacked her, signs of the scuffle remained. Wanting to believe that she had returned to another clearing, she circled around the tall cypress and the pool that it was in. Not only was there no other clearing, the entire area was muddy at best, and knee-deep pools and thicket stretched in all directions. In the entire circle that she had made, there were no clear footprints except her own. Fighting down her panic, she tried to determine the reasons Jimmy had departed. He no doubt was hunting for their supper and took the blanket roll and her knapsack to avoid having them lost. How did he disappear without leaving footprints behind? What was it Mr. Beckett had said about Indians? *"They don't get seen onless they wants to be seen."* Beth fingered the derringer in her pocket for reassurance. In her other pocket was her small jackknife. These and her notebook and pencil were her only possessions now unless he returned. Her panic came roaring back.

"Jimmy!" she called. "Jimmeee!" She was answered by the birds. "Jimmy Pantertail, I'm here!" She kept calling until her throat was dry as she wandered in larger and larger circles around the clearing where she was certain she had last seen him. She repeatedly glanced over her shoulder, afraid he might attack her from behind, but more afraid that he wouldn't appear at all.

The twilight was fading into dusk as she came back to the tallest cypress. Hope of his returning had gone. But had he disappeared for good, or was he lurking out there, waiting to creep up behind her? The panic had to be conquered, she knew, or she could die tonight by tearing herself to shreds wildly running through the thicket in the dark, or by huddling frozen in fear and being attacked by some voracious animal. Her eyes stung from the sweat of her exertion and her tears of fear and frustration.

She felt vulnerable in the clearing. Never had she felt so alone and helpless. More tears came, and Beth cried like a terrified little girl. Knowing she had to control herself and concentrate on staying alive, she gulped some deep breaths of the humid air. Now was no time to feel sorry for herself. Safety had to be her first concern with darkness rapidly closing in. She had to find a way to stay alive through the night. With a jackknife but no matches, she had no way to make a fire. A tree provided more protection than being on the ground. Looking for a tree with low branches gave her a purpose, and the panic subsided a fraction.

Of her lost possessions, her most immediate need was for a clean sanitary rag. Her one recourse was to use a part of her clothing. Modesty made her go into a thicket. All the time watching for the Indian, she kept the derringer close by her right foot. She removed her shirt, trousers, and chemise. All that remained were her drawers. She peered through the branches. If the Indian was going to attack her, now was the time. She tore off the lower half of the sweaty chemise. That had to do for the present.

After dressing, she soon spotted a gnarled tree, a pond apple, with low branches. To get to the tree, she had to wade through knee-deep water. She looked for snakes in both the water and in the tree but saw none in the dim light. Climbing up among the branches, she found a fork she was able to straddle. Whether perching here was any safer than being on the ground was questionable, but she felt better. She pushed aside the larger fears that were lurking on the edges of her consciousness. Those considerations had to be faced, but tomorrow was the time for that.

Sleep was impossible. Her mind was whirling, and the branch was uncomfortable. A protrusion on the trunk was already causing pain in her back. But what if she did fade off to sleep from exhaustion and fell out of the tree? Broken bones must not be risked here alone in the swamp. She must prevent a fall. Climbing higher, she found a crotch that was shaped like the upturned palm of a huge hand. It provided a little comfort and was broad enough to keep her from falling.

With one leg stretched out along a limb, and the other dangling into space, she was able to lean back without the fear of falling. The tiresome movement of the palm frond barely kept the mosquitoes at bay. Dusk had dissolved into total darkness. The multiple layers of foliage above kept out any possible starlight or moonlight. But she was going to be safe here, she told herself, as long as a snake or predatory animal didn't decide to climb up this particular tree.

Speaking of predatory animals, where was Jimmy Pantertail? Why had he deserted her? Had he planned to take advantage of her in the swamp all along? And then what? The answer to that was too horrible to consider. Whatever his intentions had been, the derringer had scared him off, and he was too cowardly to confront her once he knew she had the weapon. If he ever returned to Gopher Ridge, he would tell the Becketts that she had been eaten by an alligator. That lie might turn out to be the truth.

Except for an occasional outcry, the birds had roosted for the night. Several bullfrogs croaked around her, and the tree frogs cheep-cheeped. But there were other sounds. Beth tried to ignore the whine of the mosquitoes. From not too far away she heard a heart-stopping roar, and from another quarter, an answer. She had heard the same frightening sound the night before, and Jimmy had told her it was an alligator. But to her, these roars sounded like lions she had heard at the Barnum and Bailey Circus.

For some reason Dr. Worthington and his silly rhymes entered her mind. Perhaps she could raise her spirits by composing her own lines. Nothing rhymed with swamp. Words came to her, slowly at first, and then she recited aloud, her voice quavering:

"A lady who went into the Glade

Quaked at every sound that was made.

The rain heavily poured,

And the alligators roared.

Elsewise the lady would've stayed."

Was "elsewise" a word? Dr. Worthington might have appreciated her poem, but he didn't have to worry about competition from her.

Close by, another sound was just barely audible, a snuffing, rooting sound that might be a wild boar or a bear. Now the sound was under the tree. She remained motionless, allowing the mosquitoes to have their way, and hoped that whatever the animal was, it had no interest in climbing. The snuffing sound went on forever until it gradually faded off behind her.

The tears came again. She had wanted to be independent, free from Papa, Mama, and Edward Cushing. Well, she couldn't be any more independent than this. "Now look, Mr. Cushing, and see what you've made me do!" she said aloud. She wasn't about to blame him or her parents, though. Being here was her own doing—with some help from Little Jimmy Pantertail. Blaming anyone else was wrong. A long list of people had warned her not to go into the Everglades. Being here was the result of her own stubbornness.

On that list of people who had warned her was the Worthington's cook, Phoebe. She tried to avoid thinking about Phoebe. The old Negress had told her about the evil spirits and the miasmas in the swamp. Phoebe had called her a bucket flower. "Well, you should see me now," she said aloud. She felt the string around her neck, and the charm pouch that Phoebe had given her was still there. Every bit of help was appreciated, and she rubbed the little cloth bag between her fingers. She wasn't going to dwell on evil spirits any more. A prayer wouldn't hurt either, she supposed. Mama and Papa were good Presbyterians, whatever good meant, but her religious fervor had diminished during her college years.

She sometimes felt guilty for not praying more, but now she asked for God's forgiveness and His help.

The first thing she had to do in the morning was find something to eat and water to drink. For now she tried to force herself to think of something else. The last solid food had been in the early morning, and her water can had been depleted since mid-afternoon. Her immediate goal had to be to get through the night. But then Phoebe's words came back: "Watch out for the night folks."

Not too far from the tree stood a dark silhouette she had not noticed before. It was large and hardly moved, if it moved at all. It was tall, standing on his hind legs like a trained bear—or a swamp ape. Then to her horror she saw others, all shapes and sizes barely moving, standing in a wide circle around the tree, perhaps twenty of them, shadowy life forms. This was the dark ritual of the night folks that Homer had told Phoebe about, and she was to be their victim, stripped naked and roasted on a pyre of flaming logs and later eaten. Light flickered through the trees. Lightning. The shadows disappeared momentarily in the flickering light, and she breathed a sigh of relief; they were only the darker recesses of the swamp after all.

A thunderstorm must be moving through, but she hadn't heard the thunder yet. Getting wetter wouldn't make much difference. Her feet were still squishy from wading through the swamp. Her body ached from being in one position so long. Her head was too heavy to hold up any longer. She shifted carefully and rested her head back against the tree, bending down the brim of her hat in the process. Being awake all night wasn't going to help her solve her problems in the morning. If lizards lived on the tree, then they were welcome to crawl on her, too; they ate mosquitoes didn't they? The gallnippers, as Mr. Beckett had called them, were as thick as ever. She pulled up the collar of her shirt and pulled down her hat as if she hadn't done both a thousand times before. Her fan palm seemed to anger the little beasties more than shoo them away.

Being at home with Mama and Papa didn't seem to be the most terrible thing right now. She had loved their house on Dartmouth Street. Her third-floor bedroom had been her favorite place. At fifteen, moving from the room on the second floor, adjacent to her parent's master bedroom, had given her a liberated feeling. The large room was her sanctuary. Its best feature had been its access to the tower. When home from Dana Hall, she had loved to take a book up the winding stairs into the tower and read. From its windows she looked down upon the neighborhood. Papa had said that people had towers on their houses to prove that they were rich enough to afford one. But the tower served a practical function; the center space was filled by a water tank that supplied the rest of the house. How she wished she had a pitcherful now!

The tree was falling! No, she was falling from the tree! She was clinging to the nearest branch unnecessarily. The crotch of the tree was broad, and it held her safely. It was a nightmare, but her heart was pounding wildly. She had dozed off. Whether she had been asleep for minutes or hours was hard to tell. She had been dreaming of waltzing with Charlie Everett at the Ponce de Leon.

This was the first time Charlie Everett had been in her dreams, and their bodies were touching excitingly as they danced. Everyone was watching, and she didn't care. In the past she had dreams of waltzing with Mary's husband, Michael Otis. Ever since she knew that Mary and Michael were inseparable, she had hoped to find a man like Michael. Certain other men at college dances had been fun to talk to and dance with, but most were shallow and self-centered.

Daylight crept into the glen. The time was approaching when she had to face the problems ahead. Her most immediate need was water. As Beth carefully climbed down from the tree, every joint and muscle cried out in pain. Putting her full weight on the lowest branch to swing down to the ground, she felt something soft and squishy in her right hand. It was a green tree frog, its innards now spread over her palm. In shock, she lost her balance and landed on her side in the muck. Fortunately, the earth was soft enough that she was unhurt. She wiped the mess from her hand and washed it in the nearest water.

The quagmire around her was no more than a collection of stagnant, oversized mud puddles. Crossing over to a deeper pool, she searched for snakes and alligators. Staring at the reddish-brown mix, she knew that she had to drink to stay alive. The color, from tannin in the trees and plants, was harmless, but other chemicals and organisms might be deadly. She knelt down and scooped up the liquid in her cupped hands. Her mouth and throat were dry, and even the first lukewarm mouthful helped. At least the taste was no worse than the sulfurous water she had been drinking since leaving the Ponce de Leon.

A streamlet trickled down her neck and into her shirt and felt cool. Bathing would be refreshing, but the Indian might still be lurking in the underbrush. After drinking a third, fourth, and fifth handful, she filled her hat and poured it over her head. She stood up, waiting for a sign of nausea or pain, but wondered if it was too soon for that.

Feeling better for the moment, her next problem was to find food. Sharpening her walking stick into a weapon was a precautionary move, but eating a furry creature raw was another matter. One course in botany had included the study of edible and poisonous plants, and now she wished she had paid closer attention. Jimmy Pantertail would know what plants to choose, but Beth had never memorized the list—she never thought there would be a need for it, never dreamed of wandering around a swamp starving. She tried to visualize the printed page on which there was a long list of edible plants, but was able to remember only a few. Then there was another list of poisonous plants, some of which caused serious discomfort including convulsions and hallucinations. She had to look for roots, bamboo shoots, and fruit. If she were lucky, she might shoot a snake or animal. But the chances of hitting an animal with her tiny derringer were nil. Cooking was desirable, and so was the possession of salt, oil, and vinegar, but she had none. For the moment eating the uncooked fiddle heads of ferns was her immediate choice. She pinched off the tightly-wound fiddlehead and tentatively touched it with her tongue. Having no negative reaction, she placed it in her mouth. The first taste was similar to the grass she had sampled as a little girl, but the second sensation was a peppery stinging of her gums. After chewing on a handful of the fiddleheads, she couldn't imagine how this plant was going to ease her appetite. There had to be something more palatable growing here in the swamp.

Now came the biggest decision of all. Which direction should she go? Having no idea where she was made the answer difficult. Jimmy Pantertail had said it would take her four days to get to Allen River from

Gopher Ridge; he could do it in two. If she were halfway between Gopher Ridge and the Gulf, then she might as well continue on to what had been her original destination. On the other hand, if Gopher Ridge were closer, then it made sense to go back. But how was she to find her way? Retracing her footprints back to where they had disembarked from the canoe was impossible; most of that had been swampy. And what then? There had been miles of travel in the canoe in water sometimes waist deep or deeper. Perhaps the village of Allen River was a short distance to the south. The Indian would expect her to go north, and he might be lurking there ready to jump out and attack her.

Which direction was south? The sun was hidden beyond the layers of tree leaves, but this early in the morning the most light clearly was coming from her left. Heading south she had to come to the Gulf of Mexico sooner or later. After another handful of fiddle heads, she sloshed through the mud, keeping the morning light to her left. Determining the correct direction when the sun was overhead was a problem to be faced later.

Heading south in a straight line was not easy; there were vines to climb over and duck under, pools and thickets to skirt, and mud to plod through. The cypress trees presented a problem of their own with their vertical knees, some growing as high as her waist several feet out from the base. More treacherous were the ones under water, just large enough to make her trip and fall.

Without warning, a huge bird took flight at her feet, startling her. The bird was too large to be a red-shouldered hawk. He flew up to a branch not too far above her head and sat glaring down at her. It had to be a barred owl.

Water was everywhere. Beth had no choice but to wade through it. It became deeper and was soon above her knees. No matter which direction she chose, there was no way to avoid getting wetter. Mama had warned her that getting wet during her period caused insanity, a myth some college friends had scoffed at. Well, she was insane already for having attempted this journey. She forged ahead, and was soon immersed up to her waist. The anxiety over angering swimming snakes made her watch carefully. The cypress knees protruded unseen almost everywhere, and along with the clinging mud, made the going treacherous. She was grateful for her walking stick, for without it she would have fallen more often. The difficulties of plodding through water had never entered her mind before, but the movement was tiring and the progress slow. Her feet were already hurting and had been damp for two days. How much longer could she continue this effort?

Beth had been looking down as she scrambled around the flutes of a large cypress. Then, as she looked up, there was the panther. She froze. The animal was not more than fifteen feet away and was as long as she was tall. Its unblinking eyes burned into her, its sleek body motionless except for an angry tail whipping from side to side. To admire its beautiful golden-tan coat during these moments of imminent danger seemed absurd, but there stood this beautiful, sleek animal, its head lowered distrustfully toward her. She didn't dare reach for the derringer. Minutes went by. And then slowly, almost imperceptibly the animal's head moved to one side, its eyes no longer on her. Then, as if having made a decision, it was no longer interested in her, and slipped noiselessly into the undergrowth. With a long sigh of relief, she stood knee deep in water recovering her strength.

The fern fiddle heads were not satisfying her hunger. Off to her right was a fruit-bearing tree. Coco plum, she guessed. The fruit were small and varied in color from green to pink. Assuming the pinker ones were the ripest, she picked one. Its Latin name came to her: *Chrysobanus icaco*. It was reassuring to know its name, and that must make it edible. The white, juicy flesh was tart and puckery, still unripe. A peck of these wouldn't satisfy her hunger. She ate two more and was already thirsty. After filling her pockets with the small fruits, she moved on.

Then she saw the orchids, first a few and then many. Growing on the trees, those at eye level were hard to miss. In the course of a hundred yards she spotted several varieties without stopping. She had tucked her notebook inside her belt, but it had become wet and was falling apart. This was no time to be taking notes anyway. How silly! Fear, hunger, thirst, and the infernal mosquitoes made her keep moving. These alluring plants had drawn her here and now might mean her death. She had neither the will nor the equipment to stop and study them. There was so much to learn, and now that she was here, she had no time or energy to expend.

The sunlight was diffused throughout the glade, and to guess which direction was south was no longer possible. In the north it was said that lichen grew on the north side of tree trunks, but here in the deep shade it grew everywhere. She chose a royal palm or a bald cypress in the distance to keep her course straight, but from now on finding the correct direction was guesswork. It became apparent that her greatest loss in the fire had been her compass. Until late afternoon she might be walking in circles.

She came upon a quiet pool that mirrored the trunks of the nearest cypress. A cloud of black-and-orange-striped butterflies fluttered about in the glen. Here were bright flashes of blue sky between sunlit branches high above where the position of the sun no longer helped her. Around the pool were thick growths of fern. Not far away were cabbage palms and the thin trunks of leafy trees. The mosquitoes here were thicker than ever. Whatever blood she had left after her period, the mosquitoes were going to take. The welts from the bites on the backs of her hands now had welts of their own. Feeling the roughness of her once-smooth cheeks, she imagined the horrible sight she must be.

As exhausted as she was, it was impossible not to notice the wide variety of growth under the umbrella of the bald cypress—trees such as gumbo limbo, mastic, ironwood, Jamaica dogwood, and Bahama lysiloma, and smaller plants such as marsh pinks, coreopsis, tiny duckweed, delicate white flowers of arrowhead, white spider lilies, spatterdock, water hyacinths, sawgrass, maidencane, fireflag, blue flag iris, and others she did not recognize.

A silent movement to one side caught her attention. The Indian! But then the tawny shoulder of the panther passed by a small opening in the undergrowth. It was about twenty yards behind her. When she stopped, it stopped, watching her. It was stalking her! Remembering how Dr. Worthington had said he scared the fish, she spoke loud enough for the cat to hear:

"There once was a curious panther
Who asked if the lady liked tan fur.
But the lady took flight
At the frightening sight,

Which gave the panther his answer."

From time to time she looked behind her, but she didn't see the animal again.

She moved through a green chapel. The filtered light created an ethereal haze. All the shades of green in the world were collected in this one space. Something was different here. The lower trees bore leafy bromeliads on their trunks similar to the ones she had seen all morning. But these were a paler green, growing in profusion in this one alcove. Their color seemed to give off a light of its own. Beth suspected these plants were a unique variety and was torn between stopping or continuing the march she knew she had to make. If she ever wanted to come back here, how would she find this spot?

Frequently she saw snails of every color and design imaginable. She gathered some and placed them in her pocket with the mixed intentions of making a collection or later crushing their shells and eating them if she became hungry enough.

Crouching to pick a handful of fiddleheads, she had the sensation of someone touching her shoulder. The snake glided silently from a low branch down her arm and into the underbrush. It had happened so quickly she had no time to move or scream, but the aftershock left her shaking and unable to move forward for some minutes.

Pausing to satisfy her thirst every now and then, knowing she had to drink, Beth put aside the notion that it might become the cause of her death. Pond apples, with their unappealing musky, resinous flavor, and coco plums were plentiful, but neither of these satisfied her hunger. Often she saw holly trees, and some still bore a few of their red winter fruit that the birds had missed. But she refrained from eating the small berries. The names of the poisonous plants she wished she had learned eluded her except for the meaningless *Strychnos toxifera*, which repeatedly echoed through her head.

If anything, the going was rougher here. Often the choice was a pool to wade through or a thicket too dense to penetrate. She saw the alligator in time to alter her course. It moved to the right, and she moved to the left to skirt its watery hole. The log she was about to step over, without warning transformed itself into a second alligator. It lethargically opened one eye as she jumped back. The beast must have had its dinner already, for it lazily slipped into the water, leaving her breathless.

Wading in a knee-deep pool, Beth lurched forward as her walking stick failed to hit bottom, and she plunged below the surface. Gasping, she finally found footing and was able to crawl from the hidden pit.

Midday had come and long gone. She had lost all sense of direction and mindlessly plodded on. She had been walking since just after daylight with only short pauses for rest. She was beyond exhaustion, hot, wet from her plunge, every muscle painfully sore. No longer were the orchids or other flora of any interest to her. Her notes had become a soggy, illegible mess, and she threw them aside. Her feet became heavier, and she fell more often. She wanted to rest, but knew she had to keep going.

She came upon a putrefying mound of dead and bloody birds covered with swarms of flies. For a moment she stared, not understanding, and then realized that poachers had been at work here gathering plumage. It was with mixed feelings that she realized there had been other humans in this place. Did it mean she was coming closer to civilization? Her will to continue was cranked up a notch.

Her clothes had not dried thanks to perspiration. She was annoyed by flies more than the mosquitoes; their sting was vicious. Now she understood why Mr. Beckett had called them "sharpshooters."

Once again the filtered light from the sun was low enough to tell her that she must keep the waning light to her right. But the remaining light was on her left! She had to make herself realize what had happened. She was turned around and had become disoriented. Whether she had been headed the wrong way for an hour or most of the day, she had no idea. Time and energy had been wasted walking in circles. Confused and discouraged, Beth cried. She forced herself to turn around and head in the direction that her head told her was wrong, but the failing daylight told her was southward. While she had this advantage she must keep moving, tears and all. But when dusk arrived, she knew she had to find refuge in another tree for the night.

Chapter 17

*D*aylight was barely filtering through the branches as she awoke and realized that she was still alone, lost, hungry, thirsty, bone-tired, damp, and hot.

Beth's second night in a tree had helped neither her body nor her spirits. This tree had not been as comfortable or as safe as the one she had been lucky to find the night before. Her joints were so painful she cried out as she jumped the final three feet to the ground. Fear of falling from the tree while she was asleep caused her to take off the pair of Hawley's suspenders that Mrs. Beckett had given her and lash her arm to a branch with them. This arrangement had worried her, making it impossible to move out of the way if threatened by a snake or other animal.

Her first steps of the day sent fire up her legs and back. She cut herself a fresh palm frond to drive away the ever-hungry mosquitoes and picked up her walking stick. Each movement became easier as she forced herself to walk. Swinging her arms and bending helped to loosen other joints and muscles. She had made a mistake by not heading back toward the Beckett Ranch yesterday. An entire additional day's energy had been spent moving farther into the swamp. She was lost and starving and getting weaker. Yesterday she had two choices of direction. Today she had to keep plodding toward what she hoped was the south—and what might be her last chance to find civilization. Her close calls with the panther and the alligator had haunted her during the night. The concern over what might lie ahead made her tremble. But two positive facts helped to fight back the tears: her period was over, and she hadn't become crazy or sick from the water or the raw plants—not yet anyway.

"The menu for today," she announced to the trees, "will feature eau de swamp consommé, an entré of coco plum au naturel, followed by a pond apple dessert. For an appetizer we will start with fern fiddleheads." Surely the first signs of insanity had surfaced.

The light was more diffused this morning, as if the unseen sky were cloudy. Having no way to tell which direction she should take, her spirits sank further. Thunder rumbled in the distance and then crept closer preceded by flashes of lightning. Beth heard the raindrops on the leaves overhead, and a few seconds later, a fine, misty rain was descending upon her. Then the downpour started. The noise of the deluge was deafening. Each flash of lightning and simultaneous crack of thunder frightened her. Continuing to walk was foolish; she had no signs of which direction she should go. But it seemed wrong to stand still; there was no place to keep dry. After what seemed like an interminable period of crashing and popping, the lightning and thunder diminished, and soon after that, the rain abated.

Beth looked more carefully than ever at where she placed each foot. The worry of falling was coupled with the knowledge that she might lack the strength to get up again. Between bushes, spiders had stretched their webs. When concentrating on her footing, these webs caught her full in the face. With a shudder she brushed them away. On one low branch was a yellow rat snake, which she went out of her way to avoid.

She came upon a black pool. The light was dim, and the air was cooler here, even at midday. On the bank across the dark water dozed six alligators, the largest two being over ten feet long. The smallest one, about three feet in length, lay on the back of a much larger adult. They squatted watchfully, but seemed unconcerned by her presence. On the surface floated a dead cousin of theirs, belly up. On its exposed yellow underside stood a large black vulture, pecking away at the dead reptilian giant. Perched on the lower branches were other vultures watching their leader below. The usual cloud of insects hung above the pool. The storm had passed, and through the roof of the cathedral-like opening, a ray of sunlight shone onto branches on which sat several dozen snowy egrets and white ibis.

After skirting the alligator hole, while sloughing through knee-deep water, Beth tripped over a cypress knee. Her walking stick, instead of being in front, was stuck in the mud behind, and she fell flat on her face in the muck. She was drenched from the rain anyway, and the mud, except for the stink of rotting vegetation, was pleasantly cool and soothed the hundreds of itching mosquito bites.

The thunderstorm had drifted away, but the trees were still dripping cold droplets on her. She knew the air was warm, but she was soaked and chilled, and had nothing to do but keep pushing on. The water grew deeper, up to her thighs, and moving forward was harder than ever. On a fallen log not more than four feet away was a snake. It slithered into the pool until only its diamond-shaped head could be seen. He was swimming away from her, fortunately, but she could still make out the arrow-like ripples followed by the zig-zag motion of its body. She had no interest in finding out what species of snake she had encountered. After giving the serpent plenty of space, Beth climbed into the thicket, not wishing to share the water with the reptile.

Off to her left, brighter light revealed a break in the trees. She struggled through the vines and thorns toward the opening. She saw a patch of blue sky for the first time in a day and a half. Hopefully the sun would give a hint as to the direction she should take. The trees ended abruptly. Spreading before her was a broad expanse of sawgrass. She was comforted to see the open sky again. Above the narrow green spears of grass a squadron of dragonflies flitted about. In the shallows off to her left two wood storks were stalking crayfish or frogs. She heard no sound except for the loud cry of a yellow-bellied sapsucker in a tree behind her. Her boots parted the sawgrass, and below was water. Beth entered cautiously. At first the water came to her knees, but then her feet sank deeper into black, sticky mud. Every step forward was obstructed by the sawgrass, as well as lily pads, trailing vines, and other freshwater plants. Soon she was immersed up to her waist, and still the mud persisted. The horizon disappeared behind the tall, sharp blades of grass. To try to continue farther in this direction was folly. This might be the grassy river that Flagler had described.

The lily pads had something she wanted. The spaghetti-like spikes at the bottom were edible, and she pulled up a plant and tentatively tasted the rhyzomes. They weren't exactly dining room fare, but anything to help quell the hunger was welcome. After eating what she could, Beth stuffed a few spikes and unopened young blossoms in her pockets and resumed her journey.

The sun was high in the sky and was no help in finding south. Her only choice was to return to the slough. Across the small pond, the bushes were covered with largish brown birds with snakelike necks—anhingas. She was glad she was able to skirt the water here; it looked deep, and she saw an occasional alligator sunning itself on the bank. Numerous fish drifted just below the surface. Nearby she spotted a turtle she at first had mistaken for a rock. Turtle meat was edible, but the black shell, wider than her shoulders, presented too much of a challenge, and the plants seemed more palatable than raw turtle flesh anyway.

Soon Beth was back among the bald cypress, the sky again obscured by the layers of branches. An ugly opossum startled her as it waddled across an opening with two babies clinging to its back in a rare daylight appearance. A subcanopy of pop ash, swamp bay, and pond apple caused the area below to be darker and cooler, but she was chilled and wished for the sun. Around her were alligator flag, pickerel weed, the lavender panicles of thalia, swamp hibiscus, ferns, of course, and as always, plants she didn't recognize. If the sawgrass marsh was to the east as Mr. Flagler had described, then heading parallel to it might lead her south, she reasoned. She staggered on, half aware of her surroundings, hoping she was heading in a southerly direction, but never certain.

A strangler fig had killed a small tree, and the rotted stump of its victim still stood encircled by its killer. As Beth approached, a wood duck fled from a hole in the stump at eye level. Looking into the hole she counted eleven eggs. This was no time to feel sorry for the poor duck. She had never eaten a raw egg before, but here was the most nourishing food she had found. Sooner or later she was going to be hungry enough to eat the rotting bark on the tree, ants and all. One by one she lifted the eggs, cracked them open, and gulped down the contents. After eating nine of them, guilt made her leave the last two for the duck, not knowing whether the mother would return to hatch the eggs or not.

She wished for nightfall as an excuse to stop, but it was a long time in coming. Then at last came refuge in a third tree, and a third nightmarish ordeal alone. This was the end of the fourth day since leaving the Becketts. If she had been moving in a straight line south, she should be near the Gulf.

The next morning she made her most promising discovery. Pausing to rest for a moment, she happened to notice a few dry leaves floating on the surface of the water. They were drifting slowly without a breeze. There was a current! As the Charles River flowed toward Boston Harbor, this brook must be leading to the Gulf! Her discovery raised her spirits to their highest level since Jimmy Pantertail had deserted her. For the first time she believed she could get through the swamp.

Stopping to rest again, Beth allowed herself to dream of being home with good food, baths, and cool nights in a soft bed. A sting on her calf made her look down. To her horror, her feet were covered with swarming ants. She swatted at the hundreds of vicious biters, stamping her feet at the same time. Up her pant legs, down into her socks, the little pests were tenacious. She pulled down her trousers to get the ones already above her knees. Then off came her socks and brogans. The stinging slowly subsided. She had been standing on an ant hill. Another lesson learned. It took most of her energy to pull on her wet trousers. Her limbs and feet still burned from the ant bites, and her feet were sickly white and wrinkled from being wet for so long. She had no choice but to pull on her soggy socks and half-boots and move on.

The creek scarcely looked like a river at all. Every so often she came upon quiet, connecting pools with a current which was to be seen only if she studied the water carefully and watched leaves and sediment slowly drifting at an almost imperceptible rate. Tall bald cypress were standing along what must be the stream bed with the bases of their fluted trunks immersed. One of many lizards she had seen stood unmoving on a buttress, waiting for a careless water spider to skate close enough. Higher up on the smooth surfaces were lichen, moss, and leafy bromeliads. The pool's surface was interrupted by the usual vertical knees. A few yards farther back were royal palms, sabal palms, and undergrowth, including thick ferns. Vines were woven through the fabric of the brush everywhere.

The infernal mosquitoes were attacking more intensely than ever. They were in her ears, in her eyes, and up her nose. The fan palm was useless and she flung it aside. Grabbing her hat, she lashed out in all directions and slapped herself with it, but it had little effect upon the cloud around her. The little demons seemed to take delight in her actions. She fell to the ground, and they followed her. Jumping up, she ran through the underbrush, and they were still with her. They were in her mouth, and then she realized she had been screaming. She lunged into a pool—sudden relief as long as she stayed submerged. Alligators and snakes would have to wait their turn. Raising her head and gasping for air every few seconds, she lay under the surface for a time, knowing she could not remain this way for ever. The cooling water had a calming effect upon her nerves as well as her skin. The cloud of insects had disappeared, and she arose from the pool. For a while, at least, she was left alone until the beasties found her again.

The flapping of wings made her look up abruptly, and the trees whirled around. Steadying herself, the sickening movement subsided, but began again as soon as she moved. The nausea stayed with her as she forced herself to forge ahead. Her hunger pains were now accompanied by abdominal cramps.

What had caused her to feel this way? Was it the water, the plants she had eaten, the countless mosquito bites, the ant bites, the raw duck eggs, or the poisonous swamp miasmas that she had been warned about? Now she was wracked with chills in addition to the dizziness and pain. She leaned against a tree for support, unable to move another step.

She heard voices. Now came the hallucinations, she realized. Voices she had heard before had been the chatter of ibises in the lower trees that had then taken flight as she had drawn close. She had been wandering in circles, lost, and too weak to struggle on. As she sank to the mud, she heard the voices again, men's voices, and they were almost real. She forced herself to stand and stagger toward the sound.

Then she saw the two men.

Chapter 18

"Help!" she cried. Both men grabbed rifles from their canoe, seeing her for the first time.

The two men were waist-deep in water as they pushed along a dugout canoe in the same direction she had been going, their path converging with hers. The canoe was loaded with bulging burlap bags. Not convinced that what she saw was real, she waited and watched as the apparition moved closer. Every other word they used was vulgar. She learned that one man was called Roach.

"Come over here, kid, and keep your hands where we can see 'em." The man who spoke had a full beard. Both men watched her suspiciously.

"Who you with?" asked the other one. This one's beard was thin and scraggly. Both had on broad-brimmed hats, and it was difficult to make out their features, not that she cared. She was saved! She had made it through the swamp! These men would help her get to Allen River.

"I'm alone," she said, pushing her way through the water. Neither man seemed to be convinced and looked warily around as if they expected an ambush. She stumbled on a root and went under before she reached the canoe. She struggled to regain her footing and grabbed the edge of the canoe. Neither man moved to help her.

"What're you doin' out here, boy?" asked the scraggly-bearded one in a high, whiny voice.

She was about to correct his misimpression, but the scurrilous manner of these two reminded her in some vague way of Prichett, and she hesitated before answering. "I was separated from my party."

The two men waded around opposite ends of the canoe and stood on either side of her. "How many in yer party?" asked the taller one with the full beard that she saw now was streaked with gray.

"Two. My father and my—" she almost said "husband." "—brother. We were hunting."

"Where's yer rifle?" he asked.

"I leaned it against the tree. When I went back to look for it, that's when we got separated."

The shorter man with the scraggly beard spat into the water, not seeming to be interested.

"May I ride in your canoe?" she asked. "I can't walk any farther."

"What do you think, Lopez?" asked the shorter one, who must then be Roach.

Lopez answered in a foreign language she guessed was Spanish, and they both laughed maliciously. She was too tired and nauseated to care. When she put weight on the edge of the canoe, it tipped precariously. The two men hoisted her roughly onto one end. Leaning against a burlap bag, she discovered it was light and soft. Quills sticking through the fabric told her the bags were filled with plumes. These men were poachers!

Lying back on the bag of bird feathers, the dizziness and chills consumed her for a few minutes. Lopez was on her right with Roach on her left, both guiding the canoe along. They were moving in the direction she had intended to go and that was all that mattered for now.

After a while she was able to sit up slowly without having the trees whirl around. The two men were close beside her. Their clothing was filthy and torn, and their body odor was rank—just like she must be. From the gray in his matted beard, she guessed that Lopez was the older one.

His black, beady eyes, being close together, gave him the appearance of a rodent. His clawlike left hand, which rested on the edge of the canoe, had only a thumb and forefinger. Roach was shorter and stockier than Lopez. Where his right eye had been, a scarred hole remained, which made her shudder. His other eye stared wildly, and his eyebrows slanted downward toward his hooked nose. Both men had rotting teeth.

"How far are we from Allen River?" she asked.

"One day," said Lopez.

"We ain't goin' to Allen River," said Roach.

"Shut up, Roach," said Lopez.

They moved along in silence during the late afternoon and came to an egret rookery at twilight. Both men took their shotguns from the canoe and moved toward the vast flock of snowy egrets nesting in the trees. The poachers took aim and fired two shots each into the mass of birds, reloaded, and fired twice again. They repeated the process several more times as fast as they could reload. It seemed to her that they were not aiming, but firing indiscriminately into the flock. At the sound of the first shot the birds rose into the air with much uproar and confusion. The men kept reloading and firing until the greatest mass of birds had fallen or flown away. They then walked among the fallen birds, many still flapping their wings, hacked off the plumes, and stuffed them into bags. From the canoe she observed that the baby birds in many nests were now without parents to feed them. The men added the two bags of plumes to the dugout canoe and moved on.

"Hit's time we had a little party, Lopez. This here looks like a good place to stop," said Roach. They dragged the canoe onto a shallow spot where the canoe's bottom scraped on the mud. Lopez reached under the bags and pulled out a jug, tilted it above his mouth, and guzzled noisily before passing it over her head to Roach.

The two men stood on opposite sides of the dugout canoe, each with their feet still in the mud. They hesitated a moment, appearing as if they didn't know what to do next, but then Lopez seized her shoulders and Roach grabbed her feet. Having suspected foul play, she was ready and yanked out the derringer, pointed it at the man at her feet and pulled the trigger. Nothing happened. She squeezed the trigger again, and again nothing. Lopez, behind her, laughed and grabbed the little gun from her and threw it into the water.

"Turn him over," said Roach, grabbing her ankles.

"Pull down his britches first," said Lopez. She struggled, but was no match for the strength of the two poachers as they pulled off her suspenders and trousers. Almost too sick and weak to care, she fell back and groaned.

Roach had climbed up on the canoe, and was kneeling at her feet. His one eye, more fearsome than the empty socket, stared greedily at her. He pulled down his own trousers, and she saw the sickly whiteness of his lower belly compared to his darkened face and arms. Between his legs protruded the thing she had heard about but never seen. He then proceeded to pull her drawers from her grasp.

"Jesus Christ! This 'un's not a boy!"

She was too frightened and nauseated to be embarrassed or have the strength to struggle. Her stomach chose that moment to throw up a splattering of green bile.

"Hey, what's the matter with you? Are you sick?"

"Yellow fever," she said, the words popping out from the back of her mind where they had been suppressed from the first moment of dizziness.

"Yellow Jack!" exclaimed Roach, pulling up his trousers and hopping off the canoe. In almost one motion the two men grabbed her arms and feet and were about to throw her into the mud.

At that same moment a loud click that even she recognized as the sound of a gun being cocked made the two men freeze.

"Let her be," said a voice, and then she saw a third man standing above them on a fallen log holding a rifle.

Lopez released her arms, and she pulled up her drawers and trousers, only half aware of what was happening. The third man gave them orders sharply, and she was carried a short distance and dumped unceremoniously into another canoe.

"I'll get you for this, Phelps." That came from Lopez somewhere behind them.

"You're lucky to get away with your canoe and plunder, Lopez."

She was aware of the canoe's movement as she lay in the bottom, her feet near the man called Phelps. After a time the nausea diminished, and she took stock of her rescuer as he poled the canoe along a narrow creek in the fading twilight. He was average in height, clean-shaven except for a large, brown mustache. Except for perspiration marks and the mud on his boots, his khaki trousers, shirt, and broad-brimmed straw hat were remarkably clean.

The sudden turn of events was just catching up with her. Near death and starvation, the attack by those two poachers followed by her rescue by this man—all this was hard to grasp in her condition. She had made it through the swamp and was now safe.

He looked down and saw her watching him. "Can you talk?" he asked. His eyes were cold.

"Where are you taking me?" she asked.

"To my farm where you can get cleaned up and rest. My name is Luther Phelps. I'm a grower and shipper. What's your name?"

"Elizabeth Sprague. Thank you for rescuing me."

"What on earth are you doing here in the swamp?" His eyes were on the meandering creek, narrow and enveloped in mangroves, hardly a stream at all, but the most promising she had yet seen.

"I'm a botanist. I'm here to study the flora of the cypress swamp." She swatted at the mosquitoes.

"Indeed! A woman." He poled on for a few minutes as if thinking that over. "Were you alone?"

This man spoke well, and there seemed to be no reason to avoid telling him the truth. "I started out from Gopher Ridge with an Indian guide, but he abandoned me."

"Aha. What was his name? If you don't mind my asking."

"Little Jimmy Pantertail. Have you heard of him?" It made little difference one way or the other now.

"No, can't say that I have."

The way he looked off into the swamp when he answered her told her that he had.

"That was clever of you to tell Lopez and Roach that you had yellow fever. They're too dumb to know they can't catch it from you. What do you think you have?" She realized that the three men had called each other by name and must have encountered one another before.

"I don't know. Perhaps it is yellow fever."

"Have you been drinking swamp water?"

"Yes."

"Well, that would make anyone come down with the ague. Who knows what's in that water. I have a cistern of rain water at my farm."

"Are we near the village of Allen River?"

"That's about ten miles from here as the vulture flies, but there's some dangerous territory in between." She sank back into the canoe. No way could she travel another ten miles feeling as she did.

"Alligators?"

"Well, yes, but there's also a swamp ape that dwells in these coastal marshlands. It's an animal you wouldn't want to meet face to face."

Her interest rose. "I've heard of them. I was told they don't exist."

"I've seen one. This one stood about eight feet tall and was vicious, but you'll be safe at my place so long as you don't go wandering off." His tone made his statement seem more like a threat than a caution.

They came to a wider stream as dusk became complete darkness. The man seemed to know where he was going. While not as sick as she had been, she still had chills and a little dizziness. She had to force herself to stay alert. Mr. Phelps was not a man she could trust.

Chapter 19

*S*he had been in a large room of the farmhouse for several minutes before she realized another person was in the room with her. A single kerosene lamp emitted a dim light. Phelps had disappeared into the back of the house. Sitting still in one corner was a girl wearing a faded homespun dress, her bare feet tucked under the wooden chair. Too sick to say anything to the girl, she rested her head on the bare table. The chills shook her body. Her teeth chattered. The nausea was in full force, too.

"Emily, show Miss Sprague where she can sleep," said Mr. Phelps sharply from a doorway. The girl hopped up and headed for the stairs.

There was one answer she had to have before succumbing to the fever. "M-Mister Phelps, will you t-t-take me t-to Allen River?" Sick or not, she had to get to Key West and home to Boston.

"Too dangerous. You'll have to stay here," he answered.

His answer was ominous. If he had said, "You're too sick," she would have believed him. He had to have a safe way to get to civilization. What were his intentions for her? Standing and then holding on to the table for balance was too much effort. She sat down again heavily. Her intention of heading for the door was foiled by the shakes and dizziness.

Emily approached and took her by the arm without saying anything. There was no point in resisting as the girl helped her up the stairs into the darkness. She was led into a small room where she could barely make out a single bed and a dresser. She fell onto the hard bed, thankful to be able to lie down. The room spun around sickeningly. The girl stood and stared at her and then left without a word.

When she awoke sunlight was streaming though the window. She had slept through the night. Sitting up slowly, the room started to spin again, but after a few minutes it stopped. Except for the two pieces of furniture, the room was bare but clean. The walls were plain boards. Then she saw a metal pitcher and a cup on the dresser that she hadn't seen the night before. Standing slowly, she took two steps to the dresser. The pitcher was full. Not until then did she realize how thirsty she was. The water was warm, but it had to be an improvement over what she had been drinking for the past three days.

She looked up and saw the girl standing in the doorway, watching. Scarcely more than a child, the youngster wore a faded blue dress, its print barely distinguishable. She was barefoot. Her drab hair hung down despondently. The girl's eyes were lifeless, her face a picture of defeat.

"He's gone," the girl said. "You must run away while you have the chance."

"What do you mean?" she asked, filling the cup again and taking it back to the bed and sitting.

"He'll keep you here and do mean things to you like he does to me. Have some food to eat and then run."

"I couldn't run. Every time I move, everything spins around." The girl's words about Phelps confirmed her suspicions of the night before.

"Come downstairs. I'll feed you." The girl took her by the arm and led her from the room and down the stairs. She noticed that the rest of the house was as bare as the bedroom was. The girl helped her to a chair in the kitchen. Shelves full of jugs, bottles, and bags of Red Devil lye caught her eye.

The girl saw her looking at the shelves and said, "He makes moonshine and sells it to the Indians."

"My name is Beth. I'm sorry, I don't remember your name."

"Emily. Would you like some grits?"

"I'm not sure I can eat anything, but I'll try it. I think I have a fever."

"You must escape before he comes back," said Emily as she worked at the stove.

"If he is mean to you, why don't you run away?"

Emily shook her head. "He'd come after me and kill me. Besides, Luther says there's a swamp ape out there somewhere."

"Have you seen the swamp ape?"

"No. I don't believe him about that. There's a canoe out there you can take. It belonged to Martin."

"Who is Martin?"

"He used to be a handyman here, but he's dead now, and others before him," Emily said dully.

"How did he die?" Maybe she was in danger of dying from yellow fever after all.

"He fell into the alligator pen, according to Luther." Emily's tone suggested she didn't believe the story. "If you took the canoe you'd be safe except for one thing."

"What's that?"

"You might meet Luther coming upstream while you're going down." She handed Beth a plate of fried cornmeal mush and then sat opposite.

"Where did he go?" Beth noticed the dark rings under Emily's eyes for the first time.

"Chokoloskee. He'll be back tonight. He usually comes back drunk. He likes their whiskey better'n his own squeezin's."

She had heard Dr. Worthington mention Chokoloskee, one of the Ten Thousand Islands. Fishermen lived there. "Can I get to Allen River from here by canoe?" She took a small bite of grits. It had been fried in bacon grease, she guessed, but it went down, and she knew that she needed food.

"Yes, but you still have to go past Chokoloskee. Go downstream. When you come to a fork, bear right. It's all part of Deadman's Creek.

It's longer and that's where the swamp ape lives, but you're less likely to meet Luther. Luther uses Turtle Creek, the left fork. It's shorter. Both Deadman's Creek and Turtle Creek join the Turner River, which comes out at Chokoloskee. You'll find that the whole swamp is criss-crossed with little creeks that go nowhere."

"I don't think I can do it alone. Why don't you come with me?"

Emily shook her head. "I don't want to leave here."

The girl was obviously afraid of Luther Phelps and was mistreated by him. "Why don't you want to get away from him?"

"I don't want to leave my baby." The look on Emily's face reflected a deep sadness.

She was unaware that a baby was in the house. "You could bring your baby with us." She had guessed the girl was about fourteen. "How old are you?"

"Seventeen."

"What's your baby's name?"

"Suzie." Emily pulled at her long, colorless hair. "I can't take her away. She's dead."

"I'm sorry."

The tragic expression on Emily's face revealed abysmal despair. The silence that followed seemed to be begging for another question.

"How did she die?"

"She was colicky and cried most of the time. Luther didn't like it and fed her to the gators. Alive." Emily was looking down at her dress, and was wiping her hands on it as if she were trying to get them clean. The horror of the girl's answer made Beth forget her sickness. The predicament they were both in was overwhelming. Just when she believed she was safe, this man turned out to be a monster, unless the girl was imagining all this.

After recovering a little from Emily's answer she said, "How did you get here?"

"I was sold to Luther by an Indian. I lived with my family at Gopher Ridge."

A discussion the Becketts had at the supper table the first night she was with them came back. "What's your last name, Emily?"

"Jenkins." The girl stared at the table.

"I heard about you being missing when I was at Gopher Ridge. Your family is still there, and they believe you're dead. Don't you want to go back?"

Emily shook her head. "Daddy'd kill me for livin' with Luther."

"Your mother wants you back. She wouldn't let that happen. What happened wasn't your fault, Emily. If I get away in the canoe, won't Luther punish you for helping me escape?"

Emily shrugged. "I'll tell him you were gone when I went upstairs. He won't kill me, not at least until he gets another housekeeper. Besides, I pleasure him."

The significance of what Emily was saying sunk in slowly. Phelps had no need for the two of them. He might make her his new slave and mistress and kill Emily if all she had heard was true. The girl wanted her to escape to save herself. "We've a better chance of getting free if we go together."

Emily shook her head. "I want to stay with Suzie."

Beth sat looking at the half-eaten grits. She didn't like leaving the girl alone. Emily was only six or seven years younger than she was, but was so childlike in many ways. Staying with her was not a solution. If what Emily had said was true, then Phelps was planning to make one of them his next victim.

Leaving wasn't safe either. If the rumors about the swamp ape were true, meeting up with him might be even more gruesome. And the alligators, snakes, and other wild animals were out there as well. With the dizziness and chills that kept coursing through her, the risk of becoming too sick to complete the ten-mile trip to Allen River was a strong possibility.

But by canoeing to Allen River and reporting the murders, she'd be saving Emily's life—and her own. She expected to be safe as long as she kept the canoe away from the shore. The chance of meeting the mythical swamp ape in such a big swamp, was small, she convinced herself.

She stood up slowly to avoid bringing on the dizziness again. "I'm leaving, Emily, and you should come, too."

Emily perked up. "Keep on Deadman's creek, which bears right about a mile and a half down. You can wash up while I pack some food and water to take with you. I'd like to wash your clothes, but there's no time."

She hadn't washed, and her clothes were crusty with dried sweat, vomit, and mud. Emily showed her where the wash stand was out back. The sun was higher in the sky than she expected; she must have slept most of the morning. Forcing herself to strip down to her torn chemise top and drawers, she cleaned herself as well as the dizziness allowed and decided to rinse out her shirt and trousers, too. Wearing wet clothes was better than having them filthy.

After dressing again she looked beyond the washstand. The house had been built on a mound, and the brush and trees behind it had been cleared. Closest to her on the left was a cistern to catch rain water, and farther out was a field of sugar cane. A big iron pot on a fire pit stood on the right not far from the house. Beyond that was a large pen with a stout board fence, which aroused her curiosity. She walked over to the fence and looked over the top which came almost to her chin. In the center was a shallow pool, and around the edge lay ten or fifteen alligators sleepily enjoying the sun. In the mud she saw several bones. Her shivering now was from wondering with dread if they were parts of the man called Martin.

When she returned to the house, she asked, "Emily, do you remember the Indian's name who sold you to Mr. Phelps?"

Emily nodded. "It was Little Jimmy Pantertail. I thought he was my friend." The moment the Indian had attacked her in the swamp came roaring back. If the derringer hadn't scared him off, she, too, might have been sold as a slave, ending up here anyway.

Emily had prepared a small sack of food and a can of water and walked with her down to the creek where the dugout canoe rested in the mud.

"Thank you, Emily. I wish you'd come with me." The thrill of being on the last lap of her journey helped in fighting back a surge of dizziness.

She found that standing in the canoe and attempting to pole was harder than it looked. Fortunately Deadman's Creek, like the other waters she had encountered, had a barely discernible current. Before long she had become accustomed to standing and poling the boat forward without losing her balance. The canoe zig-zagged until she learned how to use the pole more effectively.

The creek was a little wider than the canoe was long, and made gentle turns. Mangroves crowded in from both sides. She watched for the fork, and was fooled by several false starts to the right that went nowhere and expended energy she could ill afford to spare. Returning to the creek each time, she pushed downstream again, fearful of meeting Phelps, and hoping she hadn't missed the opening among the mangroves.

After thinking she must have gone beyond the junction, she came to a turnoff to the left that had to be Turtle Creek, the shortcut Luther Phelps was taking from Chokoloskee. After bearing to her right, the creek narrowed and soon the branches were nearly touching her. At least she felt safer from Phelps here. She passed several swimming alligators. If one nudged the canoe, keeping her balance was going to be difficult. In places, the creek was less than twice the width of the canoe, and the mangroves brushed past her on either side.

Bouts of dizziness accompanied by the chills made her stop and sit down more and more frequently. Forcing back the illness, Beth tried poling from a sitting position without much success. The mangrove branches were interfering with her movement of the pole. Not too far above her head two buzzards sat watching her. How was it that they always knew when the end was near? She sat and waited for the dizziness to pass. She drank from the can Emily had given her. Feeling no better, she decided to wait a little longer, but then she saw a snake heading for the boat. The snake changed its course away from the canoe, and she pressed on. She might mistakenly pole her way up a dead-end creek, faint, and be eaten by flies and buzzards. The image of her skeleton lying in the canoe didn't help her spirits.

A thunder cloud accompanied by a few warning rumbles brought on an early twilight. The creek remained narrow and then farther on was blocked. A tree had fallen across the creek, and its branches had snagged floating objects, making passage impossible.

On both sides were mangrove roots growing downwards from the branches, almost like prison bars cutting off movement in either direction.

To get past the barrier, the canoe had to be pulled through the branches of the fallen tree, a task she doubted she had the strength to do even if she were well and rested. Under the mangroves it was almost as dark as night.

"Now I know why they call this Deadman's Creek," she said aloud. The trees started whirling around her worse than ever, and she was shaking. To make matters worse, a breeze came up, and raindrops began to fall. Within minutes the rain intensified into a violent downpour accompanied by flashes of lightning and loud booms of thunder like cannon firing nearby.

She huddled in the shallow bottom of the dugout canoe, shivering. During a rapid series of flashes she saw movement though the tangle of roots and branches. Again a flash, and again she saw a shadowy shape, and she was sure that it had moved. Unlike the bushes that were lashing about in the fury of the wind, the hulk was moving laterally and slowly making its way through the snarl of growth toward her. It was large, and dark, but she collapsed uncaring, unable to hold up her head any longer. The last thing she remembered were the cold raindrops falling on her face.

Chapter

20

When Beth awoke, it was dark. The sickness remained with her. She felt hot and then cold. Her clothes were soaked with perspiration and yet she was wracked with violent shaking from the chills. A dark figure stood over her in silhouette. The swamp ape. She was too weak to be frightened. Her eyelids felt heavy and refused to stay open even though the light was dim. Every bone, muscle, and joint ached. The overpowering nausea told her death must be near. Not certain whether she wanted to live or die, she let the darkness surround her again. The quicker death came, the better.

Daylight. Beth was conscious of being covered with a harsh wool blanket. The roof of the Beckett's chickee was above her. No one was about. Mr. Beckett must have gone for the doctor. She had something pressing to do, but it eluded her. She hoped the doctor was coming soon. Mama was pouring tea, and the doctor was late.

The chickee, she realized during the next period of awareness, was not on the Beckett ranch. She was in the swamp. The dark creature was there and approaching menacingly. He was tall and hairy. Her inability to sit up scared her more than the swamp ape did. He came closer and stood upright, unlike the ape she had seen at the circus side show with its hands nearly touching the floor of its cage. This one was more of a wild man than an ape, with long, dark hair and beard and patched clothes. She saw him through a haze and decided she was experiencing an apparition as he drifted into darkness. "I must save Emily Jenkins," she mumbled.

Mama was on the stage speaking to a hall crowded with excited women. Seated on one side were Elizabeth Cady Stanton and Susan B. Anthony with Julia Ward Howe on the other. Mama spoke with fervor and resolve, standing regally, eyes flashing. Gone were the jerky, nervous movements usually seen in Papa's presence. Beth watched her mother with pride from the first row as she sat beside Papa, who was smilingly admiring his wife and nodding in agreement to her profound advocacy of women's suffrage. Mama told the audience how proud she was of her daughter, who was a professional woman, a successful architect. She tried to tell her mother that she was a botanist, but the words would not come out, and she awoke with a start.

Bits and snatches of being rescued from the canoe came back. It had been raining and cold, and most of all, a sickening dizziness had overpowered her. She dreaded the immobilizing shakes that had chilled her clear through and made her teeth chatter. Now in the chickee, she was extremely weak and unable to move.

Much later she saw someone standing by a tree, and then she realized it was a shirt hanging on the trunk—her shirt! Below it were her trousers. To her embarrassment, her torn chemise, and drawers hung to one side in plain view for the man to see. Peering under the blanket, she discovered she was wearing a large, gray shirt of rough cloth that came nearly to her knees. Beth was astonished to find that she was wearing nothing else. A nurse or a farmer's wife had to be taking care of her. No other accounting was possible for having been bathed and having her clothes washed and hung up to dry. Her head was heavy from the exertion, and she lay back once again.

A heavy downpour awakened her. At the other end of the chickee sat the wild man, but wild men didn't sew, did they? The hairy man was sewing a patch on an article of clothing and not aware of her studying him. This man could not be the one they called the swamp ape; he was tall, but not as tall as the eight feet Luther Phelps had described. His trousers were faded jeans with rivets and a long-sleeved shirt with patches on the elbows. His beard was untrimmed, but it and his mop of hair appeared to be clean. She had never seen a man doing the work of a seamstress before.

His head turned, and their eyes met. "Who is Emily?" he asked, as if this had been a continuing conversation.

"Emily Jenkins. She is Luther Phelps' prisoner." She coughed weakly. "Doctor."

"The nearest doctor is probably in Key West." He scowled through the bushy opening around his eyes as he approached. "Do you want a drink of water?"

"That's what made me sick," she whispered.

"This is rainwater." She shrank from him as he came close. He handed her a tin cup from which she took a few sips and then drank greedily before sinking back.

She had closed her eyes for only a moment, but the sun was out, and the man was coming into the clearing holding a shotgun in one hand and a wild turkey by its feet in his other. His appearance was frightening. She watched him throw more wood on the fire. He turned and saw her struggling to sit up. He loomed toward her, scowling darkly. Placing a huge hand on her shoulder, he pushed her back gently.

"Not yet," he said, and offered her the tin cup. She drank gratefully, but questioned silently whether she was his patient or his prisoner.

"I must help Emily."

"We'll talk about that when you're stronger."

Awaking from a deep sleep, she recalled that Papa had been taking care of her in her dream, not the swamp ape–man. He was watchful, loving, and gentler than he had ever been. She felt better and managed to sit up for the first time. Wearing only her chemise top and drawers, she self-consciously pulled the blanket around her even though the air was hot and humid. She had been wearing a man's shirt and was puzzled by the change. The woman who had washed her entire body and cleaned her clothes was yet to be seen.

The man came over to Beth and encouraged her to lie down.

"I must save Emily. Luther Phelps is cruel to her and may kill her if he finds she helped me escape. I must get to the police."

"There's no law within fifty miles," he said.

"Then I must go and get her." She made an attempt to swing her feet to the ground, but fell back weakly instead, amazed at how little strength she had. At least the chills and dizziness had left her.

He brought her a bowl of turkey broth and fed her. The spoon was almost lost in his huge hand. The broth was the most delicious liquid she had ever tasted. His hairy face was close to hers, and his soft, brown eyes were intent upon the spoon. She noticed how gentle he was for such a large, fearsome-looking man. This time she did not fall back asleep, but watched him go to the creek and take off his shirt. As he washed himself she saw his muscular arms and flat stomach. This was the first time in her life she had ever seen a man bare to the waist and turned away, shocked that she had been staring at him.

Then a horrible realization came over her. The water and turkey broth she had consumed were having an effect upon her bladder. She sat up again, but in this partially dressed and weakened state was too embarrassed to speak frankly to the man.

"I need to get up," she said as he approached, buttoning his shirt.

"I've built a necessary behind those bushes. Can you walk there with my help?"

She understood what he meant and nodded, knowing she had to walk, thankful he had needed no further explanation. Holding the blanket around her, she slipped her feet to the ground as he held her free arm. He half-held her as she walked in the direction he had indicated. His grasp was firm but gentle, unlike Mr. Cushing's viselike grip that last night at Dartmouth Street. The walk was more tiring than she had expected, and he was almost carrying her when they arrived at the pit he had dug. She was shocked to see a simple bench made of saplings over the hole with no enclosure.

"You can't stay here," she said.

"I don't wish to," he replied. "Call me when you want to come back."

After a few minutes Beth stood, intending to walk back to the chickee by herself. She took several very shaky steps and then called, "I'm ready."

Halfway back to the chickee, she asked him, "Who bathed me and washed my clothes?"

"I did," he said.

She jerked her arm from his grasp and nearly lost her balance. "You had no right to touch a lady."

"Would it have been better to let the lady rot in her filth?"

"I can take care of myself," she said angrily.

"You haven't been doing such a good job of it lately." He helped her onto the cot in the chickee.

"How long have I been here?" She lay back, exhausted from the walk.

"This is your eleventh day." Beth realized that if this were her first walk to the necessary, this man must having been doing more than merely washing her face. This wild man had seen her in an undressed state under the most intimate and vulnerable of conditions. Being too tired to deal with the anger and embarrassment, or to account for where eleven days had gone, she let sleep envelop her.

A noise awakened her. Pitch darkness enclosed the camp except for flickering lightning through the branches. Thunder rolled around the heavens in the distance, but the sound had been closer. An alligator roared nearby, startling her. A bird screeched across the clearing. Then, fully awake, Beth became aware of another sound, so soft she sensed it as much as heard it. The sensation was hard to identify, but one thing was certain—it was here in the chickee. The sound was so faint that it could have been made by a snake slithering across the dirt floor, except for its rhythmic cadence. Then, with a mixture of relief and anger she recognized breathing. The man was sleeping just a few feet away from her. How dare he invade her sleeping space!

The Beckett's toolshed was in flames, and the smoke whirled around her face. Beth sat up with a start, but the smoke was from a smudge fire burning to keep away the mosquitoes, and she recognized that the smell had been with her ever since arriving here.

"Would you like some breakfast?" The man was walking toward her with a bowl. "Eggs."

She looked at the scrambled mess in the bowl and realized she was hungry. This time she fed herself as she sat on the canvas cot wrapped in the blanket.

"I want to get dressed," she said. She watched him move to the other end of the chickee and return with her shirt and trousers, now clean. He was twice her size, broad and tall. If he chose to attack her, she was powerless to protect herself from him. Yet he had a certain calmness about him that made her unafraid. She noticed a tear in her shirt had been sewn. "Thank you. Please turn your back. What is your name?"

He paused, studying her as if weighing whether she was capable of being trusted with his answer. "Matthew Hutchinson." Then he turned away as she slipped on her shirt and trousers.

"Tonight, Mr. Hutchinson," she said to his back, "I expect you to sleep at the other end of the chickee. Please respect my privacy."

"Yes, ma'am. I was on the other side of the table, closer to the alligators."

She hadn't thought about creatures coming up from the creek, but privacy and decency were important, too. "Alligators don't come into the chickee, do they?"

"Only when they are hungry, ma'am."

"You can turn around now, Mr. Hutchinson. You don't have to call me ma'am. My name is Elizabeth Sprague."

"Are you from Boston, Miss Sprague?"

"How did you know?"

"Your accent."

"Where are you from?"

"I live here now." Beth sensed that he had given all the information she was going to get. Something terrible must have happened in his life that made him hide out here in the swamp. Was he a poacher or a thief or a murderer hiding from the law?

"Did you say I have been here eleven days?"

"Today is the twelfth full day."

"Do you know what day of the month this is?"

"No. It's around the end of June."

"I'm worried about Emily Jenkins. I must find her and bring her to Allen River with me."

"You're too weak to go anywhere."

"Will you help me, Mr. Hutchinson?"

"That's none of my business. Luther Phelps doesn't take kindly to people messing in his affairs. If she wanted to, she could run away."

"She's young and confused. Besides, she had a baby by him that he murdered. She doesn't want to leave, but knows he might kill her."

He shrugged. "You don't interfere with other people's doings here in the swamp."

"If you're afraid, I'll go find her alone." Hurt showed in his eyes, not anger, as if she had touched some part of the reason why he lived here in the swamp. He remained silent and moved off to add more wood and sawgrass to the smudge fire.

She looked around the chickee. The dirt floor was swept clean. All his things were neatly stowed, most hanging from the rafters, including an axe, a shovel, and pots and pans. Dried meats and vegetables dangled from ropes overhead. Two guns hung from poles on opposite sides. And the skins of raccoons, a deer, and even a panther were stretched over a clothesline. Mr. Beckett had told her there was a five-dollar bounty for each panther killed. Beth felt the skins, and they were stiff, unlike the furs she had felt in stores. Beside the sawbuck table was a blanket on the dirt floor where he slept. He had given up his cot for her and had slept on the ground. She felt remorse for having been so snippy with him earlier.

It was comforting to be under the chickee roof when it began to rain.

It was hard to tell whether Matthew Hutchinson, if that was his name, was telling her the truth or not. Possibly he was a friend of Phelps. There might be other reasons why he didn't want her to leave his camp. She knew that today she was unable to go alone, but perhaps in a day or two she could get Mr. Hutchinson to reveal the way out of here. In spite of the alligators, snakes, and swamp miasmas, she would go back to Luther Phelps' place and rescue Emily Jenkins on her own.

Chapter 21

*B*eth awoke to see Mr. Hutchinson advancing toward her with an axe in his hands. His eyes were blazing, his long hair flowing in all directions. Before she could move, he raised the axe above his head and brought it down powerfully, missing the cot by inches. She rolled to one side away from him, but he failed to raise the axe again.

"Rattlesnake," he said. "They like it here where it's dry."

She looked beside the cot and saw the writhing remains of a six-foot reptile. Too horrified to speak, she looked back and forth between Mr. Hutchinson and the dead snake.

"Coffee, Miss Sprague?" As he poured her a cup of coffee at the fire, she began to collect herself and calm her heart, which was still pounding against her chest.

"Do they come around here often?" she asked as he returned from disposing of the snake.

"All the time."

She shuddered and decided to change the subject. "Where are we?"

"On Deadman's Creek. I don't know how it got its name. It flows into the Turner River, which leads to Chokoloskee."

"How far away is Chokoloskee?"

"Oh, about six miles."

As she sipped the bitter coffee, Beth looked around Mr. Hutchinson's camp. He had chosen a hammock, a slightly raised mound the shape of an inverted saucer, on which to build the chickee in the center. Around the circumference of the small clearing were three gigantic bald cypress and two majestic royal palms. She held in awe their tremendous trunks, like pillars of a cathedral. Through the lacy, pale green canopy high above filtered thin rays of the sun in the humid half-light. A pond apple and a half dozen small tree stumps remained around the chickee. Mr. Hutchinson's cooking fire blazed between stacked limestone rocks holding an iron grate. He was frying hoe cake in a pan beside a small pot of mush. Outside opposite corners of the chickee were the remains of smudge fires, one of which smoldered every dawn and twilight to keep away the mosquitoes, though not always successfully. To one side, where the sunlight slipped through, was a small vegetable patch behind a crude stick fence. Beside the fence was a thatch-roofed, homemade cage holding two chickens. A crude canvas cover was stretched loosely between four posts to catch rainwater, she supposed. Down the mild slope to the left, partially hidden by mangroves, was a creek, which meandered from what she guessed was the northeast toward the southwest. In the mud lay two dugout canoes. This creek, she surmised, was the highway in and out of the camp.

Around the hammock were mangroves to the east and south. To the north, across a broad expanse of sawgrass as even as if it had been mowed, she saw other clumps of tall cypress, slash pine, and palms. Underneath the sawgrass, she knew from experience, were several feet of water and all the creatures that loved that environment. To the west, beyond the buttonwood hiding the necessary, the clearing was bordered with ferns and alligator flag, and numerous semi-aquatic plants. Farther on, between dark pools, were gumbo limo, pond apple, and dwarf cypress.

To go with her coffee, Mr. Hutchinson brought Beth a piece of cornmeal cake. Later he ladled out a bowl of cornmeal mush. Mrs. Faraday had served oatmeal for breakfast almost every day of her life at home.

Now she longed for that cereal covered with cream, melted butter, and sugar, which she had eaten after gentle pleadings from Mama followed by loud exhortations from Papa.

"Do you have any cream or sugar?"

"No, but I made you this." He handed her a mangrove twig carefully frayed at one end. "It's a toothbrush."

She hadn't brushed her teeth since she lost her toothbrush and tooth powder in the fire and was impressed by his thoughtfulness. "Thank you."

"Do you mind if I ask you one question?" he asked.

"No. Go ahead."

"What is that packet hanging from the string around your neck?"

She put her hand to her throat and felt herself blushing. He had to have seen the packet that hung down between her breasts when her chemise was off. The red packet had faded to a pinkish-gray. She told him the story of Phoebe, the Negro cook, and the good-luck charm. "You haven't asked me why I was wandering around in the swamp," she said, taking a small spoonful of the tasteless mush.

"In these parts it's best if you don't ask people their business." His eyes were brown with flecks of gray and were at times soft and compassionate and at other times penetrating. Right now they were telling her not to ask him any questions.

"Well," she said, "I'm not running from the law, in case you've wondered. I came into the swamp to study the plant life. My Indian guide ran off with all I had, and I wandered around until I was attacked by two poachers and then rescued by Luther Phelps."

"You were probably safer with the poachers. The rumor is that people who go near the Phelps place are never seen again."

"That's what Emily Jenkins told me. I'm afraid she is being punished for helping me to escape. That's why I need your help to get her away."

He shook his head. "That was two weeks ago. I'm afraid you'd be too late."

"Nevertheless, I must try to save her. She's only seventeen and her family in Gopher Ridge thinks she's dead."

"Down here in the swamp it's better to leave other people alone.

If you go near the Phelps place again you might end up in the same situation as that girl—or worse."

"If you went there with me, we'd be safe enough."

"It's not my business."

She felt her anger rising. "Is it that you just don't care, or are you afraid of Luther Phelps?"

"If I were to go there, I'd have to take my rifle, and if I met him face to face, one of us might end up shooting the other. If I ended up dead, then he couldn't let you live to tell others about it."

"If you're a coward, I'll go alone. Just lend me your canoe and show me the way."

"That second canoe is the one you stole from Luther Phelps. It's surprising that he hasn't come over here to take it—and you. Besides, you're too weak to go anywhere." He stood up and walked away.

"Coward!" she yelled after him.

"Thief and busybody!" he yelled back.

She stamped her foot. He must be a coward. Why else was he living out here in the wilderness? He had to be hiding from the law.

Beth was strong enough to dress herself, even lace up her half-boots, and make trips to the necessary on her own. She sat up for longer periods each day and walked around the clearing. But in between these exhausting activities were naps every morning and afternoon. She was determined to walk more, and planned to pole a canoe back to Phelps' place as soon as she was able.

Until now she had learned nothing about this man. At least he hadn't killed her or taken advantage of her. There had to be another reason why Mr. Hutchinson was reluctant to rescue Emily Jenkins. To live out here among the snakes and alligators took courage. When she had been too sick to take care of herself, he had nursed her back from death. She was curious about the background of a man who could cook and sew and nurse someone back to health, but was afraid to challenge an evil man who was keeping a young girl prisoner.

The following day was a turning point. She felt much stronger, and Mr. Hutchinson had gone off with his rifle. He had shown her how to use his shotgun in case anyone came along the creek. Now was the opportune time to take the other canoe and go back up the creek and rescue Emily Jenkins. And she had his shotgun!

She put on her broad-brimmed hat and picked up the gun. As soon as she was away from the smudge fire, the mosquitoes attacked. It took all of her effort to shove the dugout canoe through the mud and into the water. After she had climbed into the canoe, the craft drifted a few feet to the middle of the creek while she rested and regained her strength. Then she realized that she was without pole or paddle. The stream being so narrow, the mangrove branches were within reach, and she was able to pull herself along. The creek was shallow, and she could get out and drag the canoe back to where she started. But then she saw the alligator's bulbous eyes bulging just above the surface, watching her, waiting for her to make a mistake. She had a choice. She could hold on to a branch, or let go and pick up the shotgun from the bottom of the canoe. Her energy was about gone, and now all she wanted to do was to return to the chickee and lie down. The canoe was not about to move far if she let go, the current being so sluggish. She bent over, picked up the shotgun and placed the butt against her shoulder as Mr. Hutchinson had instructed.

"If you fire that bird gun," said Mr. Hutchinson from behind her, "the pellets will make the gator angry, and the recoil will tip over the canoe." He poled his canoe alongside and lashed out at the alligator with his pole. The animal disappeared under the surface in the opposite direction. He stepped into the creek and pulled both canoes back to their resting place.

Mortified beyond words, she ignored his hand as she stepped into the mud.

"Are you going to shoot me with that gun or are you going to give it back?"

Beth shoved the shotgun at him and headed for the chickee without a word. She was not about to reveal to him that she was on the brink of collapse.

"Where were you intending to go?" he asked, following her.

"I was going to rescue Emily Jenkins. I'm not afraid to try." She was about to cry and turned away from him and flopped down on the cot.

"Well, if you're so hell-bent on getting us shot, I'll go with you tomorrow to see what we can see. Right now I've got a deer to dress. We're having venison tonight."

She awoke to the aroma of venison steaks sizzling above the fire. The remainder of the deer's carcass was dangling several feet above the ground from the pond apple. Sitting on wooden benches opposite each other, they ate in cool silence. Her hunger overcame the greasiness of the venison, and she savored the deep, meaty flavor along with the turnip greens and chunks of sow belly, his name for salt pork.

After she had been asleep for a while, she became aware of a scuffling sound just outside the chickee.

"Mr. Hutchinson?"

"Light the lantern—quick!" His voice came from outside the chickee in the darkness.

She fumbled for the matches and the lantern which he kept on the table after dark. The sounds of a struggle continued. At last she had the lantern lit and held it aloft to see what was happening. The deer carcass lay on the ground. Then she saw them. Mr. Hutchinson was sprawled on top of an eight-foot alligator with his arms around its middle. The reptile was writhing and snapping, trying to get at him.

"Let go, Mr. Hutchinson!" she screamed.

"I can't let go. He'll bite me."

"I'll hit him with the axe," she suggested.

"No, don't come near."

"I'll get the rifle, then."

"Good God, no! You'll shoot me." All this while the man and gator struggled. Beth grabbed the axe. In the meantime, the two combatants had rolled over. The alligator was upside down, its four legs clawing the air, its tail lashing, trying to reach its attacker. Mr. Hutchinson, underneath, gave a mighty shove, sending the beast only a short distance away. But he rolled in the opposite direction, leapt to his feet, and jumped across the deer carcass. The gator scrambled toward the creek and was lost in the darkness.

Mr. Hutchinson stumbled back to the chickee and slumped onto a bench. He was breathing heavily. She gave him a cup of water, which he gulped down. His shirt was soaked with perspiration and covered with dirt. Then she saw the blood on his pant leg. The fabric was torn and dirty.

"You've been bitten!"

"No, he must have clawed me."

"Take off your trousers."

"What?"

"Take them off," she ordered. He hesitantly slipped off his suspenders and lowered his pants. She held the lantern close and was sickened by the large gash which extended diagonally from just below his drawers to an area beside his kneecap. His thigh was bleeding, but the cut didn't appear to be deep.

"Are you going to stare at my leg all night?"

"Do you have any whiskey, Mr. Hutchinson? And rags? We have to put on a bandage."

"There's a bottle of whiskey in a box beside the table. No rags. I have a clean shirt hanging over there." He pointed toward the opposite corner of the chickee.

After getting the bottle and the shirt, she tried tearing it without success.

"Here, let me do that," he said crossly. While he was tearing his shirt into strips, she brought a bowlful of their drinking water and washed his wound with a remnant of the shirt. His body stiffened as she poured on the whiskey, but he remained silent. She applied a makeshift bandage and then wound several strips around his thigh.

"Do you have to do that so tightly?" he asked.

"You want to stop the bleeding, don't you?"

"How did you know how to do that?"

"In college, my friend Grace was an avid reader of dime novels, which she loaned to me. One story was about a cowboy who was gored by a steer, and his wife had to take care of him."

"Did he live?" he asked.

"I don't know. The story sickened me, and I didn't finish it."

Mr. Hutchinson went to his end of the chickee, and she blew out the lantern and tried to go back to sleep. But visions of the man and the alligator kept returning. What if the still-hungry gator came back for her? She was closer to the ground than the deer carcass had been. Then she remembered the partly-chewed carcass was again hanging halfway between her and the creek.

When she awoke, daylight had arrived, and Mr. Hutchinson had the coffee boiling. Beth noticed that he had changed to a clean pair of trousers.

"How's your wound?" she asked.

"The bleeding stopped. Thank you for helping me last night." He poured them coffee, and they sat at the table. "I have something for you." He reached under the table, pulled up a cloth bag, and handed it to her. If it contained bird feathers, it proved that he was a poacher.

"What is it?"

"A pillow. It's made of cattail fluff."

"Thank you." She was embarrassed by his gift. "I have an apology to make to you," she said.

"Oh?"

"I called you a coward yesterday. Any man brave enough to wrestle an alligator like that can't be cowardly. He was heavier than you are—and longer."

"I called you a busybody."

"And a thief."

"Well, you did take Phelps' canoe."

"Emily told me that it belonged to a man who had disappeared named Martin."

"I'm still surprised Phelps hasn't come looking for you."

"Emily thought that Phelps had killed Martin. Why does he keep alligators in a pen?"

"I don't know. The hides sell for around ninety cents, but as you've seen, the gators are all over the swamp." He stopped and sipped his coffee. "Do you still want to go and try to rescue that girl?"

"Yes, today, if your wound doesn't hurt too much."

Chapter 22

Mangroves stretched out over the canoe, the branches dropping new roots on both sides. She sat at the front end, facing forward, occasionally pushing branches aside. Mr. Hutchinson stood in the back and poled them upstream. Now that they were on their way to Phelps' place, she agonized over the slow pace, feeling as if every minute counted in saving Emily's life.

"Did you make this canoe, Mr. Hutchinson?"

"No. I bought it from a Seminole for twenty-five cents. They make them for a living. It's all carved from one log. He made the chickee, too."

This creek looked like all the others. At times she saw the brown-leafed bottom inches below the canoe. Off to the right was a murmuring sound as if people were talking in low tones. Then she was startled as a flock of white ibis flew up from the undergrowth and disappeared among the higher leaves above. Beth was accustomed now to a stream appearing to end in a cluster of mangrove roots, and then turning abruptly upon itself in another direction. Often several courses were open to them with none looking promising, but Mr. Hutchinson unerringly chose the correct one. The mosquitoes attacked in swarms whenever the breeze let up. An alligator slipped off the bank and into the water, and without warning the canoe pitched sharply as the monster let them know they were invading his territory. She let out a little shriek, but the canoe righted itself. Mr. Hutchinson steadied himself with the pole. Now through an opening above, she could see blue sky dotted with hawks and vultures gliding in lazy circles.

They came to a fallen tree that had been cut away to allow a passage through.

"This is where you found me, isn't it?"

"Yes," he said without further comment. There was a hollowness inside her as she realized this was the spot where she would have died if Mr. Hutchinson hadn't come along.

"Thank you," she said.

"You can thank me after we are safely away from Phelps."

After a while they came to an estuary to the right that she didn't recognize until Mr. Hutchinson told her it was Turtle Creek. All the surroundings looked so much alike. They continued upstream, and she knew they must not be far from Luther Phelps' place. Black clouds approached them from the east and soon hid the sun. At last she saw the house. It was a nondescript two-story clapboard building with a hipped roof standing starkly on a rise above the creek. There was no sign of life. The structure seemed out of place here in the wild. Mr. Hutchinson beached the canoe, picked up his rifle, and headed up the rise. When she started to follow, he said, "Stay here." She hesitated and then followed him, remaining several paces behind. She noticed a spot of blood on his pant leg where he had been clawed by the alligator.

He kicked at the ground. "This is a shell mound. The Calusa Indians made this perhaps hundreds of years ago. They'd be unhappy to know that someone has built a house here. It's an unlucky place." He knocked on the door, which seemed to her an incongruous act out here in the swamp. "Phelps!" he called after a pause.

No response.

"Emily!" she called. "Emily Jenkins!"

Silence.

"Perhaps he's out back," she said. They walked around the house and out to the alligator pen. In the mud lay the alligators she had seen nearly two weeks ago. As far as she could tell, they hadn't moved since. But then she emitted a small shriek as the horror enveloped her. Against the fence, partially submerged in the mud, was a piece of faded blue cloth muddied almost beyond recognition, but the print she had seen before.

"What is it?" he asked.

"That's the dress Emily was wearing when I saw her." She turned away from the fence and tried unsuccessfully to keep from throwing up.

"You're probably mistaken," he said, looking into the pen. "She's most likely run away. That was just a rag," he said unconvincingly.

They headed back to the house and entered through the back door which was unlocked. The feeling of emptiness surrounded her as much as the first time she had been here, and their footsteps echoed. The furniture was as rustic and bare as the house itself. She half hoped to find Emily crouched in a corner of the livingroom as she had the first time, but the room was empty. The upstairs was vacant as well, except for Phelps' clothes lying about. No sign remained that Emily Jenkins had ever lived here.

"We're too late," she said sadly.

They left by the front door. Down at the creek Luther Phelps was stepping out of a canoe. Mr. Hutchinson walked halfway down the shell mound and stopped. He switched his rifle from his left hand to his right. Phelps held a rifle, too. Both men had their weapons pointed at the ground. She stood to one side as Phelps walked up to meet them.

"Good afternoon," said Phelps. He tipped his hat as if they had met on Tremont Street in Boston. "Well, how is our little botanist faring?" His smile sent a chill through her.

"We're looking for Emily," she said.

"Yes, well, that's a sad story," said Phelps, looking up at them. "She left me and went back to live with her mother in Key West. I'm looking for a housekeeper if you know of anyone." She had told Mr. Hutchinson that Emily had come from Gopher Ridge and that her family owned a farm there. She was afraid to look away from Phelps and hoped that Mr. Hutchinson had remembered.

"When did Emily leave?" she asked.

"She went to Chokoloskee the day after you were here," Phelps answered. "Oh, speaking of Chokoloskee, I just came from there, and there's a man looking for you."

Phelps had just told them a whopping lie and she didn't care to hear another. "Emily told me she came from Gopher Ridge, not Key West," she said. Mr. Hutchinson shifted uneasily. She sensed he didn't wish to provoke this man.

"Isn't your name Elizabeth? This man was looking for an Elizabeth Sprague."

"Where is Emily?" she asked, only half believing him.

"His name is Winslow. A big, mean cuss with a large, brown mole right here." He pointed beside his nose. "He looked like he might be a bounty hunter. Are you running from the law, Miss Sprague?" He raised his rifle slightly, and Mr. Hutchinson did the same. "Because if you are, I might have to do my civic duty and tell Mr. Winslow you're still in these parts." The smile had transformed into a cocky sneer. At that moment a few large raindrops spattered around them on the ground.

Her heart pounded. The description Phelps gave fit Mr. Prichett. She didn't wish to have Prichett tracking her down any more than she wanted these two men to kill each other. The eyes of each man were locked on the other's. They both held their ground, their rifles now pointed at the other man's midriff.

"Go to the canoe, Miss Sprague," said Mr. Hutchinson without looking at her. "I'll be along shortly."

She was torn between wanting to get some straight answers from Phelps and wanting to run for her life. She feared that any rapid movement might trigger a shooting. Instead she gave Phelps a wide berth and headed down to the canoe. It was too late to save Emily. The rain started to come down in earnest. From the edge of the creek she watched the two men slowly circling as two animals might before an attack. Phelps was achieving the high ground, but Mr. Hutchinson was moving backward down the shell mound, one careful step at a time. As the distance between the two men grew, their rifles lowered slowly.

"Push off, Miss Sprague." Mr. Hutchinson climbed into the canoe first, still holding the rifle, his eyes never leaving Phelps. As she poled away from the shore, she glanced back and saw Phelps through the downpour still standing halfway up the mound watching them.

"So," said Mr. Hutchinson when Phelps and his house were out of sight, "who is this Mr. Winslow and why is he looking for you?" She was again seated in the front facing away from him.

"I thought people in the swamp didn't ask questions," she said through the downpour. Her reply was met by silence, and they went on that way for a while. Beth decided that after all Mr. Hutchinson had done for her, he deserved an explanation. "I know this man by another name, Prichett. He has been hired by my father to bring me home. Papa didn't want me to come to Florida in the first place."

After they had passed the junction with Turtle Creek, Mr. Hutchinson said, "Why should you mind having an escort back to Boston?"

"When I go back to Boston, I want it to be on my own terms. I'm not a little girl anymore."

"I noticed."

She turned to look at him, and the canoe tipped wildly.

"Sorry," he said. "That just slipped out." They continued on in silence past the place where Mr. Hutchinson had chopped the tree. The rain stopped abruptly.

Being unable to move about in the canoe bottom was uncomfortable. The exhaustion had returned, and she was eager to get back to the chickee. Once there, she could lay her head down and sleep—sleep, perhaps, if she could forget what had happened to poor Emily. The girl and her baby never had a chance at a normal life. If only they had been able to get to her sooner. She couldn't blame Mr. Hutchinson. He didn't know Emily, and he was unaware of the conditions under which she had lived. She felt guilty that she had not insisted that Emily leave with her two weeks ago.

Then there was Mr. Prichett. What if he had come up Deadman's Creek from Chokoloskee and was waiting there for her? A worse thought: Luther Phelps knew that they were suspicious of him. What if he came downstream into the camp in the dark and slit their throats?

Chapter

23

"I suppose, Miss Sprague, that as soon as your strength returns, you'll be leaving here." Mr. Hutchinson's tone was more of a statement than a question.

The thought startled Beth. She hadn't faced the idea of leaving his camp just yet.

Their trip to the Phelps place had expended her energy. She slept through the night and most of the next day. At twilight she felt strong enough to get up and eat a meal with him. He had prepared venison stew and it revived her quickly.

They ate in silence for a few minutes as she mulled over his statement. The lone sound was Mr. Hutchinson slurping his stew as if straining it through his beard. To stay here when she was too weak to move on to Chokoloskee was one thing, but now, remaining here any longer became a matter of propriety. The urge was strong to be rid of the swamp, away from the mosquitoes and the sticky heat. But she still had a task to fulfill. Her botanical notes had been lost. She had nothing to take back to Wellesley and show Dr. Adams except for the sketches she had left with the Worthingtons. To go back empty-handed would be admitting defeat and prove that Papa was right. Her eyes met his over their nearly empty bowls.

"After all that has happened, I think you can call me 'Beth,' Mr. Hutchinson."

"Then you should call me 'Matthew.'"

"I need at least a few days to go back to the Fakahatchee River, make sketches, and collect specimens," she said.

She explained everything that had happened from the brush fire at the Beckett's to the point where he had found her collapsed in the dugout canoe on the creek. She described the beautiful orchids, bromeliads, and other rare plants she had seen along the Fakahatchee Strand. "Do you know a place I could stay until I complete my studies of the swamp flora? I have nothing to show for my trip through the swamp. My notes have been lost."

He shook his head. "The closest village is at Chokoloskee, and there's no hotel there."

"How far away is Allen River?" she asked.

"I guess that Allen River is about the same distance as Chokoloskee through the swamp, but to get there by canoe is another two miles." He stood up and went to the fire and ladled out more stew for himself. When he returned to the table he said, "Do you want more stew? You're closer to where you want to go if you stay here," he observed.

"No, thanks."

"'No, thanks' to the stew or staying here?"

"Both. I can't stay here. It's not proper," she said. "If Mama or Papa knew I had stayed here with you even one night, I wouldn't be allowed back in Boston."

"Does it matter what your parents think? I thought you wanted to go back to Boston on your terms." He took down the lantern, lit it, and placed it on the table.

"Mama worries all the time about what the First Families are thinking of us, and all the while they are paying us the supreme insult—they're not thinking about us at all. In Boston it's perfectly all right to ignore someone if you don't approve of them. Boston, you see, is rich in customs, but deficient in manners." She realized that a few months ago, she, too, would have been shocked by the circumstances she was now living in.

He laughed. "And the last three weeks were proper? If my fiancée found out about your staying here, that would end our engagement."

"Your fiancée?" She hadn't expected that this huge, hairy man in the wilds had any remaining connection with civilization. She felt the redness creeping up her neck, and she got up from the table to hide her embarrassment. "I'll have more stew, but I can get it myself." What evil thing had he done to cause him to hide out here? When she returned, she repeated, "Your fiancée?"

He nodded. "Laura. She lives in Philadelphia. We're engaged, unless she's given up on me and married someone else."

"How long since you've seen her?"

"Four years." He paused and she waited, feeling that he wanted to talk. "I worked in the department store owned by her father and a partner. I had worked my way up from the loading dock to floor supervisor. I had known Laura since she was a baby. We fell in love, but neither her father nor mine approved of marriage."

That didn't seem like the end of the story. "What happened?" she asked.

"Well, it's pretty involved." He scraped out the remaining venison from his bowl and chewed on it before going on. "Laura and I became engaged without her parents' blessing. We were planning to run away and get married anyway. Laura expected her parents to disown her, and I knew I had to get a job somewhere else. But then her father was murdered."

His last sentence was so stark and direct, it shocked her. Was she living here in the swamp with a runaway murderer after all?

"It happened in the store after hours. I was one of the few remaining in the building. Everyone who worked in the store knew that Laura and I were in love and that her father was standing in the way of our being married. He and I had a loud argument the day before, and I'm sure many people suspected that I was his murderer. My younger brother, Luke, had worked in the store, too. The day after the argument, we were both fired, even though Luke had nothing to do with it. That night I went to his office to plead with him to rehire Luke. I found the old gentleman lying on the floor. He had been stabbed to death. Then I was discovered there, bending over him."

"Did they put you in jail?"

"No. I ran. I took what little money I had saved for our marriage and eventually ended up here."

"That must have confirmed everyone's suspicions," she said.

"That's what I was hoping. Luke was a hothead. It was obvious to me that Luke had murdered Laura's father for having fired us, and by running I diverted the suspicion from him."

Was this a made-up story or the truth? He had related what had happened matter-of-factly and had looked her straight in the eye. But she wished someone else was there to confirm what had occurred in that department store. Still, she felt that she was in no danger from him. He had plenty of opportunities to kill her—or worse—while she had been so weak. But he had been gentle and kind. Yesterday he could have killed Luther Phelps when he threatened to alert the authorities about her. Surely Matthew wanted a private detective or the sheriff nosing around even less than she did.

"Have you ever thought about going back and clearing your name?" she asked.

"Yes, many times. My running away must have hurt my mother and my sisters, but then there's Luke, who might have been put to death. I couldn't let that happen. That would have hurt them more."

"I'm sorry this happened to you," she said. "You should go back for your own sake and that of your mother and sisters."

"Thank you. Perhaps someday I will."

"Have you ever written to Laura or your family?"

"No. I was afraid I might give away my hiding place."

"Four years is a long time for Laura to wait for you."

"Yes, but our love was strong enough to overcome anything else."

"Except her finding out about my staying here with you?"

He laughed. "Even that. But she doesn't have to know about your being here. After all, our relationship has been proper."

She reflected on finding her clothes removed and her body washed clean. "How is it that you were so good at taking care of me when I was sick?"

"I have four sisters, all younger than I, and then Luke who is in the middle. My father was a streetcar conductor in Philadelphia, and my mother did cleaning and took in laundry. I had experience helping to bring up my sisters and Luke."

She understood how the department store owner felt. Papa would have locked her up before agreeing to her marrying the son of a streetcar conductor. Mama could never have survived having six children, let alone do laundry or housecleaning, even her own house. She could not imagine having even one brother or sister. "I'm an only child."

"Where did you go to college?" he asked.

"Wellesley."

"Did you always want to be a botanist?"

"No. I had no particular goal or real desire to go to college. My father sent me to become a better conversationalist at dinner parties. One of my professors, Dr. Alice Katherine Adams, inspired me. I think that if she had been a professor of architecture, I might have become an architect. She taught that botany was the study of the mystery of life and life's miraculous adaptations. I became interested in the wonder and majesty of plants as living things because she is such an inspiring teacher. Here in the swamp are an unknown number of genera and species yet to be discovered and understood."

He smiled. "And you want to be the one to discover them. Isn't that a man's job?"

"What do you consider to be women's jobs? To stay home, clean house, and make babies?"

"Well, I wouldn't have said it that way. But somehow it doesn't seem right to have a woman—a lady—doing what you've been doing."

She laughed. She ran her hand through her short hair. It was now getting shaggy, like Hawley Beckett's. "I don't look like a lady now, do I?"

"I figured you were a boy until I—until, that is . . ."

She laughed again. She felt herself blushing. What had been embarrassing for her before was now awkward for him as well. "I think no one ever thinks that I'm a woman because they don't expect to see one in these circumstances."

"Once all of the plants have been discovered, then what will you do?" he asked.

"There is so much to be done. We must learn the economic uses of plants as new sources of food, cloth, and medicines. We need to learn what crops grow best in which soils, and discover the best hybrids. There's much we don't know yet about plants. For example, how they use the sun's light."

"My father had started out as a horse car conductor and wanted me to become a streetcar motorman like he had been. But I had started on the loading dock at the department store at the age of fourteen and was promoted often enough to encourage me to stay there." He studied her for a moment before continuing. "So, do you want to stay here until you've completed your study?"

It was hard to fathom his true feelings. Was he just being polite, or did he want to be rid of the nuisance of having her around? She said, "I won't have any money to pay you until I get to a bank. If I stay I should help with the work."

"I don't need money. Can you cook? I don't do that very well."

"You do fine. I watched Mrs. Faraday, our cook, when I was a little girl, and I'm willing to learn. I can collect firewood," she said, remembering those two awful nights with Little Jimmy Pantertail.

He rubbed his beard vigorously trying unsuccessfully to cover up a smile. "I will need to go to Chestnut's store at Chokoloskee tomorrow and get supplies. Do you wish to come with me?"

The desire to go to a store washed over her like a fragrant wave. If the store was like the one at Fort Myers, she could smell the condiments, feel the goods, and look at all the wares for sale. Going to stores had always been taken for granted. For three weeks she had possessed nothing but the clothes the Becketts had given her. But Prichett was a problem. "That man, Prichett, or Morrisey, or Winslow, or whatever his real name is, might still be there. It's best if I stay here. Will Mr. Phelps tell Mr. Prichett that I am in the swamp?"

"No," said Matthew. "Phelps wants people roaming around the swamp even less than we do. That's why he tells everyone he sees that there's a swamp ape dwelling here on Deadman's Creek—to keep people away from his moonshine and bird poaching activities."

"He made you the swamp ape? Doesn't that make you angry?"

"No. It helps me as much as it helps him. Anyway, don't worry about Prichett. He couldn't take you away against your will. I wouldn't let him."

Beth shook her head. "You don't know the determination and power that Papa has. Somehow they'd find a way to get me to return to Boston."

"Why does he want to prevent you from completing your studies?"

"Because Papa must always have his way. And more important than that, Papa and Mama want me to marry a Mr. Cushing. They have arranged an engagement." She explained how Papa and Mr. Cushing wanted to combine their shipping companies, and how she was a part of the bargain. She then told him how Mama looked forward to the imagined advancement in social status by marrying her daughter into a blue-blooded Boston family.

"So you're engaged, too."

"No! It can't be an engagement unless I agree to it. I refuse to marry a man I detest." She described the long list of Mr. Cushing's less than desirable traits, including the fact that he was ten years older than she.

"Well, I'll go alone to Chokoloskee tomorrow and return by nightfall. Is there anything you need from the store?"

"Yes. I need clothes, and paper and pencils, but I don't have money. I need paper and pencils more than anything—and cloth."

"I usually trade pelts for the supplies I need. What kind of cloth? They have several different patterns."

"It doesn't matter. A yard or two of anything. Something absorbent." She wasn't about to tell him about her coming need for sanitary rags.

"Oh," he said, seeming to catch on; after all, he had sisters. Then a sudden change of subject: "Your father must be like Laura's father was, demanding and protective."

"Worse." She told him how her father had gained control of her inheritance. Then she told him about Papa and Miss Murchison, her long walk to Papa's office, finding them together, and how the Flaglers had met her with him in St. Augustine. She hadn't intended to tell anyone about that and was upset with herself.

They had been sitting at the table for a long time. Twilight had faded into dusk, and dusk had metamorphosed into pitch darkness that enclosed their cozy chrysalis of lantern light.

"I feel so bad about Emily," she said.

"That took a lot of grit, Beth, trying to rescue that girl and then standing up to Phelps." She felt herself blushing again when he called her by her first name.

"It was a stupid thing. I might have gotten you killed," she admitted. "Thank you for going with me, Matthew. I know that I could never have done it alone. Do you think he might come here and try to kill us? He knows we're suspicious of him."

"If he shows up here, I'll shoot him on sight. To kill him at his place with no real evidence was one thing, but if he comes messing around here, that's a snake of a different color."

"What if he sneaks up while we're asleep?" she asked.

"If he's as cowardly as I think he is, he'll stay well away from here. But if he comes, I'll hear him. I'm a light sleeper. I heard that gator," he said, as if to prove his alertness. "Well, I'm going to turn in. I want to leave early tomorrow morning—and don't worry, he won't come during the day."

"Matthew," she said, "I wish you'd take back your cot. I can sleep on the table." She expected the table to be hard, but she felt guilty. She pictured him sleeping on the table with his head hanging off one end and his feet off the other.

"That's all right. I've been sleeping well on the ground, and did so long before I had the cot. Good night, Beth."

"Matthew, there's one more thing. Can you mail a letter in Chokoloskee?"

"Yes."

"I suggest you send a letter to Laura."

"I could suggest that you do a little letter writing yourself, Beth," he replied as he disappeared into the darkness.

She had a warm feeling about their long talk. At last he had talked about himself, and what he had revealed was more than the tragic story of a man who had ruined his own life to save his brother's. If what he had told her was accurate, he had shown himself to have a great amount of loyalty and integrity. He stood out as a real man, much more mature than Mr. Everett or the other boys she had met at the Ponce de Leon in St. Augustine. And they were boys, irresponsible boys who had no goal in life other than to have fun. Matthew, on the other hand, had matured before he was fifteen, taking care of four sisters and a brother. He not only had a job and paid his own way, he had made a supreme sacrifice for his brother Luke.

What had confused her the most during their conversation was her own reluctance to leave Matthew's camp. She felt at home here in spite of the camp's rustic nature. She wasn't certain whether her desire to stay was caused by the need to complete her research project, or because of her reluctance to re-enter Papa's domain. She promised herself one thing: she must stay no longer than one week, and then with whatever notes she had, she was returning to Boston.

Chapter

24

*T*hat night Beth's sleep was troubled by doubts about Matthew's truthfulness. Everyone had warned her that the cypress swamp was a haven for thieves, murderers, poachers, and scofflaws. What were the chances that she had discovered the one honest man? But her outlook improved as the sun rose, until she discovered that Matthew had already left for Chokoloskee.

The fire was still burning brightly, and the coffee and cornmeal had been made. After her breakfast, she cleaned up the camp, including sweeping the dirt floor of the chickee, a never-ending chore. Washing the greasy pots and pans in cold water was an unpleasant task; they never came clean. She then searched for firewood to add to the pile that Matthew was forever replenishing, until she had to rest. At all times she kept Matthew's shotgun nearby.

The remainder of the day, she had decided, was to be spent committing to paper whatever recollections of specific plant life she had recorded earlier and had been lost. Matthew had given her a pencil stub and a few scraps of brown wrapping which he had stored away. After stoking the smudge fire, she sat at the table and stared at the paper. The images came slowly at first, and then more rapidly and with details as she mentally retraced her steps through the swamp. Her concern was for the accuracy of what she had remembered. To redraw the inflorescence, spikelets, bracts, and other details as they actually were was impossible.

For lunch she chewed on some cold venison. The deer meat had become dry and gamey, and she hoped Matthew was bringing back something different to eat. After eating a little of the meat and drinking some stored rainwater, she continued to write and sketch as small as she could and still make her notes legible. Nevertheless, both sides of the scraps were filled before she had run out of memories. Her notes would serve as a rough guide. Each species had to be found and rechecked.

Looking at the wet space on the table where her perspiration from her forearm had left its mark, she decided to go down to the creek and bathe. Her intentions were to cool off as much as to get clean. She removed Marian's brogans and walked down to the creek. She placed the shotgun in Martin's canoe, removed her shirt and trousers, the torn chemise, and her drawers, and dunked them in the creek as she had done once before when Matthew was hunting. After her clothes were hung on the mangrove branches, she waded into the sluggish stream which felt cool compared to the humid air. The mud was soft and welcoming between her toes. After taking a few steps she stopped and made the obligatory search for snakes and alligators. The water was shallow beside the canoe, and she waded upstream a few yards where it came up to mid-thigh. By crouching down, her shoulders were nearly covered. Every few moments she glanced around for ripples that might signal the presence of a snake or alligator. The coolness of the creek was refreshing, but to stay here too long was inviting trouble.

The sound behind her made her whirl toward the beached canoe, half expecting to see the evil eyes and snout of a gator gliding toward her. But what she saw standing in the mud where she had hung her clothes was much worse. Between her and the shotgun stood two ugly, ragged, and dirty men.

"Well, there's our little boy-girl, Lopez." Roach, the poacher, was in the water up to his knees, and behind him stood Lopez, grinning broadly. She crouched down as low as she could, but Roach was wading toward her, his evil eye glaring wildly, his mouth contorted into a lecherous sneer.

"This time no Luther Phelps is around to rescue you." It had been nearly three weeks since she had encountered them. When he came within a few feet, he reached out to grab her.

"Stop right there, Roach." She heard Matthew's voice from behind the mangroves. Matthew stood behind Lopez with his rifle trained on both poachers. A feeling of relief swept over her. Matthew's voice was uncompromising. "Get out and get moving. If either of you show up here again, I'll shoot you on sight."

"Not iffen we git the drop on you first, swamp ape" sneered Roach. But he was moving away from the creek and downstream from the camp. Matthew stood his ground until the poachers had disappeared from both sight and earshot as they sloshed through the swamp. She kept herself underwater as much as was possible.

"You going to stay there all day?" Matthew asked her. Then he froze, staring behind her. "Gator!" he yelled. She was frozen in her embarrassment, crouching in the thigh-deep stream to cover her nakedness as much as possible. She assumed his silly warning was a joke, of course. The big man plowed through the water toward her and swept her up as if she were a small child and strode back to the shore. Putting her down gently on the dry bank, he turned his back and said, "You'd better put your clothes on before we have all the men in Chokoloskee up here gawking."

"There was no alligator," she said angrily. "You used that as an excuse."

Turning toward the creek, he pointed and said, "What's that?"

She paused, holding her clothes in front of her. All she saw were the ripples Matthew had made carrying her through the water. "There's nothing there!"

"You have to know what to look for," he said with a straight face.

She looked at him again. "Where's your beard?"

"Wendell Chestnut's not only a storekeeper. He pulls teeth and cuts hair, too. I'd better make certain those critters keep moving downstream." He moved off in the direction the poachers had taken while she pulled on her clothes.

Her heart was still pounding as she trudged back to the chickee. The transformation in Matthew's appearance shook her almost as much as the poachers and alligator had. His facial hair was gone with the exception of a well-trimmed moustache, and his hair was short enough to show his ears. He could walk down Tremont Street now without notice, except, of course, for the ladies who would coyly make side glances from behind their fans.

When Matthew returned, he showed her the items he had bought. "They don't have any dresses, just cloth. I have needle and thread." He handed her several yards of cotton print. "Until you have time to sew yourself a dress, I brought you these." He unfolded a plaid shirt and a pair of trousers that looked as if they might fit. He had also remembered the paper and pencils she needed, as well as the food supplies. Then he reached into his shirt pocket. "Here." He handed her a peppermint stick.

Tears welled up. She was overcome and unprepared for feeling that way over these gifts. "Thank you," she said simply. It was the peppermint stick that made the tears come. Beth ran with her new clothes behind a bush and changed. The trousers were too long, but that problem was easily remedied. She came back to the chickee and smiled at him. "I feel like a little child at my birthday."

"Well, happy birthday, then. Mr. Chestnut said today is July seventh."

"I've missed both the Fourth of July and my birthday, but not by much. My birthday was two days ago."

He seemed almost as pleased as she was. He also brought back sow belly, flour, and canned corned beef.

"You look so—different without your beard." She had almost said "handsome" but held back. His face was pale where the beard had been. What intrigued her the most was that he looked like someone she had seen before.

"What is it?" he asked. "Why are you staring?"

"I think I've seen you before, or your picture, at least. I met a man named Gallagher. He's a Pinkerton detective who poses as a drummer, but he had a picture that looked like you, but a little younger perhaps. Everywhere he went he showed the picture and asked if anyone knew the man."

"Where did you see him last?" His smile had vanished.

"In Fort Myers. That was almost two months ago. It seems longer than that."

"A drummer?"

"Of patent medicine. The strange thing was he had met my Aunt Sarah, and she hired him to look out for me during our trip from St. Augustine to Fort Myers. It must have been a picture of someone else." Rumblings of thunder to the east presaged the coming of the customary afternoon shower.

Matthew was quiet all through the evening meal. Beth wished she hadn't mentioned the photograph. Perhaps she had been mistaken. It was hard to believe that Mr. Gallagher was a bounty hunter looking for this man. Matthew's hesitation ignited her doubts about him again, but she had even more difficulty accepting that this gentle person could be a criminal. She knew that if she ever saw Mr. Gallagher again, she couldn't tell him about Matthew.

The list of men who had a reason to come to Deadman's Creek was increasing. Luther Phelps had murdered at least two people and knew that they suspected him. Mr. Prichett wanted to drag her back to Boston. The poachers, Lopez and Roach, had vowed to seek revenge, and now there was Mr. Gallagher, who seemed like a nice enough man, but he carried a gun and was violent enough when the situation demanded it. He had killed the card player on the riverboat and shot Mr. Prichett in Fort Myers. That night she awoke at every little sound.

25

"*I*f you insist on returning to the Fakahatchee Strand, Beth, then I'm going with you. That's no place for a woman to be lollygagging around alone."

Beth welcomed Matthew's offer to accompany her back to the Fakahatchee with little hesitation. More than the snakes and alligators, the fear of being lost again made her shudder. The memory of two days with the Indian and then those three days of wandering through the cypress swamp alone still gave her nightmares. Having Matthew with her lessened the dread of encountering the snakes, alligators, and worst of all, the poachers again. The Fakahatchee was the place to see the most beautiful and unusual plants, especially the orchids, bromeliads, and other epiphytes. The time had come to go back and complete what she had come to do.

The rainy season made travel by dugout canoe necessary. Matthew had loaded his shotgun and rifle into his canoe along with supplies and equipment for five days. Instead of poling up the creek, he cut across the sawgrass marsh, the canoe parting the stalks to either side like a comb through hair as they moved forward. As Beth sat in the canoe, the tall sawgrass made it difficult to know where she was, but Matthew, standing in the back, could see ahead. Once across the marsh, they entered a narrow creek that led to other creeks, all narrow and overhung with the branches of pond apple, buttonwood, and mangrove. He had supplied her with a paddle which she learned to use when the undergrowth permitted it. With the aid of Matthew's compass, they headed northwest as much as the swamp would allow.

For sleeping, Matthew had brought a tarpaulin that he erected to make a small tent for her. Like the Indian, he slept in the open, but nearby on the only dry ground remaining. Their light blankets were more for keeping out mosquitoes and snakes than cold. She laughed at herself. She had been taught that a lady only touched her face or arranged her hair in private. Now she constantly slapped at mosquitoes with one hand while waving a palm frond with the other.

She was able to start their campfire with one match now and gradually was learning to prepare and cook the simple foods. They were unable to store meat due to the heat and insects. To provide fresh food, Matthew shot a small alligator, several marsh rabbits, and a wild turkey during the week. He still did most of the cooking while she went about her botanical chores. She endured his teasing about her hesitancy to eat the food he prepared. Swamp cabbage and sow belly were tolerable, but she barely nibbled at alligator steak dipped in flour, cooter (turtle meat fried in an egg batter), and fat used as gravy. She couldn't believe that at one time she had planned to bring fifty pounds of salt pork into the swamp with her.

She spent a good portion of each day observing the plant life and recording the salient features of each species in notes and sketches. Under the multiple canopies grew a whole world of new plants. More forms of plant life existed than she could deal with. The ferns, mosses, lichens, algae, fungi, and mushrooms each called for a lifetime of study. She squatted down among the same varieties of plants she had sketched hurriedly when with Little Jimmy Pantertail. They were her friends, quiet, unassuming, and harmless. Now there was time to examine their roots and observe the unique ways blossoms were attached to their stalks and the manner in which the leaves and petals were arranged. She sketched enlargements of each plant's peculiar characteristics. Now she was accomplishing what she had come for. A shiver of excitement swept through her. Here she was, a woman, in the midst of the Big Cypress Swamp, achieving that which everyone had said was impossible for her to do.

The orchids were special to her. Their peculiar shapes were intriguing and unique, yet each had the same integral parts that made them orchids. Every day she came upon new species. The size of their blossoms varied from minuscule upwards to several inches, and their colors ranged all across the rainbow. Each variety was different from the others. Beth was fascinated by the way their roots had attached themselves to the tree bark. Sometimes the roots were practically nonexistent, and in other varieties they stretched out in spiderlike fashion on their host tree. Without adequate references for classifying them, she gave them names that described their appearance, like Tigertail, Gray Moth, and Spider Monkey. Without equipment for keeping them intact, Beth had no reason to take specimens, either alive or dead. She pointed out to Matthew the orchids' unusual third petal, called a labellum, or "lip," and its means of preventing self-fertilization. His interest was short-lived, and he soon became restless and went off to hunt.

During the second evening as they sat on a log eating their supper, she said, "You've been working on this stew all afternoon. It's tasty. What is it?"

"What my mother used to call leftovers."

"Yes, but what? I'd like to learn how to make it."

"I call it Seminole stew."

"What's in it?" she persisted.

"Oh, snake meat, skunk intestines, buzzard, and a little bit of lizard."

She dropped her spoon. She was caught with a mouthful and almost spit it into the fire when she saw he was trying to suppress a smile. She raised her arm as if to slap him.

"Rabbit," he confessed, laughing, "and cabbage palm hearts."

On the third night it rained hard. She lay in her tent and listened to the raindrops hitting the tarpaulin. Matthew was lying outside and getting wet. She could count on him to be as gentlemanly as possible in that close space if she invited him inside, but still, propriety demanded that he get wet. Finally, her feelings of guilt for remaining dry while he must be uncomfortable and sleepless overcame convention.

"Matthew," she called into the darkness, "would you like to come inside?"

"No, thank you."

Then the rain became a downpour.

"Matthew. Come inside."

"It doesn't matter. I'm already wet." But after a short time as the downpour continued, she felt him crawling in beside her. She immediately saw her mistake. He was so much larger than she, and the tent so small, it was impossible to lie there without touching.

"You're soaking wet," she said. "Take off your shirt and get under my blanket."

"Laura wouldn't approve of this," he said as he struggled to remove his shirt in the cramped space.

"Laura will never know."

He lay with his back to her, and by the sound of his breathing she soon knew he was asleep. She had expected to feel more excitement over having a man sleep under the same blanket with her. Lying on her side was becoming uncomfortable, but she had no space to roll over. She slipped her hand under his arm and down his furry chest.

"What are you doing?" he asked.

"I can't get comfortable. I thought you were asleep."

"I'll go back outside."

"No." She held him close, and they slept that way the remainder of the night.

The next night he slept outside again, and on the fifth day they returned to Deadman's Creek.

"You know," she said, "I didn't accomplish as much as I had hoped. After a few days to recuperate, I'd like to go back again. This time alone."

"Why do you want to go alone?"

"You were bored with my work after the first hour. Besides, if it rains again, the tent's too small."

"I'll make us a larger tent. It's dangerous out there. What if Phelps or Lopez and Roach or some other poacher found you?"

After four days back on Deadman's Creek, they went on the second of four more excursions into the Big Cypress Swamp with three- to five-day rests back at Matthew's hammock each time. Every trip she added to her collection of notes and sketches while Matthew hunted and cooked. And every night they slept together in the tent, both fully dressed, and under separate blankets, a secret she vowed no one would ever learn. She found their arrangement to be most peculiar and wondered why he didn't behave like her friends at Wellesley said men were expected to act. Was there something wrong with him? Was there something wrong with her? Was it possible that he could be that much in love with Laura, whom he hadn't seen in four years? How fortunate Matthew's Laura was to be engaged to a man like him. Waiting four years for him would be worth it. What Papa had said about her becoming a spinster was turning out to be true so far. There was no way she was going to find a husband in south Florida.

While Beth attempted to organize her notes of the day, she watched him now as he plucked a wild turkey that was to be their supper. Even though he came from the family of a streetcar conductor, he outshone the young dandies in St. Augustine. He even compared favorably to Mary's husband, Michael Otis, who no man had ever surpassed before. Matthew had carved out a living for himself in the swamp. He killed animals and even wrestled them when necessary, yet he knew how to cook and sew—women's work that most men refused to go near. This big man was not only strong and brave, but also gentle and patient.

If he didn't wish to sleep with her, why hadn't he made two tents? He had undressed and bathed her while she was unconscious and had carried her naked from the creek—teasing her, because there had been no alligator, of that she was certain. They slept every night side by side now, and he never attempted to touch her. He treated her more like an equal than any man ever had, and he also treated her like a sister. She had always wondered what it would be like to have a brother, but for the first time in her life she wanted more than that.

He suddenly looked up from his work and caught her staring at him. Instead of looking away, their eyes held, and he smiled back at her. She wanted to go to him and take his hand or put her arms around him, but even now a gap loomed in their strange relationship. While it worked here in the swamp, how might they fare back in the civilized world? He spoke surprisingly well for someone from a common family, but his education had been limited by the need for him to work. He had no interest in her love of botany. When he returned to Philadelphia, he might become a department store clerk or a streetcar conductor. She had difficulty picturing the two of them having a life together in his world, and of course he must be thinking of Laura waiting for him. Her imagination made it impossible for her to concentrate on her work. Beth put away her papers and went to assist him in preparing the turkey.

The next afternoon they made their way back to Matthew's chickee. The last foray, a broader one into other parts of the Big Cypress Swamp, had been completed. While she had expected to be excited about having achieved her goal, her spirits were as dark as the threatening sky. A cloud cover had obliterated all sunlight since mid-afternoon and presented them with an early twilight. While they ate in the chickee, she said, "I now have enough research to complete my master's thesis. The data you have helped me collect can be found nowhere else in this much detail. Dr. Adams will be pleased." Then came the part she had difficulty saying: "It's time for me to return to Boston."

He took a bite of a drumstick and didn't look at her. "I'll take you to Chokoloskee whenever you're ready. From there you can get a boat to Key West." His face was impassive. "I'll pay for your passage." She was disappointed in his response, but didn't know what she had expected him to say.

A bank draft from Aunt Sarah would be waiting for her in Key West. "When I get to Key West I'll send you whatever I owe you."

"Will you take a letter to Laura and mail it from Boston? That will be payment enough."

"Yes, but you should go back to Philadelphia and clear your name."

At that moment a movement in the underbrush made him alert.

"Don't move, swamp ape." Roach appeared from behind the bushes with a rifle aimed at them. Lopez appeared from another spot, also holding a rifle.

"What do you want, Roach?" Matthew asked.

"You've got a nice place here we kin use fer our business. Comes complete with this nice little boy-girl."

In her fright, she stood up, but the poachers had their guns aimed at Matthew. His guns were hanging by their sling straps from two of the posts supporting the chickee roof. She was standing beside Matthew and placed one hand on the nearest post, inches away from his shotgun, which she doubted the poachers could see from where they were standing outside. She knew he kept his guns loaded in case of emergencies, but by the time she removed the gun, handed it to Matthew and he aimed and fired, the poachers would have time to kill them both twice over.

Roach approached the chickee, and Lopez circled around from the right and stopped beside his confederate. They were standing about ten feet away from Matthew, who hadn't moved from the bench. She edged closer to the post while both men were concentrating on the dangerous one.

"Let the lady go, and I'll give you the camp," Matthew said.

"Why should we do thet when we kin have both?" sneered Roach.

She dreaded what lay ahead unless they were able to gain the upper hand. Beth counted on their concentrating on the man at this point; they could afford to ignore her. Slipping her hand up to the trigger guard, she was still edging away from Matthew. They had no interest in a mere woman just now.

Lopez said something in Spanish to Roach.

"We're in no hurry," answered Roach. "I wanna see the swamp ape sweat."

"You don't know where my money's hid," said Matthew. "Kill me and you'll miss out on about eight hundred dollars."

"Tell us where the money is, and we'll let you go," said Roach.

"I'll need to get my shovel," said Matthew, starting to rise.

"Stay put!" yelled Roach.

She was now behind the post and had the shotgun off the nail, but it was still hidden vertically, muzzle downward, behind the post. It was heavy to hold in that position with one hand. It occurred to her that neither man could see her; Roach, the closest, was missing his right eye, and he was blocking Lopez's view.

Matthew shrugged. "No shovel, no money."

She stepped out a half step beyond the post. She was hoping that if they noticed her at all, it would look as if she were leaning against the post with her right hand. Actually, she was leaning against the shotgun. Her hand was on the trigger guard. From this angle Lopez was behind Roach, but just then he took a step forward to look at her. She lowered the gun away from the post, swung the barrels up, and fired from the hip, first one barrel and then the other. She was stunned when both men dropped their rifles and grabbed their faces. Matthew lunged at them the moment she fired and now the three of them fell to the ground with Matthew on top.

"Get me some rope," he yelled. She ran to fetch a coil of rope hanging from a crossbeam. Both victims were alternately screaming and moaning. Matthew used the rope to tie their hands behind their backs while she gingerly drew their firearms from under them. The two men were still yelling, their faces bloody. She was horrified at what she had done.

"You're lucky that was only bird shot," said Matthew to the two poachers. "If it had been buckshot she would've blown your heads off." With so much blood on their faces it wasn't clear whether or not they had lost their sight.

"What happened?" she asked. "I was aiming at Roach's knees."

"The shot spreads. You hit them both in the side of the head. The first shot hit the ground. The recoil must have made the second shot go high. Where did you learn to shoot from the hip like that?" he asked.

"I read Grace's dime novels about Western gunfighters in college," she replied and then fainted.

Chapter 26

*B*eth watched as the two canoes disappeared around the bend on their way to Chokoloskee. The two bleeding poachers had cried and pleaded with Matthew, but after she helped him bandage their heads as well as they could, he loaded them into Martin's canoe and towed it behind his own. He vowed to her that these two poachers were not about to bother her again. He would let the law handle them after Wendell Chestnut had dug out the bird shot, even if it meant taking them to Fort Myers or Key West. Soon after they departed the rain began, and she hoped Matthew could reach Chokoloskee before dark.

Beth couldn't believe how stupid the poachers had been to ignore her. Their attack had put off her move to Chokoloskee by at least a day, but that was nothing compared with what might have happened. Roach, having been the closest to her, would probably have lost his right eye if it hadn't already been missing. She was unnerved by both the assault and by having shot the men, and slept with the reloaded shotgun beside her. Several times during the night the sounds of heavy rain and a strong breeze whipping the branches awakened her.

In early morning the wind blew even stronger, but what worried her was the creek. It had risen during the night. The hammock had only been three or four feet above the creek to begin with. Now it was a true island, and the wind-driven rain was heavy. Water rose though the mangroves on the south, and into the sawgrass in the north. The creek itself, which had been about six feet wide at its widest, was now more than twenty feet across, and the chickee floor, at the top of the mound, was hardly a foot above the surrounding lake.

Matthew was somewhere out in the storm and had hopefully reached his destination. If he had encountered Luther Phelps on the way to Chokoloskee, that madman might have helped to free the two poachers, and then the three of them could have pounded Matthew to death. Shoving that ugliness from her head, Beth concentrated on keeping everything in the chickee dry.

After a cold breakfast, she stacked half the firewood Matthew had collected on top of the table to keep it from floating away. Her main concern, though, was the safety of her research notes. She placed them in a wooden box that contained supplies and placed that beside the firewood. The box had a lid, but to be doubly safe, she put Matthew's hatchet on top in case the wind blew harder.

The wind did blow harder, and she had to anchor everything down to keep it from blowing away. The rain was whipping through the chickee, stinging her face, making it impossible to look into the force of the gale. And the lake had risen higher as well. Her island had grown smaller. Matthew had taken both canoes; her only choice was to stay in the chickee. To wade into the flood meant being among snakes and alligators. Beth eyed the table and decided that if the water rose onto the floor of the chickee, the table was her best and highest refuge. She moved half a dozen sticks of firewood on top of Matthew's storage boxes to make a space to sit.

The wind had been from the east last night, but now had edged to the southeast, driving the creek backwards from the Gulf. Clumps of thatch from the chickee roof were being torn away. Her hat blew off and landed yards away from her little island. The wind-blown rain poured sideways in torrents, soaking her through even though she was under the roof. She detected a distinct scent and taste of salt in the wet air, as if the storm was blowing away the Gulf itself. The tree branches were tossing furiously before the tempest, and she was fearful one might break and fall on the chickee. She had no hope that Matthew could return today. Her entire trek through the swamp seemed insignificant now compared to the frightening aspect of the storm.

The wavelets were now lapping at the raised dirt floor of the chickee. Beth sat on the table with one arm around the box containing her notes. She clung to the table's edge with her other hand, afraid that she, too, might be blown away. A startling crack announced the breaking off of the top of the nearest royal palm. All that remained was a thirty-foot stump. The water was rising more rapidly, and was under the table. Her island had disappeared. Removing her notes from the box and slipping them into her shirt was pointless; her body was as wet as if she were under water.

When it seemed as if the wind could blow no harder, it did, now roaring up from the south. The howl of the storm was deafening, the loud roar of the wind, the smashing of the rain against everything it hit, the crash of branches. And above it all was the shrieking of a thousand women as the wind tore through the trees. She was slapped sharply in the face by a detached palm frond, and her voice went unheard as she added to the screaming.

The swamp was almost as dark as night. In an occasional flash of lightning she saw that the chickee was at the center of a large lake. Only the tops of the mangroves could be seen, and the sawgrass had disappeared. The water had risen almost to the top of the table. Beth drew her feet up under her even though her half-boots were already wet. Looking around for a higher refuge, she saw that the one accessible spot was in the branches of the pond apple twenty-five feet away, where the deer carcass had once hung. The box containing her papers began to slide off the table. She stacked the last of the firewood on top before leaving, but the pieces were like matchsticks in the wind. Carrying or floating the box with her to the tree was impossible. To save herself she had to leave her treasured creation behind.

Wading to the pond apple was no small feat. Immersed up to her thighs, the wind and rain strove to both drive her away from her destination and knock her down. She had to take two steps into the wind to make a half step of headway toward the tree. At last, out of breath she grasped the tree. The water was even deeper here, but now she could climb up several feet higher than the top of the table. All the leaves had been stripped from the branches, leaving no protection from the storm. The best she could do was straddle a limb, hug the trunk with her back to the blast, and hope the tree wasn't uprooted.

From her perch Beth could barely make out the box with her papers in it representing five weeks of research. The firewood had blown off. The box slid off the table and floated lopsidedly. She hardly noticed large chunks of the thatched roof flying away as the lid flew off the box, and her precious notes and sketches went flying into the storm page by page.

Soon after, Beth's attention was drawn toward a snake swimming toward the tree just as an unusually strong gust tore apart the nearest of the towering bald cypress columns. The tremendous half-tree crashed down upon the chickee, flattening the skeletal structure which had been totally stripped of its thatched roof. The outer branches grazed the pond apple, nearly throwing her into the flood. The wooden box containing any remains of her notes was crushed under water beneath the wreckage of the chickee and the fallen branches. She dreaded what might have happened to her if she had remained on the table. The snake had disappeared.

Hours had passed while she sat on the table, and more hours dragged by while she clung to the tree. It seemed as if the storm was going to go on forever, and she knew that if it did, she was going to die. Her will to hold on was in a contest with her diminishing strength. No longer was it a question of whether or not she was going to die; it was now a matter of when. The twilight held constant, giving her no way to tell the time. But after a long wait it seemed as if the water level was holding steady just below her feet, and either she was getting accustomed to the force of the wind, or else the storm was abating slightly and coming more from the southwest.

True darkness came, and the wind had indeed decreased in intensity and was coming from the west. Nothing could be done except remain in the tree. To climb down into the blackness was sheer foolishness.

Wading around in pitch darkness would serve no purpose. The chickee and everything in it had been destroyed. At least with the wind no longer pressing her against the trunk, she could shift her body and change her position now and then. With the possibility of falling asleep, she employed a trick she had used two months earlier and removed the galluses from her trousers and lashed her arm to a branch. Sleep? Beth almost laughed. With snakes and other critters looking for a dry place, how could she sleep?

Sound sleep never did come, but several times she dozed, then snapped awake as she dreamed of creatures climbing up her limbs. The wind had fallen off to a light breeze, and the rain had stopped. Above, clouds scudded across the black sky, and in between them sparkled a few stars, which lifted her spirits. The canopy of leaves had been blown away, and bare branches stood out starkly as they did in Massachusetts winters. The darkness beneath her hid what was happening to the water level. After she dozed between a few more fits and starts, the sky to the east became brighter, and she waited anxiously for daylight to come. Thirst and hunger made their presence known. She hadn't eaten since early the day before.

When the sky was bright enough for her to see the ground, she was relieved to see that the water, as if by magic, was gone except for the swollen creek and many puddles. She was in a different world. The chickee had been leveled by the big cypress trunk. The remaining vegetation was covered with a film of mud up to a level above her head. Everything in the chickee had been under muddy slime for hours. Any remaining food was spoiled, and her botanical notes and Matthew's belongings, including his shotgun, were gone.

Beth had no idea whether or not Matthew had made it safely through the storm. He might have been aboard a boat on the way to Fort Myers or Key West when the tempest struck. Her efforts to record the flora of the Big Cypress had been destroyed again. Her notes might have been the most detailed, accurate account of the Big Cypress Swamp ever made. But the swamp was not about to give up its secrets. She had no weapon, no matches, no food, nor anything to drink. The only clothes she had were those she was wearing. She was beyond crying. It seemed as if she might be the one person remaining alive in the entire world.

Chapter 27

Along the Turner River, August 23, 1893

Matthew might have been killed by the poachers or drowned in the storm. With everything destroyed, Beth had no reason for staying on the hammock and numbly set out to find her way to Chokoloskee and home. Papa had been right after all. This was no place for a woman. She had failed in her effort to show him he was wrong. This was a man's world full of tough men—strong, brave men like Matthew, and wicked men like Phelps, Roach, Lopez, and Prichett. The time had come to go home and admit defeat.

First, she had to get to Chokoloskee. It was risky to go near the creek, which was overflowing and no doubt inhabited with alligators and snakes. Matthew had said there might be crocodiles farther down, and they were faster and more aggressive than the alligators. But she had to stay close enough to Deadman's Creek to follow it to where it joined the Turner River. From there he had said that Chokoloskee was another two miles.

The problem with moving parallel with the creek was that the mangroves, with their tangle of drop roots, made passage impossible. The wreckage of fallen trees and broken branches made progress even slower. Everything as high as she could reach was coated with drying mud. The one good thing was the absence of mosquitoes. Either the storm had destroyed them, or the breeze was keeping them away. The missing leaves allowed the sun into places that had been in perpetual twilight. The sky was clear, and the humidity low, but the early sun was already hot on her hatless head. Her mouth was as dry as soda crackers, and she wished she had a box of those right now. But thirst wasn't her greatest problem. The going was more difficult than anything she had encountered before.

If she ever got to Chokoloskee, she had no idea how she was going to pay her way to Key West, but somehow she had to get there. Money from Aunt Sarah was waiting for her at a bank. She would eat and sleep for a month. Then there were clothes to buy—dresses, petticoats, chemises, shoes, and hats. And then a steamer to Boston!

Time had come for forgiveness. Mama certainly. She had been through enough with Papa without having an unappreciative daughter. Papa, too, perhaps. For all his faults he meant well, she supposed. He had provided well for them: the house, servants, all the modern comforts, and college, even though for the wrong reasons. He had reminded her more than once that she had been his biggest disappointment. He had wanted a son to someday step into his shoes and manage the Atlantic and Southern Steamship Company. Even so, she should have listened to him and stayed close to home.

Then there was the matter of Edward Cushing to contend with. Was she being too unreasonable? Life with Edward could be no worse than what she had experienced in the past three months. The merger of Papa's company with Oceanic would help him achieve his goal, and perhaps save the Sprague family from economic disaster. She could become a Boston matron and hobnob with all the highest families, completing Mama's dream for her. There was the Symphony, walks in the Public Garden, sailing on Boston Harbor, and trips to Europe.

The tangle of brush and branches ended, and she entered a saltwater marsh as flat as the freshwater marsh farther north. The green grasses contrasted with the bright blue sky, which predominated. The breeze had disappeared, and the air was still. It was as if Mother Nature were attempting to appease the world for having lost her temper the day before. Clusters of yellow and purple bladderworts floated in open pools. She came upon other growth she had not seen farther inland: wax myrtle, red bay, and different grasses. Although she was occasionally waist-deep in brine, her hopes rose. Once across the marsh, she was soon back in a morass of mangrove roots. At least she had not seen any snakes or crocodiles yet. Perhaps they had all fled before the storm.

Matthew must be far away from here. Beth had no doubt that he had survived the storm. If she could do it, then certainly a strong man like him had survived. He was the most unusual man she had ever met. Matthew was a mountain among the molehills of the other swampers—brave, gentle, caring, and loyal to his Laura. But he might be as far away as Fort Myers, and she might never see him again.

She did not envy Laura marrying him. Living in an apartment with no Mrs. Faraday to do the cooking, no maids, not even a carriage, Matthew's wife would have to take a streetcar to buy their groceries. There would be no Paris gowns and no parties. Laura was destined to have six children to raise and no nannies to help her. Living in Philadelphia would not provide the life she had dreamed of.

For a man who had been the son of a streetcar conductor, a part-time attendee in the public schools, and a department store clerk, Matthew spoke well. Perhaps his mother had tutored him at home. But how was that possible with her working and with six children? It was unfortunate that he had not been able to receive a formal education. With his fine qualities he could have been a successful businessman.

To her left Beth saw the creek and a muddy opening. If there had been leaves remaining on the branches, she would have missed the strange sight. Several feet above the water, caught in the tangle of brush and roots, the flood had left a dugout canoe. Her heart raced as she struggled over and under the mangrove roots. Fearing that the canoe was the one Matthew had towed his prisoners in, her chest tightened until she could hardly breathe. She was nearly exhausted, and the last few yards of wading and scrambling were a tortuous struggle. With the canoe, she could get over to Chokoloskee. The craft was at eye level, slightly tipped away from her, and it wasn't until she was holding on to its edge that she saw the body inside.

Then several things happened at once: she screamed, the body sat up, and the canoe slid partway down through the branches, water sloshing out from inside.

"Well, look who's here!" he said, blinking his eyes as he came awake.

Luther Phelps! She didn't know whether to be frightened or relieved. Even this evil man looked comical sitting suspended mid air in the slanting canoe. As she knew she couldn't get away, it was best to pretend as if she had no suspicions about his murderous ways. "Thank goodness I found you," she gasped.

"Whatever are you doing here?" he asked.

"I'm on my way to Chokoloskee Island."

"Where is the swamp ape?" He looked around suspiciously.

"He's not an ape, Mr. Phelps. He's Mister Hutchinson, and he's just behind me." Perhaps if he thought Matthew was nearby, he wouldn't kill her on the spot.

"Well, let's get the canoe in the river," he said, climbing down into the mud. "It'll be easier than what you've been doing." He pointed at her and she looked down at herself, realizing for the first time that she was covered with mud from all the branches and roots she had climbed through. "This is how I rode out the hurricane, in this bathtub jammed into the mangroves. Me and my little friend, here." He reached into the canoe and pulled out an empty jug that he threw into the bushes. "That was some hurricane, wasn't it?" He seemed friendly and at ease, and she tried to reflect the same attitude. His eyes were red, he was unshaven, and his clothes were rumpled and wet. He must have been caught in the storm coming back from Chokoloskee, already drunk and with an additional jug to console him. Once they were in the canoe, a hard object competed with her for the small space. It appeared to be a rifle or shotgun wrapped in oilcloth. She stretched out in the bottom of the canoe while he paddled, realizing her predicament but too exhausted to do otherwise.

It seemed as if she had closed her eyes for only a minute when pain awoke her from Phelps wrapping vines tightly around her wrists! She had fallen asleep, and the canoe had been beached. She struggled, but his grip was even stronger than Edward Cushing's. He then wrapped more vines around her feet, but with considerable difficulty as she tried to kick him away. The vines served their purpose well and held her securely. He removed a shotgun from the oilcloth beside her, still wet from being immersed in the canoe. For a moment it appeared as if this was the place where she would die.

"Well, it doesn't look as if your swamp ape is around. Wait here," he said unnecessarily. "I'm going to Chestnut's store for supplies—if it's still there. Everything I bought the day before yesterday got blown away."

She was lying in the canoe, and after he had disappeared, she had nothing to do but dwell upon the present dark state of affairs. She berated herself for having let down her guard in the presence of a murderer. She had been careless to fall asleep near that monster, but had little choice after a sleepless night and the exertion of the morning without food or water. Her thirst and hunger were secondary to the fact that she was about to take Emily Jenkins' place as Phelps' slave. She struggled at her bonds without success. When hearing footsteps in the sand approaching, she stopped. He hadn't been gone long.

"Holy Jehoshaphat!" The bearded man looked down at her, his eyes wide with astonishment. "What air you doin hyar?"

"Help me, please. Luther Phelps tied me up."

"Har! We figgered he'd come back atter the storm." The man paused a moment, scratched his scraggly beard, and then made his decision. He leaned his rifle against the canoe, pulled out a hunting knife, and cut through the vines binding her. The man helped her to her feet. They were standing on a sandy beach lined with palms and shrubs.

"Where are we?" she asked.

"Chestnut's store is thisaway."

She hung back. "Phelps will kill us. He's a murderer."

"Wal, let's see whut he's up ter." He picked up his rifle and trudged through the sand. She followed reluctantly several paces behind. At least this man didn't seem to have any plans for her.

He stopped abruptly. "Wait hyar. I'll be right back. The strange man disappeared through the underbrush. She felt uneasy waiting in the open. Phelps could be returning at any time. It wasn't long before her rescuer appeared up the beach accompanied by three other men, all carrying guns. He beckoned to her and then headed along the beach.

She headed after them, and before long the store came into sight. The wood frame structure on high stilts standing on the beach seemed to have narrowly survived the storm. A third of its tin roof was missing, and another section was bent up on end, giving the store a wild look, like a woman's hair blowing in a nonexistent wind. A large tree in front had been uprooted. The stairs had been washed away, and she had to climb a ladder behind her rescuer and the other three men.

She felt the tension as she passed through the door. To the right stood Luther Phelps. To the left were the four men she had followed, and near them behind a counter stood the potbellied storekeeper. All five were holding rifles pointed at Phelps who was holding his shotgun at his side.

"This 'un's gotched somethin' to tell yer," her rescuer said. She realized that for some reason she was now the center of attention although the guns were still pointed at Phelps.

"Air you the young man what sawed Emily Jenkins at Phelps' place?" asked one of the four standing near the storekeeper.

Before she could react, Phelps raised his shotgun from four feet away, aimed it at her head, and pulled the trigger.

Chapter 28

Chokoloskee, Florida, August 23, 1893

*N*othing happened except for the click of the hammer. But then an ear-splitting roar almost sent her into the next world as five weapons fired nearly in unison, and Luther Phelps fell backwards, knocking over a rocking chair as he went down. The storekeeper came around from behind the counter, through the gun smoke, and took her by the arm as she stood cowering with her hands to her face. "I'm Wendell Chestnut. Come with me, son." He guided her gently through the store and out onto a verandah overlooking the bay. "Stay here, boy. You didn't see anything. No one was in the store when you came in, understand? Don't fall off here, the railing got washed away yestiddy." He spat tobacco juice into the bay and disappeared back into the store.

Beth was still in shock and shook her head affirmatively as she sank numbly onto a bench that was bolted to the verandah floor. Deep breaths began to calm her pounding heart. The realization of what she had witnessed came back like a speeding freight train, and she was standing on the tracks. Luther Phelps had just been murdered by five men. She hadn't looked at him after he was shot, nor could she picture the faces of the shooters. Even so, that brief moment surpassed even the hurricane for terror. She shook as she remembered that split second when the cannonlike barrels of Luther Phelps' shotgun were aimed at her head. Then came the deafening roar of five rifles being fired almost simultaneously. Phelps must have misjudged how much protection the oil cloth gave to the shotgun lying in the bottom of the water-filled canoe. The moonshine very likely affected his judgment. He had referred to the canoe as a bathtub, and he had ridden out the storm in it, dead drunk.

As soon as Mr. Chestnut returned, Beth asked him, "Was Mr. Hutchinson here yesterday or the night before?"

"I don't know anyone by that name."

Of course. Matthew wouldn't have used his real name. "I mean the one they call the swamp ape."

"Haven't seen him in a week." A cold lump formed in her stomach. If he hadn't seen Matthew, then it meant that either the hurricane or the poachers had overwhelmed him, and now he was dead.

"Have you seen two men, Roach and Lopez?"

"One can get in trouble answering too many questions around here."

"Matthew was coming here the day before yesterday bringing the two poachers who had attacked us. Are you sure you didn't see him?"

"No, sir."

"You can call me Miss Sprague."

He looked at her closely, his mouth open, eyes bulging. He was about fifty, she guessed, had a large pot belly and was wearing a derby. Then he chuckled. "That old rascal."

"May I have a glass of water, please? I haven't had anything to eat or drink since yesterday morning."

He hurried back into the store without another word.

It occurred to her that Matthew must have told the storekeeper about Emily Jenkins and how they had found shreds of her dress in the alligator pen. That had happened weeks ago, and Matthew had been here several times since, but evidently he had never revealed to Mr. Chestnut that a woman was living on Deadman's Creek.

The storekeeper came back with a pail and dipper. "We wouldn't have any drinking water if I hadn't covered up my cistern real good." He watched while she drank deeply.

"I suspect Luther Phelps killed Emily Jenkins and at least one other man," she said.

"Oh, he has a history that goes way back to New York, but the less said about what happened here today the better. Justice has been served."

Beth didn't disagree with him, but the man had been killed without a trial. This was south Florida justice, she supposed. They might claim that they had killed Phelps to save her life, but that wasn't exactly true since his gun had misfired.

"If you see your man, you might want to tell him someone was here looking for him just the other day. He called himself Moses Gallagher."

Her heart skipped a beat. "He's not my man, Mr. Chestnut." That confirmed her thinking that the picture Mr. Gallagher had shown her was Matthew. First Mr. Prichett had been looking for her, and now Mr. Gallagher was searching for Matthew right here in Chokoloskee. "What did you tell him?"

"I tol' that Gallagher fellar I don't know any Matthew Hutchinson."

"I must get to Key West," she said, dipping into the pail again.

"Why do you want to go there?" She noticed he had a large wad of tobacco in his left cheek that she had missed at first because of his huge moustache.

"I'm on my way home to Boston." She took another long drink.

"There's a coastal schooner that will come by the outer islands later today if the hurricane didn't do her in. I can row you out to it when I get the mail if you want."

"I don't have any money."

"I'll pay your way to Key West if you promise not to discuss what happened here today." He seemed anxious to get her away from here.

"Luther Phelps was a vicious murderer," she said. "He deserved to die." He also deserved a trial, but she didn't say that.

Mr. Chestnut seemed satisfied.

"Are you the postmaster?" She had seen the post office sign above the entry.

"Yep. I get a dollar to go out and meet the schooner." He disappeared into the store again and came back with a basin and sponge.

"You may want to wash up before heading to Key West. I'll get you clean clothes."

She had a great sense of sadness as she looked out across the bay toward a flotilla of small mangrove islands. She imagined that behind the islands lay the Gulf, and beyond that was Key West and civilization. A few white, puffy clouds floated above, giving no hint of yesterday's hurricane. Pelicans circled lazily and then plummeted into the water after hapless fish. The sun left a trail of silvery sparkles across the calm, blue bay. Sitting here was deceptively peaceful and quiet. Matthew was dead and she was alone again.

Matthew had intended to bring the poachers to Mr. Chestnut to have him remove the bird shot from their faces. If they hadn't appeared, it meant that either the poachers or the hurricane had killed him. Matthew was gone, her research had been destroyed, and another man had been shot to death in her presence. The violence of the Everglades, both natural and man-made had taken its toll. Beth was more than ready to leave.

"We don't sell dresses," Mr. Chestnut said, handing her a new shirt, a pair of trousers, and a black, broad-brimmed hat. "These are still damp from the hurricane. I prob'ly can't sell 'em anyway. The water came up to here." He pointed to the window frame at his eye level. For the first time she noticed that the windows facing the bay had been blown in. "You can change in the back of the store. They should fit. I'll be up front with a bag of vittles from Mrs. Chestnut when you're ready."

"Thank you," she said.

As soon as Mr. Chestnut's borrowed boat left the beach she unwrapped the small package of food. Inside were a hunk of homemade bread, a square of cheese, and a thick slice of meat. Beth chewed on one piece of food and then another, stopping to take a drink now and then from the pail and dipper he had placed in the bottom of the boat. The bread was stale, the cheese dry, and the meat salty, but she had never tasted anything better. Mr. Chestnut rowed the boat, and Beth sat in the back facing him.

"I had a motor launch until yestiddy," he said. "Now pieces of it are all over the island."

"How far is it to Key West?" she asked as she rewrapped the greasy brown paper around the remainder of the food he had given her. Beth was uneasy about the rush he was in to get her off the island. When she had walked through the store no sign remained that a killing had taken place or of the four men who had joined Mr. Chestnut in the shooting. What she had noticed were water marks, still damp, higher than the countertops from yesterday's storm. Here she was, with a man she didn't know, heading out into the sun-drenched bay toward a group of small islands. She was the sole witness, and he was letting her go to Key West if she promised to say nothing to the authorities. If anything happened to her out here, no one but Mr. Chestnut would ever know.

"About eighty miles from here," he replied. "If the schooner is on time, and the winds are favorable, you will be there by mid-morning tomorrow. The winds are from the southeast, which is good, but not too strong right now. If they die out, it may take longer."

He rowed strongly and steadily in spite of his girth, with his back to the direction in which they were headed. His shirt and even his suspenders were stained with perspiration. It seemed to her he was saying too much, as if covering up for what was going to happen. He had no weapon with him that she could see, but Beth was unable to swim, so if he just left her on an island, she was going to die of thirst or starvation. But why had he given her the food, new clothes, and the hat if he planned to kill her?

"Why doesn't the schooner come right to Chokoloskee Island?" she asked, unwrapping her food again.

"Too shallow." He spat a wad of tobacco over the side, expertly missing an oar.

"When I get to Key West I'll have money, and I can mail you what I owe you," she said.

He shrugged. "Consider it a gift."

Or a bribe. "Please thank Mrs. Chestnut for the delicious food," she said. She hadn't seen the woman around the store.

"My wife says she's sorry it couldn't be more, but we were lucky to come away with what we have after the hurricane. That was worse than the hurricane of seventy-three. That food has to last you until you get to Key West. The *Hibiscus* ain't no ocean liner."

Reluctantly she wrapped up the remainder of the food. "Mrs. Chestnut was very generous."

"She's my fifth wife, and the best cook yet. I should have married her first. The other four were of no account. One died, one took up with another man, and the other two just couldn't get along with me. It's the Chestnut luck, I reckon." As if she had asked about the Chestnut luck, he continued his story while rowing steadily. "My folks never got along either. They lived together for twenty-one years without talking. He lived in one end of the house, and she lived in the other. Then one day they somehow got in each other's way, and they both went and got rifles, aimed at each other, and shot each other dead." He grinned at her, his few remaining brown teeth showing under his moustache.

"Were you there when it happened?" she couldn't help asking.

"Oh, no. By then I had shipped out to see the world. That was the year I sailed around the Horn in a four-master."

"You sailed around the tip of South America?" she asked, impressed. She had heard stories about the danger of that voyage.

"Yep. And never went back." He grinned again. "That's the gosh-honest truth. I vowed that if I ever got off that ship alive, I'd never get on another one. Hundred-foot waves for days on end. When we got to San Francisco I came back to Baltimore on horseback. That was before trains ran all the way across the continent. I went into business for myself. Me and my partner bought a coastal steamer and sailed her from Baltimore almost to Boston."

"Almost?" She had heard many stories about shipping when Papa had talked to their guests at the dinner table.

"She sank off Cape Cod."

"Many ships have been wrecked on the sandbars off the Cape."

"Oh, she didn't hit a sandbar, she just sank," he said sadly. "I had to swim twenty miles to shore." Then his face lit up. "I had to go into smuggling to regain a financial footing. Naturally I don't do that anymore."

While she was skeptical of almost everything he had said, she believed this last part the least. For all she knew, he was in partnership with Phelps, Roach, and Lopez.

They had already passed several small islands. Egrets dotted the trees by the thousands. She spotted a large, dark shape slipping past them just under the surface on the right side.

"What was that?"

"A manatee most likely. They're gentle creatures. I rode one once clear across Chokoloskee Bay." He was still rowing steadily, and they were approaching a sandy beach on an outermost island. "We'll stop here until the schooner comes—if it comes." He saw her questioning look and added, "The hurricane."

Was his storytelling a ruse to falsely put her at ease? Beth eyed the island with a sinking feeling, a few broken palms and mangroves, and mostly sand. This might be the place where her life was to end.

Mr. Chestnut rowed the boat into the sand and then climbed out and pulled it up farther. "We might as well sit on the sand." He brought the pail and dipper ashore and lowered himself onto the beach with a groan.

The sand was clean, and the sky and Gulf rivaled each other for blueness. The brightness hurt her eyes. She had been in the swamp too long. A day before she had been fighting for her life clinging to a tree. Her face burned from having been in the sun all morning.

The stocky storekeeper prostrated himself on the sand as if he were on a picnic. His paunch stood out like a minor mountain. She sat on the bow of the boat near his feet. He pulled out a large pocket watch and held it before his face. "The schooner is late. More likely'n not the skipper got ahold of some low-bush lightning." She assumed he was referring to moonshine and that the man was drunk.

"Do you have any children, Mr. Chestnut?" she asked. *If he's going to kill me, why is he lying on the sand?*

"Oh, too many to count, except for the one that turned out to be a bank robber," he said staring straight up into the sky.

"You've had an unusual life."

"More'n you'll ever know. In addition to what I've told you, I've been a fisherman, a carpenter, and the mayor of Key West."

"The mayor?"

"I was nineteen at the time. You go and ask them once you get there.

They might have forgotten, it being for only two days during a Confederate attack when the regularly elected mayor ran off." He then went on about his other no account offspring. Suddenly he pulled his heavy body to his feet. "Ah ha! Here comes the *Hibiscus*. We have to hurry now. Here, grab the pail." With relief she scrambled into the boat, and he pushed off and jumped in with much effort.

The schooner bearing down on them was the most beautiful sight she had ever seen.

"Wave your hat so they see us," he said as he rowed.

She held the outside hope that Matthew was aboard the schooner, returning from Fort Myers, but not enough time had gone by for that. Instead, once on board, she spotted the one other passenger. His huge back was toward her. He was wearing a black suit and a derby hat. When he turned toward her, his eyes were mean and frightening. But the one thing that held her attention was the large, ugly mole beside his nose.

Chapter

29

Aboard the schooner Hibiscus, *August 23, 1893*

S he pulled her hat down. Everyone had mistaken her for a boy until now; why not Mr. Prichett? Her hat and matted hair might help. The last time he had seen her, she was wearing a skirt and blouse, and her hair had been long and silky under a flowery hat. She had to find a way to deceive him until they arrived at Key West. Going back to Boston as Prichett's prisoner would be a nightmare and the height of ignominy. If she returned home, it had to be on her terms.

The schooner, which had never completely stopped, was under way as soon as Mr. Chestnut departed with one letter and a parcel. She sat on a bench bolted to the deck between the masts and watched Mr. Chestnut and his boat grow smaller and smaller. He had turned out to be a kind man after all. Mr. Prichett came over and sat beside her. She had no way of avoiding him. He was wearing the same black, threadbare suit and bowler she had seen in Fort Myers. His body odor was sickening. She was chilled as his mean, close-set eyes bored into her. His face was sweaty and unshaven.

Pulling a flat object from inside his coat, he said, "Have you seen this woman, sonny?" He squirted tobacco juice past her knee, missing her foot by inches.

Startled and speechless, she looked at a tintype of herself. The photograph had been taken just before graduation from Wellesley. She had been standing beside Mary and Grace. The picture had been cut, and her friends were gone. They had been posing before a large maple. Her blue dress and a spring straw hat with matching ribbon and flowers had not shown up well in black and white. That had been when her hair was long. Papa must have mailed the picture to Prichett since she left Fort Myers three months ago. This man had been looking for her ever since, and by a quirk of extremely bad luck, he was now sitting beside her.

She had studied the photograph too long. "She's a mighty pretty woman," she said, looking away from him.

"You can't always go by appearances," he said.

"Has she broken the law?"

"Yeah. She's a real bad one, she is."

She wanted to kick him. "I think I've seen her."

"I can pay if you have information about her."

Here was a chance to kill two birds with one stone. She looked closely at the picture again. "Yep, that's her all right."

"When and where did you see her?" He mopped his perspiring brow with a blue handkerchief.

"Just last week at Chokoloskee, only she was wearing a different hat and dress. Her name was, let's see, um, Miss Spring, no, Sprague. Sprague, that was it."

"Damn," he said. "What was she doing there?"

"She was with a man. I didn't ask them what they were doing, and they didn't say. You going to pay me now?" she asked.

"That information don't help me none. We're going in the wrong direction, and that was a week ago. What was the man's name?"

"Mr. Phelps, I think. I gave you all the information I have."

"O.K., squirt, here's a quarter. That's all it's worth. Are you from Boston?"

Her mouth went dry. "No, why do you ask?"

"You sound like a Bostonian."

"I'm from New Bedford. My pappy's a fisherman. Fishes down here now."

Mr. Prichett wiped his broad forehead again, then stood and went back to stand beside the crewman at the wheel, but he turned and was staring at her.

When she had come on board, the crabby old skipper acted about as happy to have another passenger as he might have if welcoming the plague. Mr. Chestnut had exchanged a few words with him, and she had seen money passed. Now the skipper was coming past her, and she asked him for a drink of water.

"The keg is down in the cuddy. If you want a drink you'll have to go get it. I ain't the steward." As he walked aft she heard him mutter, "Women!" She hoped Mr. Prichett hadn't heard his exclamation, but the two men were talking and looking at her. Mr. Chestnut must have explained about her when he had paid for the passage.

She reopened her package of food and consumed all that remained. There was no point in waiting. As she headed for the cuddy, Mr. Prichett stood in her way.

"What's your name?" he asked, standing over her threateningly, his eyes squinting.

She was ready for this. "McKay." Mary wouldn't mind her friend using her maiden name.

"You didn't see Elizabeth Sprague, did you?"

"Oh, yes, I surely did." Her voice quavered, revealing how she felt inside.

He tore off her hat, grabbed her jaw roughly, and held her picture beside her face. "You're Elizabeth Sprague, ain't you?"

She pushed away his hand, squared her shoulders and looked up at him as defiantly as she knew how. "You never asked me where I am going, Mr. Prichett. I am headed for Boston, and there's no further need for you to track me down and haul me back to my family like a captured animal."

He grinned down at her maliciously. "Well, I'll just tag along to make sure you get there safely—and we can have some fun on the way."

After getting a drink, she stood morosely at the rail. She had to find a way to elude this hired bounty hunter and show Papa that she was returning to Boston of her own free will. But not now. They had hours of sailing ahead, and she was tired. The cabin was too stuffy. Prichett was standing behind the crewman at the wheel, so she stretched out on the bench, not having slept since before the hurricane.

Her heart weighed her down like a cast iron anchor. It was hard to accept that Matthew could be dead. With his strength and resourcefulness he should have been able to live through the hurricane. But all indications said otherwise. If Mr. Chestnut had told the truth, the three men had not shown up at his store. Was it possible that Phelps might have ambushed Matthew and his prisoners before the storm? Or had Lopez and Roach somehow overpowered him?

He was by far and away the finest man she had known. Their two-month relationship had been peculiar. At first he had cared for her as if she was his little sister. Later he had protected her and they had slept in the same tent while along the Fakahatchee River. He had always been a gentleman. While she yearned for his love, his loyalty to his fiancée made her admire him even more. He was generous, well-spoken, intelligent, and yet presumably uneducated. It was her fate that the two good men she had known, Michael Otis and Matthew Hutchinson, were devoted to other women.

She dreamt that she was falling from a tree, and woke up with a start. She was indeed falling off the bench and sat up. The schooner was listing to starboard and slicing through the waves smartly. The water frothed up almost to the deck, but she knew this was normal sailing, and they might make port earlier than at first expected. The night was clear, and the stars numbered in the thousands. She pulled her hat down securely. The air, while not like New England, was fresh and invigorating compared to the mugginess of the swamp.

The skipper came on deck and poured out a long series of curse words at the crewman at the wheel. Then she heard a second voice. An angry exchange was going on between Mr. Prichett and the skipper. After a time the argument subsided and Mr. Prichett came out of the darkness and sat down beside her.

"That stupid skipper couldn't drive a team of horses. He's changed course. He says the wind is coming from the south. Right now we're headed for the Yucatan. The Yucatan! That's Mexico, for Christ's sake. We'll never get to Key West."

"There's no need to use the Lord's name in vain, Mr. Prichett." In their two months together, Matthew had never used profanity. She knew the schooner couldn't head directly into the wind. Obviously her captor didn't know anything about sailing. Sooner or later the skipper had to come about onto another tack.

"Well, you should hear the skipper. He's swearing at the wind." The skipper had taken the wheel from the crewman, who had disappeared into the cabin, but they hadn't changed course. Fortunately, Mr. Prichett went into the cuddy, and she was able to lie down again.

Beth lay on her back and watched the stars. She was on the first leg of her journey back to Boston and once again would be confronting both Papa and Edward Cushing. But now she had the confidence to think and act for herself without running away. Perhaps she should consider marrying Edward. Was it possible to marry him and never consummate the marriage? She could spend his money like water, have the finest clothes and travel abroad as often as she liked. Julia Ward Howe lived not too far from Dartmouth Street. If she became active in the American Women's Suffrage Association, she had an excuse to spend less time with Edward. With a name like Cushing her articles to the newspapers on women's suffrage and prohibition might carry more weight and could help to make a difference. But marriage to Mr. Cushing might mean just the opposite; he could be a tyrant and keep her locked up in the house and forbid her from even entertaining her friends.

Mama's friends must be chattering behind her back about the wayward Sprague daughter who ran off to Florida and was in confinement until the arrival of her baby. If she went back and married Edward, Papa might relinquish control of her inheritance from Grandpa Jackson, but then there would no longer be a need for the money. If there ever was going to be a way to regain Papa's love, if it had ever existed, it had to be through a marriage to Mr. Cushing, enabling the merger of their two companies. Through that move the honor and recognition that Mama craved for the family might be achieved as well. Children were supposed to love and honor their parents, and her guilt for failing them gnawed at her conscience.

But the sedentary life of a Boston matron was not what she wanted for herself. She had little interest in quilting, embroidery, water colors, or playing the piano. The whole idea of marrying Edward was repugnant and depressing. More important, she didn't want to write about women's rights; she wanted to *act them out*, to be a botanist, discover unknown plants, write books about them, and be a wife and mother, too. Her goals seemed more unreachable than ever. Her hope of showing the world that women were equal to men was not to be fulfilled.

The next time she awoke, a line of light gray lay across the eastern horizon. They were now sailing on a starboard tack, heeling to port, close to the wind. Beth decided to find out their progress from the crewman, who had taken over from the skipper again. The crewman was young, possibly twenty, with black curly hair. He grinned at her but then returned to switching his gaze between the horizon and the compass.

"When will we arrive at Key West?" she asked.

He responded in Spanish. His last word, "*señorita*," was all that she understood.

"The idiot doesn't speak English," growled the skipper as he came up from his cabin. "The wind is still out of the south. We'll be in Key West by late afternoon."

She was eager to arrive in Key West and escape from Mr. Prichett. Why he was agitated by their slow progress was unclear.

"Where's Key West?" he asked.

"Where it always was," snapped the skipper.

"I mean point to it, damn it," Prichett snarled. She dreaded being on the same steamer with him all the way to Boston.

The skipper pointed into the early morning darkness. "Over thar, somewheres."

"Why don't you go there, then? My ship is leaving tomorrow morning."

"Take yer taters outta the fire," said the skipper. "We'll be thar before the sun sets tonight. We're doin' the best the wind will allow."

Prichett sat down on the bench beside Beth, and she decided not to move away yet. There was something she wanted to know.

"Mr. Prichett, how was it that my father was able to hire you in Fort Myers?"

"All I know is a Mr. Cushing in Boston sent me a telegram. He got my name from Mr. Flagler, who I done some work for."

Her mind whirled as she moved to the rail. Mr. Cushing! All this time she had been blaming Papa. What did Edward Cushing expect to accomplish by having her brought back to Boston by force? It mattered little. Papa had probably contacted Mr. Flagler for Mr. Cushing.

The sky changed from gray to blue, then gold on the eastern horizon. The beautiful sunrise contrasted with her feelings. Added to her other problems was the need for something to eat. To compensate, she drank water, but it didn't relieve her hunger. During the morning the skipper tacked several times, each change in course accompanied by sarcastic comments from Mr. Prichett. She had nothing to do except sit on the bench and watch the undulating waves and the nearly cloudless sky. In the early afternoon the wind increased, and the skipper had the crewman reef two sails. Spray whipped across the deck from time to time. Mr. Prichett swore, but Beth found it exhilarating. At least the breeze kept the temperature lower than an oven.

She was dozing when the skipper called out. "Thar's Key West."

The sun was almost on the horizon. At first all she could see were several low lumps in the distance that might have been fog. The breeze was coming straight from the Keys, which forced the skipper to continue to tack, and their forward progress was agonizingly slow. At last, numerous islands were in view, one of which boasted tiny rooftops and spires glowing orange in the last rays of the setting sun.

All eyes were on the distant town when the boat came to a sudden stop and the sails luffed noisily. "Damned sandbar," said the skipper.

"Why in hell don't you look where you're going?" sneered Mr. Prichett.

"Must've been kicked up by the hurricane. Wasn't here t'other day."

The skipper and his crewman dropped the sails. Then they lowered a dinghy and dropped an anchor from it twenty or thirty yards behind the schooner. Beth understood the logic of trying to winch the schooner to the anchor and away from the bar, but the vessel didn't come free.

"How do you expect to go anywhere without the sails?" yelled Mr. Prichett.

"Shut up if you don't know what yer talking about," growled the skipper. He climbed down a rope ladder followed by the crewman. The water was up to their shoulders. They tried pulling the *Hibiscus* without success. "Come on down here and help us out, Prichett."

"I'm not getting wet for you, just because you don't know how to sail a boat. I paid for passage from Punta Gorda to Key West, and I expect to get it."

She saw large dark shapes below the surface circling the two men. "Are those sharks?" she called. Both men scurried back aboard as fast as moving through the water allowed.

"Too bad," said Mr. Prichett. "That was going to be fun to watch." She looked at him with disdain, shuddering at the thought of seeing blood in the water.

The skipper looked toward the town. "Maybe they'll see us and come out," he said, puffing from his exertion. But the sun had set, and the hope of being rescued before nightfall diminished quickly.

"I want you to row me into town," said Mr. Prichett. "My ship is leaving early."

"Maybe the tide will float us off during the night," said the skipper.

"Well, if you won't do it, I'll row the dinghy myself and take the little lady with me. It's only one or two miles." The notion of going with him repulsed her.

The skipper wheeled and went down into his cabin. In no time at all he was back with a rifle in his hands, which he shoved into Mr. Prichett's ample stomach.

"I've had all I'm gonna take from you," said the skipper through clenched teeth. "You go inter the cuddy and stay thar, or I'll blow yer shirt buttons out t'other side."

Prichett backed away with a growl and slunk into the cuddy. The skipper looked at Beth for a long moment as if she were to blame and then returned his rifle to his quarters. By this time the city's lights had come on in the distance, and she knew the sandbar was where they were spending the night.

In the early morning light, the skipper hailed a sponge boat which came alongside and took her along with Mr. Prichett to the docks. The Greek sailors gave them bread, cheese, and water. Gratefully chewing on the bread, she tried to think of a way to escape.

As they approached the docks, she saw several other sponge and shrimp boats as well as three steamships, the SS *Empire Builder*, the SS *Southern Pride*, and one other beyond them. In the sun's first rays laughing gulls and royal terns circled the boats while pelicans and cormorants sat on the pilings. Even before the boat touched the dock, she was ready to jump, but Mr. Prichett jumped with her, grabbed her by the arm and pulled her along the pier.

"We'll have to hurry, our ship is about to sail." He rushed her toward the *Empire Builder* without so much as a glance at the town.

"Wait, Mr. Prichett, I'm not in that much hurry to get to Boston," she said, hanging back. "I have some business here, and I'd like to buy some clothes and get breakfast." Getting on the ship with this man was not in her plans. She yanked her arm free, but she felt his arm around her waist, and then her feet were off the ground. His strength was surprising.

"This ship is leaving now, Miss Sprague. We have no choice. We might have to wait a week or two for another ship."

Crewmen were already standing by the lines as Mr. Prichett shoved her up the gangplank. He spoke to an officer in Spanish and gestured toward her disparagingly, and the officer laughed. She was free of her captor, but was unable to get past him down the gangplank. Mr. Prichett thrust a wad of greenbacks at the officer. The urgency of his movements worried her. A sixth sense told her that there was more to his concern than merely getting to Boston on the first available ship. It was probably nothing more than his anxiety over wanting to have her aboard and safely ensconced in a cabin. The officer pointed to the upper deck.

Mr. Prichett hustled her up the outside stairs. From this height she was able to see the name of the third steamship, the *City of Providence*. She knew that something was definitely wrong as he seized her arm and attempted to shove her through the doorway of the third cabin.

"There's one of Papa's ships! Isn't that the one we should be on? We can get free passage." She grabbed the railing. "I have money here in Key West. I can pay you more than Mr. Cushing has offered." He continued to pull and broke her grasp on the railing. She swung at him with her free arm, and both feet were kicking. Prichett's strength was overpowering, and she was shoved brutally through the doorway and thrown onto a bunk like a sack of potatoes.

He closed the door and grinned at her. "Don't worry, Missy. We're not going to Boston just yet. This ship is on its way to Havana. If your daddy wants his daughter back, he's gonna to have to turn over his business to Cushing."

She remembered his saying that Mr. Cushing had made the offer.

At that moment, yelling out on the deck followed by pounding on the door caused Prichett to spring at her and clasp his hand over her mouth. She kicked, flailed her arms and tried to scream, but to no avail. All at once the door flew inward off its hinges knocking Prichett across the cabin. Two men, one tall, the other short, pinned Prichett against the bulkhead. She stopped in mid-scream and looked at the intruders. To her amazement she recognized them both.

Chapter

30

Key West, Florida, August 25, 1893

*T*o be among people again was thrilling; traders, shopkeepers, hawkers, ladies in dresses in the company of gentlemen, Cubans, Negroes, rough-looking seamen, and sailors in uniform. They had left Prichett in the care of the sheriff and were riding a victoria to the Island City Hotel on William Street. How enjoyable to see the stores of Key West: a print shop, Pierce's clothing, Willacott's Restaurant and Ice Cream Parlor, and even a cigar factory. The coral limestone streets were hard and uneven, but to be riding in a carriage again was a joy.

She sat happily with the two men. Beside her was Matthew, and facing her, riding backwards, was her friend the Pinkerton detective, Mr. Gallagher. Matthew was clean-shaven and was wearing a suit, obviously new, a black hat, and shiny black leather boots. She was aware of staring at him, but was unable to help herself.

"How did you get here? What is Mr. Gallagher doing here? Where are Roach and Lopez? How did you know I was on board that ship? Can you believe that man was hired by Mr. Cushing and was trying to kidnap me to Havana? Is Mr. Gallagher taking you back to Philadelphia?"

Both men laughed. "One question at a time," said Matthew.

"You said you were going to take Lopez and Roach to Mr. Chestnut to remove the bird shot. He said he never saw you."

"That's because Mr. Gallagher found me coming down the Turner River with my two prisoners. He had rented a steam yacht here in Key West, and with a storm brewing, the pilot insisted we make haste to get back here before it got any worse. Then there were Lopez and Roach. They needed medical help and ended up with the sheriff."

"As it was, we almost didn't make it back," added Mr. Gallagher. "In the last hour the waves were mountainous, even in the harbor."

"We were lucky," added Matthew. "The worst part of the storm passed east of Key West."

"Not as lucky as you may think, Matthew," she said. "Your camp was totally destroyed. The money you had hidden probably washed away."

"I had under thirty dollars, and that was in my pocket. That talk about eight hundred dollars was an attempt to distract Roach and Lopez. As far as the camp goes, it doesn't matter—as long as you're safe. I'm never going back there again. I have to go back to Philadelphia. My mother is getting old, and there's much business I must attend to."

She turned her face toward Matthew. "Are you under arrest?" she asked quietly, hoping Mr. Gallagher didn't hear.

Matthew laughed. "No. My brother sent Mr. Gallagher with good news. The murderer of Laura's father has been found. It was his partner. I'm free to go home."

"I'm so happy for you, Matthew." For some reason Beth wasn't as happy as she expected herself to be and hoped he didn't detect her lack of enthusiasm.

"There was something about my relationship with Laura that I didn't tell you. We were in love, but no one in the family wanted us to marry. Our fathers had hated each other for years. You see, they were brothers, and Laura is my first cousin. When my father and uncle were young, they, along with a friend, opened a store. My father fought with them all the time and finally was driven from the growing business by the other two partners. He never forgave them for that, even though his cantankerousness was probably the cause. When my uncle was murdered, everyone thought

I had a several reasons to kill him. They knew I wanted to marry Laura. Then there was the family's share of the company business, and the fact that both my brother and I had been fired. Actually, I loved my uncle because he helped put me through school even though he and my father never spoke."

"And now Matthew, his brother Luke, and Laura will each own a third of the store," added Mr. Gallagher.

"And you and Laura can get married," she said, preparing herself to act indifferently to his reply.

"Except for two things," said Matthew. "Mr. Gallagher has told me that Laura has no interest in having an active part in running the store. She was married a year ago. She and her husband have a baby." He was looking at her as if to see how she was going to react.

"Oh, I'm sorry, Matthew." Beth hoped she sounded sincere. Her true emotions were in a confusing uproar. She looked up at him, waiting for what he was about to say next.

He just looked at her with a quizzical smile as the carriage stopped in front of the hotel.

"How did you find Matthew, Mr. Gallagher?"

"I wasn't looking for him, not right then, anyway. I was looking for you," he said as he helped her down from the carriage. "I felt a little guilty about leaving you alone in Fort Myers. You told me you would be doing your research on the Fakahatchee River, and since I was in the region, I had the pilot go up and down every inlet from Marco to Chokoloskee. I talked to people at Allen River and that storekeeper, Chestnut, and no one had ever heard of you. Well, I never found the right river, exactly. We were already heading back, it was almost dark and raining, and low and behold, there was Mr. Hutchinson as big as life at the mouth of the Turner River with his two friends."

"How did you know where I was this morning?" she asked as they entered the lobby.

"Pure coincidence," said Matthew. "We were walking along Duval Street near the docks after breakfast and happened to hear a woman screaming loudly enough to be heard at the other end of town."

"You heard me?" she asked, surprised. "I didn't realize that I had screamed."

"Oh, yes," said Mr. Gallagher. "But Matthew failed to tell you the whole story. He's been meeting every boat that came in since we arrived on Friday. We were on our way to the docks to charter a boat and come looking for you."

This was the first time she had seen Matthew blush. "Beth, your father is here," he said.

"Here? In Key West?" She wasn't sure if she was happy or sad. She didn't relish admitting to him that she had failed in her mission. Whether or not she was going to be glad to see him depended upon how he acted toward her.

"In this hotel," said Matthew. "Room twenty-one. Someone pointed him out yesterday, but I didn't speak to him. I wasn't sure what you'd want me to say."

She needed to work out a plan of action. She had to prove to both Papa and herself that she was free of his control. Facing Papa was better than putting it off. After making arrangements with Matthew to meet in the dining room, she went upstairs and knocked on the door of room twenty-one. Her heart was pounding. Their last exchange had been before their guests, and it came back as if no time had lapsed in between.

Papa opened the door and looked down at her. Uncharacteristically, he was in his shirtsleeves, his hair, usually parted in the middle, was mussed, and his suspenders hung down around his trousers. He paused for a moment, studying what must have looked like a street urchin to him. "What do you want?"

"Hello, Papa." She took off her hat.

He bent over and looked closely at her face. "Elizabeth?" he asked incredulously. "My God, what's happened to you? You're so peaked. Whatever did you do to your hair?" He stared at her trousers. "I hardly recognized you." His face expressed shock. They stood in the doorway facing each other. Behind him she saw a steamer trunk standing on end, ready to be picked up. "Come in and sit down."

"Is Mama here?" Beth asked, looking at the trunk.

"No, but she is well and has been worried about you." They were in the living room of a small suite. As soon as they were seated, he said, "I have some bad news, Elizabeth. Aunt Sarah passed away three weeks ago today." He sat there staring at her. Whatever sorrow he felt was hidden deep within.

The sudden sense of loss swept over her much like the hurricane had. "How did she—"

"The doctor said her heart gave out. She had been sick ever since she returned from St. Augustine."

Poor Aunt Sarah. She had a lonely life. She had always been kind, and risked the wrath of her brother by helping her escape from his control. Then it struck her. Had Aunt Sarah transferred money to a local bank for her before she became ill? Without those funds she was again under Papa's control. He still controlled her inheritance. Guilt consumed her for her selfish thinking. The aunt she had loved as much as anyone was gone.

He was the same old Papa, tall, stern, with bristling mustache and a scowl. But he had changed—or had she? He was less formidable now, physically smaller than she had imagined, and less threatening. Or was it that she was no longer afraid to stand toe-to-toe with him?

Being more than a thousand miles from Boston helped, too. She had control of her own destiny if she stood up to him, she reminded herself. No longer was he in charge of her life. No longer was she terrorized by him. Whether they were in Key West or Boston, with money or without, she now knew she was capable of making her own decisions. She could go home with the confidence that she was a grown woman who was in command of her future. The problem was that she had no money to do it. There had to be a means of returning home without being in Papa's debt.

"Why don't we have lunch together?" she asked.

"No, I'm here on business. I'll meet you for dinner." He was still eyeing her trousers. "Why don't you bathe and change into more appropriate clothing, Elizabeth? After dinner we can go on board the *City of Providence*. We sail tonight." She had been dismissed. It was as if he didn't wish to talk with her as long as she didn't meet his standards of appearance.

She had made a mistake by not finding a dress to wear before seeing him. Deciding for the moment not to tell him these were the only clothes she owned, she said, "I'll meet you here at the hotel for dinner, Papa." She had wanted to say, "Oh, I thought you were here looking for me." There had been no kiss, no hug, not even a smile. That was Papa's way. There was no, "I was worried about you, Elizabeth," or "How did you make it through the Everglades, Elizabeth?" or "Did you see any snakes or alligators lately, Elizabeth?" or "You are a strong, brave woman, Elizabeth," or even "I am proud of you, Elizabeth."

Matthew was waiting for her in the lobby. After reveling through a large breakfast in the hotel dining room, she sent a telegram to Mama. Then they went to the banks to find whether Aunt Sarah had transferred money for her. She had not. Matthew assured her that Mr. Gallagher had anticipated his need for money and was able to advance him sufficient funds. Now he was in a position to help her buy clothes and a ticket to Boston if necessary. She made him agree that he was making a loan. They went to John W. Sawyer's for a dress, Gideon Lowe's to select hats, and John McKilley's for shoes. Much more clothing was available for men than for women. In order to buy a satisfactory dress, she had to have it tailor-made. Because she had no other clothes, Matthew paid extra to have a dress ready that afternoon. Matthew had shown an interest and was conversant about women's clothing, even the unmentionables, without being embarrassed. Having four younger sisters and working in a department store explained that.

As they strolled around the town, she was amused by Matthew's enthusiastic reaction to their surroundings. Obviously he was more a city person than the wild man that she at first thought him to be. He had used his time in Key West by telegraphing his mother and brother and purchasing clothing. His new suit emphasized his broad shoulders and made him the most attractive man on the streets of the city. Beth was still wearing the trousers, work shirt, and Marian's half-boots which were starting to fall apart. They must have been a peculiar sight, the tall, well-dressed gentleman and the little boy-girl almost running beside him to keep up. She was pleased with herself to know that she no longer cared what other people thought.

They had a late lunch at Willacott's. As soon as they were seated,

Matthew said, "I suppose you're going back to Boston with your father." Was he asking a question or making a statement?

"The *City of Providence* leaves tonight," she answered.

"Have you ever been to Philadelphia?"

"No, except on the train. I've heard that it's a nice city." She hadn't heard that. No one in Boston would admit that any other city was "nice." "Who sent Mr. Gallagher to find you?" she asked.

"My brother Luke. Even though he hated our father, our uncle had bequeathed his share of the store to Luke and me. He had only Laura. Since I haven't been there, Luke has been running things. I'll probably work for him when I go back. The other partner is in prison."

"If he hadn't sent Mr. Gallagher, you'd be going back to the swamp."

"No, I don't think so. You suggested once that I should go back to Philadelphia and clear my name. That and the fact that you're so brave made me change my mind about hiding any longer."

"Brave?" she asked. "I'm not brave. I almost faint every time I see an alligator or a snake."

"That's the thing. You know the danger, yet you have the courage to do what has to be done. You came down to south Florida alone, then traversed the Big Cypress Swamp. Most people, men or women, wouldn't even dream of doing what you have done."

"My exploration was a failure, Matthew," Beth said sadly. "All my notes were destroyed in the hurricane. If I had known what the Big Cypress Swamp was going to be like, I wouldn't have come. Now Papa will remind me that he has been right all along."

"With your perseverance, Beth, you will succeed at anything you set out to do. You are the most remarkable woman I've ever met. We've known each other a short time, just two months, but I decided even before I learned that Laura had married, that I wanted to marry you even more. That was the second reason why Laura and I wouldn't be getting married. I was planning to go back to Philadelphia and break our engagement. I will be honored if you will become my wife, Beth."

Across the table from her was the handsomest man in Florida. He had saved her life, he had wrestled alligators, and stood toe-to-toe with the murderer Phelps. She knew him to be gentle, considerate, and trustworthy. He stood head and shoulders above every man she had ever known, including Mary's Michael Otis.

This was not how she had imagined a handsome prince would ask for her hand in marriage. Here she was, sitting across from him in shirt and trousers, her hair scraggly, without cosmetics or jewelry, looking like a street urchin, and he was willing to accept her as she was.

"Thank you, Matthew. I hope you're not saying this just to do the honorable thing because we shared the same tent."

"No. We both know we didn't do anything to be ashamed of, although the gossipers will have a field day if they learn we were together in the swamp for two months."

She heard herself saying, "I'll need some time to get back to a normal life before I can give you an answer, and I suspect that you need that time, too. Once we've had the chance to see where our lives are going, and if you feel then the way you feel now, we can talk."

He reached across the table and took her hand in his. "I understand," he said, smiling. This was the first time he had purposely touched her since he had pulled her naked from the creek. A surge of desire welled through her. She had never felt happiness like this before, and to top it off, they were having ice cream for dessert.

They walked around the town, looking in the shops, and buying a few incidentals that she needed. In one store a doll caught her eye.

"Oh, Matthew, do you mind if I buy and ship that doll to a little girl I know? Look, her eyes close when you tip it back." She told him about Little Maggie Beckett and how the little girl had lost her homemade doll in the fire. Then she bought a book, Stevenson's *The Strange Case of Dr. Jekyll and Mr. Hyde*, for Hawley, and a hunting knife for Billy. "There's something I want to do for their sister, Hannah, too, but that will have to wait." As they left the store, exhaustion overcame her, and they headed back to the hotel to rest before dinner, where she planned to have Papa meet Matthew. Matthew escorted her to the lobby and then went back to a men's store to make more purchases of his own.

In the lobby she suddenly heard a loud, high-pitched voice. "The name is Murchison. Some idiot has forgotten to pick up my steamer trunk. Make sure that my luggage is on board the SS *City of Providence* before sailing time or else Mr. Sprague will have you fired!" The woman was tall and well-dressed, but her screeching voice revealed a person of inferior upbringing. The hussy's skirts rustled as she brushed past her indignantly. There was no doubt that this was the same woman she had seen in Papa's office more than twelve years ago. This was Miss Murchison, his secretary, and possibly the woman Mrs. Flagler had mistakenly believed was Papa's wife.

Miss Murchison stopped and turned. "Boy!" she said, looking straight at her. "Here's two bits. See to it that the trunk in room twenty-one is delivered to the *City of Providence* in twenty minutes, and there'll be another coin in it for you. Don't stand there, dummy, hurry!"

She took the quarter open-mouthed, already knowing what she was going to do. The clerk behind the desk was berating a Negro he called Rastus for having overlooked Miss Murchison's trunk. She followed him partway up the stairs to Papa's room.

"Rastus, do you remember which ship the trunk goes to?" she asked.

"Yassuh," said the Negro. *"The City of Providence."*

"Oh, no. You've forgotten already. Take it to the SS *Southern Pride.*" She combined Miss Murchison's quarter with the one given to her by Mr. Prichett. "Here's fifty cents to help you remember." She had him repeat the name of the ship.

He stared at his small fortune. "Thank you, suh."

She should have realized that something was amiss that morning when she saw the steamer trunk in Papa's room—or was it Miss Murchison's room? Chances were that the hussy was hiding in the bedroom when she had been talking with Papa. Papa always traveled light, and he usually slept aboard, or so he had told Mama.

How did he plan to handle the presence of both his daughter and his mistress aboard the ship? The affair with Miss Murchison must have continued throughout the past twelve years. Poor Mama, she must have guessed by now. Forgiving her for having spent so much time and energy trying to elevate the Sprague name was easier now. Mama must have known that Papa, in spite of his haughty demeanor, was doing everything he could to tear down the family's reputation.

Beth's finished dress arrived at her room in time for dinner, along with her other purchases. She could now feel like a woman again after a luxurious bath in scented, warm water with no alligators or snakes. As she dressed she reflected upon how Matthew had found her on Deadman's Creek. In Boston, when introduced, the lady nodded, and the gentleman bowed. She and Matthew had missed the usual "coming to call" or "going somewhere" activities that were generally considered a part of courting. There were to be no cotillions, parties, or even private dinner dances, and a honeymoon in Europe was out. Mama and Papa always regarded the working class as common, and now, like Grace's fisherman friend, Patrick Muldoon, there was dear Matthew, the store clerk.

She looked at herself in the mirror. The dress was a simple pattern with a pink floral design on a cream background that the seamstress could have ready in one afternoon. It would be considered a house dress in Boston, but until then she'd make do. She was thinner than ever, and not much could be done with her hair until it grew longer. At least it was clean and brushed. She hadn't been able to decide between two hats in the store, so Matthew had purchased both for her. Now she chose the pink one with the broad, cream-colored, trailing ribbon. Her face was red from the sun of the past two days and still looked pockmarked from earlier mosquito bites.

Beth looked in the mirror again. Wearing a dress brought her back to another time. But this was not the naïve girl who had left Boston more than five months ago. So much had happened. South Florida was so different from what she had expected. She had learned much, but had more questions than before, about herself, her family, and the world in general. There was one thing she had learned for certain: she was tougher, more capable, and more resilient than she had ever dreamed.

In the time remaining before dinner, she wrote a letter to Mr. Beckett about poor Emily Jenkins and what she knew about the kidnapping and subsequent disappearance. She wanted to offer to take Hannah to a hospital in a northern city and have her shoulder repaired. But that would have to wait until she was in control of her inheritance again. One way was to marry Edward Cushing. There had to be another way.

Papa was already at a table in the hotel dining room. He rose to his feet as she approached. As soon as she was seated, Beth saw Matthew coming through the archway. She couldn't help but notice his staring at her. As soon as he was at the table, she said, "Papa, may I present Matthew Hutchinson? He saved my life more than once." The two men shook hands. Matthew was slightly taller than Papa.

"Then I am in your debt, sir," said her father as they sat down. She saw that Papa was already taking stock of Matthew.

"Not at all, sir. You have a courageous daughter."

They ordered their dinners from what was a sparse menu, by Bostonian standards.

"Where are you from, Mr. Hutchinson?" asked Papa. A person's background was almost as important to Papa as it was to Mama.

"From Philadelphia, sir. As a matter of fact, now that Beth is safe, I'm heading back there on the SS *Southern Pride* tomorrow morning." Too soon! Her heart sank.

"Hutchinson of Philadelphia," said Papa. "Are you related to the department store Hutchinsons?"

"My brother, Luke, is president of the company, sir."

Papa nodded. It was the first time she had ever seen her father look impressed. "That's the biggest department store in Philadelphia, and now I understand they are expanding to New York."

She looked at Matthew, forgetting to close her mouth for a moment.

"I had hoped to have a more suitable time to speak to you, sir, but since you are leaving tonight, I had better say it now. I wish to ask for your daughter's hand in marriage if she decides to accept." She was pleased with Matthew's assertiveness.

Her father stiffened. "I'm afraid, sir, there is no suitable time for that. You see, Elizabeth is already engaged to another gentleman, Edward Cushing of Boston."

She could hardly believe what she was hearing. Papa hadn't changed at all. "Papa, I was never engaged to Mr. Cushing, and I never will be."

"Elizabeth, you are my daughter, and you will do as I say. Edward and I have an arrangement that will enhance our business and will allow you to marry into one of Boston's First Families. Your mother wants that," he said pointedly. "As of now you will start acting like a civilized woman for a change."

Now was the time to say what she had rehearsed: "Papa, if I come home with you, it will be because I decide that's what's best for me and it's what I want to do. And when I get there, I will act as I please whether you like it or not." She was tempted to accept Matthew's offer of marriage on the spot just to spite her father. Papa's face had turned red, and his mustache was bristling more than ever.

"Elizabeth, this is not the time or place to have this discussion." He looked around the room, evidently embarrassed to have this argument within the hearing of Matthew and the other dinner guests. Their chowder had arrived unnoticed.

"There is no other time, Papa, and this is where we are," Beth said, starting in on her chowder. She was going to eat even if the men were not.

"Well, Elizabeth, I had hoped that several months in Florida would have helped you grow up. I've never had the son I had hoped for, and it looks now as if you will not even be half the lady your mother is."

His attack hurt, but she had expected it; that was the way he had always talked. "I'm sorry, Papa, if I have disappointed you, but I am who I am." She wasn't about to let their conversation interfere with the delicious chunks of fish in her chowder.

"When you get home, perhaps Edward can talk some sense into you."

She continued chewing on the fish, without saying anything. The moment she had rehearsed had come. If she were to take over her own life, now was the time. "I'm not coming home, Papa. I've decided to stay in Florida for now. I haven't completed my work, and I wish to do that before returning north. I'm heading back into the Big Cypress Swamp. One day while I was staying with the Worthington family in Fort Myers, I was talking with their cook, Phoebe. She used an expression that I didn't understand: 'bucket flower.' She called me a bucket flower. It's a potted plant in Negro talk, but they also use it to describe a person who had been pampered like a flower in a pot—and she was referring to me. You and Mama have taken care of me and made decisions for me my whole life. I have decided that I don't want to be a bucket flower. Whether I teach or write textbooks or continue with research, I will not be mollycoddled any longer. I intend to earn my way, Papa."

"Elizabeth, it's all for a silly little piece of parchment from a college. It won't make one bit of difference one day after you graduate."

"It's not the diploma, Papa. It's the cypress swamp—the orchids, the bromeliads, the bald cypress, and the other rare and unnamed flowers and plants. And the same must be true for the wildlife as well, the bears, panthers, egrets, roseate spoonbills, even the beautiful snails. There's no other place like this in the country, and someone has to let the people know about it and protect it."

"Protect it? From whom?"

"From people like Disston and Flagler who dream of draining the Everglades, cutting down all the trees, converting most of the state into farmland, and building hotels all along both coasts. Once they've destroyed the trees and drained the swamps, the animals and birds will be gone and it will be too late."

Papa shook his head. "That will never happen, and besides, the task you're describing is a man's job. No one will listen to a woman."

"I'm making it my job, Papa."

His facial expression changed. Papa seldom smiled, but now he smiled faintly. He must be thinking that he still held the upper hand. "How are you going to support yourself, Elizabeth? I will retain control of your inheritance from Hubert Jackson and the little money my sister left you until you come to your senses." She needed money, and she needed it now. There had to be a way to make him return control of her money to her. Papa, almost as much as Mama, had always held sacrosanct the regard the First Families had for their hallowed customs. Now she was about to find out just how dear the Sprague family reputation was to him.

"I will become a lady of the evening, Papa. There's an abundance of sailors here in Key West. When I have earned enough money, I'll continue my research." The idea seemed so ridiculous she expected him to laugh, and she would have laughed, too. She glanced at Matthew, and he was staring at her with his mouth open.

"As wild as you have turned out to be, Elizabeth, I know you couldn't sink that low. I forbid you to even talk like that. It's clear to me that you have lost your senses. The way you were garbed this morning made you even look like a strumpet."

Matthew leaned forward and cleared his throat, but before he could say anything, she said, "I'll not only talk this way, Papa, if you don't restore my inheritance from Grandpa Jackson, I'll write to everyone I know in Boston and tell them about my new profession whether I go through with it or not." None of these threats would hurt him personally. Saving the best part for last, she said, "In addition, Papa, I'll tell them about your affair with Miss Murchison."

Papa's face turned gray. "She's my secretary."

"What is she doing here in Florida?"

"She's here on business."

"Monkey business. Is business so bad she has to share a room with you?"

His stern features crumbled. "No one will believe your ugly rumors."

"Excuse me," interjected Matthew, pushing his chair back. "Perhaps I should leave." Beth noticed that Papa's food had scarcely been touched.

"No. Please stay, Matthew. I want you to hear this." She then turned toward her father. "Please don't compound your sins by lying, Papa."

"You don't understand. A man has his needs."

"What about Mama's needs? Now I understand why she had to struggle so hard to make the Sprague name respectable."

He sat silently, stubbornly holding his ground.

"And I will tell everyone about how I've been sleeping with Matthew."

He switched his glare to poor Matthew who stared back at him, neither denying nor admitting to his supposed wickedness. "My daughter is a . . ." He paused. His face was as red as she had ever seen it. He turned back to her. "If I return control of your inheritance to you, will you promise not to say anything rash?"

"I promise to do as I have said I will do if you try any more underhanded tricks, Papa. I'll need money from you before you leave to pay back Matthew what I owe him, and to carry over until you have my funds released." Her whole body shook with anger and disdain.

"This is extortion," he fumed. "You'll be exhausting your trust fund before you're thirty, Elizabeth. You'll have nothing to fall back on in your old age."

"And what do you call trying to force me to come home by stealing my inheritance? Then there's the attempted kidnapping."

"What kidnapping?" he asked distractedly as he fingered his watch chain.

"Are you aware that a Mr. Prichett was hired to kidnap me? He was going to force you to relinquish Atlantic and Southern to him for my return. He was abducting me to Havana. If it hadn't been for Matthew and Mr. Gallagher, I'd be on my way to Cuba right now."

"Cushing's man tried to carry you off to Havana?" His eyes blazed.

"I had thought Mr. Prichett was working for you."

"No. I obtained Prichett's name from Henry Flagler and gave it to Cushing. I thought he hired Prichett only to locate you." His shocked tone of voice and look of concern convinced her he was telling the truth. This news was one final straw. "From what Henry Flagler told me, Prichett was only capable of hawkshaw work. If it had ever come to Prichett demanding my firm as ransom, he would have been brokering for an intermediary of Cushing's. If I signed over the company as ransom, Cushing would have kept the firm in a hidden trust so that I would be unable to prove his involvement. I'll make him regret he ever thought of that idea." Walter Sprague slumped back in his chair. "You have no reason to remain here now. I wouldn't allow you to marry Edward Cushing even if you wanted to."

"The reasons haven't changed, Papa. I'm staying here, and I expect you to release my inheritance to me."

"All right. I'll let you stay here for your mother's sake." He reached into his coat and removed several large Federal Reserve notes from his billfolder and handed her the money. "This is your last chance to come back to Boston with me, Elizabeth. The ship leaves in an hour." He arose from his chair with effort.

"No, thank you, Papa. You say that you're 'letting me stay' because

I am of no further use to you in a transaction with Cushing. I'm staying because I've forced you to give up your hold on me."

"You should know that this means you are no longer welcome in my house, Elizabeth."

"It's Mama's house, too, Papa, and I will wait for her reaction on that matter until she learns how you held back her father's money from me." From his expression Beth could tell that he had not revealed to Mama his chicanery. She had never seen her father beaten before. For the first time in her life she gave her father a command: "On your way to the ship, stop at the telegraph office and wire whomever it is necessary to release my funds."

"Good-bye, Elizabeth."

"Good-bye, Papa." They watched him disappear through the archway and down the steps to the street.

Chapter

31

*M*atthew sat with her after her father had departed. She had a few tears, but only a few. They waited until the table was cleared.

"I'm sorry that I gave Papa the wrong impression about you," she said.

"It's all right. What you said was the truth. He interpreted it the way he wanted to. Did you mean what you said about returning to the swamp, or was that merely said for your father's benefit?"

"Yes, I'm going back to Chokoloskee. Once Papa releases my funds and after I have my supplies shipped, I'll go back, and this time I'll hire a bodyguard, probably someone Mr. Chestnut can recommend. Now that Luther Phelps has no need for his house, I'll try to buy it or rent it. Deadman's Creek will make a fine field laboratory and location from which to embark into the swamp."

"Are you sure you're not staying just to spite your father?" he asked.

"Yes, I'm sure. When I complete my work, I can return to Boston and will be able to hold my head high. My parents will no longer try to force me to marry Mr. Cushing now that they know he's a snake. I almost feel sorry for Papa, but knowing him, he might not have given up his company for me, but now he'll do his best to destroy Mr. Cushing and Oceanic."

"How long will it take you to complete your research?"

"I'm not sure, but with a laboratory and the proper equipment, I can do much more thorough research. Papa was right about one thing: the master's degree diploma isn't that important. If I wished to complete my thesis in a hurry, I could do it almost from memory and get away with an acceptable paper within a few weeks. But if I do a comprehensive job, I might have enough material for a book, maybe two or three. The Big Cypress Swamp, and especially the Fakahatchee Strand, is an undisturbed garden of rare plants, and I might as well complete my research while I'm here."

"Are you talking about weeks or months, Beth?"

"Perhaps a year or two, maybe longer. Observing nature is a process. It takes time to see how the flora reacts to changes in the environment." His eyes showed disappointment, and she didn't wish to hurt him. "Is there any chance you might come back, Matthew?"

He shook his head. "It's too early to tell. I must attend to my elderly parents. Then it depends upon how much Luke needs me, especially with the expansion in New York. Besides, what could I do in the swamp—live like I have been or become a poacher? I don't believe I could grub out a living as a farmer or fisherman. Nature is too cruel." Then he brightened a bit. "Perhaps I could open a branch of Hutchinson's in Key West."

"Something you said this morning puzzled me," she said. "You mentioned that your uncle had helped put you through school. You had told me weeks ago that you had left school at the age of fourteen."

"Yes, that's right. But later I went to night school to catch up. Then I attended the Wharton School at the University of Pennsylvania. You see, my uncle wanted to help his nephews even though he and my father never got along. Later on he sent Luke to business school as well."

"You never cease to amaze me. Why didn't you tell me?"

"The subject never came up. A business degree in the swamp wasn't worth much."

They searched for other possible alternatives to their separation

270

and found none that could meet their immediate needs. Not wanting to end the evening, they fell back on reminiscing about their two months together in the swamp.

"Tell me the truth, Matthew. The day that you rescued me from the poachers in the brook, was there really an alligator there?"

"Well, there may have been," he said with a sly smile. "You can never be sure about those buggers hiding under the mangroves." They both laughed, and their hands touched across the table. She tried not to notice that the last patrons were leaving, and the waiters were beginning to clean up the dining room as Matthew talked about the hardships she had endured. He abruptly changed the subject to sleeping back to back in his makeshift tent those nights in the swamp. They laughed at the improbability of anyone believing that their relationship had been anything close to proper. Beth felt like crying and hoped it didn't show. She was hoping Matthew would tell her he loved her, but expected that he, like Papa, could not disclose his true emotions even if he did love her. She realized that she, too, was unable to reveal what was uppermost in her thoughts.

Finally the waiters turned off the lights one by one. She knew the evening was coming to a close but wanted it to go on forever. When Matthew suggested they go for a walk, she was relieved and accepted immediately. The night air was cooler, and their being together would have been wonderful if he wasn't leaving in the morning. Matthew was quiet, and she wondered what he was thinking.

They could walk only so far, and eventually had to turn back. In a dark corner near the hotel he drew her to him and kissed her. He held her firmly, but gently. The electric moment tingled through her whole body. It was their first kiss and the third time in her life she had been kissed by a man. Even though she was breathless, she wished his kiss had been longer and wished he would kiss her again.

"Good night, Beth."

"Good night, Matthew." This was the end.

He took a half step away but then turned and said: "Will I see you in the morning?"

"Of course," she said. "I'll see you off."

"Come with me to Philadelphia."

"Stay here with me," she replied.

His next words came in such a rush she had trouble keeping up with him: "Beth-I-love-you-and-promise-to-come-back-if-you-want-me-to."

"Of course I do, darling. I love you, too."

"If I can't open a branch of Hutchinson's, I'll open my own store. I might even buy out Mr. Chestnut."

"And after I've finished my research, I'll go with you wherever you want to go."

They kissed again, longer this time. He held her tightly, knocking her hat back, and she realized her feet were off the ground.

When he finally put her down, he said, "If you weren't such a lady I'd invite you to sleep with me tonight."

"If you weren't such a gentleman, I'd refuse."

"Back to back?" he asked.

She smiled but remained silent as they headed for the hotel.

Acknowledgments

I am deeply indebted to the following people and sources that have influenced my writing of *The Bucket Flower*.

Marjory Stoneman Douglas' *The Everglades: River of Grass* stimulated my interest in the Big Cypress Swamp and the ecosystem of south Florida.

From Zora Neale Hurston's *Their Eyes Were Watching God* came the language of Florida's African-Americans. In her book the phrase "bucket flower" was used to describe a pampered person.

Two very different works of fiction that have increased my fascination for the late nineteenth century were Jacob Carr's *The Alienist* and Jack Finney's *Time and Again*.

Other works that gave me specific assistance in creating the background for this novel were Edith Wharton's *Age of Innocence* and Elizabeth Griffith's biography of Elizabeth Cady Stanton, *In Her Own Right*. Marjorie Kinnan Rawlings' *Cross Creek* helped with local color. Patrick D. Smith's *Allipattah* helped with information on the Seminoles. Also invaluable were Marc McCutcheon's *Everyday Life in the 1800s,* Cleveland Amory's *The Proper Bostonian,* and Lucius Morris Beebee's *Boston and the Boston Legend*.

Valuable articles in the *Naples Daily News* included "The Everglades 50th Anniversary," December 6, 1997; "Habitats Around Us," March 5, 1998; "The Big Cypress National Preserve," March 28, 1999; "Gliding the Glades," November 11, 1999; "Stomp the Swamp," January 9, 2000; and "Enriching Experiences," January 10, 2000.

I used numerous references at the Collier County Museum Library with the help of resourceful volunteer Marie Mayer.

Following Mike Owen, biologist, on a hike through the Fakahatchee Strand was exciting and informative.

The staff of the Naples Public Library Central Avenue Branch were very helpful in acquiring several of the above titles.

My friends Barbara Smith and Bill Katterfield have contributed greatly through their reading of and suggestions for the manuscript.

Without the help and support of David and June Cussen and Helena Berg of Pineapple Press, this book would not have seen the light of day.

I owe my daughters, Jeanne Wilson Joffe and Christine Wilson, for years of joy and encouragement and for their critiquing of the manuscript.

Without my wife, Regina, this story would not have been written. Her generosity, patience, and loving input are what make my writing worthwhile.

The assistance of all of the above is deeply appreciated.

Donald Robert Wilson
Naples, Florida

If you enjoyed reading this book, here are some other books from Pineapple Press on related topics. For a complete catalog, write to Pineapple Press, P.O. Box 3889, Sarasota, FL 34230 or call 1-800-PINEAPL (746-3275). Or visit our website at www.pineapplepress.com.

The Everglades: River of Grass, 50th Anniversary Edition by Marjory Stoneman Douglas. This is the treasured classic of nature writing that captured attention all over the world and launched the fight to save the Everglades. The 50th Anniversary Edition includes an update on the events in the Glades in the last decade. (hb)

Marjory Stoneman Douglas: Voice of the River by Marjory Stoneman Douglas with John Rothchild. Nationally known as the First Lady of Conservation and the woman who "saved" the Everglades, Marjory Stoneman Douglas (1890–1998) founded the Friends of the Everglades. This story of her influential life is told in a unique and spirited voice. (pb)

A Land Remembered by Patrick Smith. This well-loved, best-selling novel tells the story of three generations of the MacIveys, a Florida family battling the hardships of the frontier, and how they rise from a dirt-poor cracker life to the wealth and standing of real estate tycoons. (hb & pb)

The Honor Series
At the Edge of Honor by Robert Macomber. This nationally acclaimed naval Civil War novel, the first in the "Honor" series of naval fiction, takes the reader into the steamy world of Key West and the Caribbean in 1863 and introduces Peter Wake, the reluctant New England volunteer officer who finds himself battling the enemy on the coasts of Florida, sinister intrigue in Spanish Havana and the British Bahamas, and social taboos in Key West when he falls in love with the daughter of a Confederate zealot. (hb & pb)

Point of Honor by Robert N. Macomber. Winner of the Florida Historical Society's 2003 Patrick Smith Award for Best Florida Fiction. In this second book in the "Honor" series, it is 1864 and Lt. Peter Wake, United States Navy, commands the naval schooner St. James. He searches for army deserters in the Dry Tortugas, finds an old nemesis during a standoff with the French Navy on the coast of Mexico, and confronts incompetent Federal army officers during an invasion of upper Florida. (hb & pb)

Honorable Mention by Robert N. Macomber. This third book in the "Honor" series covers the tumultuous end of the Civil War in Florida and the Caribbean. Lt. Peter Wake commands the steamer USS Hunt and plunges into action, chasing a strange vessel during a tropical storm off Cuba, liberating an escaping slave ship, and coming face to face with the enemy's most powerful ocean warship in Havana's harbor. When he tracks down a colony of former Confederates in Puerto Rico, Wake becomes involved in a deadly twist of irony. (hb)

A Dishonorable Few by Robert N. Macomber. In this fourth novel in the "Honor" series, the year is 1869 and the U. S. is painfully recovering from the Civil War. Lt. Peter Wake heads to turbulent Central America to deal with a former American naval officer turned renegade mercenary. As the action unfolds in Colombia and Panama, Wake realizes that his most dangerous adversary may be a man on this own ship, forcing him to make a decision that will lead to his court-martial in Washington when the mission has ended. (hb)

An Affair of Honor by Robert N. Macomber. In this fifth installment in the adventures of Lieutenant Peter Wake, United States Navy, Wake goes farther afield than the coast of his adopted home of Florida. Leaving his wife and family behind, Peter must navigate uncharted waters in the West Indies and a Europe wracked by war and intrigue. But it is in mysterious North Africa where Peter faces his greatest challenge yet—an affair that tests his honor. (hb)